ONE TWO THREE

One Two Three

ONE TWO THREE

LAURIE FRANKEL

THORNDIKE PRESS
A part of Gale, a Cengage Company

GALE
A Cengage Company

Thorndike Press® Large Print Basic.
The text of this Large Print edition is unabridged.
Other aspects of the book may vary from the original edition.
Set in 16 pt. Plantin.

**LIBRARY OF CONGRESS CIP DATA ON FILE.
CATALOGUING IN PUBLICATION FOR THIS BOOK
IS AVAILABLE FROM THE LIBRARY OF CONGRESS.**

ISBN-13: 978-1-4328-9018-6 (hardcover alk. paper).

Published in 2021 by arrangement with Henry Holt and Company

Printed in Mexico
Print Number: 01   Print Year: 2022

For Erin Trendler, my sister
For Lisa Corr, my cousin
who is like a sister
And for Larry Hess, my cousin
who would be like a sister
if only he weren't a boy

The world is before you and you need not take it or leave it as it was when you came in.

— JAMES BALDWIN,
"IN SEARCH OF A MAJORITY"

The town of Bourne is a fictional place, not found on any map, not assigned to any state or region or people. But the crisis its citizens face, its causes and its aftermath, the battles demanded of them as a result, are all modeled on and imagined from communities and their citizens all over the country and all over the world.

ONE

My first memory is of the three of us, still inside, impatient to be born. We were waiting, like at the top of those water slides you see at amusement parks on TV, slippery wet and sliding all over one another to see who got to go first, shivering, hysterical, mostly with laughing but a little with fear. The winner — me! — streamed away from the other two, excited to slide and smug because I got to be first but also a little scared to leave them and a little left out because of the time they'd get to spend alone together until it was their turn too. Not that I've ever been on a water slide.

School doesn't start until tomorrow, and already I'm behind. Mrs. Shriver emailed us the prompt a month ago. "History and memory are unreliable narrators, especially in Bourne. Therefore, please write a 2-to-3-page essay on your earliest memory and its relation to what's true." You think I couldn't possibly remember being born — that its "relation to what's true" is something like third cousin twice removed — but maybe the reason most people don't remember is because they were alone in there. We weren't alone. We never were. Before we were our mother's or ourselves, we were one another's.

Mama was waiting outside, of course, so she can't say for sure either. Most mothers of triplets don't even try to give birth naturally. Most aren't even allowed to try. But our mother is not like most mothers.

She remembers hours of screaming and pushing and pain, and she was alone then, after him, but before us. While she waited, she made a plan to give us all *M* names with escalating syllables so she would be able to keep us straight. She named me Mab — queen of the fairies, deliverer of dreams — baby number one.

Two came kicking and screaming a quarter hour later and needed two syllables. Mama must have been tired because she'd lost track of what day it was — evening had turned to night had turned to morning by then — and when they told her it was early Monday already, she named the baby that.

And then three came too slowly, no matter how our mother pushed. Typical, though

12

none of us knew that at the time. Eventually, they had to go in and get her, but she got the good name, the normal one. Mirabel. It sounds like miracle.

It turned out we didn't need such an elaborate system, though. No one has to count syllables to tell us apart.

When we were very little, Mirabel called us with her fingers. One for me, two for Monday, three taps on her armrest or right above her heart when she was talking about herself. Monday and I used these nicknames too after a while, since she and Mirabel can't go by something shorter without invalidating the entire point, so that's our triplet shorthand. One for me, Two for one, Three for the other.

Mrs. Shriver won't believe the other part, though, that I remember being in utero. She'll say, "I asked for an essay, Mab, not a short story." But if memory's so unreliable, who is she to say? If memory's so unreliable, what's the point of even asking the question?

Except I know the answer to that one. It's important for us to exercise our memories in Bourne, to stretch and strengthen them — like brain yoga or mind aerobics — because one of the sad things that happens

when almost everyone dies is there aren't
enough people left who remember why.

Two

Even though it is summer still, it is raining so it is a green day so I take all the shades of green pencils — in alphabetical order: avocado, forest, kelly, mint, moss, olive — plus white paper, the cereal box I ate all the cereal out of, scissors, glue, and a ruler into the upstairs hall closet where I can be alone for the next twenty-seven to twenty-nine minutes until Mama gets home from work and says we have to hurry up and make dinner and eat it quickly and clean up fast so we can get ready for bed immediately and fall asleep at once as if school starts fourteen minutes from now instead of fourteen hours from now.

I cut a perfect four-inch-by-six-inch rectangle out of the cereal box which I can do without measuring but I measure anyway, and then I cut a perfect four-inch-by-six-inch piece of paper and glue it on top. If I ever went anywhere, I would buy postcards.

15

In movies, you see people on vacation look at a tower of postcards and choose just one, but I would buy them all. Since it is more accurate to say I will never go anywhere though, I make my own.

On this one, I draw trees because that is one of the best things to draw on days when it is raining and therefore green. You could also choose frogs or grass, but frogs' tongues are pink like most tongues, and grass is boring, both, like the saying, to watch grow and also to draw. But enough shades of green will make a whole forest of trees if you choose the right season (summer) or the right part of the country (the part with evergreens), and olive and forest layered on top of each other make a green-brown that works fine for trunks, branches, and green days. So that is what I draw on the front of her postcard: oaks, firs, maples, pine trees, pear trees, and one eucalyptus. I am not stupid — this will be an important point to remember — I know there are no real forests where those trees grow together. But it is not a real postcard so it does not matter if it is true.

On the back I write:

Dear One,
  Wish you were here.

Which *is* true.

With two to four minutes to spare until Mama gets home, I leave the closet and slide the postcard, picture side up, under Mab's bedroom door. It is more accurate to say it is also my bedroom door and also Mirabel's bedroom door, and it is even more accurate to say it is no one's bedroom but rather the dining room, which it used to be except now we sleep there. But I am certain that even though it is faceup, Mab will know who it is for.

And I am right because when we go to bed three point seven five hours later, I see it tacked up among the two hundred forty-six other handmade postcards I have sent her already.

When you're a triplet, every night's a sleep-over. Maybe it's not like this if you're rich. Maybe it's only true if you're a poor triplet. There's only one bedroom in our house and it's Nora's, not because she wouldn't gladly surrender it to her daughters but it's up-stairs. And I cannot go up stairs.

Every day after school for a whole week of fifth grade, Mab went into our room and cut roll after roll of gold foil into stars. Soon they covered the beds and the floor and ac-cumulated like snowflakes into piles which grew into dunes. Nora stood in the doorway and frowned at her eldest daughter — was she depressed? was she mad? was this unrealized artistic talent or latent obsession? — but didn't say anything.

Monday never stops saying anything, everything, whatever's niggling the inside of her head. Why are star shapes pointy but sky stars round and movie stars skinny, when "pointy," "round," and "skinny" are opposites? Why does "foil" mean a sharp metal sword but also a flat metal sheet when "sharp" and "flat" are also opposites? How can "round" be the opposite of both "pointy" and "skinny" when "pointy" and "skinny" do not mean the same thing?

At the end of the week, Mab swapped her scissors for a staple gun and made our ceiling into a sky full of stars. They've faded over the years, as if it's perpetually dawning now, but we sleep beneath them still.

I didn't say anything that week because it was not a good week for me, and this was before my Voice came. Out there in the rest of the world, the brazen, ignorant, nosy, rude, and clueless come right up to people who use wheelchairs and say things like "What's wrong with you?" In Bourne, no one says things like that, not because we're not sometimes brazen, ignorant, nosy, rude, and clueless, but because, at least on this front, we know it's not that simple. "Nothing" would be a true answer. So would "Many things." But it would never be a single fill-in-the-blank response. My muscles are spastic except for the ones that are hypotonic. My body is often too rigid though my neck will only sometimes support my head. I have no control over my

19

limbs except for my right arm and hand which are as finely honed as something NASA built.

Plus idioglossia. It comes from the Greek — *idio,* meaning personal, yours alone in all the world; *glossa,* meaning tongue. If you're a doctor, "idioglossia" means speech so unformed or distorted it's unintelligible. I can't articulate much more than a single, wide syllable, and even that you probably couldn't understand. But if you're a linguist, "idioglossia" means a private language, one developed and understood exclusively by a tiny number of very close speakers. The secret language of twins. It is raised, in our case, to the power of three.

My sisters can usually understand my speech. They get my grunts and expressions and hand signals nearly as well as I get theirs. They share my finger taps. And when I want to say something more complex, with my one very gifted limb and an app on my tablet, my Voice can tell them anything at all. It's not fast. I can't type like you can — not with all ten fingers, not seventy words a minute, not in that quick, deft way that sounds like pouring rain. More like a leaking tap. Drip . . . drip . . . drip. But if you stopper a leaky sink and give it a day or two, even at that rate, it will eventually spill over.

And we are in no rush. We have plenty of time.

So every night, as we fade beneath our fading stars, my sisters and I discuss all the immensities and all the minutiae, the everything and nothing of our lives. But mostly the nothing. All the intrigue that happened here — all the intrigue that happened to us — happened before we were born. We don't need something to have happened to talk about it, though. Teenage girls don't get enough credit for this, their ability to see the potential import of everything, no matter how insignificant it seems, and analyze it endlessly. It's written off — we're written off — as silly, but it's the opposite. We understand instinctively that, like me, change is slow. If you're not paying attention, you'll miss it.

For instance, the night before school starts Mab is talking about her friends Pooh and Petra, which leads Monday to note that *P* is one of the few letters of the alphabet that is also the name of a food (along with *T* and, she considers, maybe *U* if you were a cannibal talking to your lunch). Mab talks about how Pooh was cleaning out her closet and gave her a pair of really cute black leather mules with silver tassels, and Monday informs us that before there were school buses kids got picked up in carts drawn by really cute mules. Mab muses with wonder that we're halfway done with high school now, and Monday corrects her: we have been halfway done with high school all summer long.

And I tell them about what I saw on Maple Avenue this morning, the most astonishing thing: a backhoe. Maybe it just looked weird. Towering over the cars on the road, wings clutched up against its body like a bride keeping her dress off the ground, it would have been conspicuous in any town. But I can't remember the last time I saw a piece of construction equipment in Bourne. Nothing ever gets built here. So maybe it's no big deal, just more idle girl-chat.

Or maybe, like the second half of high school, something momentous is about to begin.

ONE

"Welcome back." The next morning there's a sign looped over the railing of one of the ramps between the parking lot and the front door. Otherwise though, everything looks exactly the same as it did in June.

Mirabel's wheelchair pauses momentarily when she takes her hand off her joystick to wave goodbye to me. Then she presses it forward again and glides past.

But Monday stops dead in the middle of the sidewalk. "Rude," she says.

"Oh good." Petra comes up behind us. "Irony."

"They don't really mean it," I tell Monday. It would be better if she didn't start the school year overwrought about something completely pointless. "They're just being nice."

"It is not accurate to welcome everyone back," Monday continues as if she hasn't heard me because probably she hasn't, "if no one left."

"Or ever does," Petra adds. Unnecessarily.

"Just go in the side door," I say. Sometimes it's easier for Monday to take the long way around than to work her way through.

"I will." She narrows her eyes at me. "But as my angry facial expression should tell you, I do not think I should have to."

Petra and I take another moment to stand there looking at that stupid sign before everything begins again. Not really begins, Monday would insist. Before everything continues. Before everything keeps going. And Bourne Memorial High School limps, rolls, and motors in around us as if we're not even there.

In the hallway, it's loud. Usually, the first day of school is subdued. It's not like there's much to catch up on. No one went to Europe for the summer or to seven weeks of sleepaway camp. No one interned with a senator or a software company. But this morning there's a buzz. Rock Ramundi saw Mirabel's backhoe yesterday too. Alex Malden saw a truck full of gardening tools — shovels, rakes, "those giant clipper thingies" — plus four guys he didn't recognize inside. No one can think who they could be, how they could be here, where they could be going. If there were news, we'd all have it already. But that doesn't stop everyone from speculating. Maybe Mirabel was on to something. And that's all before the first bell even rings.

First period this year is World History. Mrs. Shriver is our history teacher — this year and every year — but she does not believe in doing history in order. In ninth grade, American History, we did the Civil Rights Movement then colonial Boston then the Civil War then Ponce de León then the Pilgrims. The day we left Plymouth Rock for the Great Depression, I finally raised my hand to ask why.

She cocked her head like it was a smart but difficult question that had never occurred to her.

"Well, you don't do English class in order," she said. "You jump all around. Jazz Age poetry then Shakespeare then some god-awful Victorian novel then a short story that ran in the *New Yorker* last year."

"Or math," Rock Ramundi put in. Rock's is always the first hand up, whether he knows the answer or not.

"Math?" Mrs. Shriver said.

"We don't do math in the order it was discovered in."

"Right." Mrs. Shriver clapped her hands together. "Exactly."

"But that's different," Chloe Daniels said quietly to her notes in her notebook, the direction she says most of what she says in class.

"Why?" said Mrs. Shriver.

"Cause and effect?" Chloe guessed.

"That's exactly what it is." Mrs. Shriver nodded. "I don't believe in cause and effect. At least not in cause and effect you make up afterward. What happens next is not necessarily caused by what came before."

"Isn't that what history is, though?" Petra pressed. "Precipitative?" Petra and I have been studying vocabulary for the SATs since sixth grade.

But Mrs. Shriver was unimpressed. "Not if you teach it out of order."

At the time, we thought she was making some kind of weird point for the hell of it, like to show off, the way teachers do sometimes just because they can, not because they really believe it. Now, though, I think about the ways cause and effect might break you. Bourne is a town of unexpected consequences, a place where what no one sees coming runs you over like a truck.

This morning we start with the Treaty of Versailles, the end of a war we haven't studied yet. There's no lead-in. There's no

26

welcome-back speech. There's no preview of the year ahead. Mrs. Shriver collects the earliest-memory essays, but we don't discuss them. We have too much to do to waste time talking about it. It's true there's a lot of history in history, but that's not why Mrs. Shriver's in such a rush. It's because there's only two years left to get us ready for the world, and we're the so-called smart kids, the hope for the future and all that crap, the normal ones. There's a ban at Bourne Memorial High School on the word "normal," and I get their point, but it's not like kids don't know how adults see them, here and everywhere. Most schools call some classes "honors" or "gifted" or "advanced" or whatever, and no one objects to that, but here they just call us Track A. The dozen of us are like grocery-store eggs: full of potential in theory but really unlikely to grow into the full-fledged beings Mrs. Shriver hopes for. She plows on anyway.

Yesterday, when I should have been working on my essay but was not, my friend Pooh had me over for lunch to give me back-to-school shoes and back-to-school advice. Both were of a variety you never find in Bourne: actually cool, genuinely retro, and virtually impossible.

The shoes are beautiful, but I have absolutely nowhere to wear them.

"You don't need anywhere to wear them," Pooh said. "Just knowing they're in your closet will make you feel better."

"Better about what?"

"Whatever you feel bad about. Or if you have a date!" She clapped her hands, delighted. "That's what these will be. Your dating shoes."

"I don't need dating shoes."

"No one *needs* dating shoes."

"Maybe. But I don't need them more than most." I took the shoes anyway though, just in case.

The advice was to skip history altogether and take something practical instead.

"We don't have a choice," I told her. "It's different than when you were there."

"Bullshit," she said. "Nothing ever changes around here, especially not that school."

"There are all these required classes now." She tsked. "History's so . . ."

"What?"

"Passé."

"You graduated in 1947."

"That's how I know," she said.

Pooh Lewis used to be my service project in middle school. We had to pick a volunteer opportunity and then write a paper about

28

what we learned. I learned old people lie just as much as everybody else but for better reasons. Pooh had only pretended to be blind so someone would sign up to come read to her, and when someone (me) did, she had no desire to be read to. She wasn't really blind, so could read to herself. She just wanted the company.

"Don't you want to hang out with people your own age?" I asked when I showed up the first day and clued in to the fact that she didn't need me when I found her in her kitchen reading *Baseball America.*

"God no," she said.

"Why not?"

"Old people are boring. And they smell weird. And around here, most of them are gone anyway."

"You think I'm interesting?" That seemed to be the implication, but no one had ever thought so before.

"I don't know yet." She'd looked me over carefully, like when you're trying to buy apples and half of them are bruised. "I'll keep you posted."

It's been four years, so I guess she decided I was interesting enough. Every few months Monday demands to know why I keep going to read to Pooh since the program is over and I already graduated from middle

29

school, and I reply that I was never reading to Pooh.

This is the kind of logic required to unstick Monday from whatever she's stuck on.

"I also do not like that 'Pooh' sounds like 'poo,' " she sometimes says.

"It's short for 'Winifred,' " I explained the first time.

"I do not like when things are short for things," said Monday. As if I didn't know. "And neither 'Poo' nor 'Pooh' is short for 'Winifred.' "

"Her name is Winifred so people called her Winnie and then they called her Winnie-the-Pooh and then they called her Pooh."

" 'Pooh' can be short for 'Winnie-the-Pooh,' and 'Winnie' can be short for 'Winifred,' but you cannot combine them, and you cannot read to a blind person for your middle school service project if she is not blind and you are not in middle school."

"That's true," I always eventually agree, both because it is and because it's faster.

Pooh was four when she came to the United States from Korea with her parents. They changed their last name from Lee to Lewis to sound more American. Then they tried to pick the most patriotic name they could think of for their little girl and came up with Winifred.

"How is Winifred a patriotic name?" I asked the first time she told me this story.

"How should I know?" said Pooh. "You think you're the only one whose mother is crazy?"

Yesterday, she argued, "You should skip history and enjoy yourself. Sixteen was one of the best years of my life."

"Nineteen-sixteen?" I asked.

She swatted at me. "Do I look like I'm a hundred and two?" She does, kind of. "The year I was sixteen. At your very high school. Trust me. I've already been all the ages. Sixteen is one of the good ones."

I made a face. "Small towns were more fun back then."

"What makes you think so?"

"It was all hoedowns and hayrides."

"Neither one." Pooh shook her head. "Not even once."

"And the neighbors all pitched in to build a barn or whatever."

"It wasn't *Witness*."

"The world was small back then" — I couldn't quite find the words to mean what I meant, but I'm pretty sure she got it anyway. She almost always does — "so it didn't matter if your town was too."

"We did know the earth was round even when I was a child."

31

"Now the world is big." I spread my arms to show her. "Huge. You can't spend your life in a tiny nowhere town like Bourne."

"The world is smaller than it ever was," Pooh said. "And no matter what town they're in, sixteen-year-olds want to leave it. Nowhere in the world is big enough to satisfy a teenager."

"But it's different here from other places."

"What other places?"

"All the other places." I waved at them. "Out there where high school is the best time of your life. It's exciting. It's dangerous —"

"If you're looking for dangerous . . ." Pooh began, and I saw her point, but it wasn't the one I was making.

"Other schools are full of drama. Weekends are fun. Everyone's beautiful and startling and in love —"

"Where?" Pooh demanded.

"Out there. Everywhere."

She peered at me like I was fruit again. "What makes you think so?"

"I don't know," I tried, but eventually admitted, "TV. Movies."

Her eyebrows smugly rested their case, but she didn't say a word.

TWO

The main thing that is good about my school is it is painted yellow.

Everything else about it can be very disappointing.

It has forty-three yellow rooms and is named Bourne Memorial High School. Some students call it BM High and some call it Bourne High. Both names are funny for different reasons, and both of those reasons had to be explained to me by Mab, but once they were, I saw that she was right. She says if you have to explain why something is funny it is not funny anymore, but she explained it anyway, and it still was. Of the forty-three rooms, including not only classrooms and bathrooms but other rooms that do not contain the word "room" but still are, like the auditorium and the cafeteria and the principal's office, most are unused.

This is because most of the citizens of

33

Bourne do not live here anymore.

After what happened happened, some people died and some people left. The only people who did not die or leave were the ones who could not. So a better name than Bourne Memorial would be Left Behind High. I told this to Mab as a joke, and I did not explain it, but she said it was not funny anyway. Sometimes it is hard to tell the difference.

This morning is the first day of school, but just like every morning, Mr. Beechman sings my name when I walk into class. *"Monday, Monday,"* he sings, *"so good to me."* This is not because I am good to him but because my name shares that of a song by an old band called the Mamas and the Papas. Some mornings he sings, *"Monday, Monday, can't trust that day,"* which is the second verse of the song but which is not accurate because I am very trustworthy. I know a lot of facts. I relate them responsibly and appropriately. I never lie. I am also not a day.

Mr. Beechman is our homeroom and math teacher so he got to decide how we sit, and he decided alphabetical (which I like because it makes sense) and by first name (which is not traditional but does not matter to me since I am Monday Mitchell so would be in the middle either way). I sit between Lulu Isaacs, who is what other towns would call neurodivergent but is not stupid, and Nellie Long. Who is stupid. It is not mean for me to think this though because it is just a true fact, and also Mrs. Radcliffe says there are more important things to be than smart, like kind and trying hard.

How it works at our school is students who need extra help with their bodies are Track C, no matter how well their brains work. As an example, Mirabel's brain is smarter than anyone's. And students who do not need extra help with their brains or their bodies are Track A, for example Mab, even though Mab's brain is often annoyed, annoying, obsessed with vocabulary words, and deciding to touch me even though it knows I do not like to be touched. Our class is Track B which means the bodies of the students in my class mostly work all the way but our brains mostly do not.

None of this is a lie, but it is also not true, even though lie and true are opposites. It would be more accurate to say that in Track B our bodies mostly work like people's bodies on television and our brains mostly do not work like people's brains on television. Bourne may not be normal, but, as Mab's not-a-service-project-anymore friend

35

Pooh is always trying to remind her, television is not normal either. No one thinks our tracks are a great or fair system, but great and fair systems are expensive, and tracks-with-flaws are all we can afford.

A stereotype is that students who are Track B and do not lie and are picky about things like colors are also very good at math. I am only normal-good at math, and I do not see what math has to do with colors. But when the bell rings and Mr. Beechman gathers up his things and leaves, Mrs. Lasserstein comes in, and everything is ruined because I love books, but I do not love studying books for English class.

Mrs. Lasserstein passes out copies of *Lord of the Flies* and says this will be our fall book, but a whole season seems too long because *Lord of the Flies* is only 208 pages, and I have already read it, and it is not very interesting. It is by William Golding who won an award for showing that boys are mean and badly behaved, even somewhere nice like the beach. This seems like something anyone in the entire world who has ever met a boy could tell you, but they gave William Golding a Nobel Prize for it. While Mrs. Lasserstein is telling us the book is about the unraveling of civilization, Nigel Peterman and Adam Fell are in the back of the room shooting staples at each other, and Kyle M. and Kyle R. are doing a burping contest in the corner. This is called irony which we learned about in English class last year.

When we were in fifth grade and the state required us to do science and we could not do science, an independent contractor called Effective Education Passport was sent to observe us. Effective education was what they were supposed to make sure we had. The passport part was so they could give us each a little book to record our progress in so they could prove they were doing a good job. They thought it would be easy since our progress in science when they came was zero, so even if we only did a little bit, that would still be more, and anyone who looked in our passports could see it. But when they met with us, they discovered there were some problems.

Nellie Long would not do Dissecting a Frog because it was sticky when you touched it, and she would not do Dissecting a Fake Frog because it was sticky too. "No frogs were harmed in the making of this science experiment," Mr. Farer joked with her, but she did not laugh because her objection was not ethical but tactile and also it was not funny.

Nigel Peterman would not do the Is Your Mouth Cleaner Than a Dog's experiment or the Roast a Marshmallow in an Oven You Built Yourself experiment or the What Food Will Rot First experiment because they smelled like dogs, marshmallows, and rotten, soon-to-be-rotten, and weirdly-not-rotten food, and Nigel Peterman does not like things that smell like anything.

Lulu Isaacs would not do the experiment where you listened to your partner's heart and then you both did jumping jacks and then listened again because the hearts were loud in her ears and the stethoscope was pressing, also in her ears.

When Effective Education Passport called me into an empty classroom and asked what experiment was my favorite, I said, "Eep," and when they asked if any of the experiments had upset me, I said, "Eep," and when they asked if I had felt the need to skip any of the experiments or leave the room while they occurred, I said, "Eep," and when they asked if there was any way the experiments could be modified or augmented to make me more comfortable or able to participate, I said, "Eep," and when they asked me why I would not answer them, I protested that I was answering them by saying, "Eep," and when they asked me why I kept peeping like a duck, I pointed to their clipboards, notebooks, pencils, pens, and shirt pockets, all of which read, "E.E.P. Your passport to education effectiveness." And I also told them ducks do not say "Eep." That is when the Effective Education Passport team got up and left the room.

They did not close the door, however, so I overheard the conversation they had with our principal. It went like this:

Mrs. Mussbaum: You're leaving?
E.E.P.: I'm afraid we've accomplished all we can here. Too many of your students are special needs. Too many are on the spectrum. What you need is professional help.
Mrs. Mussbaum: You are professionals.
E.E.P.: Not the kind you need. We're sorry we can't offer more assistance. As a gesture of goodwill, we'll waive half our fee.
Mrs. Mussbaum: Half? You didn't do anything.
E.E.P.: We're consultants. We consulted. Implementation of our recommendations is the school's responsibility.
Mrs. Mussbaum: You didn't recommend anything either.
E.E.P.: We recommend seeking profes-

sional help. You'll have our bill by the end of the week.

Mrs. Mussbaum: Eep.

Before that I did not know what "special needs" meant, and I did not know what "on the spectrum" meant. So I asked Pastor Jeff.

Or, to be more accurate, I asked Dr. Lilly. Dr. Lilly is Bourne's only doctor, but he prefers to go by Pastor Jeff because he is also Bourne's only priest. He used to be a Catholic priest, but there are not enough people in Bourne anymore for everyone to have different religions. Whatever sickness you have and whatever prayers you pray, Pastor Jeff is your only option anyway. Mab, Mirabel, and I are a trinity, but we are not a Trinity — which is how capital letters work — and we are not religious, but this does not matter to Pastor Jeff. We are his flock, he says. A doctor's job and a priest's job are both to spread care and love and healing no matter what you believe, he says. Bourne could use some ministering, he says. When I was little, I hoped he would marry our mother because he is nice and because husband and father are also both jobs with lots of ministering, but he said that is not how it works with Catholic priests.

When I told him what Effective Educa-

40

tion Passport said about us, he said, "Everyone needs air, water, food, shelter, and clothing all the time, Monday. Everyone needs care when they're sick or hurt, love when they're sad or scared, someone to tell them no or stop when they're being unsafe. Everything else people need sometimes — and it's a lot — is special. All of us have special needs."

I felt happy because that made sense, and I like when things make sense.

"Do you know what a spectrum is?" he asked me.

I did not because I was only ten.

"A spectrum is a classification system that arranges everyone or everything between two opposite extremes, which means a spectrum, by definition, includes everyone. For a spectrum to be a thing, we all have to be on it."

"So E.E.P. is wrong about us?"

He shrugged. "Some people really like labels, Monday."

"I do!" I waved my hand like he was across a parking lot or at the other end of a grocery store aisle. "I like labels because they mean organized and order and control and correct."

"Sometimes they do. And sometimes they just give you the illusion of those things.

41

Giving something a label and putting it in a box makes you feel like you've understood it and accounted for it and can keep track of it, and that's great for things like paperwork or books, but sometimes things get mislabeled or misfiled, and then they get misunderstood or misaccounted for."

"That is why you have to label things carefully," I told him.

"Sure. But when those things aren't things but people, it's not just a question of careful. People are complicated. They're more than one thing. They're less than another. You, for instance. We could file you under 'Girl' or 'Student' or 'Triplet' or 'Tall.' "

"I did not think of that." Thinking about it then made my skin feel itchy.

"We could file me under 'Pastor' or 'Doctor' or 'Man' or 'Black' because I'm all of those things, but we could also file me under 'Catholic' or 'Priest' or 'Yoga Teacher' or 'Irish' because I'm those things too."

He was right, so I thought hard until I came up with a solution. "Extra labels. Extra files."

He tilted his head back and forth. "Except labels separate things that actually overlap. I'm different from other medical professionals because I'm also a religious professional. I'm different from other Catholic priests because I also practice other religions. I'm different from other Black men because my mother was white."

"I do not like when things overlap."

"Don't think of them as overlapping then. Think of them as having more than one side. We could say your preference for yellow things is a detriment in a world full of other colors, or we could say it's an advantage in a world that demands quick decisions and clarity of purpose."

"I am able to choose what to wear to school every morning more quickly than Mab," I agreed. "And it is only one color so it always matches."

"Exactly. So one good solution is we could decide not to file you at all. Some people really like labels, and some people need them to access other things."

"Like what?"

"Like medical care. But since I'm all you've got on that front under any circumstances, that part doesn't matter. And since I happen to know Bourne's spectrum looks different than most, I haven't found labels and official diagnoses terribly useful."

"Then why could not E.E.P. help us?" I asked.

Pastor Jeff winked. "Because they are not very E."

This could mean that they were not very effective or that they were not very educational, and even though I do not like when you cannot tell which, it was okay because Pastor Jeff was making a joke and both were funny.

He was also right about spectrums.

For instance, except on green days, I only like yellow things.

I only eat yellow foods. I only drink yellow drinks. (Except coffee. I drink coffee because even though coffee is brown, it is also really great.) I sleep on yellow sheets, get dressed in yellow clothes, study yellow subject matter. Choosing only yellow is not as limiting as it sounds. A lot of things are yellow. If I have to do a report on an animal, I pick a baby chicken. If I have to do a report on a fish, I pick a *Zebrasoma flavescens,* which is Latin for yellow tang. If I have to do a report on a song, I pick "Yellow Submarine" by the Beatles, which I know was written for people like me who prefer yellow because otherwise it does not make any sense. My mother says it is a good thing it rains sometimes or else I would never eat a salad, but this is not true. I would eat egg salad. My mother also tries to pass off pale orange and very off-white things as yellow, but I am not fooled.

All of which proves Pastor Jeff's point. I may be at the far end of the flexible-about-food spectrum and the normal-about-colors spectrum and the easy-to-buy-clothes-for spectrum, but on the yellow spectrum I am firmly in the center.

THREE

It's not that it's not hard to be me. Or the
mother of me. It is. Monday is a stickler for
many things, including language, which is
why she likes the term "birth defect." I was
born defective. Harsh, but true in some
ways. Monday doesn't care for "some ways."
Too vague. Mab — who is infatuated with
vocabulary and chooses longer words whenever possible — says "congenital disorders."
Nora objects to both. You are lovely just the
way you are, she insists, neither defective
nor disordered, so she goes with "congenital
anomalies," never mind that in Bourne —
the only place we ever are — I'm not even
all that anomalous. Whatever you call condi-
tions like what I have, sometimes they're
inherited and sometimes they're accidents,
and sometimes it's just because shit happens, but in my case, in all our cases, it's
none of those reasons, and that is worst of
all. There are ways, many ways, in which

Bourne has destroyed us.

But there are others in which Bourne is a blessing. Be it ever so humble, there is no place like home. There are very few stairs here, but any place that has even one also has a ramp or a lift. The shops have automatic doors, broad aisles, pull-down shelves, and low counters. All the restaurants that remain have tables that fit my chair and room enough to navigate between them without accidentally bumping someone and spilling their Chianti. We have only one place to buy clothes, the Fitwit, but it sells pants that are cute and comfortable even if you're only going to wear them sitting down, shirts that are seamless and label-free, tops that can accommodate a G-tube, belts and zippers you can do one-handed. They have a whole yellow section just for Monday. Bourne's public transportation's not accessible but only because we don't have any, which is only because there's no place to go. Even the vending machines are low down. And best of all, enough Bourners use wheelchairs that I don't spend all day looking at other people's asses.

We don't battle for medical care here because Pastor Jeff is the only option anyway, and there's no fight with the insurance companies because he struck a deal with them long ago. Maybe, in his man-of-the-cloth hat rather than his man-of-the-stethoscope one, he appealed to their better natures, or maybe he pointed out that maximum claim reimbursement was a good PR opportunity in the immediate aftermath when so many eyes were on us, or maybe it's these companies' there-but-for-the-grace-of-God knowledge that however outrageous the request, we are not faking it. Or maybe it's just that there aren't enough of us left to make it worth the haggle.

Even the equipment we need is readily available. Much was donated at the beginning. Even now, companies looking for the write-off, or eager to shed and unload, send our way their functional but misshapen seconds, their working-now-but-didn't-at-first refurbs. We aren't picky. We understand not everything that looks broken actually is. But mostly, we have Tom Kandinsky, out-of-work engineer, tool maven, fix-it wizard, whose plan, like the Cubans', is repair repair repair. He maintains a depot of spare parts — tires and screws, covers and seals, solar chargers for the tablets, hacks for lives navigated in chairs. Everything is shared, recycled, brainstormed, and upgraded. When my wheels clog with hair and gunk, Tom cleans them out. When I need to do

48

an experiment for chemistry, he swaps out my regular tray for one with extra cup holders. When I miss my mouth and spill all down the front of me, he's got scarves in any shade and style you can name to lend until I can get home to change. He gives me mobility. He gives me stain-free self-respect. And better than both of those, Tom gives me a voice. Or rather, a Voice.

My AAC — Augmentative and Alternative Communication device — used to require a whole high-tech speech-generating big to-do. Now it's an app on my tablet and Tom-tweaked speakers that go wherever I do. With my perfect right hand, I can type something in, and my Voice reads it aloud. Or, because typing is slow, I can speak with symbols. Touch the Food folder and a list of things I might want to eat pops up, and I can say to my mother, or really anyone, "Ice cream please." Touch the Daily Life folder, and a few strokes later I can say that I'm tired and ready for bed. Touch the Let's Talk folder and I can say, "Fine thank you" or "How is your day today?" Touch the Frequently Used Phrases button, and I can say, "Monday! Shut up about yellow things!" It's smart, predictive, so it's learned my speech patterns, which words most frequently follow which, how teenage girls talk,

49

how I am different from most teenage girls.

Here I am not deviant from the norm. In Bourne, we know there is no norm. But also in fact, for Bourne, I'm pretty normal. There's no need to fight to mainstream me at school because I am the mainstream, and school is set up to accommodate my needs. Well, some of my needs. Bourne High is equipped to keep students like me alive. But alive is not the same as educated. Let's just say I've read ahead. Nora says keeping up with me intellectually would be a challenge for any high school, most colleges, lots of postdocs, so no one is to blame for Bourne High's insufficient intellectual rigor. I wouldn't believe her (as far as proof you're a genius goes, "My mom thinks so" isn't especially convincing) except that it's a rare thing for which Nora doesn't think someone's to blame. Sometimes I go in anyway. Mostly I homeschool myself.

But not *at* home. I can't be home alone all day. So mostly I homeschool myself at Nora's work, a mix of independent studies and online courses, theories I research, ideas I wonder about, rabbit holes I wander down. You'd be surprised how many experts are willing to answer strangers' questions. You'd be surprised how much valuable information the internet has, too, in addition to all the lies and yelling and stuff for sale.

Nora works four jobs — to make ends meet, though her ends are many more than just food on table, roof over heads. Her main job is therapist, an important job in any town and in this one more than most, in the first place because she's the only one and in the second because everyone here has survived what happened here. She's on a team of two, the other being Pastor Jeff. One of the cruelest ironics of Bourne — a town which is full of them — is that we have greater body-care, mind-care, and soul-care needs than most places, but therefore we can only afford to hire two people to meet them all. No matter what you believe and no matter what condition you have, Pastor Jeff is your only option — for hope, for healing, for a higher power or, failing that, a treatment plan to mitigate all your earthly suffering — so Pastor Jeff does for everyone, believers in all gods and even those of us who have been forsaken by every single one of them. And if you still feel depressed or anxious afterward — and who wouldn't? — then you come to see my mother.

They share the medical clinic, which is really just a little house. Her office used to be a bedroom — there are ages and penc marks charting a long-gone child's growth along the doorframe — but now holds a nubby orange sofa across from a desk piled impossibly with paperwork, patient files, books, forms, and a decade-old computer. There are pens lying lame everywhere because she picks them up, finds them inkless, and puts them down again instead of throwing them away.

Today is a bad day for me, so I'm not just at work with her but parked in the corner of her tiny office, researching solar wind and helioseismology for the online astrophysics course I'm taking this semester. "Ooooo," I whisper. *Nora.* It sounds like the wind. The regular kind. Even on a good day, I can only manage simple syllables, and since Mama, Mab, and Monday alliterate, I call our mother by her first name. Even when I can only say the middle bit, she understands.

Chris Wohl peeks his head around the door. Nora waves him in. He sits in the middle of the orange sofa and makes himself small.

"Hi, Chris, it's good to see you," Nora begins, and when that gets no response, "As you can see, Mirabel's come in with me today. If you feel more comfortable, she's happy to sit in the waiting room."

Most of the time most of her patients say

yes, please, they would prefer me to sit in the waiting room. I used to take offense, like they thought I couldn't be trusted. Then I realized it was a great compliment. In other places, kids who can't walk or talk or always hold their own heads up are imagined to be stupid, imagined to have minds that don't work either, imagined to be something less than human. People think of them like dogs, and half the fun of dogs is you can tell them anything. People think of them like furniture, and who censors themselves in front of their sofa? So Bourners' unwillingness to spill their guts in front of me is actually high praise.

But Chris raises his eyes from the floor and gives me a tiny smile that seems like it might be his first all week. "I don't mind if you stay, Mirabel." He shakes his head, wispy hair flying away in spots, matted down in others. "You're a good listener. Maybe you'll be a therapist like your mom when you grow up."

He's just making conversation, but there's no way I'm going to be a therapist when I grow up. I've already sat in on — or waited outside of — more therapy appointments than any sixteen-year-old should.

"How are you this week, Chris?" Nora says gently.

"I haven't used, if that's what you're asking."

It isn't. This is obvious, even to my untrained eyes. He is sweaty, despondent, leaky — nose running, eyes running, teary. When he's used, he's happy, euphoric even, and jittering like a lightning bug.

"Good for you." Nora keeps her voice neutral.

"Leandra's giving me shit because she thinks I scored. She's not mad I have it; she's mad I'm not sharing. But I'm clean."

"What made Leandra think otherwise?" Nora is very careful to keep any suspicion, any doubt, off her face, out of her tone, but the wife is rarely wrong in these cases.

"These two enormous delivery trucks drove right by the house the other day." Chris seems like he's answering a different question. "Some kind of restaurant supply company." He looks up, clocks Nora's skepticism. "That's what Leandra thought too, but I swear. I called her to the window to see, but by the time she got out of her chair and made it over, they were long gone."

He pauses for a moment while we all three picture how long it takes Leandra to cross a room these days.

"She said I was lying to screw with her. I

54

said she knew I'd never do that. So then she said I was tripping, and what was I on. I said I wasn't on anything, and the trucks were real. They had pictures on the sides. One was a fancy fridge with a screen in it. One was this sprawling stove with like ten huge burners. But she said did I know of some kind of magical new restaurant going in around here. And I said maybe it wasn't a restaurant. And she said what else would two restaurant supply trucks be doing here. So I said there was probably enough gas in that stove you could use that shit to escape the planet in case of the apocalypse. I was just trying to make her laugh."

He laughs a little himself, but not like he thinks he's funny. More like he's embarrassed he thought Leandra would.

"And what did she say to that?" Nora prompts.

"She said, 'Too late.' "

Nora nods grimly.

But I'm thinking of his delivery trucks. I'd be with Leandra and Nora on this one except for that backhoe Rock Ramundi and I both saw and the truck full of strangers and tools Alex Malden did. Leandra's right that it can't be a restaurant opening. For one thing, a restaurant never opens here. For another, we'd have heard about it. But there've been too many strange sightings for this just to be something Chris imagined while high.

But Chris isn't thinking about the trucks anymore. "I can't help her if I don't use. You know? I can't help her."

"You can't help her if you do."

"That's not true. You know that's not true."

Nora nods. She means she understands what he's saying, not that she agrees. But I do. I agree. Chris and his wife Leandra both worked at the plant. She got cancer and lost her arm and shoulder and much of her upper torso. She looks like she's standing half out of a door even when she's in the middle of the room. Maybe if she'd been born with only one arm, like Violet Alison and Otto Mathers in my class both were, she'd have had no trouble doing without, but she was too old. Now she needs help.

Chris has too much pain to help. Maybe it's physical pain like his nerves are on fire, like his joints rub against each other like sandpaper, like needles are poking him. This is what he tells us some days. Or maybe it's emotional pain like his job is gone and his town is dead and his body hates him and half his wife is missing. Or maybe it doesn't matter which. The cure is the same. And

56

now if he doesn't come see Nora once a week and pee clean in a cup — one of the terms of his plea bargain — the state will send him to jail. So actually the cure does not exist.

"They help me. And they help me help her. And otherwise?" His question is not rhetorical. He is really asking. Otherwise what? If not drugs, then what?

Nora has an answer to that. "How are you fixed for dinners?"

He looks up from the floor again as if dinner is not something that ever occurred to him. From the look of him, maybe it hasn't.

"I'm going to freeze you a bunch of casseroles and bring them over Wednesday evening," Nora says. "Can you both be home at seven?"

Baking is Nora's third job, and she does a lot of it. It's not really a job, though, because no one pays her to do it. When she says "a bunch of casseroles," she means two or three, but also a few batches of cookies, a few batches of scones, half a dozen pies, a couple of cakes. It's true Chris and Leandra need fattening up, but this is the scale of baking Nora prefers under all circumstances.

She looks almost as skinny as Chris. Partly that's because she wears my dad's shirts and they're too big for her. Partly it's because at dinner she is often feeding me instead of feeding herself.

When Chris leaves, I try to tell her that cooking for the Wohls is not her job, that he has to learn to do life without drugs but also without her, that there are hurts she cannot fix and holes she cannot fill, but there are no preprogrammed Pep Talk folders and it's a lot to type, so I tell her with my rolling eyes, sideways from my lolling head.

"I know," she answers me. "But what can you do?"

ONE

Two years ago, on the day we started ninth grade, the first thing we did as high schoolers was herd into the auditorium for a welcome meeting and getting-to-know-you games. Mrs. Radcliffe said we were young adults now, with opportunities and responsibilities. She said high school was an adventure we were lucky to be embarking upon. She acknowledged that this would be the last school many of us would ever attend. She said we were rockets sitting on a launch pad, and from here, we would blast off to college or to careers or to parts unknown, worlds unexplored, mysteries unfathomable. We were all pretty sure she got this speech from a book because there was no way she wrote it for Bourne High. Then she had us write down and sticker to our shirts two adjectives that best described us.

Mirabel's words were "perspicacious" and

"immured." If Mirabel were studying for the SATs, she wouldn't have to study for the SATs.

Monday's were "yellow" and "yellow."

Petra's were "here anyway," which now I'm pretty sure are adverbs, but it was only our first day of high school so we didn't know much yet.

Mine were "bored" and "boring."

Bored because it is dumb to play get-to-know-you games with a bunch of people you got to know at birth which is true not just of the ones I shared a womb with but everyone else in that auditorium as well. Bored because there is nothing to do in Bourne. Bored because high school is supposed to be a fresh start, and there were no fresh starts happening that day. Or any day.

But much more than bored, I am boring. If you asked anyone I know to describe me, they would say, *She's the normal one.* I'm not short or tall, skinny or fat, buff, buzz cut, braided, or dyed. I'm not pierced, tattooed, or even mascaraed most days. I'm a boring straight white girl, but I don't think much about race. (Maybe so. I'm a boring straight white girl *so* I don't think much about race.) And my sexuality doesn't matter since there's no one in Bourne for me to date anyway. I am ordinary, unremarkable, average, your typical American teenager. Picture a high school girl. That's me. That girl in your head right now? Me exactly. I could not be more normal if I tried.

But here? That makes me weird. "Weird" would also have been a good adjective to describe me.

If Mrs. Radcliffe had chosen my word for me, she'd have gone with "indebted." Track A has a tutoring credit, one of those requirements Pooh was so skeptical about, like we have to take history and we have to take English and we have to take math. We have to tutor. Since it's after school, you'd think they couldn't make us, but you'd be wrong. Some of us get out of it because there's football practice (never mind it's only touch because no one here wants to risk a head injury, and it's only intrasquad because there's no one else to play). Some of us get out of it because we have after-school jobs (never mind after-school jobs are discouraged in Bourne where there aren't even enough jobs for the adults). There aren't many of us left after that, but the rest of Track A tutors a few days a week after school, in pairs. So at least Petra and I get to do it together. It's not that I don't get how many birds this kills — the kids wh need job experience get job experience;

kids who need extra help get extra help; the kids who need occupying and distracting after school get occupied and distracted — but even free labor is only worth the cost if you know what you're doing. And none of us do.

When Mrs. Radcliffe explained that first week that it was Track A who would staff the tutoring center after school, there was a lot of whining and moaning and protesting and complaining until she cut us off by hissing, "You are the lucky ones. This is the least you can do," and stood before us, arms crossed, daring us to disagree. We would have, vehemently, for Bourne is nothing if not a study in how it's not that simple, but there is no arguing with overworked, underpaid guidance counselors, and we accepted our lot just like everyone else.

Today when Petra and I walk into the tutoring room five minutes after the last bell, Nellie Long is sitting at her desk, gazing at the ceiling with a huge smile on her face as if there's something wondrous up there. (I check. There's not.) But I ruin her good mood as soon as I suggest we get to work.

"I don't want to read *Lord of the Flies*." She scowls at me like I assigned the book.

"Why not?"

"It has nothing to do with my life."

"It seems like it's just about boys," I concede, "but really it's about the human condition."

She looks at me blankly. "I am not a fly," she says.

"Or a lord," Petra adds from across the room. I glare at her.

"How about your history essay?" I offer Nellie.

She sighs and agrees to this reluctantly, hands me her essay, watches the worry accrue on my face as I read. "See, what I'm trying to say," she explains, "is that even though World War II happened thousands of years ago, it's still relevant now."

"Okay," I say. "How?"

"How?"

"How is World War II still impacting our lives today?"

"Obviously because" — her expression suggests maybe I'm the one who needs tutoring — "I have to write this big report about it."

Kyle M. and Kyle R. are wrestling on the floor instead of letting Petra help them with geometry. Petra is doing her nails. When Mrs. Radcliffe shoots her a dirty look, Petra says, "I'm not getting in the middle of that. I'm a pacifist." When I shoot her a dirty look, she raises her eyebrows and says, "Trade you?"

I look at Nellie's essay. She's written "World War Too" a dozen times already, and she's only got three paragraphs.

"Deal."

The Kyles are likelier to pay attention to me than Petra anyway because they want to get in good with my sister. They like Mirabel. Everyone likes Mirabel, but them more than most. They've had a crush on her since we were little, though it would take a lot more than being nice to me at tutoring for her to be interested in either one of them.

I stand over the Kyle-ball and try to be as fierce as possible though I am small and they are huge, though I am one and they seem many, though I am standing still and they are rolling around like drunk puppies.

"Liar," Kyle R. spits.

"You're the liar," Kyle M. retorts.

"Liar," Kyle R. says back. Limited vocabulary. They should study with Petra and me. Actually, I guess that's what tutoring is, but it doesn't seem to be working.

"I saw it."

"You didn't."

"My dad saw it."

"Then he's a liar too."

Petra rolls her eyes at me. I smile at her.

She smiles back.

"Go for it," she tells me, because sometimes the only way out is wading over to the other side.

"What did you and your father see?" I ask Kyle M.

They stop, part, and sit up, panting, still drunk puppies.

"Moving truck," he wheezes. "We both saw it. Down by the library. A moving truck."

Petra's mother does not leave her house. It might be that what happened broke something in her brain, or it might be that what happened honed something in her brain so that she realized she was safer inside, but in any case, it's been five years since she went outdoors. She used to leave on Sunday mornings to go to church, but she's Sikh, and though Pastor Jeff did his best, she felt she could do just as well on her own at home. She's perfectly loving and involved in her daughter's life, but only in her house.

Petra's father lives in New Jersey but works in New York, which he calls "the city," as if there's only one. This sounds glamorous, and might be for all I know, but Petra reports that he lives in a dark one-bedroom apartment with a view of a parking lot, spends hours commuting on a train that smells like summer feet, and then does other people's taxes all day for not even enough money to be able to afford to get an apartment large and non-gross enough that his only child could at least visit more often.

Since Petra's mother only lives in her house and Petra's father only lives in New Jersey, they bought Petra a car. It is older than we are, at least fifty percent mold, and also smells like summer feet, but it is better than my car which is a bicycle.

After tutoring, I climb into the passenger seat, and with absolutely no discussion, Petra heads toward the library.

If I could have one wish for Bourne, it wouldn't be enough. It would be too hard to choose. But in the running would definitely be a coffee shop. Maybe it would change everything, having a warm, bustly place to sit and chitchat wittily in oversized cushy chairs and make smart observations about the world going fascinatingly by, someplace to get a part-time job, know all the regulars, find yourself the recipient of all the good gossip, and save some money so you can leave one day.

But we don't have a coffee shop.

We have a donut shop. Ham Roland's imaginative name for the place was Donut

Shop, but the sign he ordered arrived with a typo. They told him they'd redo it or he could have a refund, so he got his money back and kept the sign as is, and now we go to the Do Not Shop sometimes after tutoring. But it's not the same.

We have a pizza place, but even though I have nothing to compare it to, I still know it isn't very good. I wave at Lena behind the counter as we drive by, but she doesn't look up from her book. We have a hardware store and a laundromat, a diner, a drugstore, a grocery, and a church. Donna's Nursery and the bar and the Fitwit.

Downtown Bourne was modest even before. That was part of its charm I think: compact and cozy and cobblestoned (this was before so many of its citizens needed wheels). There was never a coffee shop, but there used to be other kinds of shops — knickknacks, knitting supplies, candy — plus an ice cream place and a couple cafés. Those storefronts are still there, waiting patiently, hopefully. Emptily. What's left full is threadbare and torn maybe, but still kicking.

At the far end of downtown, the stores peter out and then the asphalt does. The church is the last thing before there's nothing. It's got peeling wood siding, a giant white spire, an oddly short red door that must have been put in before the whole building was finished or even planned out all the way because it's nowhere near center. It's hard to decide if those long-ago Bourners were so eager and enthusiastic they put the door in first, or more like too clueless to realize you don't need a door if you don't have walls yet, but it's nicer to think of them as just that welcoming.

Petra steers onto the gravel, lets the clutch out with the car still in gear, and stalls to a stop. In front of us is the bridge: stone, weathered and impressive, bearing in iron the name of its benefactors, Grove — the old wealthy family who used to own half of Bourne back when Bourne used to have old wealthy families — and its construction date, 1904, to remind you they built this thing without computers, cordless drills, even a pocket calculator. It spans what we call the ravine, which makes it sound like the kind of place teens wreck their cars trying to leap over when they're drunk or at least like some kind of picturesque valley with sheer cliffs and dramatic waterfalls. It's not that. It's more like a ditch, a greenbelt maybe if you're feeling generous, with a tangle of vines, thorns, and dead brush. And there, on the other side, is the library.

The library is beautiful but closed now, empty like the storefronts, pretty and vacant like cheerleaders on TV. The building kind of matches the bridge — worn and majestic — and makes you think there must have been a time before. It has a giant stained-glass window like a church, but this one shows people with books: a couple reading on a tandem bike, a bunch of people reading under a tree with books dangling from its branches, a family — mom, dad, and three little kids — all reading on a picnic; even the dog is holding an open book in its paw. It's a building you would call noble, even historic, but it's been closed for over two years now, dark and shuttered, its hedge brown and crumbling, weeds commando-crawling up from the banks of the ravine and threatening to consume the place completely.

At least that's how it was last week. Now suddenly it's different — except nothing is ever different in Bourne — and even though I'm seeing it, I still don't believe it. This is why people have reported construction equipment but no construction, delivery vans but no deliveries. The library is on the far side and the opposite shore of a mostly empty town, and since it's closed, no one comes here anymore, but now we can see that we've missed something. The weeds have been hacked away; the desiccated hedge is gone like it was never there. Fresh dirt you can actually smell, dark and damp, surrounds the front walkway and harbors something new and green and blooming. Every light is on, every door ajar. The library looks open, in use, alive. In the parking lot, two enormous moving vans idle like teenagers. We watch out the windshield and cannot say a word, but eventually we have not said a word for long enough that Petra's engine has cooled, and she climbs out of the car and onto the hood. I follow. The hood is still warm through my shorts as is Petra's leg where it presses against mine — it's a very small car — but I can't stop shaking.

"You're bouncing," Petra complains.

"Your car's bouncing."

"Because you're bouncing it."

"I'm shivering," I admit.

"It's ninety degrees out here."

"I'm algid."

She turns to look at me. "Have you been doing SAT prep without me?"

"Only a little."

"Does 'algid' mean crazy?"

" 'Algid' means cold."

"You're not algid" — we are sweating

70

against each other — "but you might be crazy."

"Pusillanimous," I offer.

" 'Pusillanimous' means fearful. I've known you for sixteen years. You're not fearful. Timorous maybe."

Shit. "I forget 'timorous.' "

"That was in last week's flash cards. Do them again."

"I will," I promise. This is my pact with Petra. We will get into college. We will get out of Bourne.

"Afraid," she supplies.

"How is that different from fearful?"

"You're not afraid as a personality trait. It's just weird as shit what's happening over there right now."

We're quiet, watching. We can just make out people moving inside. "I think 'pusillanimous' and 'timorous' might mean the same thing," I say.

"Maybe."

Petra grasps my hand in hers, and I slowly stop shaking. We watch a little longer, but there's nothing much to see. We can't tell how many people there are or anything about them. We can't imagine who they might be, and we *really* can't imagine what it might mean that they're here.

"Heteroclitic," I say finally.

"What?"

"Week before last," I remind her. "Weird as shit."

We lean back against the windshield and shift our hips away from the wiper blades and watch in silence as our lives change forever.

TWO

There is no right way to systematize the arrangement of books. Some people like Dewey decimal classification, but that is usually nostalgia because that is how their childhood library was organized. Some people like the Library of Congress classification system, but that is usually elitism because that is what academic libraries use. And that is only if you want to organize by subject. You could alphabetize by author's last name or first name. You could alphabetize titles or even keywords. You could arrange books by color, and that would be nice because if it was a rainy day you could go to the green section and get a rainy book. I bet Melvil Dewey never even thought of that.

I do not have a system though because I do not need one. Once I put a book somewhere, I remember where that somewhere is. And also because to have a system you

need to have a large storage apparatus —
usually bookshelves — which I do not.

Instead I have books under my bed, under
Mab's and Mirabel's beds, under Mama's,
on our bedside tables, under our kitchen
and coffee tables, on our countertops and
next to our sinks, though you have to be
careful because books, like huskies, do not
like to be wet. I have piled books on the
sides of the stairs because our stairs are
thirty-four inches wide, and you only need
fourteen inches to walk up. Mama bakes a
lot, so I cannot put books in the oven, but
she says you cannot bake in a microwave,
and she does not trust the microwave
anyway, so I put books in it and just take
them out and hold them if someone wants
to heat something up and Mama is not
home to object. They are on top of the
kitchen cabinets, between the blankets in
the upstairs hall closet, in the spaces beneath
the sinks between the water pipes and the
walls, under the sofa, inside the fireplace,
on the corner of the porch it does not rain
on. They fill the unfinished attic and the
even less finished crawl space. They are
stacked tightly around the chimney, which
is good because that means they could also
help hold up the house if there is an earthquake or mudslide.

My mother keeps all the law books in her room.

Mr. Beechman told us all about how taxes work the year we were doing percents in math. Instead of each individual paying for her own teacher and her own school, her own roads and her own sidewalks, her own books and her own wars, each individual pays taxes on her home, land, income, investments, and holdings, and that money goes to the government, and then the government buys one teacher and one school and one road and one sidewalk and one library, and everyone shares. The government hosts a war, and everyone just comes to that. This is called efficiency, and it means you cannot have your own war. You can only join someone else's.

This is also why the library is at my house instead of at the library.

The residents of Bourne do not have investments and holdings. We do have homes and lands, but they are not worth any money. Some Bourners do not even have jobs because lots of our stores closed and most of our restaurants too. We still have a pizza place, and it is called Bourne's Best Pizza which is technically true but not that impressive since it would be just as accurate to call it Bourne's Worst Pizza since it is also Bourne's Only Pizza. A lot of people worked at the places that closed, and now they do not have jobs.

And of course all the plant workers. Most of them are unemployed. Or dead. ("And/or dead" is more accurate. Some are both.)

Eventually, we did not have enough money to have a library, but the library building is Historically Significant (which means more than when it is just historically significant which no one cares about), so they left it right where it was — or, to be more accurate, where it still is — but with nothing inside. They tried to sell the books, but there is a very small market for used library books. What they could, they sold, and donated the money to Mr. Bergoff's scholarship he set up in memory of his wife. The rest, Mrs. Watson, the former librarian, gave to me.

Now I am the librarian.

I take this job very seriously. I take all jobs very seriously, but this is more important than other jobs because Bourne citizens are stupider than other citizens — I am not being mean; this is just a true fact — and the way to get less stupid is to read more books. You might argue we need books more than we need extra ramps.

That is what I did argue.

That is how I convinced Mrs. Watson to give me all the books.

Straight after school I go home and wait for anyone who might come. Maybe they will want a good mystery to occupy their mind if their body is not working well. Maybe they will want a memoir by someone else who overcame odds. Maybe they will want a book about computers so they can get a better job. There are not a lot of jobs in Bourne, but if you knew computers, you could work somewhere else.

When the doorbell rings today, the person ringing it is Pastor Jeff. The person ringing it is often Pastor Jeff. As I have said — and as should be obvious — stupid people need to read books in order to get smarter, but unfortunately people who like books are usually smart already, and stupid people do not read. Maybe this is tragic irony, or maybe cause and effect. I do not know. What I do know is that Pastor Jeff is not stupid. But sometimes he makes stupid book requests.

"I need a book about how to sew wheelchair and walker parts," he says when I answer the door.

"I have no books about how to sew wheelchair and walker parts," I regret to tell him.

"How about a book on how to sew car parts?"

"I do not think that book has been written."

Like everything else in Bourne, the church is underfunded, but because it was built a long time ago by Bourners who were richer than we are, it is also very big. Therefore there is enough room inside for God *and* fundraising. On Saturdays, Pastor Jeff does not have clinic services or service services, so he teaches yoga and aerobics classes in the back of the nave. In the rectory, which is attached to the church, he has machines which you can use for a small fee to copy documents, keys, and old videotapes. In the church basement, he has a wheel and a kiln and teaches pottery classes. Every summer, he goes on a thrift-shop tour around the state, and this summer he bought an old sewing machine. He was going to teach sewing classes, but it turned out he did not know how to sew.

"Ham Roland needs snow tires for his walker before it gets cold," he tells me. "Donna Anvers is having trouble reaching the bag on the back of her wheelchair. I'm sure Tom has something at the depot that would work, but I thought I could help. A hubcap bag that fits over the wheels instead.

Some kind of extra-grip, anti-slip device I could stitch."

"Those are good ideas," I compliment him.

One thing that is good about librarians is they listen to what you need and want and think of a way to help you which sometimes is by ignoring what you need and want. Maybe they do not have the book you requested because their library is nothing but leftovers. Or maybe what you requested is wrong — people often are, even smart people who read — but it is okay because librarians have witchlike librarian magic to pick the right book for you.

For instance, Pastor Jeff's cheeks show red which means he is embarrassed because he does not know how to sew. Pastor Jeff's belt shows holes which means he is skinny and should eat more. Pastor Jeff's hands show twisting all around themselves which means he is worried, so even though he did not ask for cheering up, I know cheering up is what he needs and wants.

"Wait here," I say and return four and a half minutes later with a book on decoupage which is the closest thing I have to sewing, an owner's manual for a 1995 Honda Civic which has sections on both snow tires and hubcaps, and a novel about a woman who finds inspiration in fattening and joy-inducing (and, it can be assumed, non-embarrassing) pies. That is how to be a good librarian.

When I get back to Pastor Jeff in the kitchen, he is at the sink where he fills a glass with water, drinks it down, refills it again, drinks it down again.

Just like books, there is no right way to systematize the categorization of people. But in Bourne, one good way is by water usage. Or, to be more accurate, lack of water usage. Some people use their tap water for laundry but not for cooking. Some people use it for washing their bodies but not their carrots. Some people will flush toilets with it but not wash their hands in it afterward. I do not do sports because there are germs in locker rooms, and when Mrs. Radcliffe said I could shower afterward at home instead, I could not do that either because I only shower for three point seven five minutes at a time, and that is enough to wash off a regular amount of germs but not an athletic amount of germs. Petra and her mother shower for as long as they like but only on Wednesdays and Sundays. They separate their laundry not by lights and darks or deli-cates and regulars but innies and outies, like belly buttons. If the garment hardly touches their skin like it is a sweatshirt or a cardigan or a skirt they wear with tights underneath, they wash it in their washing machine with Bourne's own water. If it is underwear or socks or T-shirts or a bra, they wash it in their bathroom sink with bottled water. If it is jeans, they just let them air out and wear them again, even though they only shower twice a week. (Petra's mother does not leave her house but does not care about germs that might be in there in her jeans with her already.) Our mayor, Omar Radison, has the water tested every year, and he prints out the results and posts them all around downtown so we can all see it is safe now, but even Mayor Omar drinks bottled water.

Not Pastor Jeff, though. Pastor Jeff looks both ways before he crosses a street, wears his seat belt in his car, applies sunscreen in summer, and chooses pretzels instead of chocolate bars from the vending machine. I know. I have seen him do all of these things. I have seen that he jogs on Monday, Wednesday, and Friday mornings which he must do to increase his longevity because that is the only reason a person would jog. All of those things are doctor things. But when you ask him why he drinks tap water, he says he has faith, which is a pastor thing.

81

He says he knows God would not send poisoned water to Bourne. I ask him if he means God would not send poisoned water to Bourne *again,* since he already did once.

"That wasn't God, Monday," says Pastor Jeff.

"Well then how do you know whoever it was will not do it again?"

"Because I believe," says Pastor Jeff.

"In God?"

"Yes, in God."

"But what about last time?" I ask.

"The Lord works in mysterious ways," says Pastor Jeff and all pastors everywhere when presented with completely logical but impossible-to-answer questions like mine.

"But if God will protect you from poisoned water, why will he not protect you from getting run over by a car?"

"I believe he will," says Pastor Jeff.

"But if God will protect you from getting run over by a car," I press, "why do you look both ways before you cross the street?"

"Because, Monday" — he winks at me — "that's just common sense."

Mab says you cannot argue with people about religion, and this is why.

After his tap water, Pastor Jeff turns, looks at the books I chose for him, and chuckles. "Impressive selections as usual, Madam Librarian."

"You are welcome," I say politely. "Is there anything else I can help you with today?"

I meant something having to do with library business, but he replies, "Yes, now that you mention it: I was hoping you could warn your mother about something."

Warn her? My toes and knees start to buzz. "Why do not you do it?" I ask him. Pastor Jeff works in the room next door to my mother so sees her a lot almost every day.

"I don't want to tell her at work."

"Tell her what?"

"Well . . . word is we're getting new neighbors."

"Neighbors?" The buzzing catches fire. I am immediately alarmed, and Pastor Jeff looks worried because he has seen and heard me in all my states including the alarmed ones.

"No, no, not like next-door neighbors. Sorry, Monday. I mean we've heard there's some new people moving into town. I don't know who but —"

"Why?" I interrupt.

"Why don't I know who?"

"Why are they moving here?"

Sometimes I ask the wrong question because the point is not what I think it is.

But Pastor Jeff nods slowly. "I have no idea."

I think of the other *W* questions you are supposed to answer at the start of an essay and ask, "Where?"

Pastor Jeff winces. "The library."

"The library!"

"That's what we heard."

"*My* library?"

"That's the one. That's where the moving trucks went."

I am dancing now, the buzzing flames in my toes turned to happy sparks. "You saw moving trucks at the library?"

"I didn't. But others did."

"It is reopening!" I am jumping and spinning. If it did not mean touching him, I would hug Pastor Jeff.

"No, Monday, that's not —"

"They are moving all the books back in. They must be."

"All the books are here." He waves his hand around at them.

"The ones they took."

"They sold those."

"They bought them back."

"Monday, I don't think they're reopening the library." He is being very gentle of me. "I don't think that's what's going on here. I think —"

I am ready for Pastor Jeff to leave, but it is

rude to say so, so I put on yellow oven mitts so I can push him out the door without touching him. "I will tell her." I wave both yellow mitts goodbye as he stumbles outside. "I will tell my mother and everyone. They are reopening the library!"

There is still cereal in the cereal box, but it is in a bag and the bag is clear, so you can see what is in it and do not need a box to tell you, so I remove the bag and cut the box into an extra-large postcard. I do not put anything on the front because I plan to tack it up on our door so no one will be able to see that side.
On the back I write:

Dear Citizens of Bourne,
   Good news! The library is relocating to the library.

Then I think that sentence might be unclear or confusing for some people so I cross it out and clarify:

   The library is re-relocating to the library.
                                   Your librarian,
                                   Monday Mitchell

Many of the things that happen next can

be chalked up to the fact that Pastor Jeff, a representative of both science and the Lord, has gotten my hopes up.

THREE

Norma's Bar is owned and operated by a man named Frank Fiedler. He doesn't know why it's called Norma's. It was called that already when he bought it. From a man named Todd. It is why he hired my mother, though. He said she had no experience, too many little girls (we were kindergartners at the time), and a face that did not inspire people to drink. Is that a good thing or a bad thing, she said. He said wasn't it her job to talk people out of drinking away their problems. Only during the day, she said. He said she would have to take off her dead husband's shirts and wear a uniform and he knew she wouldn't do it. She said bartenders don't wear uniforms. She said Frank, I need the money. She said my name is on the place. He said off by a letter. She said closer than Frank.

She's been working here ever since. Her second job.

When we were little, we all three used to hang out at the bar in the afternoon. There's no one here who cares about underage kids in bars and no one to enforce it if anyone did. Besides, Nora had to work — everyone understood that — so we had to come along. Now though, Mab tutors after school, and Monday runs the library, but much of the time I still come in with my mother because this is my second job too. After I finish my first (homework), I do Frank's accounting. They started as one and the same, in fact — I assigned myself Frank's books as math practice in eighth grade — but now he pays me a little bit, and, Nora observes, every little bit is a little bit.

"Maybe you'll be a CFO or something when you grow up," Frank says this afternoon as I get organized.

I think of Chris Wohl saying maybe I'd be a therapist. Everyone's thinking about me growing up today. There's no way I'll be a CFO either though. Too boring. I'd never do it as a career, only as a favor. If I didn't do his books for him, Frank would do them himself — he doesn't have enough money to hire someone who's actually qualified — and he's lousy at it.

It's a quiet evening, good for bookkeeping. Ours is the sort of town where there's only one bar, and it's as likely to be packed at eleven a.m. as eleven p.m. Nora works only a few hours on weekdays, filling the ones that come between getting off work at the clinic and getting home to eat a late dinner with the three of us and get me ready for bed. She picks up more hours on the weekend, but these quiet afternoons hardly seem worth doing. That's the deal she made with Frank though, and the guys who are here are always glad to see her.

And it's always guys. Other times of day, the bar could be filled with anyone. These twilight hours belong to her boys.

Zacharias Finkelburg works the night shift thirty-one miles away at the Greenborough 7-Eleven, so he comes in late afternoons for one for the road. I used to object that that was like having beer for breakfast, which seemed gross, or beer for driving, which seemed worse, but Nora would say, "It takes the edge off," which is what she always says. Zach used to be a line supervisor, so you can see where 7-Eleven night manager is a job with edges that could use removal. He got some kind of rare bone cancer in his ankle and lost from his left knee down. The doctors said he had to find a new line of work where he wasn't on his feet all day, and Zach replied he needed a new line of work where he wasn't on his foot all day, that maybe he would get a peg leg and start calling himself Zach-*arrr*-ias. We always laugh when he tells these stories, but he says the doctors never did. They gave him an ordinary prosthesis, and the Greenborough 7-Eleven gives him a stool to sit on behind the counter.

Here, the stool next to his is empty, and on the one next to that is Tom Kandinsky, almost always, except for the hours he's in his depot soldering old wheelchair parts to older wheelchair parts to get new wheelchair parts or making the talking calculators talk slower and louder. Tom also has only one foot — nerve damage — and he and Zach like to quip they should pair up for the two-legged race. That Bourne could actually hold such an event does not make this joke funny to anyone but the two of them.

Tom nods to me when we come in this afternoon. "How's that new caster wheel working out for you, Mirabel?"

"Love it," my Voice sings.

"Ooh, new speakers too?" Zach asks.

"Better." Tom's thrilled he noticed. "I put a DSP into the audio to eliminate noise and enhance the sound quality. You know how much math it takes to do voice? It's not like you can just roll off a few dBs at 250 hertz.

Much clearer, right?"

Why a chemical plant employed an electrical engineer, I do not know, but I also can't imagine what we'd do if Tom weren't one.

Hobart Blake sits a couple stools farther down. I find this strange, but Nora says it is the way of men everywhere, not just here. She says in any empty bar anywhere, three women will pick a table in the corner and squeeze into it all together, lean in to hear one another over the music, close as possible. Even if they're strangers, she says, they'll sit at neighboring tables and exchange shy glances that turn into awkward smiles that can be dispelled only by one getting up, introducing herself, and joining the other. But men who are lifelong friends, who have been — are still going — through hell together, will still leave an empty stool between them if possible. When I ask her why, she says she has no goddamn idea.

Hobart has what would be a rash if it ever went away, but it never does. He won't call it a skin condition, though, because it's only permanent going forward. He didn't use to have it, wasn't born with it, didn't grow up with it, only developed it after the water in his shower started coming out brown and putrid. That he's stuck with it now does not turn it into a condition, he says. That appropriate rash terminology is a perfectly reasonable discussion to have over beer and pretzels tells you everything you need to know about Norma's Bar.

When I was little and learning about the body, I used to worry for their livers. But when I told Nora, she snorted. "Nothing can kill these guys. Trust me, they tried." The male species is endangered in Bourne. The plant employed more men than women, so more of them died, quick and early and before my time. Or theirs. But the other sad truth about Bourne is anyone who's here is here because they couldn't leave. That was another thing I didn't understand when I was little, why you wouldn't just pack up and move somewhere else. "Lots of people did." Nora nodded. Then added, "Some could not."

Hobart stays because raw pink lesions and welty skin would draw stares in any town but this one. Zach and Tom stay because Bourne has lots of accommodations that make life with only one leg easier than it would be other places. And because here they have each other. Frank stayed because he owns the bar. Predictably, it's the most profitable business in town (though still nowhere near profitable enough to hire a real accountant). When you ask Nora why she stayed, she says Bourne is her home. She says she has happy memories here. She says she'll be damned if she lets those bastards run her out of her own town. But really it's because of us. Bourne is a good place for Monday to be Monday. It's a really good place for me to be me.

And never mind all that, she stays not just for us, but for all of us. For Nora's fourth job — for which she also does not get paid, for which, in fact, she herself pays handsomely — is truth-prover, justice-seeker, retribution-guarantor, and wreck-herder. Every hour she is not working or baking or mothering, she is holding Bourne's class action lawsuit together with both hands. She has a fancy, big-city lawyer, Russell Russo, and a crowd of plaintiffs — nearly everyone left has signed on at some point or another. She has piles of research, interviews and testimony, documents, affidavits, and absurdly high hopes. What she does not have, however, in sixteen years of trying, is sufficient admissible evidence to prove what she absolutely knows to be the case. Not yet, anyway.

When the old oak door opens and a little light spills into our dankness and with it Bourne's mayor, Omar Radison, everyone holds their breath, but I am the only one

93

who sets off an alarm. My apnea monitor starts shrieking like a banshee on the moors, and this is a good thing actually because it reminds everyone to breathe again and gives Nora something to do.

Omar comes running over to help me, but Nora beats him there. Still, it was sweet of him to try.

"Christ, is she all right?"

"She's fine," Nora snaps.

"Are you sure?" Omar's hands are out to help, but he doesn't know where to put them. Nora's propped my head and checked my airway and is fiddling with the monitor, trying to get it to stop shrieking. I am telling her with my eyes I'm fine.

"Yeah, I'm sure." Some days Nora is too tired for sarcasm. Today is not one of those days.

"Okay, jeez, just . . ." Omar trails off. *Making sure? Trying to help? Unable to muster the will to live with that alarm pummeling my eardrums?* Who knows how he meant to finish that sentence. But the pealing finally ceases.

"She's fine," Nora says again.

Omar's outstretched hands rise up like he's under arrest. "Sorry, sorry. A beer when you get a chance."

He chooses the farthest stool at the end.

Her eyeballs look mere degrees away from being able to set it aflame. She returns behind the bar and pours unrequested refills for Zach, Tom, and Hobart. "On the house," she says. Then she starts polishing glasses.

Frank sighs and pulls Omar a beer, takes it over to him.

"Sorry, Frank," says Omar.

Frank nods. "Not your fault, man."

Everyone in the bar closes their eyes and takes this in. Everyone winces. Everyone thinks the exact same thing. There is an unspeakable amount for which Omar is at fault.

"So, um . . . I have some news." Omar doesn't look up from the beer Frank has just handed him. He sounds sorry — for opening his mouth at all — but also a little bit excited, proud even, to have something to report. There's not much he can give us — his wards, his citizens — but this is one thing. Some news. An offering. "Donna Anvers saw a moving truck."

"I heard it was a delivery truck," Nora says, also without looking up. "Kitchen supplies or something."

"That too," Omar says. "But that's not what Donna says she saw. A moving truck, she said, for sure."

Nora's incredulity is such that it overwhelms her abhorrence for Bourne's mayor. She looks to see if he's kidding or lying, teasing her, mocking her, tormenting her, manipulating her. He is not. Finally she asks, "Where?"

"She saw it go by the nursery."

The plants never really came back here, so neither did Donna's Nursery. It's still open, but mostly she sits in the front window all day and watches Bourne go by.

"Must have been on the way somewhere else," Nora says, sure.

"Where?" Omar asks.

It's a good point. Bourne is on the way to nowhere. No one, nothing, goes through Bourne.

"No shit." Frank gets away with penetrating commentary like that because he owns a bar.

"Can't be," Nora says but adds, despite herself, "Can it?"

Omar smiles at her. Omar shrugs. Omar looks like hope. So does Nora. It makes them both unrecognizable. His shoulders rise up toward his ears. "Maybe?"

Nora considers this a moment. "I doubt it's true." Then her face shuts down. "And even if it is, we don't want them here."

"You don't even know who they are."

She goes to anger faster than an exhale.

"Who would move here, Omar? I wouldn't. You wouldn't. We're broken."

"Nora, that's not —"

"And anyone who came willingly, who actually chose this, would be brokener still."

"This is a nice town —"

"Used to be."

"We have some challenges but —"

I don't get to hear what comes after Omar's very mayoral "but" because Nora interrupts again.

"And whose fault is that?"

Omar nods, resigned, closes his mouth and every other part of him, sips his beer. He and Nora have had countless versions of this conversation countless times, but this is where they all end. Speaking of going nowhere.

ONE

In the morning, I wake up like usual, groan out of bed, pee, pad back to the bedroom still half asleep to get Mirabel up, take her to the bathroom. (Monday helps lift and carry, but she won't do the toilet part because: germs.) While Monday gets dressed, I find clothes for Mirabel (Monday can, but Mirabel sometimes likes to wear clothes that aren't yellow), and then I get dressed while Monday helps Mirabel into the outfit I've picked out (no germs). When Mama's appointments start early, sometimes she's gone before we're even up, but she always leaves coffee in the pot and breakfast on the table for us. Monday helps Mirabel (without touching her mouth) while I eat. If Mirabel's head is steady, she can brush her own teeth, but this isn't one of those mornings, so I brush mine, then hers (so many germs) while Monday eats. An ordinary morning.

But that is the last thing in my day — my life — that's ordinary.

Mrs. Shriver is standing in front of the blackboard as we file in, twisting a piece of chalk in her hands. She looks nervous. It's weird. "Good morning, everyone. Take your seats quickly this morning, please. I have some news."

History teachers can't be used to reporting news.

"Class, we have a new student."

I can barely breathe. Mrs. Shriver either. She sounds like she's repeating something she got from a book. She's been teaching for almost two decades, but those words have never come out of her mouth before.

And it's not just me and Mrs. Shriver. We're all wiggly like when we were second graders. We're all paying attention. Chloe Daniels is not falling asleep on her notebook. Evie Anders has pulled back the hood of the sweatshirt she wears so ubiquitously I'd forgotten what color her hair is. Rock Ramundi's phone is nowhere in sight. Mrs. Shriver walks over to the door and opens it with a little bit of a flourish.

"Allow me to introduce —" The kid standing there looks embarrassed then alarmed as Mrs. Shriver suddenly stops talking and starts looking panicked. It's her big moment, and she's forgotten the kid's name. I try to imagine day one in a new school where everyone already knows everyone but you. I try to imagine day one in *this* school, without having grown up here, and cannot. I consider what he sees. Bodily — like, as a body but also physically — we're varied as a garden, one of those weedy ones where anything that grows goes. For a small nowhere town, we're pretty diverse, I guess because not that long ago Bourne was on the rise, a good place for fresh starts and young families, open to anyone because not that many people were here yet. Mrs. Shriver, who is a Black woman married to a white man, says that's why they chose it, so her family would belong, so her kids would fit in no matter what they looked like. But it turned out not to matter because Mrs. Shriver and her husband couldn't have children. Maybe after six miscarriages, they gave up. Or maybe they realized having kids in Bourne wasn't safe after all, no matter how diverse we are.

So we look different. But we're all poor. We're all poisoned. We're all tired — of this place, each other, our options. Our sisters. We're all here, and we're all stuck, and we're all stuck here. Not that you can tell any of that from looking.

The kid leans in from the hallway and stage-whispers his name to Mrs. Shriver.

"River Templeton."

And at once, we all understand the look of panic on her face.

Petra's eyes have doubled in size.

"No. Way." I grab her hand under the desk.

"Phantasmagorical," she whispers back.

Alex Malden stops sharpening his pencil mid-point. Peter Fabbelman's squeaky felt tip falls silent mid-doodle.

Apparently, insanely, in all the flurry of the morning, it had not occurred to Mrs. Shriver when she saw it written down on the paperwork. Not until her lips were on the cusp of mouthing his name did she figure out exactly who River Templeton must be.

There is a jolt through the whole of me, like some kind of acid has been pumped out from the middle of my chest, down my arms, around the horn of my fingertips to pool into my stomach. I look down and expect to see smoke. I look around and notice that River Templeton is the only one in the room with his mouth closed. He uses it to smile.

He looks like a movie star. It's not the perfect skin or the bright teeth or the hair so labored over I can see neat furrows like he plans to plant seeds. It's not that he's so overdressed in brand-new khakis with a sharp crease down the middle of each leg, black dress shoes shiny as silverware, a light-blue shirt, clearly ironed within the hour, buttoned all the way down around his wrists and within one of his neck, never mind it's supposed to hit ninety-three degrees today and is not much cooler than that now in our classroom. I suppose no one thought to tell him we don't wear uniforms. Or have air-conditioning. But I can see that under his outfit he's just a kid playing dress-up, trying too hard, itchy in his clothes. So it's not that. It's something else.

"Do you want to introduce yourself?" Mrs. Shriver finally stammers.

He turns to us and smiles again, then swallows that smile like it embarrassed him. "Hi. Um. Hi. My name is River Temple-ton." As if it's nothing. "We. Um. My family and I. We just moved here. From Boston. Um." He falters, then goes with "Thank you for having me." Winces. Sits with polite relief at the desk Mrs. Shriver waves him toward.

It is hard to be objective now that I know his name, but mostly what he looks is new. It is strange, his newness, and hard to describe because here is a weird and horrible thing about me: I never, ever see anyone I haven't already seen before. When Monday and Mirabel and I stop by the Do Not Shop on Saturday afternoons, we know everyone there. On the way there, on the way home, no matter how long we dawdle, we know everyone we pass. At the pizza place, at the laundromat, at the grocery store, at any of the shops still in business, we know all the patrons. At the bar where Mama works, there are no regulars because everyone's a regular.

So some of why I've forgotten how to breathe is this kid's newness. But that is not the problem. Because he is new, it is true. He is new. But his name is not.

"Yesterday we finished up the Treaty of Versailles." Mrs. Shriver takes a deep breath and dives in. "So now we turn our attention to the Italian Renaissance."

We're used to history as backgammon, all shakers and dice throws. But River looks around like maybe it's a trick or some kind of weird performance art we're all in on. Of course he's not familiar with Mrs. Shriver's out-of-order approach to history, and of course he doesn't know her own — how she and her husband and her brand-new teaching certificate moved to Bourne when the plant did to start a new life as a young married couple in a safe town where property was still affordable but on the rise and good new jobs were plentiful. Now her history includes all those miscarriages, a husband with migraines bad enough he can't work, and a house into which they poured all their savings that today is worth nothing. So you can see why she would want to take history by the throat and shake it, what happens and what happens next, how one thing leads to another thing without any choices ever being made. Petra would say unassailably. She might even say incontrovertibly.

When River determines it's not a joke and we are, in fact, advancing our study of history by going five hundred years in the wrong direction, I watch his eyes cloud with the possibility that what he must already be thinking of us — provincial, backwater, small-town hicks — isn't the half of it. He has no idea.

But he rolls with it. He shrugs then leans over and pulls a leather-bound book out of an expensive-looking bag that is not remotely a backpack and starts taking diligent notes.

Right in the middle of Mrs. Shriver's lecture, he raises his hand to make a point about the way fair trade and international commerce were sparks for democracy and religious equality. He raises it again with a question about the role Catholic Rome played in the rise of Venetian capitalism. He cites a book he's read. He makes a joke about a gondola which is almost dirty and actually funny.

We are paying attention, if not to Renaissance history, at least to the history being made in this room right now. We are slack-jawed — with incredulity, with implication, with the audacity of this kid — or maybe just because we are exactly the unbright yokels River must imagine us to be.

We're not actually dumb though. Which means some things are clear to us at once.

River is normal. This is what normal looks like. Not normal for here, normal for out there, normal for everywhere else — bright, educated, untroubled, unworried. Whole. And us? We're not normal, not for anywhere.

And some things come clear more slowly, to us and to bright, clean, sparkling River himself. He knows much about the world out there and, apparently, the world which built it and the worlds which came before, but about our world here, the one in which he finds himself now, he knows nothing. Not even who he is.

Two

"Templeton?" says Nellie.

"Templeton," I affirm. I have heard it from three different people now, and that is how many sources Mrs. Lasserstein says you need before you can put a fact in your research paper.

"The rat in *Charlotte's Web*?"

The Kyles laugh at Nellie because we are sixteen, and she is not remembering *Charlotte's Web* from her childhood or reading it aloud to a younger sibling but is actually studying it with her supplemental reading group. But the Kyles should not laugh at her. One, because it is mean. Two, because we all read at different levels, and different does not mean smart or stupid, and everyone has their own strengths as well as their own challenges. Three, because *Charlotte's Web* is a good book regardless of how old you are. But mostly, four, because she is right.

"Yes," I tell her and the Kyles. "A rat. Exactly."

Because I have also confirmed that River Templeton is *that* Templeton. His father is Nathan, not Duke, but only because Duke is his grandfather. I have only one source on this rather than three, but since the source is River himself, that makes it a primary source rather than a secondary source, and sometimes you only get one of those. You could also interview his father, but of course he did not come to school. You could also interview his father's father, but he would not grant you an interview. I know because Mama tried. A lot.

What happened was that I saw Mab in the hallway looking weird.

"One," I said, and she did not even look up.

"One!" I said louder, and many other people looked up, but Mab did not.

"One," I came up and said in her ear, and her head snapped over to me, and her eyes met my eyes and told them something was terrible. "Something is wrong?" I guessed.

She nodded.

"You feel sick?"

"No."

"You thought of something sad?"

"No."

107

"You got a bad grade on something?" This was a stupid guess because Mab never gets a bad grade on anything.

"That's him." She pointed with her chin at the walking-away back of someone. I could not see his front, but I still knew who she meant because there was only one *him* we had discussed recently: the new person living in my library.

"He is a kid?"

"He came with his family."

"He is Track A?" I asked even though I was pretty sure because otherwise how would Mab know?

"Sure. He's not from here."

"Some people who are not from here also are not Track A," I said.

She did not say anything because that was true, but that was not her point.

"Was he mean?" I guessed. She looked at me for the first time in the conversation. I looked away.

"No. He was fine."

"What is his name?" I asked.

Mab's expression was hard to identify. Closest was proud. She looked proud of me. Like I had finally asked the right question.

"River," she said.

"River?" I wrinkled my nose. It was a weird name.

"River Templeton."

She made big eyes at me, so big I had to meet them, and then I had to look away.

"Are you making a joke?" I asked because Mab is often making a joke, and it is hard to tell.

"It *is* a sick joke," she said. And first I felt relieved and then I felt strange because one, it was not funny, and two, she did not look like she thought it was either.

That is when I got my other two sources.

"Alex Malden," I called to him politely. "Can you tell me the full name of the new student in your class please?"

Alex Malden looked at me like I am weird but said, "River Templeton?" His voice went up at the end like a question, but his question was not whether the new student's name was River Templeton. He knew the new student's name was River Templeton. His question was why I was asking, why I was asking *him,* and why I am so weird.

No one knows the answers to these questions, so I turned to Petra.

She started nodding before I could even ask the question. "For real, sister," she said, and she meant me, even though we are not sisters, because my sister is like her sister which makes us like sisters too. That is the transitive property which I learned in geometry.

"Maybe it is a different Templeton," I said.

"Wait'll you see him," Mab breathed all in a rush.

But I could not wait. I watched the back of the student weave off down the hall and then into the bathroom, and then I could not go in the bathroom because it was the men's room and I am not a man, so I stood right outside the door. When the door opened and the front of the new student was behind it, what he looked was surprised, probably because I was a girl and not a boy and also probably because I was standing so close he could not get out.

"Excuse me," he said which was polite.

I did not want his eyes to look in my eyes, but I did want to see his face, so I looked and did not move.

"I . . . have to get past," he tried, and I saw what he meant, but I still did not move.

"Can you . . . um . . . scoot over a little?" he said, and that is when I saw what Mab meant about him. He had the same eye shape and the same lip shape. His nose spread out the same way from his cheekbones. The same lines, but less deep, came down from his nostrils to his mouth which raised at the corner in the same way. It was confusing. It is true I have only ever seen that face before in newspaper clippings and on the computer, but I recognized the sameness anyway.

So he would not see me or see me seeing him, I looked back at the ground and asked him my questions.

"Did you just move into the library?"

"Yes." What he sounded was surprised. He is new so he did not yet know what a small town Bourne is or how fast word travels around it. "Why?"

I did not want to tell him why. "Is your name River Templeton?"

"Yeah." Again, surprised with a little bit of something else. "Why?"

"Is your dad Duke Templeton?"

"No," he said, and then he added, "My dad is Nathan. Why?"

"Do you *know* Duke Templeton?"

"Yeah, he's my grandfather," he said. And he did not ask why.

That is when I knew all I needed to know, so I let him out of the bathroom, turned, and went back to my class.

"I don't get it," Nellie says, which she does not need to because it is obvious. "River is a weird name for a boy."

"Not River." Kyle R. looks and sounds scrunched-up which means exasperated.

"Templeton. Like Duke Templeton."

Nellie's face stills shows confused.

Nellie is usually confused — that would be rude for me to say out loud, but it is okay for me to think because it is just a true fact — so she might not be smart enough to know who Duke Templeton is, but she might also never have been told. Lots of Bourne parents do not tell their children what happened because it is hard to say to your baby girl, "Baby girl, you are real dumb. It is not your fault, but it also cannot be changed," and it is also hard to say to your baby girl, "We needed the jobs so we did not mind for a while that we were all being poisoned." A lot of parents never told their children what happened. They did not want them to know, or maybe they just did not want to talk about it.

As a contrast, my mother has talked about it every day for the sixteen years I have known her which is my whole life. She has shown me and my sisters her notes for the lawsuit so many times that when the grandson of Duke Templeton walks out of the boys' bathroom at Bourne Memorial High School seventeen years after what happened happened, I recognize him in the blink of an eye without even meeting his.

My mother calls Duke Templeton the AIC

of Belsum Chemical which stands for Asshole in Chief, and this is probably accurate but technically wrong because really Duke Templeton is the president and CEO.

"You know that abandoned plant on the other side of Bluebell Park?" I say to Nellie.

She shakes her head no even though it is the biggest building in all of Bourne, and she has driven by it at least 11,680 times which is twice a day for sixteen years, and since her birthday was in May, that is an underestimate.

"There is an abandoned plant on the other side of Bluebell Park," I begin again. "It belongs to Belsum Chemical. They turned the water smelly and brown and said it was still okay to drink, and then they turned the water very bright green and said it was not okay to drink after all or even use or even be near, but by then it was too late."

"Wow," Nellie says, "I don't remember that."

"Because you were not born yet."

"Oh." She frowns. "Did they say sorry?"

"They said sorry like when you punch your sister, and she yelps, and you are glad it hurt her because she is annoying, but your mom says say sorry, so you say sorry, but you do not really care, and she knows it."

"I don't have a sister," Nellie says.

113

"They said sorry, but they did not mean sorry," I clarify.

"How do you know?"

"I know they did not mean sorry because they did not do anything to make it better."

"What *did* they do?" Nellie asks.

"They left," I say. "They did not do anything."

She thinks about it. "Except send you their grandson."

Nellie probably does not understand what she means, but this is a good point. Mab said who he was, but Mab did not say the most important things which are what is River Templeton doing at Bourne Memorial High School and why is he living in my library. It does not seem possible that Belsum Chemical sent their grandson to live with us. But I cannot think of a thing which does seem possible instead.

After-school tutoring is canceled because, Mrs. Radcliffe says, "What with everything." I do not know what her words mean, but what her actions mean is Mab can leave school with me. On the way home, we stop at her friend Pooh Lewis's apartment because even though Pooh Lewis's eyes work, her legs do not, which means it is not accurate to say she cannot read without a

114

reader (Mab), but it is accurate to say she cannot read without a librarian (me) because Pooh can read but only if there is a book already in her home.

I have chosen for her a book about King Philip II of Spain because King Philip II of Spain had a wheelchair, even though it was the 1590s and even though really he could walk if he wanted to, and that makes him a good subject for Pooh who also uses a wheelchair and also was born a long time ago and also can read without help but pretends she cannot.

But before I can give the good news about the book, Mab opens Pooh's front door and calls in, very loud and happy about it, "You were wrong."

"So what else is new?" says Pooh Lewis. I look at her face to see if she is mad or sad about being called wrong, but she does not look like she minds. "About what?"

Mab tells her about the moving vans at my library and how there was a new student at school and how that new student's name is River Templeton.

Pooh Lewis says, "Oh!" She claps her hand over her mouth which means surprise or shock, but I can see under her hand that she is smiling which means happy which is weird. When she stops smiling and holding her mouth, I think she will ask what is he doing here or what does it mean that River Templeton has moved to Bourne or what happened when he was introduced at school. But instead she says, "So! What does he look like?"

"That's what you were wrong about." Mab is bouncing a little bit. "When you said real life isn't like the movies anywhere? He looks just like a movie star. It is *exactly* like the movies out there."

Pooh Lewis makes a noise like a squeal and claps her hands. "That handsome?"

"Not handsome. More like . . ." Mab does not finish saying what she is saying.

"What? What?" Pooh is very impatient. I know how she feels.

Mab says, "Well lit."

Pooh says, "Well lit?" because she does not understand what Mab means which makes me feel better because I also do not understand what Mab means.

"Glowing like," Mab says. "Shiny."

"Greasy?" Pooh is guessing because Mab does not make sense. "Radioactive?"

"Healthy," Mab says. "Whole."

"Ahh," Pooh says to show she understands. "Well, sure. He must be rich."

Which makes me feel glad to have something to contribute to the conversation. "It is not accurate to ascribe a correlative relationship between being rich and being pretty," I inform them. Mr. Beechman is very big on the difference between correlation and causation.

"I don't know what that means, honey," Pooh Lewis says, "but being rich has everything to do with being pretty."

"There are many ugly rich people," I point out.

"Name one," Pooh Lewis says.

I cannot name one, but I cannot name any rich people, ugly or pretty.

Pooh Lewis says, "If you have money, you can get your hair curled or straightened, darkened or bleached, thickened or removed. You can get the fat taken off your ass to fill in your wrinkles. You can get your teeth pushed in if they're pushing out, straightened if they're crooked, whitened if they're beige. Clothes, nails, shoes, jewelry." She waves all up and down herself. "You can replace the whole damn thing if you have enough money."

This is a weird thing to think about. I do not have any money. But if I did, there are a lot of other things I would do with it.

But Mab is not thinking about that. "He's sixteen," she says.

Pooh Lewis snorts like a horse. "You'd be

surprised what rich people let their kids do."

But Mab is shaking her head no. "It's more like he's been . . . I don't know —"

And Pooh Lewis fills in the end of her sentence. "Drinking clean water?"

I do not know what this has to do with being rich or being pretty or being River Templeton, but Mab's eyes get big and Mab's cheeks get red and Mab whispers a whisper and her whisper is this: "That's it, Pooh. That's what it is. That's it exactly."

I look at my sister's face, but I cannot say if she is happy or surprised or mad. Mrs. Radcliffe says these are very different emotions, and it is easy to tell them apart if you remember to look. And even though happy, surprised, and mad are like the points of an equilateral triangle — all far apart from one another — I think Mab might be all three.

THREE

"I'm never going to get to sleep."

I knew she was awake still — Monday too — but I'm relieved to hear Mab's voice in the dark.

"Muh," I say. Me neither.

"It is not accurate to say you are never going to get to sleep," Monday says, "because people who do not sleep go insane or die, and you are not insane or dead."

"Not until they stop sleeping." I don't know why Mab bothers arguing with her. "So the fact that we are sane and alive now just means that we've slept in the past, not that we will in the future."

This is the kind of logic Monday usually likes, but now it sends her into a panic.

"You cannot be insane or dead! How will I survive alone?"

Mab sighs. "One night's not going to kill us."

But Monday can't take that chance. *"Hush*

little baby do not you cry," she sings. *"Two is going to buy you a hook and eye."*

"That's not right." My Voice has that one saved because it applies in so many conversations.

"Please stop," Mab begs, but she's laughing, maybe at Monday for concluding all that stands between us and madness is a good night's sleep and all that stands between us and a good night's sleep is a lullaby. Or maybe at herself for imagining she can head off this lullaby before three more verses at least.

"And if that hook and eye will not hook, Two is going to let you borrow a book," Monday sings in the third person. Actually, come to think of it, that song is always in the third person.

"It's okay to be worried" — my Voice has this one saved as well — "but there is no immediate cause for concern."

"And if that book is overdue, Two is going to hit you with her shoe."

"And angry," Mab adds. "It's okay to be worried and angry — when we have such good reason to be worried and angry — without having our ears assaulted."

"Because keeping books beyond their due date is not nice, therefore when you do you have to pay the price."

120

"Truth or dare?" my Voice says, and Monday stops mid-inhale.

"I'm too tired," Mab whines.

"Lie!" Monday declares. We have upped the Truth or Dare stakes by merging it with Two Truths and a Lie. "You just said you could not sleep."

"Just because you can't sleep doesn't mean you're not tired. When you can't sleep you're more tired."

"Truth or dare, Mab?" my Voice clarifies.

We play this game like comfort food, like other sisters drink mugs of cocoa or gorge themselves on mac and cheese and chocolate-chip cookies.

"Dare," Mab tries, pointlessly.

"I dare you to stick your foot in the toilet." My Voice has had that saved for years.

"Germs!" Monday shrieks. Every time. "I dare you to wash your feet in the bathtub with warm water and soap for at least one hundred and twenty seconds and then wash your hands that washed your feet for another one hundred and twenty seconds."

So, "Truth." Mab changes her mind. As she always must.

I type. "What did you think of River?"

"Asshole," Mab says instantly.

I would like to say "asshole." Saying "asshole" seems like it would make you feel better. Whereas typing it — or tapping the folder of curse words I've saved and titled "I Swear" — is completely unsatisfying. My Voice is such an asshole.

"Lie," Monday pronounces.

"Truth," my Voice insists.

"You did not even meet him, Three. He was nice."

"Yeah, right," says Mab.

"He was. He was polite. He was not angry I was blocking his way out of the bathroom even though there are many germs there. I would become alarmed if someone tried to trap me in a bathroom."

"Duh," I say, my one word you don't need triplet-sense to understand.

"Plus he answered all of my questions."

"Lie," Mab says, and I giggle. "No one could ever answer all of your questions."

"I am not playing right now," Monday says. "I am making the point that River Templeton answered all my questions I asked him on the way out of the bathroom. And also he cannot be blamed because he was not even here when what happened happened because he was not alive yet."

"Point," I type.

"Exactly, Monday, that *is* the point. He wasn't here. We were all here. We were all living with the consequences of what his family did. And where were they? Safely elsewhere. They protected themselves. They protected him. They kept their distance. And now look at him. He's attractive, intelligent, fully mobile —"

"Truth or dare, Mab?" my Voice interrupts.

"It is my turn," Monday says.

"Attractive?" my Voice presses Mab, but she ignores me.

Monday has turned on the light and is kneeling up in bed to look at herself in the mirror over the bureau. "I was born here, and I am attractive."

"Lie." The Voice is not great for comic timing, so it takes its opportunities when they come.

Monday knows she's being teased, but Mab reassures her anyway. "It's not that he's attractive and we're not. It's that he's whole." *And we're not,* she does not add. Does not need to add.

"Is the reason you said River Templeton is an asshole because he stole my library," Monday asks, "and now I have to write a retraction postcard announcing that the library is not re-relocating to the library after all?"

I smile at Mab, and she smiles back. "Truth or dare?" she asks me.

"Truth." It is my only option really.

"Is River Templeton an asshole because he stole Monday's library" — Mab turns the light back off — "or is there another reason?"

I tap the picture of the adult woman. "Nora," my Voice says but leaves the rest unspoken. What about her lawsuit? I shouldn't say hers. She wouldn't like it. It's all of ours. It's what she's doing for us all, not "us all" her progeny, "us all" her entire town. This has been her obsession — you might say addiction — but also her solace for almost two decades. And though we don't know what the Templetons' reemergence into our lives means, we can be certain Nora will think it is very bad news.

We three lie in separate beds in the dark, considering our mother.

Finally Monday says, "Do me."

"Truth or dare?" Mab asks, unnecessarily. Monday always chooses truth. For one thing, she'd rather die than stick her foot in a toilet. She might die if you tried to make her stick her foot in a toilet. But mostly, she thinks she's incapable of telling a lie. This makes her feel like she's winning the game.

"Truth."

"What will we do when Mama finds out they're back?"

"She cannot find out," Monday says.

"Lie." Mab sounds resigned, exhausted. "She's going to find out."

"It is not a lie, but it might be incorrect," Monday admits. "It is more accurate to say we cannot be the ones to tell her."

Monday tells her first thing the next morning. The coffee has not even cooled enough to sip before she blurts out, "We have a new student at school, and he is living in my library, and that means the library cannot move there, and that means my extra-large postcard was a lie, and his name is River Templeton, and his father is Nathan Templeton, and his grandfather is Duke Templeton, and it is not a different Duke Templeton but the exact same one."

Nora's expression passes from confusion to laughing because she's sure she's being teased to anger to horror, like a magician flipping over one card after another after another. She lands on the saddest face I've ever seen. "My Duke Templeton?" she whispers finally, the opposite of how Monday says "My library," desperate to disavow ownership rather than claim it. She looks at Mab for confirmation because sometimes Monday doesn't realize when someone's kidding or lying or being sarcastic. Mab has

125

to look away from our mother's broken face, but she nods at her shoes.

Nora squeezes her earlobes for some reason then drops her hands to her chest. "Christ," she says and doesn't say anything more, and neither does anyone else until finally, what feels like an hour later, she says to, I guess, all of us, "Why?"

Mab shrugs, and Monday shrugs, and I make a motion with my hand that means what a shrug means. We do not know.

"They canceled tutoring" is all Mab can offer.

But Nora nods. "Like when someone dies."

Mab and I exchange glances. It's not that we don't have the same question Nora does — *Why?* — it's that that question is over-whelmed by the ones it presages. Nora is worried about what possible reason the Templetons have for being here. We are worried about our mother.

She sits, pale and not closing her mouth all the way. Her eyes are scary, somewhere else, like her mind is whirling away from us. She keeps shaking her head no, seeming about to speak, changing her mind. She leaves for work without another word.

But over scrambled eggs and summer squash for dinner, Nora is new, smile tight and bright, hopeful, which is not a thing we ever see her be, so it would be strange regardless. As it is, it's alarming. Creepy. When she speaks, what she says, finally, beaming and to all three of us at once, is "You can find out."

"What can we find out?" Monday asks, but I can see Mab feeling the same sinking feeling I am.

"The kid knows something," Nora says. "Everything maybe. But maybe he doesn't know he knows, or maybe he knows but he doesn't know we don't know, or he doesn't know he isn't supposed to know or isn't supposed to tell."

"*I* do not know," Monday says. What our mother's talking about, she means.

But Nora doesn't get it. She's grinning like the villain in act two of a superhero movie. "No, but you can find out. You can find everything."

The next morning, I get up and go to church, seeking not salvation but alone time, which is nearly as elusive and just as holy. Mab and Monday rose not long after the sun and left before Nora even got me out of bed. Sometimes this eats at me. Sometimes them together without me seems as cruel as if my own legs went walking off and I had to wait for them here. But it's hard to be forever one of three or half of two, a third of triplets, a dependent daughter. These solo Saturday mornings are my only time alone, so they're painful but they're also precious, and I'm grateful as a nun to be on my way somewhere as well.

Before bed last night, we made a reluctant plan. Nora's probably wrong that we'll be able to find out anything never mind everything, but she's even less likely to be able to let this go. Mab and Monday will go to the library this morning to see what they can learn there. I'll go to yoga and do the same.

Everyone at Pastor Jeff's Saturday-morning yoga class is there for enlightenment, but not the spiritual kind. Whatever gossip there is in Bourne, it gets discussed at Yoga for Seniors. Mostly his students lie in savasana and whisper loudly mat to mat while Pastor Jeff demonstrates a variety of dogs from the dais. If anyone in town knows anything new about the Templetons, church will be the place to find out.

I get Nora's rancor toward Omar for his epic dropping of the mayoral ball once upon a time, but he deserves props too. On my way this morning, I find curb cuts at every intersection, wide, smooth pavement over every inch of sidewalk, extra-long reds at the stoplights. Nora's point is let's not lionize people for cleaning up messes they made themselves — especially if they're not so much cleaning them up as straightening a little and shoving what can't be mended into a closet or under the sofa and hoping no one notices — but in fact, at least as long as I've known him, Omar has quietly been doing a hard job well.

It's early still, drizzling, but fresh air and agency are an intoxicating combination. Tom fashioned rain gear for my chair long ago — an elaborate tangle of poncho, glove, and plastic bag — and being outside and unchaperoned is so lovely, I don't mind getting a little wet. The smell is mossy and cool at the back of my nose. The world looks spit shined: green washed and water slick. The raindrops feel good on my skin. Nora got me dressed but let me go without socks and shoes — I'm not walking, after all — and the wind in my toes rivals the wind in my hair as far as the feel of freedom goes. Some of the kids in my class who can't move their legs also can't feel them, so though I sometimes have pain, I am grateful to have feeling at all. I wave good morning to the few early risers I pass, and they wave peaceably back.

When I get to the church, it's cool and

dry inside and Saturday-morning loud. Pastor Jeff's dog is downward. Everyone else's is abuzz. Busybody Dog. Pooh has traded her wheelchair for her mat but isn't stretching anything. Instead she's telling everyone what Mab reported about River. Donna Anvers is telling about the moving vans. Mrs. Radcliffe and Mr. Beechman are telling what happened at school. Everyone is talking about the Templetons, but no one knows anything, which is itself noteworthy. Aside from enrolling the kid in school, the Templetons are lying low. Or else in wait.

Pastor Jeff comes up to standing, lowers his hands to heart center, takes a deep inhale, and, without opening his eyes, calls, "Mirabel Mitchell. You are not a senior."

True. Not that I can do much yoga anyway.

"So stop spying on my yogis for your mother," he adds on the way to his toes.

Maybe it's years of doctoring the widest range of patients, maybe it's years of ministering the widest range of parishioners, maybe his mind is focused from all the yoga, but it's hard to hide things from Pastor Jeff. Plus he knows my mother almost as well as I do.

When he finds me skulking near the chancel after class, his first question isn't a question. "You can only chase your own demons, you know." Strange advice from a pastor. "You can't chase your mother's."

I don't need to plead the fifth to plead the fifth, but I make my face look as innocent as possible.

Because Pastor Jeff has to doctor during the week and lead services on Sundays, Saturday is his only day off, and he usually starts it, after yoga, at our house for breakfast. He and Nora don't talk shop over the weekend, and my mother doesn't let him preach to her, but she does like to feed him. All those pastries have to go somewhere. So after he puts all the mats away, he wanders back toward home with me. For a while, we're both quiet. Then he asks his second question, an actual question at least, if at first it seems like a subject change.

"Did I ever tell you my mother was almost a nun?"

Pastor Jeff's parents met in Mississippi during Freedom Summer. He doesn't talk about that time much — he wasn't born yet, after all — but we know all about it anyway from Mab's ninth-grade history class. Mrs. Shriver said Pastor Jeff was descended from royalty, that his parents, whose only relation to Bourne was raising a son who later moved here, were the most monumental thing that ever happened to this town. And that's saying something.

"She saw injustice and felt called to help, and she'd been told all her life the path to righteousness was God. She was beloved at church, and love feels holy. *Is* holy. But mostly, she wanted to be a teacher, and every teacher she'd ever had to that point was a nun. So that was her plan: graduate high school, go to college, become a nun."

"What happened?" my Voice asks.

"She met my dad. Learned there were other ways to be beloved and other kinds of holy. Learned there were as many paths to righteousness and as many ways to serve as there are fights against injustice."

I wait, but he doesn't say anything else, so I type, "Point?"

He winks. "Not all teachers are nuns."

I consider this. "Point?" my Voice repeats.

"Just because your mother's cause is just and right, doesn't mean you have to fight her fight. And if you do, it doesn't mean you have to fight her way."

"If you knew something, you'd tell me, right?" Nora's waiting at the door for us and plows right in. "You wouldn't keep it from me so I don't start yelling like a crazy lady?"

"You are a crazy lady, Nora."

"Exactly. So there's no need to lie."

"Lying is against the code," says Pastor Jeff.

"What code?"

"Medical ethics, religious leader, take your pick."

"I went to yoga," my Voice tries to reassure her. "No one knows anything. Maybe there's nothing to know."

"I don't need yoga." She snorts. "I know why the Templetons are back."

Pastor Jeff has filled his mouth with pineapple scone but raises his eyebrows at her.

"They're here to bury evidence." She gives a little shudder. It's glee.

He humors her through crumbs. "Evidence?"

"Something we're close to finding. Something that would break the lawsuit wide open."

His eyebrows turn to waggle at me. *Your mama's nuts,* they say. I grin at him.

"If they've come in person, it must mean they're scared. If they're scared — finally, after all this time — it must be because we're closing in. We've always had a critical mass of people signed on to the suit. We've always had tons of evidence. So far, they've been able to spin it as circumstantial or inadmissible or unreliable or biased or fabricated or ambiguous. So now we must be close to something they know they can't deny, something they won't be able to get dismissed. Something that could really hurt them. Point is, they never come in person. They must be worried."

Nora's so charged she's trembling, shimmering at the edges, not so far gone as optimistic, but something's changed, at least it's starting to, and it's been so long since anything has. Maybe they know something we don't and they're here to hide it before we find it, but at least that means it exists. Maybe their being here at all is evidence they're hiding something, the smoking gun she searches for like the Holy Grail.

Pastor Jeff swallows his mouthful and echoes my thoughts. "Maybe."

She rolls her eyes. "You're not a Zen priest, you know."

"I do," he intones, exactly like a Zen priest.

"You can pass judgment."

"I could if I had any basis for one."

"Jesus, Jeff —"

"You're right, Nora," he interrupts because he knows it's time to stop teasing when he's driven her to blasphemy. "It could be the lawsuit. It could be there's evidence you're about to uncover, and they're here to better bury it. It could be Russell and the firm have got them scared finally. Maybe. But I think it would be prudent not to get your hopes up."

"I don't give a shit about prudent, Jeff."

"I noticed." He smiles at me from inside his coffee. "Maybe you're on to something. Or maybe they're going to find whatever they're looking for before you do. Or maybe there's nothing to find."

"Of course there's something to find," Nora scoffs. "We're not pretending they fucked us. They did fuck us."

This. This is Nora's religion. I have solo Saturday mornings. Pastor Jeff has God, the Catholic Church, and any number of other denominations he borrows from liberally in order to meet his congregants' needs and practices. Nora's faith is just as fervently held, just as life guiding and path determining, and for the same reason: she believes in her soul it will save her.

And this is her central tenet: They did fuck us. Therefore there must be evidence of this fact somewhere. Therefore she has only to find it. Then justice will be served, the wicked unmasked and punished, the good and faithful rewarded for their patience and fidelity.

Why else do people believe in God?

ONE

We are not girl detectives. We're not plucky like that. We can't hide. Maybe this would be true anyway — there are three of us — but there's also Mirabel's inability to walk, Monday's inability to lie, my inability to go places without them. The lack of places to go. Under our folded clothes, our dresser drawers are all lined with Nancy Drews — Monday likes to keep them there because their spines are yellow — but Nancy's got skills, resources, and horizons we can only dream of. Suffice it to say, some kind of teen-spies thing where we get wigs and fake mustaches and sit outside the library pretending to read a newspaper (Petra would say "surreptitiously") is not an option.

Last night, in response to our mother's mania, Mirabel suggested a fact-finding mission, but it's not even fact finding. More like information gathering. Situation determining. It doesn't make sense to think we'll

137

find the elusive, conclusive proof Mama and Russell have been searching for for entire lifetimes — our entire lifetimes — simply by befriending River Templeton. If her lawyer can't, what chance do her teenage daughters have? So let's just say we're getting there first. Not before anyone else in town — no one will care as much as my mother, and everyone knows it. Getting to the Templetons before the Templetons get to us.

It's overcast, which makes it seem dark still, dawning, and drizzling hard, almost raining, so it feels closer to floating, or maybe sinking, than riding bikes. Monday and I fly down Baker, the hill steeper than it is on foot and slippery with wet, just the hint of fall in our noses. The wind and rain tease our hair. Snaggled grass whips our legs. Our tires throw up gravel and pebbles like popcorn. We close our eyes for a moment, two, and I could not stop now if I wanted to. If I had to.

And then — like a sign spontaneously generated by flying too fast downhill — the road curves up again past the cemetery. It's tragic but apt that this is the one place in Bourne that's as it should be. It has soft, deep-green grass and meandery paths between sprawling trees. There are all these old, weathered gravestones because, hard as it is to remember, Bourne's citizens died even before Belsum came to town. It's hilly, and at the crest of a ridge are the showy monuments: giant angels, giant crosses, tombs that look like houses that would be cramped to live in but are probably plenty roomy if you're dead, the same few family names over and over — Grove, Alcott, Anderson — town founders, our ancestors, our history. We used to ride by fast so we could hold our breath as we crossed, but now Monday slows as we pass, and I see her eyes seek and find our father's grave.

This is the part of Bourne's cemetery that is not as it should be. They had to dig it too fast without making any kind of plan. Mrs. Shriver says that when demand is greater than supply, it makes the economy stronger, but in our cemetery, it just made things overcrowded and chaotic. Maybe that whole supply-demand thing only applies to the living. And it's sad, which makes sense for a graveyard, but ours is sadder than most because the years on either side of the hyphens are too close together. Bourne was not prepared for all our sudden dead. Maybe no town ever is, though.

Our dad lucked out. He is under a giant oak tree. Some of the trees in Bourne go straight to brown in the fall now, but his still blushes as if embarrassed. It's already pinking a little as we go by. Monday closes her eyes too long, and I know, I know she doesn't like to be touched, but I'm worried she'll crash. I reach out and tap her arm as lightly as I can, but she still snatches it away from me like I burned her.

Her eyes snap open. "Why can it not be yellow?"

"What?"

"His tree. Many trees turn yellow in the fall. His turns red. It is not fair."

"No," I agree, "it is not fair."

We continue down the hill, brake into the curve on Main, stand to pedal hard over the slight slope by the Do Not Shop, wobble off the end of the pavement and through the gravel, climb up across the bridge and over the ravine and pull, breathless and sticky-damp from drizzle and sweat, into the empty parking lot of the library.

Well, almost empty.

The moving vans are gone, but there are two cars. One is a shiny, black BMW, new, immense, almost uncomfortable to look at. (Petra would say "carnal," "corporeal," "lascivious," "lubricious" — it's weird how many vocabulary words there are to describe kind of gross and inappropriate cars.) The

140

other is the same, only gray. Cars in Bourne are mostly not the shiny luxury variety. More like dented, rusted, ancient pickups or sad sedans with doors of different colors. Or tricked-out, million-year-old wheelchair vans.

Heaped at the far end of the lot are a dozen of those squat little library stools, some of them tipped over, like maybe they were bowled out the front door, their casters spinning uselessly up at the sky.

"Motherfuckers," Monday curses.

Monday never curses. Which makes me think we can go home now. That word coming out of that mouth says it all really. My mother will be disappointed when we return without a single shred of new evidence, our holsters empty of smoking guns, but my mother is used to being disappointed. It was a dumb plan anyway. I'd maybe buy that River's just a kid and can't keep a secret. It's that he has any confidences to betray that's hard to believe. When you're obsessed with something, as my mother is, it's hard to remember that everyone else isn't obsessed with it too, but I think about how healthy and whole and normal River seemed — oblivious, ignorant — and I'm certain we already know all we're going to. We can leave now. But before I can explain this logic to Monday, the front door opens.

River Templeton stands in the doorway with an older version of himself. His father. Must be. My in-breath is quick and loud, and Monday's head whips around from them to me again.

"Why did you gasp, One?"

"He looks just like his father," I whisper, "who looks just like —"

"Why are you whispering?" Monday interrupts. "They are too far away to hear."

Our river has washed away more even than we think. More even than our lives and livelihoods. It's not just that we are pale, whittled down, water worn, corroded. Our actual DNA is weaker than theirs. Monday and I barely look related. Triplets are rarely identical, but the three of us don't really even look alike or all that much like Nora either. River is a copy of his father who's a copy of his. It's like our genes are not just infirm but mutated, like we've sloughed off our essential natures. They're shiny and strong and cloning themselves. We're eroding toward gone.

Shiny Nathan Templeton claps his son's shoulder and then gives him a little shove, and River stumbles out the door in our direction, slow and sheepish, like a cranky toddler.

"He is coming, One!" Monday shrieks, drops her bike, and tries to hide behind me. She is five inches taller than I am.

He stops a foot away from us. He looks more normal than he did at school — he's got on a T-shirt and shorts and mussy Saturday-morning hair, but he still has that glow. It might, like Pooh said, be a lifetime of wealth, clean water, high (and met) expectations. Or it might be more a shimmer than a glow, like when it's hot and it looks like there's water pooling on the asphalt up ahead, but when you actually get there it's flat and dry and empty.

He's also carrying a top hat. And a wand. He's bright red, trying to hide the wand by shoving it into his back pocket, and having about as much luck — for about the same reason — as Monday.

If he were my friend or even my sort-of friend, I'd be embarrassed for him since he was clearly in the middle of something private when his father pushed him out the door like a two-year-old. But since his family's basically my family's sworn enemy, I'm thinking it's okay to laugh at him.

What Monday's thinking (and therefore saying) is "There are no dance classes in Bourne," her first words to him since they met on his way out of the boys' bathroom at school. "There used to be Miss Molly's when we were little, but she died and that was only ballet."

He has no idea what she's talking about. Even I have no idea what she's talking about.

"So you better change," she peeks out from behind me to add.

"Change?" He has a funny look on his face. Is he confused or contemptuous? ("Supercilious," Petra would say.) I admit Monday's not making sense, and he's probably used to people making sense. Still. He came over to talk to us, even if he didn't want to. We're on his lawn, yes, but it wasn't his until this week.

"Out of your dance clothes," Monday explains.

He looks down at his ratty T-shirt, up at me for help, back to Monday. "These aren't dance clothes."

"The top hat." She waves at it, her arm emerging over my shoulder alongside my ear. "The tiny dance cane."

"Oh." He blushes again. "It's not a tiny cane. It's a wand. I was" — it seems like he won't finish that sentence but then concludes it's too late anyway — "practicing magic."

"You are magic?" Full of wonder.

"No," he says at once. Then, "Well, you know."

"No." She does not. But she's stepped out from behind me to get a better look at him.

"I'm just practicing. Messing around. An amateur magician or whatever."

"A wizard apprentice?" Monday's eyes are open as prairies, splitting the difference between impressed and afraid.

"No, just for fun." He can't decide if she's making fun of him or not. "Or like for little kids' birthday parties maybe."

"Is that why your father made you come here?" This is the first on-point question she's asked yet.

"What? No." But he answers a different question, the one he thinks she's asking rather than the one I wish she were. What she actually means is anyone's guess. "He saw you ride up and thought the well-bred thing to do was come say hello. Dad's big on well-bred."

"He wants you to use your dark arts against us." She scuttles behind me again. I can feel her trying to keep it together. I can also feel little flecks of spit flying out of her mouth onto the top of my head.

He assumes she's joking, starts laughing, sees he's the only one, trails off. We have run out of things to talk about already, and

145

I'm glad because I'm ready to leave now. Past ready. Creeping toward desperate.

But then the library front door opens slowly — it's still wired for wheelchair access to come ajar, ghostly, at the press of a giant square button — and we see Nathan again, standing in the doorway, smiling. In fact, his whole body is smiling. He's wearing new-looking, tech-flaunting hiking boots, but you can tell that if you could see his toes, they'd be smiling too.

"Guests! Welcome!" He waves from the doorway for us to come in like when the lifeguards hear thunder at the pool, and then he turns and goes back inside, that confident we'll follow, as the door closes slowly behind him.

I know that talking to Nathan Templeton is my best shot at finding out something my mother could use, but I have exactly no desire to do so. I feel many things, but one of them, embarrassingly, undeniably, is frightened.

River rolls his eyes. Then he reaches into his back pocket and retrieves his wand, waves it over us, makes his voice deep and cavernous. "The Raging River commands you to come inside."

"The raging river?" says Monday.

"You know" — his voice back to normal

— "like the Great Houdini. Or the Powerful Oz. Get it? Because a powerful river is raging, but raging also means —"

"Thanks for the offer but . . ." I interrupt then trail off with a tone and facial expression which I hope finish the sentence for me. *Thanks, but you can't command me to do anything, and I would rather drink actual tap water than spend my Saturday morning with your family.*

But Monday is bouncing on the balls of her feet and doing a little dance with her fingers because, be it from the devil incarnate, or at least his grandson, an invitation to get back into her beloved library is not one she is going to refuse.

TWO

It has been two years and three months and some number of days since the last time I was in this building. I study Mab's pulled-together eyebrows and pulled-down lips and conclude she does not want to enter River's house, but I want to enter my library so I accept, even though those two places are the same place at the moment. River Templeton taps the wheelchair square with his wand, and the door glides open. If this were my first time here, I might think this is magic, but it is not my first time here, and the door opens with the same little puff and ding as it always did, whether you use a wand or not.

As far as my nose can tell, it is exactly the same: the dusty odor of the books, the musty odor of the carpet, the hot-wood smell from bookcases heated by years of sun streaming through windows. This is the most beautiful, perfect building in our town or probably in anyone's town.

At the bottom of the staircase up to Reference and Research, River's father has an expression on his face which I do not know what it means. It is not sad or mad or worried or embarrassed. It is also not happy or excited or surprised. If you do not know the answer to what a facial expression on a facial-expression card means, Mrs. Radcliffe says to first decide is it a happy expression or an unhappy expression, but I look at River's father's face and cannot tell. What River's father looks to me is smooth, but smooth is not an emotion. His face is smooth and smiley, and that smile is smooth and white, and his hair is smooth and shiny and puffy, and his clothes are smooth and neat. He reaches a hand right at me while he is also walking right at me, and that hand is also smooth, but it also wants to touch me, so when he says, "Nathan Templeton. Very pleased to meet you," I hide behind Mab who does not mind when smooth hands or any hands touch her.

Mab shakes the smooth hand, but she does not say anything, I think because you are supposed to say you are pleased to meet him too and she is not.

Then he says, "Welcome to our home," very big and loud and smooth.

149

So I say, "Ha!"

So Mab says, "Monday," in a tone which means warning.

"River's father is making a joke," I inform Mab, "because this is not his home."

"Please, please" — River's father holds his arms out and I panic that he is going to hug me, but he just stands there like that — "call me Nathan."

"Nathan!" I call.

"A teenager who takes direction." River's father laughs. "You're a wonder . . ."

He trails off, so Mab says, "Monday."

"Monday? Oh! I didn't realize when you said just now . . . well, uh, delightful! What a great name. Let me guess, Monday. Your parents are artist types."

"Wrong," I say because he is, and I am about to explain, but Mab says, "Monday," again in her warning voice.

"Best two out of three," says River's father, which is when I realize he plays Truth or Dare and a Lie as well. "You grew up in this library."

"Lie," I say. "No one grows up in a library."

"Not so!" He claps his hands and lowers his voice but not his smile, like he is going to tell me a secret and he is very happy about it. "Some of my best friends grew up

150

in libraries. But I can see that you like things literal. I like that too. What I meant was I bet you spent many happy hours here as a child reading beloved titles."

"Truth," I admit. "The insides too."

He laughs like I have made a joke. "Right you are, Monday. I can tell all those hours reading have paid off. Nothing gets by you. You're sharp as a tack."

"Lie." I am neither sharp nor a tack. He has three lies and a truth so far, which is not how you play the game, but he is laughing and happy anyway.

"River here has been worried about being the new kid. You know, making friends, fitting in. I'm pleased to see he has such fine, smart classmates."

I look at River's classmate, who is Mab, but River's father is still grinning at me. Mab coughs a cough that does not sound like her usual cough.

"Well, see ya," she says to I do not know who, but it is probably not me. She turns around like she will walk out the door.

"No, you can't go yet," says River's father. "You know who bought muffins fresh this morning?"

I do not know, but I am preparing three guesses when a woman appears hurrying down the staircase. She is wearing clothes

151

to exercise in and has white and gray smears I can assume are dust all over them and her arms and face and hair.

"Here she is!" River's father's voice sounds surprised. Maybe he did not know just like I did not know that this woman was in the library. "How was the attic?"

She shakes her head at him, but I do not know why because "How was the attic?" is not a yes-or-no question.

"Find anything?" He makes his voice lower as if he hopes we will not hear him even though she is still on the stairs whereas we are standing right next to him.

She shakes her head again, and even though I do not know what she was looking for, at least that is a question to which "No" can be an answer.

"You," I say.

"Huh?" says River's father.

"I am guessing who bought muffins fresh this morning."

"Ahh." River's father's face does a big smile. "Nope, not me. Even better." He points to the dusty woman. "It was this lady here, my wife, River's mom, the lovely Apple Templeton."

Except for the dust, River's mother looks like a woman on television, not a television mother with aprons and cookies, but a television woman with shiny lips, curly eyelashes, and long hair that does not move when she moves. Whereas River's father looks smooth, River's mother looks pointy. River's father smiles at her. She does not smile back.

"Let me tell you" — River's father is still talking — "she has great taste in baked goods. We'd love to get to know you both, hear a little bit more about Bourne Memorial High. What are the hot clubs to join? Who's the cool teacher? Where do the popular kids eat lunch? We want the inside scoop." He turns to Mab. "We haven't even been introduced."

River points his wand at my sister like he will turn her into a toad. "This is Mab, Dad. She and Monday are sisters."

"Mab! What an unusual name. Are you sure your parents aren't artists?"

"It's Shakespeare." This is a truth, and it is the first thing River's mother has said, but she says it very quietly. She looks surprised, and he looks at her, and then he looks surprised.

But then he claps his hands together and turns back to us. "Mab and Monday! Wonderful! Delighted to meet you. So glad you're here. Come on in."

He turns and waves to us over his shoulder

which means "Follow me," and River's mother does and River does, and Mab and I do not know what to do so we do too, and he walks past where the checkout and return counters and the library card desk should be, but they are gone. And he walks into the Children's section, and my eyes see what is there, and they cannot believe it because in the Children's section, a kitchen has bloomed. It has a white-and-navy floor made out of shiny diamond tiles. It has a giant refrigerator with a screen right in the door. It has a range with six burners, two dishwashers, two sinks, two ovens, cabinets so blended right in you can almost not even see them, and countertops covered in appliances that look like no one ever used them before which might be because no one knows what they are because they are not obvious things like a toaster but non-obvious things with chutes and dials I cannot identify.

The Children's reference desk is still there like when you see a documentary about the Roman Colosseum but there are people with cellular telephones all around it. It has become shiny on top and grown a rack on the side for also shiny knives and hooks with dish towels. There are tall stools along the back like a saloon in a movie. My eyes see the Children's section they met before they can even remember, and they also see River's not-even-cooked-in-yet kitchen which looks like a kitchen in a magazine, and they cannot believe it even though they should not be so surprised because Chris Wohl said he saw kitchen delivery trucks, and my eyes can assume this kitchen is what they were delivering.

River's father motions us to sit on the tall stools, and he puts out three glasses, and he fills the glasses with orange juice, which I will not drink because it is raining and orange is not green, and he puts out a big bowl full of blueberry muffins, which I also will not eat because blueberries are also not green and because I am a baker's daughter and can tell that these muffins will not taste good. I feel a howl starting to build in the back of my throat.

But before it can come out, River's father does the most amazing thing. He walks over to the sink and fills a glass with water straight from the tap and drinks it all down!

Mab is staring at him with her mouth open. My howl is shocked into silence.

"Are you a pastor, priest, rabbi, or reverend?" I ask instead.

"Me?" River's father says or, to be more accurate, yelps. "No one's ever accused me

155

of that before."

"I am not accusing you," I correct him. "But the only person in Bourne who drinks water from the tap is Pastor Jeff, and he has faith as a man of God."

"Ahh. I see. Well, I don't trade in faith, but I do believe."

"In God?" I ask which he must have been hoping for because he smiles.

"I believe in Bourne. I believe the water and everything else here is pure and clean and safe as houses."

"Are houses safe?"

"Very, Monday. They're very safe. Clean. Clear. Healthy. Perfect. I believe Bourne's going great places."

"Where?" I ask.

He points his finger up, but when I look, all I see is they painted over the mural of rainbows and clouds which is usually on the Children's section ceiling. Now it is just beige. "The eaves?" I guess. "The roof?"

"The sky, Monday. The sky's the limit."

I do not know what this means or what it has to do with the tap water, but before I can ask more questions, River interrupts his father.

"Come on," he says. "I'll show you my room."

I do not think Mab will want to see his

156

room, but she gets up so I do too. I have a guess that she follows him because she does not like him less than she does not like his father who sounds kind but feels like something else.

"Thank you for coming by to welcome us, Monday and Mab," River's father says as we leave the Children's section.

"That is not why we came," I say.

"Then we were both surprised," he says. "How wonderful."

"Lie," I say, but I do not think we are playing anymore.

River leads us past the New Releases section where there are three fat, puffy chairs that sit up or lie down with their feet out, past the Mysteries and Thrillers section where there is a fancy, old-fashioned dining-room table with lots of wooden curlicues and knobbly legs ending in carved feet with actual carved toes, plus three equally old, toed chairs. (You could also shelve mysteries and thrillers in General Adult Fiction, but Mrs. Watson made them a separate section because sometimes people are dead on the covers of mysteries and thrillers, and a lot of readers in Bourne feel traumatized by looking at dead people without warning like if they were just browsing for a book all the characters live through.) In the Audiovisual section are stacks of boxes and pictures in frames and lamps — I guess because the Templetons moved in only recently and have not yet unpacked — separated into three groups. It is like *Goldilocks and the Three Bears.* It is also like *Apocalypse Now.* Both of these are movies I checked out approximately four feet away from where I am currently standing. I slide my gaze over to Mab who looks like her eyes are having the same problem mine are, and I am glad to know I am not overreacting or upset by myself. I can feel my howl trying to come back.

"That's my dad's office." River waves as we walk past the big study room. It is the biggest, but it is not the nicest because it is also the smelliest, but maybe his father does not know that yet, or maybe, like Mr. Beechman, he has lost his sense of smell. A more accurate name than study room would be loud room anyway since what people did in it was be loud. Bourne kids used to hang out and talk in there because you have to be quiet in all the other parts of the library. Bourne adults used it for holding organizing and task force meetings, back when there were more adults besides Mama who still wanted to organize and force tasks. The door is open, and inside I can see a giant chair and a giant desk and a giant painting of a giant.

"Who is that giant?" I ask.

"That's Uncle Hickory." River keeps walking and does not even look where I am pointing. He knows what "who" I mean. Maybe he really is magic. "His eyes follow you everywhere. It's creepy."

"Why is he a giant?"

"I don't know. That's just how portraits were back then I guess."

"Why is everything in your father's office so big when your father is a normal size?"

"Overcompensation," River says, and Mab laughs for the first time since we came inside the library, but I do not know what that means.

"My room's upstairs," he says, so we follow him up the grand staircase to Reference and Research where the dictionaries and encyclopedias are, and the tables and chairs are laid out in a grid system of rows with enough spots for many people to sit and read but enough space for wheelchairs or walkers or people with an armload of books to maneuver without accidentally touching anyone. I used to have to borrow one of the dictionaries to sit on, but now my feet touch the floor and my elbows touch the table and my butt touches the chair all at the same time, and this is good because butts put germs on dictionaries.

But at the top of the stairs, instead of the shelves and sets of books and the perfect seating grid, there is a twin bed with a brown comforter and two blue pillows, a dresser with twelve drawers, and a coatrack on wheels that should be downstairs by the elevator in the lobby for winter but instead is up here holding a bunch of flannel button-downs and sweatshirts. The far wall is naked except for the scars where the bookcases were bracketed, and in their place is a television tall and wide and flat as the world map which used to hang up here. (The map was not life-size of course — you cannot fit a life-size map of the world on the world — but I remember when Brazil was taller than I was.) There is one singular solitary beautiful lonely bookcase left, but it does not hold books because instead it holds a cape, five balls, two decks of cards, one stack of boxes, one pile of coins, and ten tied-together red and blue handkerchiefs.

My howl spills over. I drop to my knees, then my side, hands clamped over my ears, howling. Shrieking, to be more accurate. Dozens of the tables and chairs — I would count how many to be exact but I cannot stop screaming — are heaped atop one another, some broken and some scratched, pushed and piled into the corner as if they were washed there by a storm at sea. I can smell them through my screaming and also in my memory, a deep gold smell. Deep gold is practically yellow.

Mab grabs my wrists and tries to pull my hands from my ears. She is saying something to me, but I cannot hear her because I am shrieking. She is saying something to River too, but his hands are over his ears as well. She grabs me under the arms and hoists me upright, pushes me toward the stairs, and I start running, hands still in protective place, and she is running after me, and we go down down down, past the mother coming up the stairs with a tray of brown drinks and orange chips, past the checkout desk, past the father who emerges from New and Notable Releases to stare at us openmouthed with what looks like terror and fear, though I am bad at reading faces, but why he should be afraid of me, instead of the other way around, I cannot tell.

THREE

Raining again. Darkling though it is only early afternoon. After Pastor Jeff left this morning, Nora and I had only an hour of quiet before Mab and Monday arrived home red, breathless, muter than I am. We looked up alarmed when they slammed into the kitchen, hair untamed as tigers, cheeks the same color outside as in.

"Where have you been?" Nora toppled her chair when she stood. Mab shot us warning eyes, but Nora either didn't see or didn't care. "What happened?"

Monday kept her eyes on the ground and rushed past us to her shoeboxes of home-made card catalog. She wedged herself between them and the wall, a tiny space she fits in only by mashing knees to shoulders, thighs to breasts, and started flipping through the cards, but way too fast to read.

Mab looked tired and fed up and possibly scared. She met my eyes and shook her head. Then she went to our room and slammed the door.

Now Nora, who has learned again and again not to push these daughters, is baking bread, baking cake, baking tarts: sugary things, sweet things, any things to keep her hands busy, muttering under her breath, earbuds in deep as sunken treasure.

Someone paying less attention than I do, than I have to, might think Nora bakes to feed her fellow citizens. Her attempts to help run up against so many walls she's like a mouse in a maze. She can't keep Chris Wohl off drugs or give his wife Leandra her right side back, and she can't give the guys she abets in the bar a reason not to drink too much, and she can't give Bourne's citizens fresh water or fresh history. But she can bring them all cookies. And that is also love.

But that's not why she bakes.

Or you might think she bakes because it's something she can control. She couldn't protect her husband or her friends, her neighbors or her town or her daughters, but through precise measuring and careful assembly and attention to detail, she can make muffins that teeter at the serrated edge between sugar and butter, pillowed perfect sweetness you taste at the sides of your tongue like an afterthought, like you imagined it but imagined it vividly. If you're careful, and she is, muffins are entirely in your control.

But that's not why she bakes either.

Nora bakes because baking doesn't involve water.

Before a cow becomes a hamburger, it drinks a dozen gallons of water a day. Before a chicken and a bunch of onions and carrots become stock, you have to add a potful. Fish made it their home. Vegetables and fruits have to be rinsed in it before consumption, and that's a lot of bottled water literally down the drain.

Whereas what's wet in a batter is probably nothing more than melted butter and whipped eggs. The water that made the wheat that made the grain that made the flour happened so far away as to be another planet. So to ensure our good health, to keep us well and strong, Nora insists we eat cake. Cake and cookies, muffins and crumbles, danish and donuts and croissants. Some Saturdays she feeds us nothing but brownies and a multivitamin. When she relents, we have dinner from a box or can.

Timeworn wisdom prescribes food whole and unprocessed, slow and locally grown, low on sugar and light on butter. But Nora loves us, and if she boils boxed macaroni and cheese in bottled water then adds yellow beans from a can and bakes a cake, nothing involved has anything to do with our river or our soil. We all choose the terms of the desperate bargains we make with the powers that may be, which baseless beliefs and decaying wisdoms we cling to, and which we discard as superstition or sorcery or the ravings of misguided zealots. Which is to say: it may not make sense all the way, but it makes sense enough.

Some days Nora has to tear coffee cake into tiny pieces and feed it to me like a bird. Or she sits on a bag of potato chips and places the crumbs on my tongue where they dissolve one at a time. Some days that's all my system can manage. Some days I subsist on the smells from her oven alone.

That is what I am doing all afternoon while my sisters stew, sitting and smelling as our mother cooks, redolence as nourishment. And then the doorbell rings.

On the front porch, soaking and sorry, is a boy I can only presume is River Templeton.

Mab is right that he looks exactly like his grandfather, so much so that Nora seems barely to be breathing.

Mab is right that he is perfectly attractive

and whole-looking.

Mab is right that there is something deeply unsettling, and not unexciting, about how new River Templeton is, how odd it is to see a person you have never seen before.

Nora can't get her breath back.

River can't decide what to do with the panting, speechless adult whose pasted-on greeting smile is falling slowly past shock to scorn.

"I'm, um, here to . . ." River stammers. He peers around Nora, for help presumably, for a hint as to what to do next, but sees only me, stares, looks away, stares again. Nora pants.

"Is, um, does Mab live here?" he tries. "Or Monday?"

It's that "or" I think that does it. It is pity and newness and his cheeks covered in rain and his hair soaking tendrils down his face, but mostly it's that "or." Like either girl would do as well as the other. Like maybe Mab and Monday don't even live together. Like maybe we three are three and not one. With that one tiny word, all at once, I am in love.

Just so you don't get the wrong idea, I am not usually so easily beguiled. The Kyles both wooed me for years, but I remained unenthralled, probably because their displays of affection mostly manifested as wrestling with each other, and a girl wants wit as well as charm. At least this girl does. Technically, I went to the fifth-through seventh-grade dances with Rock Ramundi, but really everyone just stood along the walls and felt shy of one another. Rock and I still text sometimes though. It's not Abelard and Héloïse as far as passionate correspondence goes, but then she was cloistered in an abbey whereas I am only cloistered in Bourne. The point is I'm not one of those girls whose head is turned by every boy who shows up at her house, though not that many boys do show up at my house, but nor am I a total newbie to the tangles of the heart.

But before I have a chance to process my own alarming and probably misguided emotions, I have to deal with Nora's.

"It's you." She finds her voice finally, but it's dreamy. She sounds awed, wonderstruck, but I know it must be something else.

"It is?" he asks.

"Come in," she says, still dreamy, like she can't believe it. "Come in."

He wipes his feet, but it's only a gesture because he's dripping all over the entryway. He looks all around at everything except for me. And there's not a whole lot else to look at. Books everywhere. A scratched kitchen table, mismatched chairs. At the moment, and most moments, the kitchen is buried beneath a mudslide of dirty mixing bowls, baking pans, wooden spoons, and measuring cups, plus the pastry knives, flour sifters, whisks, and rolling pins which mostly just stay out for there's no place to put them away because the cabinets are full of books. But beneath all that, somehow, you can still make out stained countertops, cheap linoleum, cabinets without handles, drawers without pulls. Through the doorway into the living room, there's matted, worn carpet the uneven but unrelenting gray of winter skies, a faded sofa roughly the same non-color, an upturned packing crate masquerading (unconvincingly) as a coffee table, Monday's lumpy yellow recliner, which hasn't reclined in years, leaking stuffing onto a pile of romance novels. There's a fat old TV on top of the plywood bureau that holds Nora's clothes right there in the living room since it doesn't fit upstairs. Our house smells like a bakery but looks like a thrift shop. We have none of the grandeur of the library, none of the glory or the soaring space, none of what his family must have with which to fill it either. Only the books.

And here, they are out of place.

And then Nora finds her real voice, her sense, her purpose at last. "River, is it?"

He nods, dripping sheepishly.

"Tell me this, River," and I brace myself, but instead she says, "Are you hungry?"

The promise of cake lures Monday out of her corner, the promise of drama Mab from our room. I am parked at the head of the table like a queen. The middle is piled with rainy-day baked goods: zucchini muffins, crème de menthe brownies, and a red velvet cake dyed green instead. There's coffee, and Nora's poured some for everyone then opened another bottle of water to make more when she sees River blanch.

"Oh, sorry," Nora says when she takes in his face. "Do you not drink coffee?"

"I'm sixteen," he says.

"Can I pour you a glass of milk," she offers solicitously, "or make you some cocoa?"

Mab smirks at him over the rim of her mug, but I can see her considering whether she's cool and he's childish, or if it turns out sixteen-year-olds who drink black drip are yet another Bourne anomaly and she just never knew.

I sip mine through a straw from a cup gripped by a snaking hose clamped onto

169

the side of my chair.

River tries not to stare at me.

I try not to stare at River. But not that hard.

"So, River, what brings you here?" Nora is not used to guests, but somehow she knows what to say anyway.

"She left screaming" — River points at Monday — "so I thought I should check if she was okay."

"Thought you should, huh?" says Nora.

He nods and looks at his plate of baked goods, says nothing.

"She's fine," Nora says lightly, as if worry over someone who had to be bodily removed shrieking from his home makes him something of a fussbudget. "She's just —"

"How did you find us?" Mab interrupts.

"I asked at the laundromat. It was the only place open."

"Lots of downtown's closed these days," Nora muses, as if idly.

"I asked the guy at the counter —"

"Rich," Nora puts in helpfully.

"— if he knew where two sisters named Mab and Monday lived." He looks pleased with himself for this bit of sleuthing. It seems not to have occurred to him that I must be a sister as well. "I felt bad because my parents can be kind of . . . off-putting."

170

"You don't say." Nora is expending so much energy on her nonchalance, I expect her to collapse from the strain.

"And I don't know anyone here, so . . ."

He trails off, and I wish he wouldn't. I want to know what he intended to say. *So I'm settling for the two of you? So I'm really invested in our quarter-hour of friendship so far? So even though we've barely met, running through the rain as if at the climax of the kind of TV movies that air Sunday afternoons seemed the way to go?*

"Plus you were on your bikes, and" — he waves at the window — "it's raining again."

Mab and Monday are dry as deserts. River is wet as his namesake, a puddle formed on the floor beneath his chair.

"That's not what I meant," Nora says.

Mab squeezes her eyes shut. River looks lost. Meandering.

"Pardon?"

"Not what brings you here to our home this afternoon. What brings you to town. To Bourne."

Ahh.

"Oh." He smiles, relieved. Here's a reasonable question it's reasonable to expect a reasonable adult to ask. "My dad got transferred."

"Really." A statement from Nora, not a

171

question.

"His company sent him here."

"What company is that?"

"Belsum Basics?" River's voice sounds like a question.

"Belsum *Basics*?" Nora has stood up.

"It used to be called Belsum Chemical?"

"I remember." Her voice is rising.

"But they changed the name."

"Why?"

"Why?"

"Yes, why?" She's stopped being reasonable.

"I . . ." He looks lost again. And slightly alarmed. "I don't know."

"You don't know?"

"Mama," Mab interrupts, and waits for Nora to look at her. "He doesn't know."

Nora blinks. She blinks again. She sits. This is true, of course. He doesn't know. He's just a boy. He doesn't know.

But then he says, "Maybe something about the reopening?"

No one moves. No one even breathes.

"The reopening?" Nora says.

"The reopening of the plant?" Earnest, trying to be helpful. "A new start and everything? I mean, I'm just guessing. No one tells me anything. But, you know, the sign on the roof?"

172

The plant is topped with rusted, wind-racked metal letters taller than our house that spell out B-E-L-S-U-M. Kind of like the "Hollywood" sign.

"What about it?" Nora has bright red spots on paling cheeks.

"Well, it just spells 'Belsum,' so I guess they could change the second half of the name without costing anything or inconveniencing anyone, you know?" He shrugs and goes right on, sparing us all Nora's answer to that question. "A whole bunch of stuff got messed up when they decided to reopen the plant, so I guess they wanted to leave whatever they could the same."

"What got messed up?" Nora keeps her voice low, steady, but she's got her hands balled into fists so tight they look permanent.

"Well, *my* whole life for one thing." He laughs. "Not that they care. You know?"

"Yes, indeed I do." Nora starts laughing too, but hers is more of a cackle really. "Welcome to the club."

Mab's eyes meet mine then flick back. We want the same thing, she and I, for River Templeton not to be here to watch while our mother loses her mind.

"It's totally not fair," River is saying. "I had to change schools, leave all my friends.

Boston's a lot . . . bigger than Bourne." I notice that pause, take it to heart, the adjective he went with politely rather than the ones that must have presented themselves first. He's not thoughtless, just oblivious. He doesn't know. He can't possibly. He's just trying for banal conversation with a slightly weird adult.

A slightly weird adult who's turning colors.

Monday's confusion is about to spill over into questions it's not polite to ask in front of guests. Especially when they concern the guest. River is talking about how unjust it is that there's no marimba elective at Bourne Memorial High nor even one available for him to continue his practice on as an independent study.

He needs to leave now. But how to effect this graciously? Or how to tell Mab without him overhearing? My Voice is about as inconspicuous as I am.

I tap my finger once, and my sister's eyes shift instantly from River to me as if I've poked her with it.

My finger points at Mab. It points at River. It points at the door. Mab, River, the door. She nods once.

"River," she says, and he turns to her, but

her eyes are still holding mine. "Let's take a walk."

ONE

We are the last house before the woods. That's why my parents bought it. My mother thought it was too small, even though they were only two at the time, because they planned probably to have a baby someday and maybe even another one after that. Who could see that many years in the future? "We'll build an extension," my father promised. "There's so much room here." She thought the house was too dark, but my father said he'd cut holes in the walls and fill them with glass. When she told me this story when I was little, I pictured smashed windshields and wineglasses swept up and piled into big gaps punched in the walls. At some point, years later, I realized he'd meant windows, and it blew my mind — that a window was nothing more than a hole cut in a wall and filled with glass, that even something as stable and permanent as a wall was no more solid or nonnegotiable than anything else.

In the cramped kitchen she wasn't sold, but he turned her around by the shoulders and pointed her toward the woods. Think of wind blowing through summer branches, he said. Think of our kids jumping in piles of school-bus-colored leaves. Think of the forts they'll build and the exploring they'll do and the trees they'll climb and the make-believe they'll make believe out there. There's no place better to be a kid than the woods. No place safer.

I have played in his woods, but I have mostly played alone. If Monday did not fear the dirt, the disorder, the potential to get lost. If Mirabel's chair could more comfortably cover ground stippled with roots, branches, puddles, mud. If Mama hadn't come to see danger lurking everywhere. If he had himself survived. But that's a lot of ifs. And besides, there was no place safe here after all.

Pooh used to be our next-door neighbor, back before we lived here, years and years before I was born. It's maddening that I missed this merely by arriving six decades too late. When she was a little girl, she lived in the house next door to ours, and the people who lived in our house were an older couple called the Perrys who used to invite her over after school for fruitcake.

"What's fruitcake?" I asked the first time Pooh told me about them, my ghost roommates.

"Old-fashioned holiday loaf that tastes like shit. That's why they foisted it off on me. But it tastes like shit because it keeps forever so they'd get half a dozen at Christmas and saw off one tiny slice every time I came over. It'd last almost until summer."

"Why'd you eat it?"

"Even bad cake is still cake when you're little." She shrugged. "It's a shame you didn't live here then. They'd have liked to know the four of you."

"The house would have been pretty crowded at that point."

"They'd have appreciated your mother's baking skills. But mostly, they liked kids. Never had any of their own. I think they didn't mind not having kids, but they hated not having grandkids. That's why they liked me. That's why they'd have liked you."

"Is that why you like me?" I ventured. "Because you don't have any kids of your own?"

Pooh snorted. "I don't like kids. Having no kids isn't why I like you. You're the exception."

"Everyone likes kids," I said.

178

"No." She looked over her glasses and down her nose at me. "Children are a pain in the ass. Look at your poor mother. No offense."

"I'm not a pain in her ass," I protested.

"Oh, sweetie, I love you, but of course you are. That's the whole point of children — they keep you grounded, but another way to say that is they weigh you down. Grandchildren are probably better, but it's not like you can start with them so you have to lie."

"Lie?"

"To your kids. If you let them know how much they wreck your life, your kids won't make you any grandchildren." She stopped pulling at her fingers and pointed one at me. "You remember that now, Mab. That's good advice I'm giving you."

"I'm not having kids," I said.

"Of course you are."

"How?"

"Mab Mitchell, Bourne Memorial High School may not be Eton, but I know you don't need me to answer that question."

"I don't mean *how* how. I just mean . . . I'm never going to meet anyone here I want to . . . you know."

"What's wrong with here?" She threaded her fists through the armrests of her wheelchair to plant them on her hips.

"Among other things —" I was, in contrast, lolling on her sofa, one leg long along the cushions, one stretching over my head — "there is no one here I would want to raise a child with, never mind, you know, make a child with."

"I think there may be some lovely babymakers in Bourne. Not now, of course. Not soon, even. But there's no need to rule all of them out forever."

"I've known everyone here too long. They're practically related to me at this point. It's gross to have a baby with someone you're related to."

"Well, inadvisable anyway," Pooh conceded, "but don't knock friends and neighbors who are like family. That's the best thing about Bourne."

"It's a short list."

"Maybe, but that's a big thing. It's why I stayed."

"No it's not."

"The hell it isn't. Why do you think I'm still here?"

I sat up to look at her. It had honestly never occurred to me that she had a choice. "I thought you . . ." I trailed off.

"You thought I couldn't leave. You thought I was stuck here. Well, I'm not. I like it here.

180

It's small —"

"Too small," I interrupted.

"Other places have more people," Pooh said, "but the problem with people is lots of them suck. You limit the population, you limit the assholes too." Then it seemed like she changed the subject. "You know what growing up Korean in America in the thirties and forties was like? Even with the name Winifred?"

Especially with the name Winifred, I thought.

"Here I got teased and picked on and called names, and Bobby Euford's mother wouldn't let us go to prom together, but that was pretty much it. I had cousins in Los Angeles, San Francisco — big, beautiful cities — who got beaten, who got deported, who owned houses and businesses that got destroyed. Anyone tried to deport us? They'd have had to answer to all of Bourne. We were here so we were one of them. We were part of the community. Bourne was small enough that's what mattered to people here. *Matters* to people here."

I saw her point — that life can be terrible anywhere, that there are lots of ways besides ours to get screwed and lots of ways to be evil besides Belsum's, that sheltered has its

181

perks too — but instead I was thinking about how much wider her life had been than mine. How much fuller and farther flung. "Maybe a small town has fewer assholes," I said, "but it has fewer cool people too."

"We have plenty of cool people. Neighbors you know will be there when you need them. Neighbors who get you and what you've been through. A sense of place. Shared history. None of that's easy to find. Or easy to give up."

"I guess not."

"You'll leave, I'm certain, and out there, you'll have your absolute pick of fellas, but afterward, maybe you might surprise yourself. Maybe you'll come back."

I wanted to ask her how she knew for sure I'd be able to leave, never mind return. I wanted to ask her where I would go and what it would be like. I wanted to ask her why anyone would fall in love with me when I didn't know anything about anything. Instead I said, "Fellas?"

"Oh yes." Pooh rubbed her hands together like a bad guy in a cartoon. "Fellas falling all over themselves to make Mab Mitchell's babies. Now that I'd like to see."

Which got me thinking about how she probably never would. That's the part Petra and I don't talk about when we talk about the SATs. If we get into college, we'll go. We'll get to leave Bourne, but we'll have to leave everyone we know. And the difference between get and have is everything.

"Why don't *you* ever serve cake?" I asked Pooh at the time, around the lump in my throat.

"Child, your mother bakes three a week. You don't need me for cake. When you come to me, you get protein." Bulgogi is an unusual after-school snack, but Pooh is an unusual friend.

Now Pooh lives in an apartment so she doesn't have to negotiate steps, and there's no one in the house next door to us. Most of our block sits empty, in fact. River turns to head back the way he came in, but I reach out and tug his sweatshirt sleeve, careful not to actually touch him, and pull him the other way.

It's wet in the woods, but from below rather than above — the ground is sodden and muddy, but the leaf cover is thick enough that I lower my hood. River does the same, seems surprised it's not raining in here, as if we've passed into some parallel dimension, and then looks at me, full on, like for the first time.

He puts out a hand — also to my sleeve,

also not touching me — and says, "Wait."

I do. I stop. I don't say a word. Just look at him. And wait.

River is panting lightly, like we've been running. His color is high, red cheeks, bright eyes. He seems to be buzzhumming underneath where you can quite hear like the overhead lights at school.

What he says is "Your sister."

"Yeah," I say.

He shakes his head. Then he adds, "Is this whole town . . . ?"

He trails off.

"Yeah," I answer anyway.

"Whyyy?" He draws the word out. Not an idle why. A what-the-fuck why. A how-on-earth why. The *why-God-why* kind of why. Like he actually doesn't know.

"Do you actually not know?"

"Know what?" he says.

How could they not tell him?

How could they tell him?

How can I tell him myself?

Seventeen years ago, your family built a chemical plant, killed a lot of people, ruined my whole generation, destroyed our town, mumbled a half-assed non-apology, packed up their shit, and left. And now, apparently, you've come back to reopen the plant and do it all over again.

184

"What's . . . wrong with them?" he manages and then blushes. "I mean, sorry, it's probably not cool to say it like that. What do you say? From what do they suffer?"

"If you're in Elizabethan England."

"What ails them?"

"You talk very strangely," I can't stop myself saying.

"So I've been told." And then he tries again, more simply. More gently. "Are they okay?"

"Who?" He needs to narrow his question down.

"Everyone. Your sister."

"Which one?"

He looks more stunned, takes this in, can't think quite how to proceed.

"Mirabel developed brain damage in utero," I begin. "She has lesions on her brain. Some days are better than others. But she'll never walk. She'll never talk so that many people besides us understand her. She'll never be able to live on her own." A swallow swoops low overhead. We must be too near her nest.

"God." He pauses, forgets I'm there, takes this in too. "Is that what they all have? All those kids at school?"

"No. Some of them do. Some of them have other stuff."

"Other stuff?"

"Cerebral palsy, spina bifida, hearing loss, blindness, microcephaly, heart defects. Missing limbs. Pastor Jeff's not big on labels, official diagnoses, that kind of thing, but we've got it all."

"Pastor Jeff?"

"Town doctor," I supply, and because that stuns him into further silence, "Have you noticed all the buildings in town have ramps? Have you noticed most of the parking is wheelchair parking?"

"Why?" Bewildered again, full of appalled wonderment.

"There's a lot of people who use wheelchairs."

"No, *why*?" he explains.

"Or it's intellectual disabilities," I continue without answering. "Or learning or emotional ones. Or low birth weight, cognitive impairments, disrupted endocrine system, central nervous system toxicity, thyroid disease, high blood pressure, a whole lot of really nasty cancers. Not that there are any especially pleasant ones."

"I don't . . ." He has stopped looking horrified and started looking scared. "Mab, I don't understand."

He doesn't. This is obvious. So our eyes look at each other, but our heads are both flooding with too many impossible details. He has no idea what's going on here, how he's landed in a town of people like this, how a town like this can even exist. He must be thinking of all the science fiction movies he's ever seen, all the fantasy he read as a little kid. Maybe he fell asleep and woke to a new reality. Maybe he wandered through an invisible veil between worlds. Maybe he fell through a portal to another universe where everyone seems normal at first until you look more closely and realize something is very, very wrong.

And me? I can't believe his parents brought him here without a warning about what we're like, how we got this way, and their family's role in making it happen. Even if they dispute the facts, even if they want to spin it differently for their kid, sending him into a den of wolves as if we're only poodles seems mean. And shortsighted.

Plus now *I* have to tell him. Maybe that was their plan all along. Make someone else break all this to their son. Make someone else lay out the facts and the cause and effect. And then when he brings home the wild accusations, they get to deny and laugh them off and say, "Oh, of course not, don't be silly," and say, "Does that sound like something we'd do?" and say, "These people have too much imagination and too little sense."

But I don't know what else to do. I don't know how to keep talking without telling him. And besides, he needs to know. Of course he needs to know. For his own safety. For his own comprehension. If he's going to be lonely, shunned, and tortured — and he is — he should at least understand why.

And never mind all that, it's his birthright. I have the speech ready. I have heard it often enough from my mother. I can recite it like other people's children can recite Scripture. It starts like the Bible, in fact. In the beginning. Felled innocence, followed hard by retribution and terrible fury. "Twenty years ago, Belsum scientists invented a chemical called GL606."

But I realize, hearing myself incant it, that that makes it sound inevitable, handed down remotely and anonymously, no one to blame, too long ago to have anything to do with us here right now, and since none of that's true, and since its not being true is the most important point really, I give up on the speech. We find a log and sit on it, and I try to figure out where to start if not at the beginning.

"You know at first it was great, I guess." I'm not looking at him, but I can feel that

188

he's not looking at me either. "You —
Belsum — brought a lot of jobs, a lot of
business to town. You had big plans. GL606
was something to make something else better or cheaper. I never totally understood
how or what. Before you even started
production, though, you had dozens of
companies signed up to buy it to put it in
whatever they made. It was one of those
things, between one thing and another
thing, you know?"

"Not really." He's not touching me, but
he is sitting a little closer than seems normal.

"You weren't making a thing or selling a
thing. You were making and selling a thing
— this chemical — for other people to put
in other things they were making and selling."

"Oh." He looks confused. I've never had
to explain this to anyone before, and the
dark spots in the story my mother's told
again and again reveal themselves slowly to
be holes.

"That was nice," he adds, "to make something for others."

I am telling this wrong.

"My mother says the smell came first."
There's no reason to tell him fast. We're not
in a rush. We have nothing else to do.

There's no reason not to tell it all except it's overwhelming. It's hard to explain something that's completely foreign to the person you're explaining it to but has always been true for you, like when you try to describe color to someone who's blind or if you had to teach a frog to use its lungs when it had spent its whole life underwater using its gills. Or a toad. Whichever one is the amphibian. "When you ask my mother what it smelled like, she says chemicals. When you ask her what the chemicals smelled like, she says death. Sometimes she says it's not what it smelled like, it's what it stopped smelling like — wisteria and honeysuckle because everything stopped blooming all at once that spring, and then fresh-cut grass because people couldn't be outside long enough to mow due to the reek, and eventually snow because sometimes it fell but never enough to freeze over the stench. And she also remembers how they had to cancel Fourth of July that year because the stink stank too much for anyone to go out and grill or roast marshmallows or watch fireworks. She remembers everyone kept their windows shut tight and just sat around sweating in their houses because the air was too foul to let inside. She remembers when it was over ninety degrees every day for three and a half weeks, but they wouldn't open the pool because this yellow dust fell out of the sky and settled over the water half an inch thick."

"Gross," says River. "What was it?"

"No one knew" — I am playing tic-tac-toe with myself with a stick in the mud — "but then the smell stopped being just outside and came inside because the water smelled bad coming out of the tap, and it looked bad too — brown or oily or murky, like maybe there was something in it — and then you could taste it. People filled bottles and jars and took them down to the plant. At first, they just wanted to raise the alarm or whatever, like of course no one realized what was happening, and if they knew they'd do something immediately. And when that didn't work, people stopped complaining and started, you know, panicking."

"Why?"

I stop playing tic-tac-toe and turn to look at him. I make sure I'm looking at his eyes. "You — Belsum — didn't stop. You kept doing what you were doing. You just kept saying the water was fine. It was fine for water to smell like that and taste like that and be that color. Perfectly safe."

"Maybe it was," River says hopefully.

I press my sneakers into the game I've drawn and pull them up again, watch water seep into the pattern the treads have left behind.

"My parents had a dog. Sparkle. Stupid name for a dog. This was before we were born. Sparkle was like a practice kid for them. He was a rescue dog, and he was like the son they'd never have. Not that they knew that yet. He got a lump one day." I have one in my throat telling River this. When Mama gets to this part of the story, Mirabel always cries. When we were little, you'd think Mirabel wasn't even listening, maybe not even hearing, and then Mama would come to this part of the story and tears would start to fall right out of Mirabel's eyes without her making a sound. "Sparkle got a lump one day and then lots of lumps in the days after that, but Mama couldn't get an appointment at the vet because suddenly the vet was full."

I stop because probably he gets it, and what happens next is terrible and better left unsaid.

But he doesn't get it. "Was one of the vets away? We had a cat for a while in Boston, and there were only two vets in the office, so it took forever to get an appointment in the summer because one or the other was always on vacation."

"Doc Dexter wasn't on vacation. It was hard to get an appointment because so many people's pets were having seizures or bleeding from their mouths or growing tumors. Sparkle just lay in the kitchen with his tongue out on the tile all day long, trying to cool off in the closed-up-tight house."

"And then what happened?"

"And then he died."

"Holy shit!" He keeps looking at me, at my face, I think because he expects it to crack into a smile any moment now. Like I'm going to punch him in the arm and laugh and say, *I'm just messin' with you,* or, *Kidding! Gotcha!*

But all I say is "Yeah. I know." I do. It's hard to hear. I get that. I would like to stop. I would like not to tell him the rest. I would like there not to be a rest.

"So what happened?" he asks, like we are indeed at the end of the story, like dead dogs is as bad as it gets, and all that's left from here on out is the epilogue where everyone learns a lesson and cleans up the mess and moves on. But this is not that story. And this is not the end.

"The animals got sick and died. The pets and also whatever was living in the river — dead fish washing up all along the shore, dead frogs." I take a deep breath and let it out slowly. "And then the people started getting sick. People who never had asthma before suddenly had it a lot. Rashes and burning. Seizures. Stomach problems. Headaches and coughs that didn't go away."

"Jesus."

"And then people started getting cancer, and that didn't go away either."

"Shit."

"Yeah."

"No, I mean . . . shit."

"Yeah."

I let him just sit with it for a while. It's a lot to take in. It'd be a lot to take in anyway, but it's probably more if it's your fault. His eyebrows have pulled into one in the middle, and he's rubbing the spot between them as if easing them apart will also erase what's drawing them together.

"Everyone?"

"Everyone what?"

"Did everyone . . . get sick or whatever?"

"No. Not everyone. 'Increased incidence.' 'Statistically higher than average occurrence.' 'Greater than expected number of cases.' Those are the words they use. But lots of people. Especially the people who worked in the plant. My dad."

"Got sick?"

"Died."

"He *died*?" Like he never met anyone who died before. Maybe he hasn't. "When?"

"Six weeks before we were born."

"That's horrible."

I nod. It is. "And then when we were born, well, there were some . . . unexpected challenges."

"I mean three is a lot of babies." He looks relieved to be back on solid ground conversation-wise. "My mom said she didn't sleep through the night for three months after I was born. And she had my dad to help out. Whereas your mother . . ." He trails back off his solid ground.

"Not just for my mother." I make sure to keep the irritation out of my voice. "Challenges for lots of families because another thing there was an increased incidence of was congenital anomalies."

"Congenital anomalies?"

"Birth defects."

His eyes are wide now. Wild. "And it was because of the plant?"

"Well, not the plant itself. The chemical. Or the runoff from the chemical. Or the runoff from the process of making the chemical. I'm not sure exactly. I don't know if anyone is. Point is you dumped a ton of shit in the river. And it turned out, among other things, it also caused congenital anomalies."

I don't want to talk about this anymore. I think he probably doesn't want to talk about it anymore either. But I also don't see how we're going to talk about anything else. He's looking at the patterns my sneakers are making in the mud in front of us, hands laced behind his head, chin pressed into his chest, forearms clamped against his ears like it will block out what I'm saying. After a minute he says, "You and Monday are fine."

As if this were consolation enough. Two out of three ain't bad. As if Monday and I are fine.

"Monday doesn't seem a little . . . high-strung to you?" I'm genuinely curious. He's like a visitor from outer space or one of those naked kids they find who's been raised by wolves.

"Why? Because she got kind of upset at my house?" At first I think he's being snarky with that "kind of," but when I meet his eyes, I realize he's genuinely confused. I nod, also confused. "Oh no, I totally get that." He waves his hand in front of him like my concerns are cobwebs, that slight (Petra would say "attenuate"), that easily wiped away. "It's got to be a shock when you've been going to your hometown library your whole life, and then one day it's some dude's bedroom."

I think of her shrieking on his floor, fists clamped over her ears. "And how she wouldn't eat the muffins?"

I don't add the reason — they were the wrong color — so maybe that's why he says, "We had tons of kids like that in my school in Boston."

"You did?"

"Totally. My best friend growing up was like that. Super weird about his clothes and his headphones and this one cartoon he was obsessed with. But crazy smart and really fun as long as you didn't let any of the foods on his plate touch." He pauses to think about it. "We mostly ate at his house, and it was fine."

Which makes it my turn to be stunned. There are Mondays in Boston?

So it takes me a minute to remember what we were talking about when he asks, "When did they figure it out?"

"Figure what out?"

"When did they figure out it was the GL606? It was the plant? Belsum."

"You knew all along."

"Would you stop saying 'you'?" Annoyed. More than annoyed. Angry almost. "It wasn't me. I wasn't there. Here. Anywhere."

Something changed in him while we were talking about Monday, opened maybe or relaxed. He was just a kid for a second there. Now he's closing back up again, guarding himself, defensive as if I'm the one who's dangerous.

"*They* knew all along," I amend.

"What do you mean?"

"They claim they didn't, but —"

"What are you talking about? You think Belsum knew all along GL606 was getting into the water and making people sick?"

"Yes."

"Yes?" He's watching me so hard.

"Yes."

He can't believe it. He so thoroughly can't believe it he's sure he's misunderstanding what I'm saying.

"They — we — wouldn't do that," he insists. "No one would do that."

I hate to break it to him. I'm desperate to break it to him. But also there's this small but loud (Petra would say "niggling") part of my brain realizing for the first time this is how I'm supposed to be. A teenager. A kid. Not jaded and scarred and wise about all the shit. For the first time in my life what strikes me as tragic is not what happened to my family or my town. What breaks my heart is that I regard another sixteen-year-old's faith that a company wouldn't sacrifice human life to make a profit as hopeless youth and pitiable naivete. I almost never feel sorry for myself — I live with everything I need to ward off that particular vice — but that's what I feel now.

"That's why they put the plant here," I say. "We're just a small nowhere town. No industry, no tourism, no money, no prospects. No one to object or really even notice if things go bad. Maybe they — you — weren't sure it would kill us, but you weren't sure it wouldn't."

My mother would hate to hear me admit even this much, even as a possibility. Negligence means failure to take reasonable care like a normal person would. Lawyers have fancier language than that, but that's their point. It's easier to prove, but you can only claim compensatory damages — here's how much my medical expenses were; here's how much income I lost.

Whereas if you want to hurt them as much as they hurt you, if you want to make sure they can never do it again, if you want to punish them into oblivion, if you want to send a warning to others, if you want to make sure they don't decide that your measly compensatory damage award costs them so little compared to what they make damaging you that they're thrilled with the trade-off never mind that an award that was *actually* compensatory would bankrupt them forever because your suffering is high as the moon, and your town and your family and your whole entire life will never be the same ever again, if that is the case, you don't settle for negligence. You go for recklessness, maybe even intent. That's how you get punitive damages. That's how you shut a company down. That's how you see justice served.

If they knew what could happen before they started doing it, if they knew how bad it would be and did it anyway, then they can be made to pay. My mother, therefore, has spent the last two almost-decades searching for incontrovertible proof they knew all along, something no one can deny.

River's not buying it. He's not even understanding it. "So by the time they figured it out" — he so wants this to be a tragic trick of timing — "it was too late?"

"The early signs — the off water, the smell, dead plants, sick pets — those went on for months while you said we were imagining things. Then you said there was no proof. Then you said you had the water tested and it was perfectly safe. And then people started getting sick, and you still

200

wouldn't listen."

"So what happened?"

"We went to the town council. We went to the press. We went up to the capital and talked to our representatives. We wrote letters to the governor. You know. The things you do."

"And it worked? They closed the plant?"

"No. The river turned green."

"Like algae?"

"Not that kind of green. Not a green found in nature. Green like green neon, like green Easter egg dye, like St. Patrick's Day souvenirs. It glowed."

"Wow. That's . . . ." He considers it and settles finally on "terrible."

"No, actually, that was a good thing, the one good thing, because finally, *finally,* everyone saw. People came and saw and listened. People paid attention to what Belsum was doing and how it was killing us. Reporters came and government officials and scientists and activists and experts, and since people were finally watching, they closed the plant."

"And then what?" He can't wait to hear what happened next, like I'm telling him the plot of a movie he's not allowed to see.

"Belsum moved on and the government moved on. The scientists and activists and environmentalists moved on. The journalists moved on. But Bourne did not move on. Bourne stayed right where it was."

His eyes look like they're shivering. Can eyes shiver? It's too much all at once. What would I have him say to all this? He can't think of anything. Neither can I.

"Let's walk some more." I stand up.

"What?" He startles, looks up at me like he's forgotten who I am, where he is, what we're doing here.

"It's okay." I make myself smile at him, at least a little. "It's not your fault." I remind myself that this is true.

He nods. A beat. Another. "Wait."

I do.

"What do you mean it's not my fault? Of course it's not my fault. It's not true. Mab! Tell me you know it's not true." He's not quite yelling, but he's close.

"It is true." Sad. Petra would say "atrabilious."

But he's neither. He's mad. "Bullshit. You're crazy." He peeks at me. "Are you crazy?" He's genuinely asking now.

I laugh. "Nope, afraid not."

He laughs too but not because he thinks it's funny. In fairness, that's not why I laughed either. "Everyone in this town is crazy. Your mother obviously is. Your sister.

202

I get it now. There's something wrong with everyone here."

"Well, that's what happens when you're poisoned," I agree.

"Stop saying that!"

"Your family. Poisoned. Us."

"Look, my grandfather's kind of . . . I don't know . . . but he's not, you know, the devil. He doesn't go around poisoning towns and giving dogs cancer just so he can buy a sailboat. Or whatever."

"Your grandfather owns a boat?"

"Three."

"Wow." Dry as week-old breadcrumbs.

"But that's not the point."

I disagree. "I'm pretty sure it is."

"I mean yeah, he's rich. There's no law against being rich, you know. But he didn't kill anyone or hurt anyone or poison anyone. Jesus, this isn't Shakespeare. Where are you going?"

I am not going to stand here in the sodden woods being scolded by River Templeton, so I set off for home. He should follow me because there's no cell reception out here, and I know my way only after sixteen years of practice. He could starve to death before he found his way out. He'd have to resort to drinking the groundwater, which I really wouldn't recommend. He could rely on my goodwill to come back and fetch him before nightfall, but I wouldn't recommend that either. He seems to intuit this and comes loping after me on his long boy legs.

"Hey, wait up. Hey!" He reaches out and grabs my sleeve, spinning me to a stop. "What the hell?"

"Get off me."

"I'm not on you. I'm touching your sleeve."

"Don't touch my sleeve."

"Why are *you* mad at *me*? I'm the one being accused of all sorts of insane shit no one would believe, no one obviously *does* believe."

"Everyone I know believes it," I say.

"Yeah, but no one outside this town, right?" One minute he's appalled and offended. The next you can tell this is fun for him, sparring, arguing, twisting logic all around then ramming home his point. "That must be true. No one must believe you."

"Not no one." I sound pathetic.

"Because you said seventeen years ago." He talks right over me. "If you had proof, everyone would know it by now."

"The wheels of justice turn slowly," Russell always says, my mother always repeats, and I echo now.

"Plus, now the plant's reopening," he reminds me.

"So?"

"So they wouldn't risk doing it again. If they're reopening the plant, they must know everything's fine. They must know everything's been fine all along."

"Oh, I see now," I say. "I get it too."

"Get what?"

"Why you're saying all this."

"Because it's obviously true? Because you besmirched my honor?"

"Because you're just like your grandfather." Besmirched his honor? Who is this kid? "Evil must run in your family."

"And crazy must run in yours."

"We might be crazy," I admit, "but it's not hereditary if you've been poisoned."

His mouth is open, silent. His hands are open, disbelieving. But the rest of him is closed as a walnut, his face shut against all I've told him, all I am, all of us.

He doesn't want to walk next to me. He doesn't want to follow behind me. But he doesn't know where he's going. So he walks ten feet or so to my left through the trees, off the path that's half natural, half worn by me over the years, his foot twice sinking up to his ankle in wet mud, his clothes snagging every other step on climbing thorns he's walked through instead of around, rainwater spilling down the back of his hoodie every time his head brushes the overgrowth, snapping twigs and branches like what you can't see in a horror movie, the monster that's coming, invisibly but (Petra would say) inexorably through the trees to get you.

TWO

Often when Mama says she wants me to help her, it is more accurate to say she wishes I would change my personality. She will say, "Monday, I need you to help me by being a little bit more flexible about food today," or "Monday, I need you to help me by not fighting with your sister about whether it's necessary for her to wash her hands before washing the dishes," or "Monday, I need you to help me by not eating twelve bowls of Corn Pops just because you want to cut the box into postcards," and if you reply, "It is more accurate to say you need me to help you by not eating twelve bowls of Corn Pops *mostly* because I want to cut the box into postcards but *also* because they are yellow," she will point out that this also is not helping her.

But today, after River leaves with Mab, Mama says, "Monday, I need you to help me by working your librarian magic."

And that means she really does need my help.

"Maybe River Templeton is wrong. Maybe River Templeton doesn't know what he's talking about. Most teenagers aren't as smart as the three of you, you know." Mama is making her voice sound jolly, but I look at her face and even I can see it is pretend. "But just in case, let's see what we can find out."

"Just in case what?" I ask.

"Just in case River's on to something."

"Find out about what?"

"Belsum's plans."

"How will you do that?" I wonder.

"By asking the librarian." Mama kisses the top of my head, even though I do not like germs or touching. "Even if it's bad news, better to know. Knowledge is power. See what you can find, love. Mirabel and I have to go to work."

Mama always says that — "Knowledge is power" — but she also says knowledge is depressing, demoralizing, soul crushing, mad making, and despair inducing, so I do not know if it is worth it. She says knowledge is power, but she also says there is such a thing as knowing too much as well as such a thing as too much power, depending on whose. Mama says knowledge is power but only if what you know is actually true.

She used to have an alert on her computer to tell her when Belsum was in the news so she could have all the knowledge about them for her lawsuit, but too many of the alerts alerted her to things that were not true. She was alerted to news articles by scientists who said GL606 was harmless, but Russell discovered those scientists were being paid by Belsum. She was alerted to news articles by chemists who said the level of toxicity in our river was so low it was undetectable, but Russell discovered those chemists were being paid by Belsum too. She was alerted to news articles by researchers who said there would be no short- or long-term damage to the people of Bourne, but she looked around at the people of Bourne and didn't need Russell to discover who those researchers were being paid by as well. So she took the news alert off her computer.

This is one reason we did not have any warning about the Templetons coming to town or the plant reopening. Another is because we were facing the wrong way. Mama was looking backward, toward the past, at what happened before, but the important part was getting ready to come. And now it is here.

I like to research in books because they smell nice, tell stories, and are in my house. But I also like to research online because you can set your screen to show yellow text on a black background or black text on a yellow background. You cannot do this with books. I have a lot of books, and none of them have yellow words or yellow backgrounds. And if what you read online is upsetting, you can turn both the words and the background yellow. You cannot read yellow words on a yellow background. Even for me, that is too much yellow.

So while Mab is off with River in the woods and Mama and Mirabel leave for work, I go online. It is slow because internet in Bourne is slow, but slow is better than intermittent and unpredictable which is what cellular telephone service is in Bourne, and when your cellular telephone does not work you think if only you wave it around or stick it out the window or climb on a roof it might, but this is false hope because it never does and also because climbing on a roof is dangerous, whereas if your internet is slow you might be sad but you are not in peril.

Ninety-eight minutes later, I have read and learned, which are two things a librarian is supposed to do, but I am more confused than I was before so I might not be the kind of librarian Mama needs.

I find out that Belsum Basics is officially registered as a wholly owned subsidiary of Belsum Chemical. I find out there is a new slogan, and it is trademarked, and it is "Belsum Basics for Life" which makes sense since "Belsum Chemical: We Might Kill You" is memorable, which is one thing Mrs. Lasserstein says a slogan is supposed to be, but not a major selling point, which is the other.

I find out a company called Harburon Analytical, the most exacting, state-of-the-art independent testing and chemical analysis company in the world, says Bourne's water supply is one of the safest in the nation. I find out they gave Belsum a grade as if Belsum were a student at Bourne Memorial High School, and that grade was an A-plus.

I find out Duke Templeton thinks of the citizens of Bourne like family, and Duke Templeton is so certain his plant is safe that his own son has moved to town to head up resumed operations, and Duke Templeton feels touched and honored because the citizens of Bourne are all so thrilled Belsum is back.

Which means I have not found out anything at all.

I find a picture of Duke Templeton on a horse, but there is nothing in any of the articles about a horse. I find a picture of Duke Templeton with big scissors cutting a big bow, surrounded by seventeen people the caption says are new employees of the new Bourne plant on opening day. I go downstairs and find the *Oxford English Dictionary* under the double boiler in the cabinet and take its domed magnifying glass upstairs with me and look at each of the faces surrounding Duke Templeton and grinning at the camera and excited about their new jobs, but I do not recognize a single one which means either they were lucky and left and are living elsewhere, or they were unlucky. And living nowhere.

I find a picture that looks like a crack in the earth after an earthquake or a portal to hell lined with lava or a gushing, sliced-open artery in the body of an about-to-be-dead giant. But really it is our river on the first day it turned green. The photograph is black and white so you cannot tell it was green unless you know, which I do, but you can tell that it was very, very wrong.

I print out the pictures and cut them all up into tiny tiny tiny pieces until they look like grains of rice but, more accurately, are

212

confetti made out of Duke Templeton's words and face and horse and ruined plant and ruined river. I have been saving a box that used to contain banana pudding mix, and I cut it into a postcard, and over the side that lists ingredients and nutritional information, I glue the Duke Templeton confetti, shards of his giant scissors, halves of letters, sometimes a comma or period, but no pieces large or neighborly enough to make a whole word, even a short one.

And on the other side, I write:

Dear Mama,

I have gained some knowledge, but I do not think it has given me power. Duke Templeton can lie and does lie, and I cannot and do not, so I do not know why he is CEO of a company and I have to take classes to learn what facial expressions mean. I am sorry I was not able to help you.

Your librarian and daughter,
Monday

THREE

Saturday evenings at the bar are my favorites. They're most crowded so I'm most forgotten. They're most normal, like what I imagine regular bars in regular towns look like on regular Saturday nights — drinking that seems more fun than depressed, laughter that seems more genuine than sarcastic — what's supposed to be rather than what is.

All the way over, Nora's reassuring herself while pretending she's reassuring me. "There's no way, Mir. None. No way. He's wrong. He's just a kid. He doesn't know what he's talking about. A company that size is never going to tell its secrets to a sixteen-year-old, even if he is the CEO's grandson. Besides, Omar would never let it happen again. It's got to be that the lawsuit's got everyone panicked. That has to be it, don't you think? I know you do. You're so smart, Mir-Mir. Don't you worry. Everything's going to be just fine, Mirabel, my belle."

Her nicknames get more inane the more manic she gets. It's good Mab's still out and Monday has a job to do. Otherwise Nora would have left me home, and clearly she needs a chaperone tonight. My plan for the evening had been biochemistry homework. I realize that doesn't sound Saturday-night exciting, but pickings are slim as splinters around here, and anyway I've started a project on vertical farming (no soil, little water, perfect for Bourne) that's at least as thrilling as most teenagers' weekend plans. The wifi at the bar is no worse than the wifi anywhere else in town, so I'm happy to den-mother my mother while I work.

But when we arrive, I see my presence won't be enough to keep her sane because there, at the end of the bar, is Omar. Norma's is already as crowded as it gets, even though it's only just five, and, we can hear from the back entrance, loud, but as Nora emerges behind the bar, a hush falls over the whole place. Everyone's eyes dance back and forth between Nora and Omar, Nora and Omar. Frank passes behind her, rests his hands lightly on her shoulders for a few beats before moving on. *I'm on your side,* his hands promise. *Don't start a scene in my bar,* they add. Everyone waits to see what Nora's got in store for Omar tonight — this is what passes for entertainment in Bourne — but everyone (except Omar) is disappointed.

"Omar!" She forces a smile. "Just the man I was hoping to see." She pours him a beer, even though he has a nearly full one in front of him already. He looks at it nervously.

"You were?"

"I was."

"To yell at me?"

"No!" She laughs. "Well, maybe. Depends what you say. But probably not. I hope not." She's grinning now, but even she doesn't quite look like she's buying it.

"Me too."

"You too what?"

"I hope not." Then he turns to me. "Whatcha think, Mirabel? Is she going to yell at me?"

"Signs point to yes," my Voice pronounces, a saved joke because my Voice sounds kind of like how you imagine a Magic 8 Ball would if it could talk. Omar throws his head back and laughs, a real laugh. "You're a funny, funny girl. And probably a correct one."

People are turning back to their own drinks and conversations but much quieter

216

than before, one eye on their beers, one on Omar and Nora, so they won't miss it if fisticuffs break out.

"I heard an appalling, ridiculous rumor this afternoon," Nora begins lightly, like she's going to tell a joke or a story.

"From whom?" Omar goes back to looking nervous.

"A little birdie."

Omar raises his eyebrows to mime *Who?* but the rest of his face falls. He knows.

"What little birdie?" Hobart asks.

"Well, see, that's an interesting story itself." Nora nods. "You'll never guess who stopped by my house this afternoon." She takes a breath, maybe to build suspense, maybe just to give everyone one more moment before she delivers the bad news. "River Templeton."

A pause.

"Who the hell is River Templeton?" Zacharias says.

"Well, wouldn't you know it" — no one is buying, but everyone is made edgy by, Nora's extreme good cheer — "Duke Templeton has a grandson."

"And he came to your house?" Zach says.

"He did."

"I don't get it."

"Me neither," Nora says.

"They named him River?" Tom's trying to catch up.

"They did. Can you believe that?"

"Apt." He smiles at his beer.

"Because they destroyed ours?" Nora says.

"Not like a river. Like one who rives."

"What'd he want?" Frank asks.

"To flirt with my daughters," Nora says darkly.

I wish.

"What did he say?" Omar just wants to get it over with, I think.

"Well, that's where it got weird." Nora's taking her torturous time. "I asked what brought him and his family to town —"

"Good question," Tom says, but it's everyone's.

"And he said Belsum is reopening the plant."

I hear the bottoms of beer glasses hitting the bar, forks and knives clattering onto plates, a few scattered gasps, and then that falling sound that is no sound at all, everyone's conversations lapsing into silence at once.

"No fucking way," someone says.

"That's what I said." Nora nods.

"What did he say?"

"Well, I didn't say it until after he left. Mirabel made Mab take the kid for a walk."

"Lucky kid," Hobart says, and everyone grins at me, picturing the alternative: Nora dismantling the Templeton scion with her teeth.

"But I told the girls he was an idiot. Had to be wrong. Or lying. Or screwing with us. Something. Because there was no way Omar would let it happen. Not again. Never. Didn't I, Mirabel?"

I work hard to nod, but no one's looking at me because everyone's looking at Omar, Nora included, who looks at him — it must be said — with surety, certainty. Faith. This isn't a setup or a trap. In fact, it's Omar's moment of redemption, and she holds it out to him like a prize he's won off her fair and square. Her look is equal parts proud of him for earning it at last, grateful to him for doing so, and slightly sheepish for all the shit she's given him in the past, and mostly, it is beyond-a-doubt confident of his fealty and good sense.

Which is why what happens next is heartbreaking. Not because of what he says. Because of the gap between what he says and what she vividly finally imagined he would.

In fact, at first he doesn't say anything at all. But the hesitation tells her all she needs to know. The whole bar is holding its breath (except for me; I am pointedly breathing, deep and steady, so as not to distract from the scene playing out before us).

Nora is the one to break — her will, this silence, and a great deal more. "You said yes to them again." Halfway between a question and a keen. She is furious. Of course she is. But beneath that, her face shows something else. She is betrayed. She so believed deep down, beneath all those years of animosity she's held toward Omar for getting us into this mess in the first place, that he wasn't really the bad guy here. And he failed her, deserted her, broke her faith and trust which, however small, were hard won. She looks heartsick. Him too.

"Worse." Omar can't look at her. He sees what I see in her face. "I didn't say yes again. This was in their contract to begin with."

She pales. "How is that possible?"

"The land is theirs. And when we zoned it, we zoned it for them. We gave them their designation and land-use rights for a hundred years."

"A hundred years!"

"As a gesture, obviously. To show them we were all in, we'd support them now and into the future."

"Why?"

220

"We wanted them to stay." Omar shrugs miserably but raises his head to take everyone in. He is our leader, after all. "And we didn't want to give them a chance to renegotiate the deal five years down the road when they were employing half the town and could demand whatever terms they wanted. I thought we were being smart. I could envision them wanting to leave us behind. I never imagined there'd be a time we wouldn't want the jobs. I never imagined we would want to get rid of them."

"Or keep them from coming back." Nora looks, more than anything, exhausted. "Fucking hell."

"Yeah," Omar agrees. "But listen —"

I would like to. Everyone would like to. Even Nora, if only out of desperation, would like to. But no one gets the opportunity because the door opens and in walks Nathan Templeton.

He stands inside the doorway for a moment, letting his eyes adjust, being seen, and my brain pulls up from its cloudy nethers the second half of that "Speak of the devil" saying. Both the rest of the aphorism and the man himself seem conjured not from thin air but from its opposite — thick opaque substances: mud, sludge, primordial stuffs — like they were there all along, only dormant, lying in wait to rise up at the merest suggestion. We conjured Nathan Templeton by speaking of him. As usual, it feels all our fault, never mind that, as usual, there was no avoiding it and nothing we could do.

We have not seen him before, any of us, but there is only one man he can be. I suppose that's why the saying isn't "Speak of the devil, and some dude shows up with goat feet and a flaming pitchfork, and you're all, 'Who the hell are you?'" He is a clean bright light in Norma's sticky dankness, and I see what Mab means. There is something strong about him — something whole, something sure and neat and well rested — that no one else in Bourne possesses. Nora literally recoils, and all the blood drains from Frank's face, and everyone falls silent as snow.

"Norma's Bar." Nathan Templeton opens his arms into the gloaming. "No wonder everyone speaks fondly of this place. I can see I'll be a regular."

His smile is a lightbulb in the gloom. He looks around quite pleased — with himself for discovering such a gem of an establishment, with all of us for being in the know, with Nora and Frank for doing a fine job running the place — and not at all bothered

222

that everyone's staring at him. He ambles from door to bar slowly, stopping to shake hands with the few bewildered people dotting the tables in the middle of the room — both of his soft ones grasping one of theirs, looking into their eyes — and inserts himself on the empty stool between Zach and Tom.

He reaches out and puts one hand on one man's shoulder, one on the other's.

"Great to meet you guys." He looks and sounds like he means it. "I'm Nathan Templeton."

They nod mutely. Nora hasn't closed her mouth in minutes.

"So" — Nathan picks up a menu and looks it over — "what's good here?"

Zach considers the lately frozen neon wings before him. "Nothing?"

"Hey!" says Frank.

Nathan winks at Frank and laughs with Zach. "Now, I'm sure that's not true . . ."

"Zach," Zach supplies.

"Zach." Knowing. Proud of him. Like Zach is a perfect name. Like Nathan is certain Zach must be a wonderful man to have such a wonderful name. "Pleasure." He turns the other way. "How about you . . ."

"Tom." Tom looks surprised to hear his own voice.

"So, Tom, you seem like a man of taste. What's the best thing on the menu?"

"Beer?" Tom guesses.

Nathan laughs, loud and warm. "Isn't it always? You're a wise man, Tom." He turns to Nora. "Beers for everyone, if you please, Madam Barkeep. This round's on me."

She stands there, frozen, and Nathan's smile wavers just slightly.

"Nora," Frank's voice warns.

She shakes her head, blinks, shakes, and starts pulling each of the guys' favorite beer. As she puts them on the bar, she leans in and whispers, "On the house."

"No, hey," Nathan protests, "let a guy buy another guy a beer. I'll buy you one too, pretty lady."

She takes in a breath deep as a sea trench. I watch her brain flip through thousands of clamoring options in search of where to start her response, but Frank leaps in first. "Frank Fiedler. Owner. Very generous of you." They shake.

"And look!" Nathan crows. "It's my main man — and yours — the great Omar Radison." He comes down the bar and shakes Omar's hand. "Good to see you again, man." So I was wrong. None of us have ever seen this man before except Omar.

224

"We were just talking about you," Omar admits.

"All good things, I hope," Nathan says in a tone that suggests he's never in his life doubted it. But as he turns to make his way back to his beer, he trips over my footrest.

It is normal to regard something you've tripped over with surprise. After all, if you'd known it was there, you would have walked elsewhere. But the look he gives me is less surprise than shock, shock verging on horror.

Which, to be honest, is interesting. It is probably true that people who use wheelchairs in the rest of the world get appalled looks and disgusted stares, but not here. Here, no one looks at me twice.

But the look is fleeting. I catch it for only a moment before Nathan Templeton wrestles his smile back into place. "Well, hi, hello there."

I give him a little wave. He waves back.

"I'm learning everybody's name tonight." He's talking too loudly. Maybe he thinks I might be hard of hearing. Or maybe he wants to make sure everyone notices him talking to me. He needn't worry about the latter. All eyes in the place are on him. "So tell me who you might be."

I have to type in the first part: "I might

be" — then tap my name — "Mirabel."

He is dumbfounded at first by my Voice but recovers quickly. "You might be, eh?"

I nod.

"Are you one of the famed Mitchell sisters?"

I might look surprised he knows — I am — or he might just be showing off because he laughs too loudly, goes to clap me on the shoulder, changes his mind, and brags, "I keep my ear to the ground, don't I?"

I don't know what to do but nod.

"You look too young to be in a place like this, Mirabel," he says. "Must be clean living."

Frank watches Nora consider breaking a bottle over the edge of the bar and impaling this guy. He redirects. "So, Nathan, what brings you to town?"

Nora is so angry she's shaking, but I see her take this question in, see how she wants this answer more, if only just more, than she wants to exsanguinate this man. She finds my eyes and shakes her head: No. No what? It could be anything. Then she finds emptied pint glasses to wash and pretends to turn away. Frank passes behind her and brushes lightly between her shoulder blades as if accidentally. She nods nearly imperceptibly and keeps her eyes on her dirty dishes.

"Many things, many things." Nathan puts his hands back on Zach's and Tom's shoulders. "Among them, I'm here to offer these good men jobs."

Nora looks up and blinks.

Omar drops his head into his hands.

I remind myself about slow deep breaths.

And no one says a thing.

"All of you, actually." Nathan swings an arm out wide to take us all in. "If you're a hard, honest worker —"

"Honest?" Nora chokes, but Nathan keeps right on as if he hasn't heard her.

"— we'd love to have you on board. We've got jobs for all skill levels, all education levels, all" — the pause is infinitesimal — "ability levels."

"Where?" Frank says breezily, like Nathan has mentioned a really good deal he got on curtains. Later, Monday will wonder why Frank asked when Omar already told everyone. It's the kind of thing that bugs Monday, but it's a fair question. He needed to hear Nathan say it? He thought the rest of us needed to hear Nathan say it? He wanted to help Omar out, transfer the earlier ire away from our mayor to where it belonged?

"Maybe he wanted to pretend he didn't already know and hadn't already heard," Mab will guess.

"Why?" Monday will press again.

"Didn't want to give him the satisfaction," Mab will posit, "of thinking we've just been waiting all these years for their return. Didn't want him to think he'd just pick up where he left off?"

Whatever the reason Frank asked, Nathan's answer seems canned. "Well, friend, you may have heard of a little company called Belsum. It's a new day for us. New plan, new facilities, new name — Belsum Basics — but old stompin' grounds. We're renewing the old plant from the inside out, building our operations better than ever, and we wouldn't dream of doing it without the good people of Bourne. So what do you say? Anyone around here need a good job?"

Nora looks like she's going to cry. Nora looks like she's going to scream. Nora looks like she's going to smash the teeth of Nathan's lightbulb smile from his mouth. She's got her hands flat on the bar now, probably to stop them from shaking, but she looks like she's going to vault over the top, take Nathan in her mouth, and shake him until blood and hair and guts rain down and his neck snaps and she spits his limp body into a broken heap on the bar floor and retreats to her corner to lick the gore off her haunches. Her eyes are on me, and I give her a small smile, a we-will-figure-this-out-too smile, a remember-we-have-each-other smile, an I-believe-in-you smile.

And maybe that's why or maybe she's lost her mind, but what Nora does is laugh. She throws back her head and laughs. She throws back her head and holds her belly and wipes her eyes and laughs and laughs and laughs.

Nathan laughs along with her. "What's so funny?" He's friendly, a little kid eager to be in on the joke.

Then she stops laughing. "Get out of my bar." And when he doesn't move, she leans across to him to add, "No matter the salary, no matter the job description, no matter how desperate, there is not a single person in this bar or in this town who would ever work for Belsum Chemical again."

Nathan props his elbow on the bar before her and proffers his pinky finger. "Wanna bet?" Still smiling. All in good fun.

She struggles to hold on to her mirth.

"It's a new day, Nora Mitchell. Even your daughters came to visit. Even they're on board." How does he know her name? How does he know Mab and Monday are her daughters?

"Get. Out. Of. My. Bar." Her cool is slipping off her like snakeskin.

"My understanding is it belongs to my friend Frank here" — Nathan holds up both hands — "but I get it. I do. Didn't mean to rattle you. It's Saturday night. You're busy. A handsome stranger comes to town and shakes things up." He winks again, possibly at me. "Just wanted to say hello, buy some friends a beer, and check out the hottest place in town."

Without looking, he takes two hundred-dollar bills out of his wallet and lays them on the bar, shoots in-cahoots smiles all around, and disappears with a whiff of brimstone which is probably just my imagination, but I look at Nora looking at me and wouldn't swear to it.

"Never." She starts cleaning up — wiping down the bar, clearing still half-full glasses, sweeping around her shell-shocked customers — all the while, under her breath, "Never never never never."

And no one disagrees.

But I remember that other saying about the devil, that idle hands are his playthings. And honestly? There are a lot of idle hands around here.

ONE

For a couple weeks, we ignore each other. Really, though, everyone's ignoring him, not just me. He sits alone at lunch. He sits alone in class too. We've always had more space than students, a (Petra would say) surfeit of chairs for all the kids who should be here but aren't, and either he's picking seats with wide margins of empties all around or the rest of us have made an unspoken agreement to keep him marooned. In chem lab, no one will partner with him, so he has to determine the caloric content of a potato chip all on his own. In debate prep, no one will partner with him, so he has to argue about the relative merits of human cloning with himself. In English, no one will partner with him, so he has to do Romeo *and* Juliet.

Then, slowly, we stop ignoring him. The Kyles walk past in the hallway and shoulder River sideways into the lockers. Adam Fell pushes him out front before school and then taps his own chest, showing River how to come back at him. Nigel Peterman sneaks out of his classroom into our lab and singes the hood of River's sweatshirt and the back of his hair with a Bunsen burner. At first they aren't ass-kickings. They're short shocks to teach the mouse to stop touching the buzzer, stay in his own corner, and consort with no one. They're short shocks to teach the mouse he is unloved.

Then, soon enough, they are ass-kickings. One day, River has a cut on his lip, bright red inside, crusty at the edges. Then his left cheek is one raw pink scrape. Someone drops a book in history, and he flinches, his face darkening all at once like clouds moved in fast. The next week one of his eyes is swollen, bright and tight.

His other eye looks at me hard when we get to Mercutio's Queen Mab speech, but I pretend I don't see. Twice he tries to come up to me in the hall, but I turn around and walk the other way. He goes to Petra and asks her how he can get me to talk to him, and Petra says, " 'Deny thy father and refuse thy name.' "

Not that River and I are going to be Romeo and Juliet. Juliet's problem is she loves Romeo, and he's cute and passionate and says a sonnet with her when they meet which makes him the perfect guy for her in every single way except his parents, so all he has to do is disavow them, and her objections go out the window. Romeo does not call her crazy. He is not rude and smug and a rich snob. When Romeo realizes he's done something wrong, he says sorry, and even if it was something pretty big — he did kill her cousin — at least he's not planning to do it again.

But halfway through World History one morning, there's a rustling, some ripple in the fabric of Track A, and under the desk, Chloe Daniels shoves from her hand into mine a folded-up piece of paper which when I unfold it reads, "I might have been somewhat wrong. You might have been slightly right. I may be a little bit sorry."

So, not completely unlike Romeo.

I look over at him. He's already looking at me. His eye's less swollen but more bruised, mottled purple all around, a sick yellow at the edges. His lip's almost healed in one spot but newly split in another.

I show Petra the note. "Chicanery," she pronounces.

So I write back, "Is this a trick?"

I watch the note make its way across the room. I watch him unfold and read it. He looks up and makes shocked eyes at me. Why, the very suggestion! I watch him write on the note, watch him fold it back up, watch it make its way back to me. I unfold it.

"No," it says.

Petra rolls her eyes.

"What made you maybe slightly somewhat change your mind?" Writing. Passing. Unfolding. Reading. Furtive glances at Mrs. Shriver who is talking about Britain outlawing slavery in 1833. Writing. Passing. Unfolding. Reading.

"Magic."

At lunch when he comes over and sits down with us, Petra is assembling a sandwich she's brought in pieces — English muffin, strawberry jelly, potato chips — by using one of the sturdier chips to spread the jam.

"According to my calculations," he says, lisping a little around the cut in his lip, "that potato chip is approximately eleven and a half calories."

"It's not a potato chip." Petra doesn't even look at him. "It's a jam spreader."

"Like a knife?"

"Exactly."

"Why don't you make lunch at home where you have an actual knife?"

"If I put the chips on at home, they'd be soggy by lunch."

"I thought you were just using them to spread the jam."

"Not just," says Petra. "After I use them as knives, I put them in the sandwich."

"Why?"

"They're crunchy" — she shrugs her braid over her shoulder — "unless you're dumb enough to assemble your sandwich at home."

He considers this logic.

"Are you okay?" I ask. I do not ask, "What's happening to your face?" because it seems rude and like something better left unspoken. As if it's not noticeable. As if not noticing would be a kindness. Kindness is not my goal anyway, but something has shifted here maybe, and I want to get him to tell me what it is.

"I'm fine." He tongues the raw inside of his cheek and keeps his eyes on Petra's sandwich.

He doesn't look fine, but I was just being polite anyway. If he doesn't want to tell me, there are more pressing things to discuss. "So. Magic?"

"Well, misdirection anyway." He smiles, winces, embarrassed or maybe it hurts his face to move it that much. "More like old-fashioned spy tactics I guess."

We wait.

"Cell reception sucks in this town," he says.

"We're aware," says Petra.

"We had to put in an actual landline." He looks appalled. "But then I realized the most amazing thing: if you pick up the phone upstairs, you can hear what's being said on the phone downstairs, and no one else on the phone call can tell you're listening because it's not really a shared call. No one invited you to join. No split screen. Nothing. It's like a technological marvel."

"We're known for that here," Petra says.

"The phone rings a million times a night, and it's always my grandfather, and he's always yelling, and my dad is always agreeing and apologizing and ass-kissing. So last night, I went upstairs and picked up the other phone and listened."

"And?" I try not to sound too eager or expect too much. "What did they say?"

He blanches. "I don't want to tell you."

"Tell us!" Petra and I demand at once.

"I can't. It's not nice."

"They're not hiding in the school cafeteria." Petra peeks theatrically under the table. "You're spying on them. They're not spying on you. They'll never know."

"Not not nice to them," River says. "Not nice to you."

"We can take it," I assure him because maybe this is it. I've watched my mother fight this battle a long time. I'm not naive enough to think that mean things River overheard his father say would make a difference. But maybe he overheard something that would, something we could tell Mama, and Mama could tell Russell, that would finally move the lawsuit in front of a judge who would at last be presented with evidence that could not be ignored or denied.

"I came in in the middle of the call so I missed the beginning," River hedges. "Plus, it was the third call of the night."

"That's okay," I say too fast. He seems nervous and reticent, and I don't want to scare him by being too intense and desperate, hungry. But I also don't want to seem so nonchalant he decides not to tell me.

"My grandfather said my dad has to get started before anyone in town realizes."

"Get started on what?" I say. "Realizes what?"

"I don't know." He won't look at me. "And he said my dad shouldn't be worrying about buying beers and kissing babies. He should be worrying you'll find it."

My breath catches. So there is an *it*!

Something to find, something they don't want us to find. "Find what?" I manage.

"I don't know." He shrugs with just his right shoulder, arms down by his sides. "And he said . . ." He trails off.

"What?"

"My dad said he felt bad about, you know, you." He blushes slowly. "But my grandfather said you're your own fault."

"We're our own fault?" I feel like Monday. I understand each of the words, but together they make no sense.

"He said probably you drink nothing but cheap beer and two-liter sodas and eat nothing but white bread and chips, and probably you've never even seen the inside of a gym." His face is getting redder, hotter, like he's dawning. "And my dad said that's not your fault because your grocery store doesn't really carry much produce, never mind an organics section, and the only yoga studio's in the church. And my grandfather said if you treat your bodies like that, what do you expect."

I think of Mrs. Shriver, but her inversion of cause and effect is on purpose. I mean Duke Templeton's probably is too but not so we'll grow as learners.

"And my dad was worried you'd figure it out," River says miserably.

"Figure what out?"

"I don't know, but my grandfather said you wouldn't because you're . . ." He trails off again.

"What?" I know I have to keep him talking, and I also know I don't want to know what he's about to tell me.

He says it so low I almost don't hear. "Inbred."

"Inbred?"

"So my dad shouldn't worry you'll outsmart him."

"What the f—"

"And that he shouldn't feel bad anyway because really you guys screwed us." He looks up and meets my eyes for the first time. Clears his throat. "Belsum invested all this money, and you guys sabotaged us and then lied and faked disabilities to scam us out of more cash."

"He thinks all that?" It's absurd, but it's so absurd it's hard to take seriously enough to get your feelings hurt.

"I don't know," River says again. "Maybe not." His expression has crossed over from embarrassed to more like ashamed, which is something I guess. "Maybe he was just talking trash. Psyching my dad up. Shooting down his objections. Trying to get him to do what he wants him to do."

239

Petra and I are speechless. If she weren't, she would say "aphonic."

Finally it occurs to me to wonder, "What did your dad say?"

"Not much." He shrugs again. "He never does."

"So what's he going to do?" Petra asks. "How's he going to get started on whatever it is before we find whatever he's hiding?"

"I don't know. And I can't ask him because then he'd know I was listening."

But that's not the right question. "Why?" I ask.

"Why what?"

"Why did you eavesdrop on your father and your grandfather?"

He slides his eyes away from mine. "Lots of reasons."

"Enigmatical," Petra says to me.

"Agreed," I agree. "When last we spoke" — I turn back to River — "you said I was crazy."

"Yeah. Hoped you were crazy is maybe a better way of putting it. You have to admit it's a little far-fetched. My grandfather knew his chemical was going to poison the town but he made it anyway? My grandfather saw it was killing everyone but refused to stop? Crazy."

"The story's crazy," I agree. "But I'm not."

240

"I couldn't get it out of my head. I thought there's no way it could be true. But . . ."

"But?"

"But something's going on here. Obviously." He waves vaguely around the cafeteria. "There has to be some explanation. And I couldn't think of one. Well, of another one."

"Yeah," I breathe. The fact of us. Our irrefutability.

"I wanted you to be wrong. I wanted to prove you were wrong. My dad can be a jerk, but mostly he's okay. But my grandfather. I mean he is my grandfather, but he's pretty mean. He's kind of hostile. And . . . rude. But everyone always does what he says without asking any questions. That's kind of his thing actually. Authority and respect and all that. Anyway, I couldn't stop thinking about what you said." He raises his eyes to meet mine. "I couldn't stop thinking about you."

It's such a cheesy line. I feel blood rushing to my face like I've been turned upside down, but I'm not embarrassed for me; I'm embarrassed for him. It's not my fault I'm so jaded. (If she weren't grinning like a demented clown and kicking me under the table, Petra would say "disentranced.") It's his fault. Or at least it's his family's fault.

241

So I'll be forgiven for being too worldly-wise to fall for his romantic-comedy schtick. I'll be forgiven for being overly critical of his diction like what was important about his sentiment was word choice. I'll even be forgiven for being kind of grossed out by his earnestness.

But in the high court of celestial judgment, when I go before whoever evaluates souls in the end, I'll be condemned anyway for the thought that bubbles to the top of this stew of squeamishness: I can use this. I can use *him*. If he can't stop thinking about me, if he wants me to know he can't stop thinking about me, I can get him to do what I want. I can get him to find what we need.

"Prove it," I say.

"That you're on my mind?"

"That you're on our side."

"How?"

"I don't know, but your grandfather being a jerk isn't proof of anything. We already knew that. Get us something that matters, something we can use. Help us find whatever your dad and your grandfather don't want us to find."

I'm not proud of this willingness to manipulate him, but times were desperate, I will testify before the soul tribunal, and the lawsuit needed me, and being cruel doesn't count if you're the wronged party. I will introduce into evidence all my mother and Russell haven't been allowed to and all they haven't been able to find.

And even if the soul tribunal isn't swayed by my logic, I still like my chances. I've learned not to have that much faith in the justice system anyway.

TWO

Mirabel is having a good day today, so she came to school with us instead of studying at work with Mama. She meets me after the bell rings, and I say let us go home, and she says let us wait for Mab to be done with tutoring, and I say what if someone comes to the library, and she says we can do palm reading so I say okay because I like palm reading. She does not mean telling each other's fortunes by looking at the lines on our hands because that is just pretend. She means a game we invented together when we were little. How it works is I close my eyes and hold out my palm, and Mirabel uses her finger to draw a picture on it, and I read what the picture is, and then she uses her finger to erase and draws another. Why I like this game is it is peaceful and soothing with only a little bit of touching, and Mirabel, unlike everyone else in the entire world, is always soft with her fingers. Why

Mirabel likes this game is she is as good at it as anyone.

We play in the hallway outside the tutoring room. Mirabel starts easy. "Rainbow," I guess, and I know I am right because she erases it to draw another.

She draws a face so I know it is a person, and then that person gets lots of hair so I know it is Mama even though the face is smiling and Mama usually is not.

She erases, and the next one is easy. Three lines straight up and down. "Us!" I say. Mirabel squeezes my finger. I squeeze her finger back.

She taps on my palm many times for rain which means green which is an adjective which is an advanced level of this game because most players can only do nouns. (It is more accurate to say most players *would* only be able to do nouns because there are no other players.) (That is just how it is when you invent your own game.)

Then I hear Mirabel gasp.

I look up from my palm to her face right away. "Why did you gasp, Three?"

She draws lots of squiggles.

"Snake, worm, string," I guess. "The letter *S*," I guess. "Skunk smell. Slippery road. Approximately. *Sin x.*"

She pulls on my finger so I will look at

her face again, and she uses her eyes to signal a signal to mine. I look where she is looking. And then I see what she was drawing. A river.

He is running down the hall. At first I make an assumption he is running to us, and then I make an assumption he is running to the bathroom because he has blood dripping out of his nose and down his lip and chin and neck and onto his shirt. Then I realize he is not running to us or to the bathroom because the Kyles come around the corner and they are running too, so I make an assumption that River is being chased by the Kyles. It is possible they are all three being chased by someone else and River got a head start, but that is not the assumption I make because the Kyles do not have blood dripping out of their noses.

River is running fast, but I can still see that in addition to the nose blood there is a scratch on his forehead and a rip in his shirt and a scrape near his eyebrow. River is running fast, but he gives a little wave to me and Mirabel as he goes by which is very polite under the circumstances. Then he is gone.

Left behind is the memory of his face which was scared and hurt, the echo of his running feet, loud on the linoleum, a dotted line mapping his path, like in a cartoon, except it is drops of blood, and Mirabel's facial expression, which is shocked like mine must be and upset like mine must be and something else too, but I cannot figure out what because there is a howl building up in my throat, and I know it will be loud and I will not be able to make it stop, but before it can arrive, a very surprising thing happens.

Mirabel takes her hand from mine and steers right into the middle of the hallway where the Kyles are thundering down.

"Move!" shouts one Kyle.

"Shit!" shouts the other Kyle even though Mrs. Radcliffe does not like us to say swears.

One Kyle swerves to avoid Mirabel, slams against the lockers, and falls down. The other Kyle does not see Mirabel because the first Kyle did not swerve away in time, so the second Kyle runs right into Mirabel's wheelchair and falls down too. Mirabel's wheelchair does not fall anywhere because it is heavy, and Mirabel gives them both a look that means smug, embarrassed for them, and they should be ashamed of themselves, but they are not her sisters and were not paying attention when Mrs. Radcliffe was doing facial expression cards this week so they might not notice.

"Why did you park there? We were in the middle of kicking that kid's ass," says Kyle.

Mirabel does three quick taps on her tablet. "That is why."

"Now we have to start over," says the other Kyle.

Mirabel starts typing out a reply to that, but the first Kyle says he is hungry, and the second says he is too. They have had feelings of love for Mirabel for years, but these are not as powerful as the feelings of hunger they have had for seconds. "We'll bring you back a donut," they promise her. Then they leave.

But the running feet and falling down and slamming into lockers made a lot of noise, so the tutoring-room door opens, and many people look out.

I take three deep breaths to help my surprised howl stay away, and then I tell everyone about River and the chasing and the blood and the Kyles, but I can guess they do not care because they do not say anything and they all go back inside.

Except for Mab.

Mirabel looks at her.

"Don't look at me like that," says Mab.

"Like what?" I ask. I can see how Mirabel is looking at Mab, but I cannot see what it is like.

"Why do you even care?" Mab says.

"Care about what?" I ask.

Mirabel keeps looking at Mab the way she was looking at Mab before.

"Not his fault," Mirabel's Voice says quickly, so I can guess that was what she had started to type to the Kyles before they got hungry.

"What is not his fault?" I ask. I do not ask *Whose fault?*, even though Mirabel did not say, because I can guess it is River, and my sisters do not like when I ask too many questions.

"I never said it was," says Mab.

"Help him," says Mirabel's Voice.

"How?" says Mab.

Mirabel's Voice does not answer that question but instead answers a different question. "You can."

"Not my problem," Mab says anyway.

I do not say anything because that is true but it is not kind, and Mirabel does not say anything, maybe for the same reason, so Mab says, "I'm like half his size. If he can't stop them, how can I stop them?"

"Numbers," Mirabel's Voice says.

Even Mab does not know what this means which it is nice when I am not the only one.

Mirabel sighs, which means frustrated, and types, "Safety in."

"Two is not a number," Mab says.

"Lie," I say because two is a number.

"You know what I mean," Mab says.

"Lie," I say.

Mab turns to me. "She thinks River's vulnerable alone, but with me by his side, surely we can take them."

"Who can you take?" I ask.

"Exactly," Mab says.

Which does not answer my question so in case she is not in a question-answering mood, I decide to skip right to the important one. "His face is sad and hurt and bleeding, One. Why would not you help him?"

"It's complicated." She looks confused, but I do not know why she would be. "You know?"

"No," Mirabel's Voice and I say at the same time.

"He says he can't stop thinking about me. He writes me notes in class. He's always looking at me."

Now it is my turn to sound confused because I am confused. "Why does that mean you do not want to help him?"

"He's evil," Mab says.

"It is more accurate to say his family is evil," I correct.

"And he said he was going to find some proof or something," Mab says, "something we can use."

Mirabel's hand flips out, palm up, which means *So what?* which is a good question.

"So if he does . . . I don't know . . ." Mab says. "I want him to do it because it's the right thing to do, not because he likes me."

"Why does it matter why he does it if he does it?" I ask.

"Because otherwise that makes *me* the jerk." Mab pulls the sleeves of her hoodie down over both of her hands as if she is cold. "Otherwise, I used him and manipulated his feelings to get what I want."

I consider this. "That is bad," I say. "But it is not as bad as letting him get beat up."

"I'm not *letting* him." She waves her hands around but her hands are all tucked in so she waves her sleeves around instead.

"Maybe his family is evil," I say, "but ours is not."

Mirabel points at me which means I am correct. "Right thing to do," her Voice says.

"According to who?" Mab asks, but I do not know why since she knows who Mirabel's Voice speaks for.

Mirabel holds up her hand with her fingers out wide. Five. Two plus Three. She means according to her and according to me.

Mab's sleeves flop into a shrug. "Who died and put you in charge?" she says, but then she stops saying anything because she does not need to be in a question-answering mood for us all to hear the answer to that question in our heads anyway. She tucks her sleeves under her armpits. "Sorry," she says. She does not mean because she does not want to help River. She does not mean because he is getting beat up. She means because she accidentally said that hard, sad thing, and it made everyone feel bad.

"It is okay," I say so she will not feel worse. But Mirabel is typing. "I know how you can make it up to me."

THREE

I spend a lot of time listening. As a result, I might be the world's leading expert on annoying conversational tics. The list of irritatingly misapplied clichés people utter would take me more hours to type out than I have left to live, but near the top is the conversational gambit "There are two kinds of people in this world . . ." There *are* two kinds of people in this world: the ones who split the world into two kinds of people, and the ones who know that's reductive and conversationally lazy.

With this exception: There are two kinds of people in this world. People who can expect to, strive to, feel entitled to be happy. And people who cannot.

The rest of the dichotomies are meaningless beside that one. Look through history for the latter. Look around your town or city. You will find us everywhere. We are legion.

Of course, everyone's unhappy sometimes. But some people's barriers to happiness are considered surmountable. They resolve to get in shape, find a therapist, make time for family, read more, go back to school, save money. We advise them, if they are our friends or our family, to find a new job, go to yoga, quit drinking, move out, try online dating, hire a personal stylist, buy a bigger house. You deserve it, we say. Put yourself first for a change. You be you.

Whereas some people are unhappy and that's okay with us. It seems unreasonable, in fact, that they should expect to be anything else.

Mab should fall in love. She should have friends, adventures, and a family of her own (by which no one means me, never mind I share a significant percentage of her DNA, her home and history, every single blood relation, and a onetime womb). We all agree: Mab should leave Bourne for limitless horizons. Mab should have joy, excitement, aspirations she strives for then accomplishes with much fanfare and personal gratification. Mab will go forth and be loved and fulfilled. Happy.

But me? No one really thinks that. I am lovable, yes, but not, people would say, in that way. Not like I might find myself hand

254

in hand with a crush on a moonlit night, or spill a long friendship over suddenly into more, or feel passion that simply must be answered. People imagine I will have no relationship more passionate than a pen pal.

So when I say I love River Templeton, I fear you misconstrue. You think it's cute or silly. Or pitiable. Or deluded.

But that misses the point. Love does not come from the likelihood it will be requited. If it seems reasonable, even inevitable, that soon enough Mab will fall in love with River, it must be because he is lovable. Should we not conclude, then, that I would love him too?

Or perhaps the inevitability has nothing to do with River himself and more to do with Mab being a teenage girl with a budding sexuality and nascent awareness of herself in the world. And am not I that as much as she? After all, they say the most sexual organ in the body is the brain, and by that logic, I am pretty well-hung. I do get that sex is corporeal too — I'm a virgin, not an idiot — and though relaxed muscles under your very own control must help, I am told that losing control is at least part of the point. Turning parts of my body over to others without feeling squeamish about it is some-thing I must have more experience with than most teenagers. I can communicate "yes," "no," "stop," and "more please" as well as anyone, even without my Voice, as long as you're paying attention. And as for the other body parts involved, those are some of my most functional ones: earlobes to nibble, a navel to graze, warm lips and flushed skin and bated breath and a quick-beating heart, pheromones and erogenous zones. All the parts inside. I can feel my body move even if I can't move most of it myself. And yes, I'll have to find partners who will listen to me, who will focus on what my body wants and can do instead of what it doesn't and can't, who will look at me and really see, who are patient and gentle and kind. Will those partners be easy to find? No. Does anyone in any body think those partners are easy to find? Also no.

So perhaps the assumption that I could not possibly really love River is not about him and not about Mab and not about me and what I can do, but only about what I can't, what I shouldn't. A be-grateful-for-what-you've-got sort of argument. A learn-to-be-happy-with-settling-for-less approach. This logic reasons that after sixteen years trapped in a body in a chair, I should be used to it. I should know my bounds and strive for no more. I should lower every expectation to the bottom of a well.

I should shut up and find sufficient joy merely in being alive.

But, Monday would point out, those things are opposites.

Forgone happiness foregone concluded, that special state of resigned discontent we're not supposed or even allowed to question, is a curse I share with my hometown. In whatever bougie Boston enclave the Templetons left to move here, everyone expects to be happy, and everyone, one imagines relatedly, expects not to be poisoned. If the water were contaminating wealthy Bostonians, that would be unacceptable and addressed.

But Bourne? Bourne is completely disposable. Like me, my town is not expected to aspire to happiness. We have neither right nor reason to expect we are not being poisoned. And that is not a coincidence. That is the reason Belsum chose Bourne for their site. That is the reason they did what they did to our water and soil and citizens so cavalierly. That is why I am the second kind of person in this world.

So this is where River and I part. At least one place. And I am not naive. I know he's probably a spoiled brat. I expect he has unexplored, unrecognized privilege and an ego you could see from space. But that doesn't mean I can't love him. They say opposites attract. They say find what you lack in another. They say two halves make a whole. And besides, he's just a kid — not his father, not his grandfather — so it's premature to write him off. He can learn, and that's even better. It means more if he's kind of clueless and sort of a jerk, and then he realizes what his family did to ours, and then he realizes what families like his always do to families like ours. And then he sets out to change, to change himself and then his legacy and then the world. They say you cannot change a man. But they say I cannot do all sorts of things it turns out I can, including fall in love. And anyway, he's not a man. He's just a boy, and those are ripe for change.

This is why I made Mab promise to help him. Not because I feel sorry for him. Not because it's the right thing to do. Not because what happened in Bourne is not his fault.

Because I love him.

That is why.

Support on this point comes from an unlikely party.

The doorbell rings just as we're finishing

258

dinner — Caesar salad and spinach quiche because it's pouring. Mab answers then steps back without a word so Nora can see who it is. Monday sees too and scampers back to our bedroom. Among the many things Monday does not like is conflict.

Mab forgets her manners. "What should I do?" she asks our mother.

"Let him in." Nora sounds tired already.

"Enter." Mab makes a gallant sweep with her arm. "At your own risk."

Omar Radison comes in and drips on our threshold.

"You have homework," Nora says to Mab, but me she ignores. I have more than done my homework.

Nora puts on tea. Omar takes his jacket off in the front hallway and hangs it on the doorknob. It won't dry — there's no heat in the entryway — but it won't drip on our kitchen floor either.

"Hey Mirabel." He walks over, takes my hand, squeezes it, an act of generosity — not many people touch me just casually. "How's tricks?"

"I am well, thank you," my Voice says. "How are you?"

"Can't complain." He drops his voice and winks at me. "Well, I could, but I won't because I need a favor from your mother."

I wink back at him.

"I'm not doing you any favors, Omar." Nora has dog ears.

"I thought maybe I'd catch you at the bar." He sits on the very edge of the sofa. She stands in the kitchen watching the kettle.

"Not working tonight."

"Yes, Frank told me."

She says nothing. Waits.

"That's why I'm here."

"To drink too much beer in my kitchen?"

He smiles but then says anyway, "We have to talk, Nora."

She nods without looking at him.

"Someone's beating up his kid," he says, and my heartbeat quickens.

"Not me."

"Of course not you. But Nora . . ."

"What?"

"We have to make them feel welcome."

"Like hell we do."

"Sorry. I know." Hands up like she might hit him. "That's not what I meant."

"That's exactly what you meant."

"It would be better if you could be nice to them," he over-enunciates.

"Better for whom?"

"Better for everyone."

"Better for you and for them and for not

a single other person in this —"

"Jesus, Nora, enough." He draws in a deep breath, lets it go. It's shaky on the way out. "It's time to move on."

"Easy for you to say."

"It is not easy for me to say." Omar is standing now and loud. Omar is never standing and loud. Omar is always cowed before Nora.

"Here's a game the girls love." She is so good at pretending to be calm. "Truth or dare?"

"God, Nora, I don't know."

"Well, just for variety, how about you tell me the truth for once? You're the one who arranged for them to buy the library."

I have figured this out already but am surprised Nora has as well, having far less time than I do to dwell on the issue.

He hangs his head. "Not arranged for. But yeah."

"What do you mean, 'Not arranged for but yeah'?"

"I didn't offer it to them." He throws out one hand, helpless, or like it doesn't matter. "But I didn't say no when they asked."

"No to what?"

"They came scouting for housing. They didn't tell me who they were, but they didn't hide it either. I knew the last name of course, and then I took one look at the father, at the kid, and knew for sure who they must be. They flat-out asked if the library was available. Said they drove by and noticed it was empty." He looks up from the ground at her, waits for her to meet his eyes. "I said I'd ask."

"And?"

"And the person it turned out I had to ask was me."

"Why you?"

"Because for what it's worth, and it's not much, I'm still mayor."

"I noticed."

"You want the job?"

"You wish."

"Exactly."

In a town where irony literally flows right down the middle, this is perhaps the saddest instance of all: Omar Radison, once and future and eternal mayor.

Twenty years ago, Omar ran on the Belsum platform. His opponent, Carl Castillo, moved away soon after he lost, and died — of old age, mind — soon after he moved, but before he did either of those things, he ran on a platform of tradition, staying the course, honoring the old ways, and keeping Belsum out. He wanted the town to stay as it was: small, historic, closed.

Because he was eventually vindicated as Galileo, we don't talk much about whether what Carl Castillo really was was a xenophobe and a racist. He wanted to keep Bourne for Bourne residents. He wanted to keep our money in our community. He wanted things to stay the same.

Whereas Omar was twenty-five, back in the town where he was born and raised, armed with a brand-new college degree and the unearned optimism of quarter-centenarians. He campaigned for change, growth, increase; he ran for new citizens, new jobs, new opportunities. He painted a picture of a Bourne thriving with the influx of money from Belsum, money from clearing land and paving fields and building factories, from working at the new plant, from feeding Belsum employees and their families, entertaining them, getting them drunk, selling them things they needed and things they didn't. There were tax incentives and growth incentives and investment opportunities.

Think of our past, said Carl Castillo.

Imagine our future, said Omar.

He won by a landslide. I make the whole thing sound like a political maelstrom, which is how it's been presented to me, but we aren't a big town. Both candidates went door-to-door, sometimes together. In lieu of a debate, they played a couple friendly games of pool at Norma's. We few thousand people went and voted for change. And change we did receive.

Conventional wisdom says when the populace is angry, the incumbent gets voted out, whether or not he's to blame. But Omar is more like Coleridge's Ancient Mariner, doomed to live out an error in judgment for the rest of his days, endless witness to the suffering he's wrought. After it all went to shit, no one wanted to be mayor of Bourne. There weren't enough people left. No one knew how to clean up the mess. No one was willing to take on the burden of figuring it out. And besides, who volunteers to captain a ship with a hole in the hull so wide it could be a portal to another galaxy? If only.

So Omar is stuck with the job.

"The library is city property. As mayor" — he winces — "the decision as to what to do with the empty library was mine."

"So you gave it to them?"

"Sold it to them, yes."

"Your pound of flesh?"

"Not flesh." He shakes his head, but not especially vehemently. "Money. We need it."

"How much can that library possibly have

gone for?"

"It's a pretty building."

"In a moldering town."

"A pretty moldering town," he says.

"So you were just faking before?"

"When?"

"In the bar last month. When you had big news and the big news was Donna saw a moving truck."

"She did." He shrugs. "I was trying to ease you in. Besides, I knew they bought the place, but I didn't know when or even whether they were coming, what they wanted it for."

"And then it turned out you already gave them permission to reopen the plant two decades ago, so the library was just the gravy on the potatoes." The fake cheery tone she's wrestling into submission looks like it's paining Omar physically. "And conveniently, of course, you've never signed on to the lawsuit, so no conflict of interest there either."

"We've been over this." They have. Nora thinks it would send a strong signal to Bourners if they knew Omar was joining their fight, and to Belsum if they knew the mayor himself had added his name to the class action. Omar thinks that's not his place as mayor and that he needs to be available to everyone as go-between should Nora and Russell ever get that far.

"We have," she agrees. "You like to be nice to them, and you'd like me to be nice too. Make them feel welcome and at home."

"Not make them feel welcome." He throws out his arms, frustrated, begging her. "Just don't go out of your way to piss them off."

"How am I doing that?"

He gives her a look, arms still out. "We hold zero cards here. We've got no power at all. If these guys don't come in angry and defensive, if they like us, that's our best shot at them treating us right."

"We were down-on-our-knees grateful last time." Nora gets down on hers to demonstrate. "We hailed them like war heroes. We were so happy-they-picked-us welcoming we were groveling. And that didn't inspire them not to poison us. Now they're back as if nothing happened, as if they didn't ruin everything" — her voice breaks, and I can see it break something in Omar too — "as if we've all forgotten, and you're asking us just to let it alone?"

"Yes." Clear but soft.

"You're asking me?"

"Yes, Nora." He joins her on the floor so that they're kneeling face-to-face, and he reaches out and takes her hands. And she lets him. "It's not fair, and it's not right, and God knows it's not easy. But it's happening anyway, so not kicking the man out of the bar is our best chance of making it happen well."

"Why should I want it to go well for them? Why aren't my fingers and toes crossed that they're burning in the flames of bankruptcy hell within a month of resumed operations?"

"Not go well for them. Go well for us. Protecting our citizens, making Bourne as good as it can be, this is my job."

She wrenches her hands from his. "Congratulations on finally figuring that out, Omar."

He winces again but says anyway, "No, Nora, I've known it all along. You think any of this was my plan? My hope for this place?"

"No, I think you were shortsighted and greedy, which is worse." She stands, but he stays on his knees, so now it's like she's talking down to a child. "I think you went with a get-rich-quick scheme instead of doing the hard work to find the good and honest ways that would have shored us up instead of tearing us down. I think you failed to protect us."

"I did fail to protect us." He sits back on his heels, hangs his head, but then looks back up at her. "That I did. But I'm not sure the rest of that's fair. I didn't foresee what was going to happen. No one did."

"They did." Nora snorts. "You know Belsum knew GL606 wasn't safe."

"Maybe they did. But I didn't. I wanted to grow this place. New jobs, new opportunities." He stands finally and ranges around the living room while he talks, the politician in him walking the stage. "I thought we'd start slow, open a handful of new places to eat, to shop, and the plant would grow, and new families would move in and good doctors to treat them and a movie theater, and eventually there'd be nice hotels and shopping centers and four-star restaurants, and Bourne would thrive and all of us with it. That was my plan. It wasn't quick and shortsighted. It was the opposite of that. It didn't work out that way. I'm not saying it wasn't an unmitigated disaster. I'm not saying I wouldn't change every single thing if I could. But you can't say my heart wasn't in the right place. I was wrong, and it was my job to be right, and I failed at it. Miserably. But I was trying to do the hard, right thing." He stops in front of her. "I just didn't know, Nora. They lied to me too."

She sighs and she waits and then she says, very quietly, "I know that, Omar. I do."

"And I'm still trying." He reaches for her hands again, but this time she won't let him, so he clasps his own in front of him, pleading, almost praying. "If I could keep them from coming back, I would. But since I can't, I'm working with what I have here, and that's treating them well in the hope they treat us well back, being nice so they'll be nice in return. It's not much, but it's all I've got."

"How am I not being nice?" Nora's palms are upturned like she's not asking Omar, she's asking God.

"They're beating his kid," he says again.

"That's not me."

"You're riling people up."

"I'm not," she protests.

"I hear different."

"From whom?"

"Everyone." His voice is rising again. "Everyone knows, Nora. It's always you. You are the town crazy lady who just can't let this go."

She looks at him, and her eyes fill, and of the three of us, I don't know who's most surprised.

"And here I've been thinking it's the rest

269

of you who are crazy," she says when she can speak again. "But maybe you're right. Maybe it's been me all along." She balls her fists against her chest like she can't decide whether to fight or to grasp her heart in her hands. "They poisoned us, Omar. And when they realized it — or realized we knew it — instead of stopping, they denied it so they could keep poisoning us because poisoning us was making them money. And when finally, finally they couldn't deny it anymore, they just left. Didn't try to help. Didn't try to fix it. Just left us ruined. In ruins. In the face of that, is it crazy to chase after them for sixteen years, or is it crazy to just move on? Is it crazier to demand some kind of restitution, even though restitution is impossible, or to pretend all is well and everything's fine when nothing is or will be ever again?"

"I don't know," Omar says quietly.

"You think I don't know I look crazy?" She's quiet too. "I know. You think I don't know what this crusade is costing me? But what does it cost to think we never deserved any better, and this is just the way it is, and there's no point in fighting?"

"Maybe it'll be different this time." He wraps his fingers around her fists.

"It's too late."

"Only for us."

"Who else is there?"

"Them. Unfortunately. And they don't owe us anything."

"They owe us everything."

"All we can hope for is their good grace."

"Well, in that case" — Nora unclaws her hands from under his — "we are truly, truly fucked."

ONE

The point my sisters ganged up on me to make in the hallway outside tutoring yesterday is the one it always is: it's the least I can do.

It's not that Mirabel inspires me in some sparkly-disabled-sister-inspirational-rainbow way. More like she shames me in a regular-sister-who's-both-smarter-and-nicer-than-I-am way. It's the least I can do, not the way Mrs. Radcliffe says when she makes us tutor: I am blessed so I should serve. More like: Mirabel can't, but what's my excuse? If Mirabel could, she would shout down the kids kicking River's ass, demand protection for him from the school administration, use her body to shield his, use her fists to give as good as River got. I guess it makes sense Mirabel feels a kinship with anyone at the mercy of bullies, circumstance, their own physical limitations, and shit they inherited from their parents that isn't their fault, but the only way she can help is to make me do it for her.

You know that saying "Easier said than done"? This is true even when you can't talk.

Still, I was convinced. Am convinced. Can you be reluctantly hell-bent? I am that. What I can do and whether I should do it for River Templeton may be in question, but anything I can do for Mirabel, I do, if not always gladly then resolvedly.

So I submit that into evidence. Okay, yes, a part of me is thinking that if I help him, he'll help me back, actually do what he said he would, spy harder on his father, get us proof we can use. But part of me — a bigger part — decides to help him because I love my sister. Petra would call this exculpating.

Our last class of the day is English, and River's knee bounces through the whole of it. He sits one behind, one over from me, and I can feel him through the floor. When he catches me looking back at him, he smiles then winces. His bottom lip is split again.

The bell rings, and he's up like Pavlov's dogs, but I was prepared for that, so I meet him at the door and push him back into the classroom as everyone else files out.

"You don't look so good," I tell him.

He makes bodybuilder arms. "How about now?"

Flirting with me. Because he likes me or because he wants me to like him? Because he likes me or because he doesn't want to talk about how he's getting his ass kicked?

"Your arms look fine." They do, actually. "It's your face that concerns me."

"Fine?" Mock offended. "Feel these."

I do. Flirting back, I suppose, but what choice do I have really? And anyway, I don't know what I'm feeling for — it's the first biceps I've squeezed that I'm not related to — but I see his point. "Better than fine," I admit. "Nice."

"Nice? That's even worse. We're looking for mighty. Epic. Awe-inspiring."

"They make your head look tiny in comparison," I offer.

"That's my only goal," he says.

"I think you should expand it."

"My head?"

"Your goal. I think you should shoot for tiny *and* intact."

"I don't want to get greedy."

"Let me help you," I say.

"Help me what?"

"Survive high school."

"Depends how. Are you going to disguise me?"

"A disguise will never work." It's hard for me to say because I don't do this very often, but whether he's flirting or evading, I think he's pretty good at it. "You're too distinctive. What with all those big muscles." Me too, I'm pretty good at it.

"True, true." He pretends to stroke his pretend beard thoughtfully. "Will you fashion some kind of unbreachable transport for me to take back and forth to school? Like the popemobile?"

"Not unless you're the pope."

"Can you cast a protection spell?"

"I don't know. Let me ask someone who does magic." I can feel my cheeks are flushed. "Hey River, can you teach me a protection spell?"

His cheeks are flushed too, though whether we're embarrassed or enjoying ourselves I couldn't say. "I can teach you how to pull a really long scarf out of your armpit."

"Pass."

"Then I don't think you can help me," he says.

"I have to."

"Why?" He's suddenly serious. He moves a step closer to me — and he was pretty close already — looks hard into my eyes. "Why?" he says again, softer, and waits for me to say because I like him or at least because I care about him or at the very least because it's the right thing to do. Instead I tell him the truth. Well, some of the truth. "I promised my sisters."

He blinks. "Okay." Takes a step back, but only one. "For your sisters, I agree to let you try to stop everyone from beating me up."

"Thank you," I say.

"You're welcome." He puts a hand on each of my shoulders like he's going to pull me in and kiss me. He does not. "So what's the plan, fairy queen?"

It's a good question.

The only answer I can come up with is this: I can't run circles around these guys, but I can talk circles around them.

I decide to start with the Kyles. Two birds and all that. At tutoring, I try begging them. "Just leave the kid alone."

"No," they say.

"Please," I wheedle. "For me."

"Still no." Everything the Kyles say, they say together.

I try flattery.

"But you're so much stronger than he is."

"True," they agree but can't see why this

isn't an argument *for* beating him up rather than against.

I try an appeal to fairness.

"It's two against one."

"We take turns," they assure me.

I try reason, but reason is not their strong suit.

"It wasn't his fault. He's our age."

"He is?"

"Of course. He's enrolled in high school."

"Who cares if he's our age?"

"Because what happened with Belsum happened before any of us were even alive."

"That's why you're so vacuous," Petra puts in from where she's doing multiplication tables with Nellie in the corner. But the Kyles aren't studying for the SATs so they don't know what "vacuous" means, which, come to think of it, is probably for the best.

I summon patience. "If he wasn't born yet, it can't be his fault. And besides, how much control do you have over your parents' actions?"

"Huh?" they say.

"If your dad does something stupid, is it your fault?"

"Yeah," says one.

"Usually," says the other one.

I resort to platitudes.

"Violence is never the answer."

And it's like a clearing, like a wind blows the storm clouds from their brains and suddenly you can see for miles.

"It is," they say.

"His dad's gonna give my dad a job, Mab," Kyle M. says.

"Mine too," says Kyle R.

My legs pretzel, and I fold right to the floor. They cross theirs nimbly and join me, crisscross-applesauce on the carpet like when we were in kindergarten. My brain is screaming: *It's starting. It's started.* And also, quieter, *She won't survive this.*

"My dad said the whole place is a shit show," says Kyle M., "but maybe it'll be better this time."

"My dad said the whole company's corrupt, lying assholes," says Kyle R., "but a job's a job."

"So we did what we had to," they say together.

"What do you mean?"

"Maybe our dads can't stand up, but we can." Kyle R. looks so earnest it's like he's still a kindergartner. That was the year he started an adopt-a-slug program at recess with the slogan "Even the slimy deserve a family."

"Maybe our dads can't stand up," Kyle M.

— adoptive father to the vast majority of re-homed slugs — adds, "so we have to. You know? Their way didn't work, so now it's our job."

I nod. I do know. But then I shake my head. "But River's on our side. He's helping us."

They look skeptical. I know how they feel. "How?"

"I don't know yet. I'm working on it. But I can't get him to help us if you won't leave him alone."

"Are you sure he's helping?"

I'm not. "I think he's trying."

"He might be lying to you, Mab."

"Maybe," I admit.

They consider the matter between them.

"Plus, Mirabel says," I add. My ace in the hole.

Their faces light up. They emerge from their huddle, nodding.

"We'll stop for the moment," says Kyle M., "if you promise to let us know when it's time to start up again."

"And," adds Kyle R., "if you promise to tell Mirabel we did what she said."

On my way home, I stop by Pooh's to bring her a loaf of zucchini bread my mother put into the oven when it was raining but didn't remove until after it stopped, so Monday wouldn't eat it. Pooh, of course, doesn't care.

"Who pooped in your piña colada?" she says when she buzzes me in and sees my face. I follow her into the kitchen where she opens her fridge, inserts the zucchini bread, and swaps it for a heap of meats and sauces she starts piling on the counter.

"Tutoring sucked," I tell her.

"Poor baby. You need animal flesh." She puts a plate of galbi — her mother's recipe — in front of me, then starts setting up a steamer for dumplings.

"I don't think that's the problem."

"Then what?"

"The Kyles are beating River up because his dad gave their dads jobs."

She nods. This makes sense to her, a strange kind of warped Bourne logic, whack-a-mole revenge. "And you want to save him." She's grinning at the bossam she's wrapping in cabbage leaves. "That's very sweet."

"Not me. Mirabel."

"Bullshit. You love him."

"You wish." Everyone could do with a little excitement around here. "I'm telling you it's Mirabel. She pled his case. She begged me to help him."

"Why?"

"She's nicer than I am."

"Well, that's certainly true. Whereas you, you think you'll let the kid keep getting the shit beat out of him?" She's half teasing, half making a point, though I don't know what point.

Until I say it out loud, I don't even know it's in my head. "He thinks we're so fucked up."

"I bet. Who cares what he thinks?"

I do. "He thinks we're this tiny backwards, backwoods, backwater town, stupid and pathetic and hopeless. Crazy. South of crazy. Beggarly. Lugubrious."

"You and Petra might have studied enough now."

"He feels sorry for us." I sound bitter as orange rind.

"Not sorry enough," she says.

"It's not his fault." I keep saying that.

"Not yours either."

"Sure, but no one's blaming me."

"You inherited his father's father's mess," Pooh says, "and so did he. It should be his burden at least as much as yours, don't you think? He needs to see what we are. He needs to know it in his bones. Maybe the Kyles'll knock some sense into him."

"The Kyles don't have enough sense to

knock between them," I say, and she nods, and she's quiet, and then she says, "But you know what else?"

"What?"

"He needs to see how we're broken maybe. But you? You need the opposite. You need to see how we're whole."

"A hole?"

Pooh has been in Bourne as long as anyone. She needs a wheelchair just because she's old. You forget, living here, that some of us falter before it's time, but if we're lucky and live long enough, we'll all wind up there in the end. What's different about Pooh is she's so old that even though she's been here forever, she hasn't been here forever. There was a time before. Pooh has lived in two different countries and four different states. She's visited family in Korea, California, and Hawaii. She went to college and drove cross-country once with her roommate. She knows about the world out there. She's the only one I know who does. Except River.

"Bourne's on the small end of town-sized and a bit too powder-keg-y at the moment for my taste, but there's a lot that's really nice about this town. We're not especially wonderful maybe, but we're not especially miserable either. How it is here is how it is everywhere."

I raise an eyebrow at her. "It's really not."

"Yup, it is. It was just the same for him in Boston, I promise you."

"What are you talking about, Pooh? Boston has museums, historic stuff, parks, baseball, millions of people, nontoxic bodies of water —"

I'm just getting started when she interrupts. "He was sick of all the kids he'd known since grade school, the ones he never liked but his parents made him hang out with, the ones who were there when he accidentally called the kindergarten teacher Mommy and remember when he got hit in the face with a volleyball in sixth grade and cried so hard they had to send him home. He wants a million things he doesn't have. He wants everything. He thought there was no one new to meet and no one he wasn't bored to death of and nothing to do on Saturday nights and nowhere left to go. He felt trapped there like he'd never get out. And then suddenly? He got to come here. He doesn't think Bourne's lame. He thinks it's exciting."

"No way." I'm laughing now, shaking my head.

"Maybe not Bourne itself, but all the new people, new school, new possibilities."

"They're beating him up," I remind her.

"Exciting!" She shrugs. "Roils the blood. Muddies the waters. I bet he loves it."

"He doesn't. He's terrified."

"Because you know what else it does?" It's like she hasn't even heard me. "It makes pretty girls feel protective of you. It makes pretty girls stand up for you in front of everyone."

"You're crazy, Pooh."

"I'm not. I'm telling you. Here's not so different from anywhere. You can't see that now but you will. When you leave, you'll see. And River Templeton? He's not so different either. Teenage boys are teenage boys. I bet you anything he's over the goddamn moon to be here."

"How could that possibly, possibly be the case?"

"Easy," Pooh says. "You're here."

Two

Mab kicks over a stack of checkout cards, and I know she did not mean to, but she should be more careful because the checkout cards go everywhere, and that is a whole afternoon of work wasted. If you think it is ridiculous that I am using cards and pencils to track library books in this day and age, you are correct. If you think I am too stupid to know how to use a computer instead, you are incorrect. When Mrs. Watson gave me the books, she did not give me the scanner you use to catalog, lend, and track the books. I asked, but she said it got sold. Leave it to humanity to think the book scanner is more valuable than the books.

Mab says she is sorry about my cards, but she does not look sorry about my cards.

"Come downstairs," she says.

"What is downstairs?"

"Mirabel."

"Mirabel is always downstairs."

"Exactly. We need to talk. All of us."

"Why?" I ask.

"Three heads are better than one."

"Like Cerberus?" There are two books about Greek mythology inside the microwave.

"Yes," Mab says. "Exactly like Cerberus." But she is being sarcastic enough that even I can tell.

Downstairs, she is all red and talking with a lot of extra breath. "I did it."

Mirabel high-fives her.

"What did you do?" I ask.

"What you wanted me to."

"You picked up all my checkout cards and put them back in the right order and placed them neatly in a neat pile with something heavy on top so they will not go everywhere if someone kicks them accidentally?" That is what I wanted her to do, but I do not see when she could have done it since it just happened.

"The other thing," she says.

But I cannot think of another thing.

So she rolls her eyes and says she talked to River, and she talked to the Kyles, and she told the Kyles to stop and to spread the word and tell everyone else to stop too.

"Thank you," Mirabel's Voice says, and her eyes might have tears in them, and her face might show happy or it might show relieved.

"Why do you look red and panty then?" I wonder to Mab.

"We need a plan," Mab says, "and a sister pact."

"I vow to always eat your creamed spinach," I say immediately. Neither of my sisters likes creamed spinach. "As long as it is raining."

"Not that kind, Monday," Mirabel's Voice says at once so she must have it saved, but I do not know why she would. Then she adds, "Thank you," which is polite. Then she adds, "Stop."

"Stop what?" I say.

But Mab says, "Exactly. You're right."

"Right about what?" I say.

"We have to stop them. Don't say who, Monday, I'm getting to that. We have to stop Belsum."

I wait, but neither of them says anything else, so I ask, "Stop them from what?"

"Opening the plant," says Mab. "Reopening the plant."

"How can we?" I ask.

"I don't know," says Mab.

"We do not have a lawyer," I inform them. "We do not have any money. We are just kids no one listens to."

"So we won't sue them, buy them, or convince them," says Mab. "We'll do it a different way."

"What way?"

"Our way."

"Oh. What is our way?"

"I don't know," Mab says again.

"If Mama cannot," I say, "we cannot too."

I put my hands over my ears, but I can still hear Mirabel tapping at her screen. Then her Voice says, "She is one. We are three."

"And plus, we have River," says Mab.

"We do?"

"Now that we've saved him, he owes us," she says. "Mama and Russell and the lawsuit have never had that."

"Had what?"

"A man on the inside."

"River is not a man," I inform her.

"You know what I mean."

"Lie."

"I'm saying River might have access to all sorts of things Mama and Russell don't even know to look for."

"He could sabotage his father from inside the house!" This is an exciting good idea, but Mab and Mirabel both laugh like I am making a joke. So I explain, "He could hide all his father's shoes so he could not go to

288

his meetings, or if he did go to his meetings he would be barefoot so no one would listen to him. He could hide the giant scissor because his father cannot reopen the plant without a ceremony and he cannot have a reopening ceremony without a giant scissor. If his grandfather comes to visit, River could hide a minor poison in his food so Duke Templeton could see how he likes it, and he would not like it and change his mind."

"I was thinking more like next time River listened in on a conversation he could record it on his phone," Mab says.

"My ideas are better." It is not polite to brag, but it is objectively true that my ideas *are* better.

"Fine," Mab says which means the opposite. "Let's just say we need to consider all the ways we can use River and what we want him to do for us."

"Why?" I am always asking why.

Mirabel types. "It's our turn."

I open my mouth to ask our turn to what, but Mab has guessed this already. "Our turn to fight, Monday. Look, Duke Templeton said they should be worried we'll find it, and they have to do whatever they have to do before anyone realizes it."

"But we do not know what 'it' it is," I say.

"Lie," Mirabel's Voice says.

"We *do* know what 'it' it is," Mab explains. "*It* is what Mama and Russell and all the people signed on to the suit have been looking for all these years. Proof. A smoking gun."

"How do you know?" I ask.

"Because otherwise why is Duke Templeton so desperate to keep it out of our hands?"

"I do not know," I say because I do not. "How will we get it?"

"We don't know," Mab says, "but we know it exists. That's the important thing. Now all we have to do is find it."

"That sounds hard," I say.

"Truth," says my sister's Voice.

"Truth," says my other sister's voice. "Hard but not impossible."

THREE

Russell E. Russo, Esquire, knocked on lots of doors before Nora's. Some people did not answer on principle; they did not open their doors to strangers wearing neckties. Some quietly or not-so-quietly closed the door in his face when he introduced himself. Some let him in and heard him out and deposited his card in the wastebasket before he'd finished backing out of their driveways. By the time Russell showed up, people in Bourne had a deep distrust of outsiders. But to be honest, people in Bourne were probably never going to be much for lawyers anyway. He kept saying he was here to help them, but why would he? If anyone were going to care, they'd have cared already. If strangers came when people were in need, they'd have come long ago. Since the answers were never honest, no one in Bourne was fool enough to ask the questions anymore.

Except for Nora.

When Nora opened her door, her hair a cloud of tangles encrusted variously with vomit, snot, and milk, wearing a robe liberally splattered with some previous night's dinner, holding two screaming two-month-olds while a third howled from a laundry basket lined with towels and deposited in the middle of the kitchen floor, Mr. Russo introduced himself and inquired without irony whether she had any complaints regarding the recently shuttered Belsum Chemical plant. She handed him one of the babies — me — not in answer to his question, but because she imagined that with one hand free, she could put on coffee, and while that wouldn't solve the problem, it would at least help matters. And matters needed helping.

He came in. He sat down. He took all three babies into his lap. It is true we were very small, and he was — is — a large man with big arms and a lot of real estate on his lap when he sits, but we still have trouble picturing all four of us piled together. Though Monday has many times pressed Nora for specifics as to how he managed it, our mother is vague on the details. She was sleep deprived and also breathtaken. Here her knight in shining armor had shown up at her door. Had she been limitlessly granted her most wondrous, most extravagant, most dearly held dream, there was nothing she would have wished to open her door to more than the offer to join a class action lawsuit against Belsum Chemical, especially one with an extra set of hands who wasn't put off by a house full of screaming babies.

Russell Russo was gentle and kind and surprisingly good with children. He talked so quickly Nora's ears ached trying to keep up. He informed her, deadly serious, that Belsum Chemical had wronged the citizens of Bourne. He broke this to her as if she didn't know already, as if she wouldn't believe it unless he explained it to her like a child or someone not from Bourne, someone unBourne, but she didn't feel talked down to. She felt broken open with gratitude that it was just that simple, just that clear, and to someone from out there in the rest of the world. It wasn't just in Nora's head, the crimes done unto her, the crying-out sense that justice should be done, at least some, at least trying. He made it so she could put down the burden of being the only one who knew.

Russell Russo spoke of wrongful death, criminal negligence, perjury, failure of oversight, buried memos, biased reports, and attempted cover-ups. He had spoken already to many of her neighbors. He had a pledge from the senior partners at his firm that he could take the case on contingency. He had associates and paralegals and interns back at his office who were already wading through boxes and boxes of documents. He was certain that somewhere in them was the smoking gun, the damning evidence, the indisputable proof of what Belsum knew and when they knew it that would force them to hand out significant, much deserved, desperately needed, only fair cash settlements which, Russell admitted, would not make up for her losses, for nothing could, but which would make it easier to get on with her life, both financially and the part where she didn't walk around all day long feeling like she'd been royally fucked and no one gave a shit. He was smart and passionate. And handsome, of course. Was there any chance she was not going to fall in love with him?

There was not. It was the knight-in-shining-armor stuff. It was that he was intelligent and kind and going to save her. It was that he eased her way and carried her load. It was that he had never seen her other than she was now. It was that her husband was well and truly gone. And though the same could not be said about Russell's wife, that wasn't Nora's fault because she didn't know he had one. At least not at first.

"Belsum has wronged you," he told her, but of course she already knew that, "so they have to pay."

"Why?"

"Why what?"

"Why do they have to pay? You're saying otherwise it's not fair?"

"It's not fair."

"It's not, but things usually aren't. You're not a five-year-old, Mr. Russo."

"Russell," he corrected her.

"You're not a five-year-old, Russell. 'It's not fair' isn't a reason for adults."

"It's the best reason there is." Russell truly believed this.

She found his conviction touching, but she didn't buy it. "This is really about money," she guessed. "Not fairness."

He kept his eyes on hers — would not allow them to wander over her meager home — when he said, "You're going to need it."

"I don't want their money."

"Sure you do. Besides, it's not theirs. Money belongs to whoever has it. Don't you think that should be you?"

"They can stick it up their ass."

"You need it, Nora. These girls are going

to need, well, many things. Three kids on a single mother's salary would be hard no matter where you lived, but —"

"What's wrong with here?"

"Not a lot of job prospects."

"And whose fault is that?" said Nora.

"Belsum's! That's what I keep telling you."

"So you're doing this to make up for my dead husband, my wronged children, and my poisoned town?"

"No."

"No?"

"No. Nothing can make up for that. No one's talking 'making up for.' I'm talking money."

"As compensation?"

"To meet your significant, egregious needs. Significant, egregious needs for which they are at fault."

"And you get a cut?"

"If we win, yes, I would get a cut."

"For your pain and suffering?"

He shrugged. "This is my job, Nora. You get paid for yours, don't you?"

"This is why people are slamming the door in your face, Russell."

"Why?"

She laughed at his earnest confusion, real laughter. "It sounds an awful lot like the deal we started with."

"The deal you . . . ?"

"The one we're still getting fucked by."

"How? I'm on your side! I'm making you money."

"So was Belsum."

"No they weren't. Belsum was never on anyone's side but Belsum's."

"They pitched us exactly what you're selling. We'd all be rich. Sure, they'd make money too, of course, but that just made it win-win. Without them we'd get nothing. With them, there'd be jobs, growth, opportunity. There'd be infrastructure improvement, increased services, a bolstered local economy."

"That's completely different."

"How?"

"They're a giant corporation. Of course they don't have your interests at heart." He looked at her, considered. "Okay. It is about the money, but not the way you think. If we fought, if we won, you'd make some, and your neighbors would make some, and my firm would make some, enough to continue to do this kind of work. It wouldn't make up for what's happened to you, but it would make things easier." Maybe he took her hand while he said it. Maybe their eyes met and sparked. "But none of that's the reason to do it. The reason to do it is to prevent it from happening ever again. And the only way to do that is to punish them severely enough for what they did. And the only way to do that is to make them pay. Literally."

She smiled then. "You should have led with that."

"Prevention?"

"Revenge."

He laughed. But then he was serious. "It's the only thing that works. Legislation doesn't. Corporations like Belsum just ignore it, knowing enforcement is years away, if ever, or they buy politicians and, with them, favorable policy. Citizen pressure doesn't work. These issues are impossibly complicated, way too complex for the public to understand, and besides, Belsum can spin it and sound bite it into anything they like. Public shaming doesn't even do it. People's memories are too short. Corporations just wait for everyone to get over it, and we do, quickly. What works, the only thing that works, is simple math. It has to cost them more to ruin your life than it costs them not to. That is what we have to do."

"How?" Nora said simply.

"Well, first you say yes to letting me help," said Russell E. Russo. "And then we get to work."

Around her days at the clinic, they did get to work. Many of the people who said no to Russell said yes to Nora. Together, they held meetings at the then-library. First, people came to air grievances.

" 'They killed my husband' is not a grievance," Nora objected. " 'I have only one leg now' is not a complaint for the company comment box."

"First things first," said Russell. "People need to talk, be heard. They've been ignored long enough."

They were long, weepy meetings, half the town, more, filling all the chairs in the Reference and Research section then sitting on the tables, packing in hip to hip, then standing along the encyclopedia shelves at the back of the room, boots tracking ice and mud into the carpet, everyone sweating beneath their winter coats because it was over-warm in there with all the people, all their rage. Nora stood at the podium and called on her friends and neighbors and even the ones she'd never liked much, for everyone who showed up was an ally, and everyone who showed up deserved to be heard, and everyone who showed up had a story that would help their cause. Russell sat beside her in a folding chair, hands between his knees, head bowed, concentrating.

"Don't you want to take notes?" Nora asked, early on.

"No." He shook his head. "I want to listen."

We three were parked in strollers on Nora's other side because in those days Mab and Monday required wheeling around too and because our mother had nothing else to do with us but bring us along — anyone who might have babysat was there. I think of us like mascots, but we were more like crying, shitting irrefutable proof.

The people of Bourne all knew what had happened, knew one another's horror stories, knew what was lost and what was left behind, but there was something different about saying it out loud, in front of a stranger, in service of a cause. And if the stories had a dull repetitiveness to them — my water smelled funny for months; I ran the tap into a bottle and it was silty and brown, but when I brought it in, they sent me away; I'd cough and cough all night; my wife found a lump; the doctors said nothing could be done; when I asked for more information they refused — taken all together, taken aloud, taken from a private hell to a public record, they began to give off heat, to sweat, like onions.

Nora held these meetings for months. Eventually, with Russell's help, they switched gears and started organizing people, signing them on to the suit, taking statements. At night, after work, after meetings, she was elated. He was worried.

"It's working," Nora would whisper.

"Not yet," Russell insisted.

But Nora could not see how that could possibly be true.

She read over the notes Russell had started keeping on everyone's evidence and documentation, piles and piles of it. Records of doctors' visits. Lists of medications tried and failed, tried and exacerbated. Hospice intakes. IEPs. Explanations of diagnoses. Consultations. Second opinions and then third and fourth. Birth certificates. Death certificates. Before and after photos.

Dr. Dexter, Bourne's only vet, told Russell on tape that Belsum had offered him money to tell people their dogs' tumors came from insufficient exercise or buying cheap dog food. If called upon to do so, he said they said, testify that any number of things can cause a young, seemingly healthy animal to develop cancer, even a lot of them in a very small town.

Zach Finkelburg, one of the few guys

who'd worked at the plant from the beginning to survive, said Belsum told employees they'd help them secure home loans, pay for their kids' college, offer generous salary incentives if what happened at work stayed at work, if they had absolutely no contact with regulators, scientists, advocates, supporters, journalists, or any of the community members leading protests, demanding answers, or asking questions, if any requests for contact were not only rebuffed but reported immediately to management. If employees refused in any way to any degree — if, say, they went to a barbecue with a neighbor who'd brought a jar of cloudy tap water to the Belsum front office, or attended church with a fellow congregant who'd signed a petition for an independent water tester — Belsum would find them in breach of contract, punitively fine them, and take away their health insurance. And given how many of them were coming down with mysterious and alarming ailments all of a sudden, that was inadvisable. Zach said Belsum did, however, recommend changing out of work clothes before leaving the plant, not wearing those clothes home to where wives and children were.

So Belsum knew, Nora said, triumphant.

But it is true that many things can cause

302

cancer in dogs, Russell devil's-advocated. It is true that it's not necessarily illegal to give your employees incentives or disincentives, especially if you're smart enough not to put it in writing anywhere but to confine it instead to rumors in the hallways.

Three scientists at the state university, three more from the regional office of the EPA, another two independent evaluators sent Russell pages and pages of tests which proved, they explained, repeatedly and conclusively, that the parts per billion of contaminant in the water downstream from the plant was a hundred times greater than was safe for human consumption.

But Belsum had scientists of their own, Russell said, who told them one of the chemicals was safe and another present in amounts too small to impact human health and another unregulated, legally the same substance as the water itself.

Russell subpoenaed documentation, permits, feasibility studies, environmental impact analyses. He requested from Belsum the tests they claimed to have done. He requested the health studies, the medical reports, the internal correspondence from Belsum's own scientists.

So Belsum sent over boxes and boxes and boxes of paper, hundreds of boxes, packed to overflowing with five hundred copies of a memo with instructions for how to set up voicemail on the new phone system, with an invitation to a baby shower for one of the admins in HR who was not finding out the sex so please only yellow or green clothing, with receipts for printer ink, staples, wastebaskets, toilet paper, with email threads about whether they should order ham or turkey sandwiches for the board meeting and Doria was a vegetarian so could they please order green salad instead of tuna and the sandwiches with the meat on the side. It was possible the documents which provided clear and convincing evidence that Belsum knew what their plant was doing to Bourne and its citizens and kept doing it anyway were in those boxes, but the odds of finding them were thin as a new moon, Russell warned. Moons wax, Nora said, and started looking.

Night after night, Nora would put the babies to bed then make a quick batch of cookies or open a bottle of wine or heat up something easy for dinner and look through boxes while Russell pored over records and transcripts. One night a song came up on shuffle, and he didn't even look up from his paperwork when he said, "This was the theme song at my senior prom."

"Mine too!" Nora said.

And he looked up at her then and removed his glasses and came around the table and took her hand and led her out onto the dance floor, which was just the other side of the kitchen table, and took her in his arms and pressed her to him, and very, very slowly they danced, and when the song was over he drew back to look at her, and she whispered, "I did not dance like that at my prom," and he whispered, "Me neither."

I think I remember that, though I couldn't possibly.

They fell asleep working sometimes, but Russell did not otherwise spend the night. He had a hotel room when he was in town, but usually he wasn't. He had a wife at home of whom Nora had been surprised but relieved to learn, surprised because he knew everything about her life and it turned out she knew so little about his, relieved because unrequited love of one's lawyer seemed more likely to result in good legal counsel than the requited kind, and that was a trade she was willing to make. His office was in New York, a city he described as loud and bustly and smelly compared to wide, green, open, quiet, poisoned Bourne, and he told Nora, "I wish I could stay here," and Nora told him, "Stay then," but after a few days of work, he always left.

Still, surely it didn't stop at dancing. I don't know the details because I was a child and because I was *her* child, but I know it happened. For a while. And then his wife got pregnant.

Russell is a good guy, the adultery notwithstanding, but it wasn't the prospect of becoming a father that stopped it. It was actually becoming a father.

One morning he knocked on the door, soaking and lost. He wasn't scheduled to be in town — he'd been coming less and less — so when Nora opened the door and found him on her front step, she was surprised then delighted then worried in very short order. It was pouring, and he was drenched, but he didn't even look up when the door opened.

"Russell?"

"Nora."

"You're here."

"Yes."

"I'm so glad."

Nothing.

"Come in."

Nothing.

"Russell, you're soaking. Come inside."

"I can't."

"Why not?"

Nothing. Then finally he looked up from his sodden shoes. "The baby was born," he said.

"Oh, Russell," she gasped. "I'm so glad." And she looked it. That's what I remember from that moment: she was truly glad, truly happy for him, like he was her best friend and not her lover, which, I suppose, he was.

"No," he said.

"No?" she said.

And then Russell whispered, "He has Down syndrome." Her face fell, and he dropped to his knees right there on the front porch, and she bent down over him, an attempt to shield him, which did not work.

"Did you know?" Nora asked, as if that were the point.

He shook his head. "Sarah said no to all the tests. The midwives told us they were unnecessary."

"Is he okay?"

"Who?"

"The baby."

"No, Nora." His eyes focused on her clutching him in the rain. "He has Down syndrome."

"Yes, I know," said Nora, "but is he okay?"

"I don't know." His eyes were wild. "I don't even know what that means."

"As long as he's healthy," Nora said, "as

long as Sarah's okay, you'll be okay. You'll all be okay. There are so many worse things than Down syndrome." Maybe this was fumblingly put. Heat of the moment and all that. Shock and sadness and no time to pick your words over like lentils, looking for stones. And to her credit, her eyes did not so much as flicker in my direction. But I know she thought it all the same. Me. I am what's worse than Down syndrome. Among other things.

"We were wrong," Russell said.

"Who?"

"You and I."

"About what?" said Nora.

"It wasn't the water. It wasn't the chemicals. It wasn't the plant. Who knows what it was."

"What are you saying?"

"So many things can ruin a baby. So many things get broken on the way. No one can ever say why."

Nora stood upright, backed away a step. You'd like to think she was appalled by his words, the horrible things he was saying, or maybe appalled by the state he must have been in to utter them. And maybe she was. But mostly I think she was stumbling under the dawning realization of what he was going to say next. "Why are you here, Russell?"

"To tell you it's over." He did not specify what it was that was over. Everything, maybe.

But it wasn't that simple.

For one thing, no one understood as well as Nora what Russell was going through. He felt at first that he could hardly stand under the weight of loving his newborn son but that his heart was also broken because no one else ever would. What we know now — that Sarah had shock and postpartum depression, not lack of love, that Matthew's teachers and neighbors and doorman and the guy who runs the bodega downstairs and the two women who own their favorite coffee shop and all the kids at the Ninety-First Street playground would adore everything about him, especially his smile, wide as the arc of the swings — Russell could not see at the time. But I could. And Nora could. She was so thoroughly, entirely, in-all-the-world the right person to talk him off this particular ledge it seemed like a miracle to Russell that he'd ever met her. But, of course, that was why he'd left the hospital and driven through the night to show up at our door. That was the one thing, the main thing.

But the other was this: Letting go of Russell was heartbreaking and devastating and left a hole like a canyon, but it was possible. Letting go of the case against Belsum was not.

Actually, that's not quite true. It was possible for Russell, who let it go like a weight sinking to the bottom of the ocean with him holding on. He released it and then floated right to the top where air and light and hope are. He watched it spiral down below, doomed, but doomed without him, his sadness eclipsed utterly by his relief. Or maybe it was just that he didn't have enough hands anymore.

But Nora hung on like life while the case sank toward death, down down under the waters. She fought the waves and swells by herself, though she lacked expertise and experience in law; she lacked her partner in commitment and enthusiasm; she lacked someone with whom to share the highs of discovery and the lows of what she knew goddamn well but could never prove. But that didn't mean she stopped. She never stopped.

There was no money for a new lawyer, one who hadn't sought them out, wouldn't work on contingency, would have to start from scratch. So Russell still helps. Still takes her calls. Files necessary paperwork. Keeps her apprised of developments. Does the minimum to keep the suit pending. But it's on the back burner. Of the neighbor's stove. Nora does the bulk of the work now — researches, reads, compiles notes, remains vigilant. She cheerleads too — stokes her neighbors' anger, encourages when they despair, reminds when they forget. She's kept the lawsuit alive, kept up with everyone signed on to it, kept after the elusive proof that will finally be enough. She has done it all. And she has done it mostly alone.

In the end, this is another of the many things my mother and I share, not just unrequited but unrequitable love, stories we know from the start will not — cannot — have happy endings. An unusual thing to turn out to be hereditary. Happy is not an option for us. Nora understands this. But she imagines fair is still on the table.

ONE

Fall comes for real. The world gets a little chillier, dark a little earlier, a funny, buzzy feeling.

"Mercurial," Petra calls it.

"Serotinal," I offer.

"Just barely." We actually needed sweaters this morning. "Isochronous."

"Seasonal?" I check.

"Or occurring at the same time. Either might show up."

"Variegated," I reply.

She high-fives me. "Good one."

Even though it's an easy word unlikely to show up on the SATs, what fall in Bourne usually is is anticlimactic. The color of the leaves changes but nothing else does.

Except this year. River's face is healing. You can see it changing slowly like the seasons from bruised to mended, from broken open to whole. Other things are changing too — maybe also breaking open, maybe not — but they are harder to see.

He sidles up after English one afternoon. "Wanna go somewhere?"

"For what?"

He peers all around — I don't know if he's nervous or just pretending to be nervous — and drops his voice. "I might have found something."

"Tell me!" My first instinct is to hug him.

"Not here."

"Where?"

"I don't know. Somewhere we can talk."

"I can't leave. I have tutoring."

"Why do you get tutoring?"

It's interesting, now that I think about it, that no one has pressed River into Track A tutoring servitude. He's not doing football or an after-school job. So it turns out there's this additional dispensation — you don't have to tutor if the tutees might try to kill you.

"I am the tutor."

"Oh. Who are you tutoring?"

"Kyle M. and Kyle R."

"My favorites." He rolls his eyes. "Does it help them?"

I laugh, not because it's funny but because it's true, and I never thought of it before. Years of tutoring to make up, I guess, for getting more than my fair share, and does anyone even think it's helping? I shrug. "It's the least I can do."

His eyebrows snag. "Can you skip?" he says.

"I can't."

"Why not?"

I open my mouth to answer him, but suddenly I can't think of a single reason.

Somewhere to be alone.

Somewhere to be alone together, which is not alone, which is the opposite of alone.

That's how we find ourselves at Bluebell Park. It's pretty there, with the lake and the path that loops around it, picnic tables and gnarled trees blazed orange and yellow and red now it's firmly fall. Leaves cover the ground and the walking trails and a multitude of sins because the grass and flowering plants never really came back here, so in spring and summer, when it should be green and bright, Bluebell Park is brown and dead-looking, sparse scrub and bleached-out ground where nothing grows. But the trees are older, more established, hardier. Autumn here looks like autumn on a greeting card.

We follow the path around the far side of the lake until we come to the dam. River follows me as I climb out onto its concrete ridge, a spine along the top of a body of rough wood beams and rocks and cement. Like everything else in Bourne, it's a little the worse for wear, and you can see trickles of water leaking brown tendrils down from cracks along the wall. The lake is pretty, but when we reach the middle of the dam and sit, we have to have our backs to it because it's rained a lot and the water is high.

Instead, looking out from up here, we can see the plant. That's why, even though this is the prettiest spot in town, I knew it would be empty. The plant is ugly. It is also mammoth. I forget that. It's loomed over my hometown all my life — it's loomed over my life all my life — so I don't really see it anymore. River won't look directly at it. I don't know if that's guilt or shame or because it's loomed over his life all his life too, even from hundreds of miles away, but he averts his eyes.

It's a hard thing though to ignore. (Petra would say "elide.") Except for those giant rusted letters on top, it's aggressively gray, not a spot of color on its whole enormous hull, like it's sucking up the light and life all around and trapping it away. There are hardly any windows, so the walls soar on and on, all the way up, all the way over, sprawling, smothering. This massiveness must be purposeful. It could be to make you feel walled off, enclosed within, protected from what's outside, like a fortress whose members-only club you're desperate to join. Or it could be to make you feel despairing, like you've joined already, and now it's too late and there's no escape. It works either way. It takes up the whole sky, like the clouds you see when you look up must be part of the plant too. Or maybe the clouds are just the half of it because the plant has the feel of taking up the whole world, earth and sky and everything else, and in many ways, it did, it does. It looks exactly like it always has except the ground's been all torn up, muddy, tiretracked. There are a couple dump trucks and a dirt-caked bulldozer out front. No one's there, but someone has been. And it's clear someone's coming back.

Beside me, River nods over his shoulder with his chin. "Can you swim here? In the summer I mean."

"You're allowed." It's such a Boston question. There's no rule you can't swim in Bluebell Lake, but there doesn't have to be. No one in this town would ever think to swim in its water.

"I bungee jumped off a dam once." He's bouncing the backs of his heels off the wall of ours, his right then his left, his right then his left, so it sounds like when Mirabel taps Monday's name. "In Switzerland. You ever done that?"

I don't know if he means have I ever bungeed? Or have I ever jumped off a dam? Or have I ever been to Switzerland? I shake my head no.

"They strap this elastic cord to your feet and you just dive into thin air, headfirst, arms wide. It's like flying. That's what they say, anyway."

"What?"

"That falling is the same as flying."

"Falling seems like the opposite of flying."

"No, you know like things in orbit. Satellites or whatever. How it seems like they're flying in space but really they're just falling and falling around the earth."

"How big is this dam?" I ask.

"It's like seven hundred feet high."

"Oh." I start to see how what I'm picturing is different than what he's talking about. I start to see where our perspectives diverge. "So if it's high enough, falling is like flying?"

"Well, it's not like you're going to crash into the bottom. You've got the wind in your face and the view all spread before you and nothing keeping you on the earth."

"Except the cord."

"Right, except the cord. But not while you're falling. It doesn't kick in until the end when it yanks you back up."

I'd have said that the difference between falling and flying is everything. Like the difference between a home and a library. Like the difference between broken and whole. Like the difference between a seven-hundred-foot dam you can fly off and this one. His legs are longer, but from where we're sitting on the top, even mine dangle nearly a quarter of the way down, the silver tassels on Pooh's mules glinting in the sun. It's not seven hundred feet high. More like ten maybe. You could jump down without a bungee cord or anything else and you'd be fine, but it would be nothing like flying.

"Sorry I made you skip tutoring." He's got a magic coin in his hand which looks solid but flips open to reveal a secret hollow inside. He's practicing clicking this open and closed with one hand, open and closed, clear blue sky above, fall trees getting naked all around us.

"You didn't make me." I want him to tell me what he has to tell me, but I don't want to seem overly eager or overly selfish or overly anything.

"It's nice of you to do that. Tutor."

I snort.

"It is," he insists.

"It's the least I can do."

"You keep saying that."

"Everyone keeps saying that. They've been saying it my whole life."

The coin clicks open, shut.

"Because you're normal?" he asks.

"What's normal?" I say. "Besides, it's a Track A requirement for pretty much everyone but you. But yeah. Because I'm normal."

"That doesn't mean you owe everybody."

"That's not why I owe everybody."

"Why then?"

Click.

"Because I'm going to leave them." It's out of my mouth before I've decided whether I'll try to explain this — to him or even to myself.

In third grade, Petra and I started planning to go to college together and share a dorm room, and then get jobs together and share an apartment, and then marry brothers and share a giant house with a swimming pool. We were eight-year-olds when we concocted this plan, and, of course, it's nuanced over the years, but we still plan to go, together and far away — we talk about it, study and prep for it, all the time — and how did I imagine that was going to happen while I stayed here with my sisters and my mother? I didn't. I couldn't have. But somehow, my brain disconnected that from leaving, not like I thought there was a way for me to be elsewhere and still here, like I thought there was a way for me to be elsewhere and still with them, a way for me to leave without leaving my family.

I glance over to see if River is appalled because it is appalling.

"Sure." He is the opposite of appalled. "I mean, it's not like you can go to college here."

"Or maybe anywhere."

"Anywhere?" Like he never knew anyone who didn't go to college. "You might not go at all?" Like I said maybe after high school I'd still have earlobes but maybe not.

"It's abstruse."

"Abstruse?"

"Hard to understand. Complicated."

"Oh." Then, "Don't worry, there's financial aid." He opens his fingers to reveal the coin sitting on his palm. Like all you have to do is turn your hand over to find it full of money. Maybe that's true for him. "Or you could get a scholarship. You're really smart."

I turn not just my eyes, not just my face,

but my whole body toward him. "I am?"

He laughs, closes his fingers over his coin again, jostles his shoulder into mine like we're joking together. "I guess maybe not that smart if you don't know it."

I do realize that this is embarrassing and also that we're getting off topic, but he's an opportunity I can't pass up. I've been told I'm smart all my life, but it's closer to accusation, recrimination, than compliment. I'm not smart like Mirabel. And I may not be smart for the rest of the world. I may only be smart for Bourne.

"How do you mean?" I fish.

He shrugs. Can't quantify how. "You know, smart. You'd get into college no problem."

"And flunk out?" Because I could probably get in somewhere. Petra and I still had a few baby teeth when we started studying, and my grades are good. But an A at Bourne High is what at a normal school? If I got in, would I be able to do the work once I got there? Up against kids whose brains were fed by blood cleaner than mine?

"You'd be fine. I bet you'd love it after, you know . . ." After living here, he means.

"What about you?" The wealth of options open to him takes my breath away. "Where are you going to go?"

"Who knows? My dad's all about the 'Family Legacy.'" He deepens his voice and scratches the air with two fingers as if family legacy is a strange and complicated concept I might not be familiar with. There are a lot of things in this conversation I'm not familiar with, but family legacy isn't one of them. "He wants me to go where he went and his father went. My parents are both Ivy Leaguers so of course they have these expectations . . ." Jesus. Ivy League. "I have the same problem you do, I guess. Not sure I can cut it. Not even sure I want to."

"Yeah," I breathe. It's all I can do. To have all he has and be just the same as me. But though I do not know the cause of his doubt, I am certain it is nothing like mine. "I don't know if I can leave them." I don't even know why I'm telling him this.

"Of course you can. You have to." Then he adds, "Who?"

"My sisters. My mom. This town."

"You'll visit. You're not leaving forever. But you can't spend your whole life here, Mab." He doesn't even say this convincingly, persuasively, just throws it off like it's the simplest thing in the world. Nothing more or less than true. "You know they want what's best for you."

Like there is a best thing for me. Like

there's no question what that thing is. Like that thing can't possibly be family and sticking by them and putting their needs first. Like when you're stuck in Mirabel's body — or stuck caring for Mirabel's body — there's enough room left to consider what's best for anyone.

Like when Bourne runs through you, there's any way to leave it behind.

"Anyway" — he clicks the magic coin open again — "thanks for bringing me out here. It's pretty."

"And quiet," I add so he remembers he has a secret and the reason we're here is so he can tell me without being overheard.

When we sat down, we were not touching. Now, somehow, we are, just a little. I can feel his leg through my jeans, through his jeans, like he's giving off heat. Or I am.

"It's good to have a tour guide," he says. "You're like my Virgil."

"Virgil?"

"You know, Virgil? Dante's guide through hell? In Dante's *Inferno*? You guys didn't have to read that in tenth grade?"

"No."

"Oh. We did. It's pretty good."

Wait a minute. "Does that make Bourne hell?"

"Well, kinda." He laughs. "I mean, there's

323

nothing to do. I got beat up a lot. The water might be poisoned, and you and your sisters are my only friends. Plus the pizza's lousy."

He's trying to make me laugh, I think, and it's probably not fair to be offended about something you yourself believe. Bourne is hell in lots of ways, but with at least one important difference.

"But people go to hell because they sinned," I point out, "and we're not here because of sinning. At least, not our sinning."

"No, I get that."

"Your sinning," I add, in case he actually doesn't.

"Well, my family's, yeah."

Also, he thinks we're his friends, and I don't know if we want to be his friends.

But before I can decide, he takes a deep breath. "Okay, so." He lets it out, doesn't say anything else for a while and then finally does. "I have to tell you something."

And at last, this is it. I wait and try to slow my own breathing.

And he says, "My father's only pretending to be drinking."

I think of Mirabel's report from the bar when he tried to buy a round, when Tom said beer was the best thing on the menu, when Nathan started to share a pint with the guys before my mother kicked him out. "Why would someone pretend to drink?"

But that's not what he's talking about. "My dad wants anyone who comes by the house to see him drinking water straight from the tap." And I remember that from when we were there, how shocked Monday and I were. "But he's faking it. It's bottled. He gets Hobart Blake to make a run into Greenborough once a week. He brings back a bunch of those giant five-gallon jugs and hooks them up under all our sinks. My dad doesn't drink the water. He doesn't even shower in it."

I knew it! And I still can't believe it.

"I was thinking I could take pictures," he offers.

My head is spinning. Maybe Mama's been approaching this all wrong for years now. She's been looking for evidence that's two decades old, proof of intent to harm and recklessness in the planning stages before the plant even opened, but it's hard to find things that have been buried for twenty years, especially if you've already been digging for sixteen. What if, instead of looking back and then, we started looking here and now?

But River's still talking. "I tried his birthday, mine, my mom's. Their anniversary. I even tried the days before and after their anniversary in case he forgot. But it's none of those."

"What?" I try to refocus on him.

"His laptop," he explains and when that doesn't do it, "It's password protected."

"Oh."

"But his phone isn't."

"His phone isn't what?"

He reaches over, I think to touch my cheek, but instead he pulls the magic coin from behind my ear. "Password protected."

I wait before I reply to make sure he's saying what I think he's saying. "You'll look on his phone?"

"Yeah." He sounds slightly nervous, but only slightly.

"For us?"

"Yeah." A little more sure.

I breathe out and can't breathe in again. "What if you get caught?"

"What can he do? Ground me? It's not like I'm getting invited to lots of parties, hanging out with tons of friends, going to all the good clubs."

I try to smile, but my face is frozen. "Won't it feel like a betrayal?"

He looks at me. And then he takes my hand. I feel it all the way up into my chest. "I think it would feel like a betrayal not to."

TWO

Mab comes home and has two pieces of news, and she says they are very exciting, and she is all panty and red and cannot wait to tell.

The first piece of very exciting news is Nathan Templeton pretends to drink tap water but actually drinks bottled water, and River is going to take pictures of the bottles and also look on his father's phone for more evidence.

The second piece of very exciting news is River's parents went to Ivy League colleges and so did his grandfather so River is probably going to go to one too.

It is a very disappointing afternoon because these are the two most boring pieces of exciting news I have ever heard.

Everyone in Bourne drinks bottled water, and everyone in Bourne knows the Templetons are liars so all aspects of the first piece of news are the opposite of exciting which is dull, predictable, or depressing, and this is all three.

"Ho hum," I say because that is what people do in books when they think what you said is not interesting.

"Don't you see?" Mab is so excited she is wiggling which is not a facial expression but a whole-body expression. "We can prove Nathan Templeton isn't really drinking the tap water."

"Not drinking the tap water is not illegal," I regret to inform her.

"We can prove he's making a big show of drinking the tap water — and showering in it, doing his laundry, washing his vegetables — but really it's all lies."

"Pretending to use the tap water is also not illegal," I tell her.

"Subterfuge!" Mab insists.

"Ho hum," I repeat.

And no one except Mab cares where anyone else goes to college. Only the people who also go there are impressed, and you already know them so they will be evaluating you on your other merits or lack thereof anyway.

But *talking* about where other people are going to college is something people do care about, and it is contagious like yawns or strep throat, so Mama gets mad at me for not doing my homework, and the person whose fault that is is River.

"Monday," she says while I am cutting up a box that pasta came in. "What are you doing?"

"I am cutting up a box that pasta came in," I tell her although I do not know why since that is obvious from looking at me which she is.

"You need to do your homework," she says.

"Lie."

"I'm not playing a game," Mama says. "You need to do your homework and get into college."

"I am not doing my homework because there is no point," I tell her, "and I am not going to college."

"Of course you are," Mama says.

"Which?"

"Both."

"There is no point doing Spanish homework because I do not speak Spanish," I explain patiently, which is nice of me because we have already had this conversation many times. "There is no point writing an essay about what Emily Dickinson meant when she wrote, 'I heard a Fly buzz — when I died' because if she meant to be understood she would not have written something so impossible and untrue."

"Oh, Monday" — Mama closes her eyes — "it's so true."

"If she were dead, she would not hear anything. Or write any more words."

"Well, it's poetry," Mama says, like that is an excuse to not make sense. "What did you write in your essay?"

"I did not write anything in my essay because there is no point in doing my homework, but if I were going to do my homework what I would have written is 'Emily Dickinson means for me, the reader, to be confused. I am. So she has done her job. And so have I.' "

"What does Mrs. Lasserstein say when you hand in essays like that?" Mama asks although I do not know why because she knows the answer.

"Mrs. Lasserstein says I am being too literal, but there is no such thing as too literal. Literal does not come in degrees. That is like being too seventy-seven point four. That is like being too bicycle."

"Monday, you do not know everything."

"There are many things I do not know," I agree.

"Just do your homework. I'm not arguing with you about it."

"Lie."

"You're being too literal."

"There is no such thing as too literal!"

Mama has two plans, a first-things-first plan and a then-save-the-world plan. Her first-things-first plan is to win a class action lawsuit against Belsum and make them pay for what they did. You would think this would be an easy goal to achieve because so many things are obviously true facts. It is an obviously true fact that our water used to be clear and then it was cloudy and smelly and then it was green, but Belsum said water did not need to be clear, odor-free, and colorless to be safe. It is an obviously true fact that my father did not use to have cancer and then he did, but Belsum said he ate a lot of red meat and felt a lot of stress, and that was probably why. It is an obviously true fact that a lot more babies were born with birth defects than before Belsum came or than in towns where Belsum is not located, but Belsum said we were eating chemicals in our food and putting chemicals on our lawns and wearing chemicals in our clothes and sitting on chemicals in our sofas, and probably those were the chemicals that were causing our problems and not Belsum's chemicals at all.

Then Belsum said they had scientists study GL606 and those scientists said it was perfectly safe, but that was because those scientists worked for Belsum, but that turned out not to be illegal. Then it turned out Belsum measured the amount of GL606 that was in the water and issued a statement saying that amount was the amount that was safe, but that turned out not to be illegal either. Then it turned out that it is very expensive to run for government office and the people who had done so successfully had had their campaigns paid for by Belsum. And they were the ones who decided whether or not things were illegal.

That is how I know Mab's idea to get River to take pictures of the bottles of water under his sinks will not work. Russell says *notoriously.* These cases are *notoriously* hard to try successfully. That means cases like ours are famous for failing.

That leads Mama to her second plan, her then-save-the-world plan.

"Go to college and become lawyers," she says to all three of us, even though you cannot become a lawyer by going to college but have to go to college and then go to law school.

"Go to college and become lawyers and make the world a better place," she says, even though lawyers do not make the world a better place, and even though she has a

332

lawyer, Russell, who is already not making the world a better place or even removing Belsum from it.

"Go to college and study hard and learn everything," Mama says, "and get far, far away from here."

And if you say, "I do not want to get far, far away from here. I want and have to live at home because that is what home means. It means where you live," Mama will say, "Then move somewhere else, and home will be there."

But she is being too literal.

THREE

Winter is hard for me. Cold makes my muscles stiffer, less flexible, less predictable than usual. Snow makes even Bourne's ultra-accessible sidewalks and streets impassable or — worse — not quite impassable. You think you can make it. You are making it! Sidewalks have been cleared and salted. Snow has been shoveled and removed and not just a tiny strip down the middle but edge to edge. Your power chair is powerful indeed . . . until suddenly a tree branch laden with ice and snow snaps and falls across your path, or you swerve right to avoid black ice and wind up stuck in a snowbank.

Saturday morning is not cold enough to snow. The temperature will hit sixty by noon. But chilly mornings remind me my precious solo outings are numbered, at least until spring, and at the bar last night, Tom promised he had wonders in store if I stopped by the depot. So first thing this morning, that is what I do.

When I get there, he's all the way under a huge touring van with "The Dendrites" airbrushed on the side. He says band vans are the easiest to convert into wheelchair vans — it's all the extra room they left inside for drum kits and visits from groupies — and he can get them cheap because there's always a surplus. Engines may not last forever, but they last longer than rock bands and are easier to fix. I tap Tom's foot gently with my front right wheel, and he rolls out from under.

"Mirabel! Excellent." He stands and shoves out of the way the ambulance stretcher he repurposed as a mechanic's creeper. "Come on. Your pile's over here."

I follow him through the converted old garage, past what look like stacks of junk but are really citizen-specific solutions Tom's collected, built, and repaired. There's a stack that's five deflated inner tubes, a coil of wire, and one of those orange hazard cones. There's a stack that's clothesline, a box of extra-large binder clips, and a heap of dog tags. There's a stack that's nothing but two balls of twine and fourteen two-liter soda bottles with their ends cut off.

My pile is a solar panel, four black mats,

four wooden boards. I smile at him, hold my hand to my heart. It's gratitude plus a Christmas-morning sort of excitement. My items aren't wrapped, but they might as well be. They're gifts. And their purpose — at least for the moment — remains a mystery.

"The boards are for the ramp into the house," Tom explains. "Replacements. You've got rot. I know your mom likes the wood, but there are so many more durable materials out there for a wheelchair ramp."

"Natural materials are healthier materials," my Voice mocks my mother. It can't do impressions, but Tom's heard this from Nora enough times it doesn't have to.

"As I keep telling her" — he laughs — "that's only true if you're licking them. If you're just rolling over them, wood is not ideal."

"What else is new?" Sarcasm is also hard for the Voice, but in Bourne, ideal is too high a bar.

"I also rigged up a portable solar charger, just in case of power outages or, I don't know, a zombie apocalypse. It won't work when it's rainy. Or at night. But on sunny days, you can attach it to the back of the chair, and it'll collect energy as you go."

"Enough to outpace zombies?" my Voice asks.

"Well, they're slow," Tom says. "But don't go too far, and make sure you save power to get home. You don't want to get stranded when the sun sets."

Always good advice for an apocalypse.

"I also found some weighted rubber mats to help you navigate cords when you do have power. I'm giving you a few because they'll work for anything. You can just lay them down over whatever's in your way and get right over."

If only.

"Thank you," my Voice says.

"My pleasure."

"Thank you," my Voice repeats in the exact same tone, no change of inflection to mean the difference between polite appreciation and the ocean-deep gratitude I owe Tom for making my life a life. But he gets it anyway. After all, my Voice is largely his work as well.

He starts to load what will fit into the giant sack he attached years ago to the back of my chair like a luggage rack but finds it already full. Nora's sent him three dozen pumpkin cupcakes. He makes the swap, and we fist-bump. When I turn for home, I'm giddy with my prizes.

And as if all that weren't miracle enough, just outside Tom's door, I all but run over

River Templeton.

"Mirabel!" A flash of panic as he leaps out of my way but then, undeniably, delight to see me.

"Sorry!" my Voice says.

"No, no, *I'm* sorry," he says.

"Sorry!" I tap again. It's the first time he's been alone with my Voice, and I wonder if he'll think it's strange — I'm strange — to have a conversation with.

"No, it was definitely my fault." He does not seem to think it's strange. I remember when he came to the house and couldn't stop staring. The novelty of me has worn off, I guess. Other girls would be unhappy about this development, of course, but I am not other girls. "I was distracted."

I type, quickly but there's still a lag. "By what?"

"The limitations of your hardware store." He indicates it with his chin as if there might be more than one hardware store in town. There is not. "My mom wants an extra key for the side door, but your hardware store doesn't have a key-copying machine."

"Church," I tap.

"Huh?" he says.

So he has to wait while I type. "The key-copying machine is in the church."

He waits for me to amend that statement, like maybe it's auto-correct's fault. It's not. Then he waits for me to explain, but it'd take me till winter to type in a thorough gloss of Pastor Jeff's fundraising schemes.

"Weird," he says eventually.

I don't disagree.

"I was also looking for spoons to practice bending with my mind," he adds, speaking of weird, "but your hardware store doesn't carry spoons either."

"Do they in Boston?" my Voice wonders.

"Well no, but there's a separate store for everything in Boston. Whereas your store seems more . . . general. It had this" — he opens a brown paper bag to show me his purchase: a cookbook thick as a thigh — "which is also an odd thing to have in a hardware store, so I thought maybe there was some kind of culinary section."

"You cook?"

"No." He grins. "That's why I bought a cookbook. But I figure cooking's like magic. You follow the directions, stir a bunch of stuff together, and presto! Poof! Dinner! Plus if your brain could stir the spoon for you, think how much time you would save."

I consider what a difference telekinesis would make in my life. So that's another thing River and I have in common.

"Can I walk with you?" he says, and I nod and push my joystick forward, and he falls into pace beside me, and we take in the perfect October morning, that lovely-all-over feeling of being outside and neither sweating nor shivering, though I am shivering, just a little, the smell of leaves drying or dying or whatever that smell is that comes when the trees turn and the seasons change and the whole world shifts toward what comes next.

But then he says, "Oh, Mirabel," and blushes hard. "I shouldn't have said 'walk with you.' I'm so sorry. I didn't mean . . . I just meant . . ."

"I know what you meant," my Voice assures him. I did, but that's not what's remarkable. What's remarkable is that he even noticed. And having noticed, he could have just pretended he never said it. He could have just ignored it. Instead, he was brave. Awkward and brave.

"Thanks," he says, which is sweet, thanking me. "I need to expand my vocabulary. I should study with your sister, come up with some other words besides 'walk' to mean, you know, wander around next to you. Traipse? Ramble? Take the air?"

I laugh.

"She's great at the whole synonym thing,"

he says, then scoffs, "And she says she's worried about getting into college."

I nod, agreeing that this is silly, not her worry but *that* worry. She'll have no trouble getting in.

"Seems like smart runs in your family," which is a nice thing to say but nothing compared to what he says next. "Do you think you three will go together?"

We three?

I stop to look at him. So he stops and looks at me. He reads the confusion on my face. "You know, to college?"

I type. "I will not go to college."

He laughs. "That's what your sister said too. You're both crazy."

This is not as miraculous as telekinesis, but it's close.

When even my Voice is speechless, he says, "Maybe it's like the hardware store."

I raise my eyebrows.

"Different in Boston."

Isn't everything?

"At my old school, everyone goes to college. Everyone wants to get out of town, and our town's a lot more . . . you know, than yours."

I try to nod.

"And you're smart, you and your sister. Your sisters. So, you know . . ."

He trails off, but honestly, I *don't* know. Not whether or not I'm smart — I know that, obviously. What I don't know is why he thinks smart has anything to do with leaving town. What I don't know is why he's not smart enough to realize that the options open to him and his Boston classmates and even Mab and even Monday are not open to me.

"Anyway" — he keeps talking because I've stopped — "what are you doing all weekend?"

"Don't know." My Voice finally finds its voice. "You?"

"Same. Maybe I'll make something from my cookbook. Maybe I'll practice bending something else with my mind."

"Start easy," my Voice advises.

"Like what?"

"Noodles."

He laughs. "Even I don't need a cookbook to make noodles."

"To bend," my Voice explains. "Just add boiling water."

He stops in the middle of the sidewalk again, looks a little stunned. "Forget what I said about college. You don't need it." He grins at me. "You're a genius already. That's the best idea I ever heard."

I take the long way home and try to decide whether the fact that River thinks I'm as likely to leave home as my sisters puts him on the side of the angels (big-hearted, faith-filled, and not just faith in general but faith in me) or the demons (completely oblivious). It was only a few years ago it occurred even to me to wonder how — literally how — I will someday live when Nora does not. Maybe I'll go on her heels, like a broken-hearted lover, from grief but also lack of care. I need a lot of help to be me. It's not that I couldn't hire people. I could, of course. It's that no one on earth could ever do it as thoroughly and thoughtfully and devotedly as Nora. Mother love is a powerful force. She is so essentially a part of me — like a limb, an organ — that maybe without her, I will simply cease to be.

But it's bigger than that. Maybe we'll all find Bourne was only ever for a little while, and as our beleaguered parents age away, the next generation will peter into nothing. We'll leave if we can, stay if we can't, but many of us won't survive, won't live without our platoon of parental carers, won't have children of our own, and Bourne will shed its citizens softly like trees do their October leaves, green fading to gold fading to brown, then quickly, quietly, returned to dust. The remaining shops and suppliers will go, the post office and Tom's depot. Some of us will die almost at once without meds, filled G-tubes, emptied catheter bags. Some of us will go up in flames when there's no one to help with the stove or herd us away from steep stairs or run baths with no more than four inches of not-too-hot water. Others will go more slowly as our wheelchairs shudder to still without anyone to repair, push, or recharge, as our implants stop whispering, our joints no longer bend, our Voices fall silent. And then, sooner than we imagine, when there's no one left, the plant will finally close again forever. Our homes will crumble back to dirt, our buildings rot to stone and soil. The library will overgrow with trees who remember when all those pages used to be theirs. Our streets will bristle with weeds. Maybe the flowers will come back. And the river will flow on, as rivers do, as rivers must, and if its waters eventually run clean again, it will not matter anyway because there will be no one left to drink.

It sounds dark, I know, but it will happen to you too, to you and your family and your town. It sounds dark, but that's apt for somewhere that's had its day in the sun. These places, they don't last long. They don't stay. But while they're here, they're safe and whole, like cocoons, like eggs, on the way to somewhere else, yes, but for the moment, a world entire.

Of course River doesn't see this. Of course my soul is older than his. Think of the world he's grown up in versus the one I have. Think of the body he's grown up in versus the one I have. So you see why he imagines that, like him, like Mab, like anyone, I will head toward unbound horizons with no fear of darkness brought by storm clouds or by night nor any need to save my power to get back home. His assumption is not naivete. It's not unheedful. It's not disregard. At least, it's not only those things. It's also him seeing me, how smart I am, yes, but also how capable. Sure, it's a little oblivious and myopic, but it's also empathetic and generous and kind. And, mostly, unexpected. That I'm seen and treated as normal by everyone else here is only because I am normal to everyone else here. That River sees me that way too is miraculous and magical. Like if he really could bend spoons with his mind.

ONE

Everything feels different.

It is a new feeling, difference. That difference should feel different makes sense I guess, but it means I feel it twice, once because you get to the other side and find everything's changed, which is probably what change means, but what I didn't expect was how change feels while it's going on.

I am not explaining this well.

It's a little because of River. When I catch him looking at me in calculus, I forget the integral of 1/x, and when I catch him looking at me in World History, I forget who built the Suez Canal, and when I catch him looking at me in English, his eyes make me remember how Juliet says, "If love be blind, it best agrees with night." I have not forgotten what his family did to mine. I have not forgotten he comes from a different world than I do. But I can't ignore how he's helping us, how he's choosing loyalty to my family over loyalty to his own, how he promised to find us information and is doing so.

It's a little because work is progressing so quickly at the plant, construction equipment everywhere, a new welcome center that went from hole in the ground to solid structure over what seems like the course of a week, like it was built by ants or bees or whatever, whichever the super-industrious one is. But honestly, once the initial shock wore off, Belsum's return seemed predictable as mud after three days of rain. It's funny how something can be both shocking and inevitable, which Monday would here point out are opposites.

It's a little because of the sister pact we've made to make certain Belsum's decision to reopen the plant is shocking, inevitable, *and* ultimately futile. Monday would object that this is yet another opposite, and besides, Monday would further object, you can't have three opposites, but somehow I seem to have found them.

So it's a little bit those things. But also it's this: maybe surreptitious bottled water isn't illegal, but if Nathan's lying about that, think what else he's probably lying about, and River's promised to get his father's phone and find out. What feels so different is having, for the first time in my life, in our lives, a little bit of control, a plan, some sense that what happens next might not be something done to us but something, for better or for worse, we do ourselves.

Everything feels different.

And different changes everything.

I start skipping tutoring more often than I go. It's embarrassing, actually, that I never thought to before. The only person ever helped by tutoring was River because, since I talked to them, the Kyles have left him alone and made everyone else leave him alone. Tutoring itself was never doing them much good. It was never dulling my guilt, only sharply insisting I had something to feel guilty for. Someone is at fault. Someone should feel ashamed. But for the first time in my life, I realize it's not me.

See? Everything is new.

So I stop going.

Petra is happy to skip tutoring but not to skip studying. "You should excogitate upon the matter."

"I am convinced of this eschewal," I assure her.

"What about college?" Ironically, none of our SAT vocabulary words have anything to do with higher education.

"I have other, clamant things on my mind now."

"It's our way out," she says. "Our only way out."

"Let's take a peregrination," I compromise, and make her drive me all the way to Greenborough — thirty-nine minutes there, forty-two back — for an ink cartridge.

"Why can't he just forward you whatever he finds on his father's phone?" Petra says on the way to her car.

"He wants to print it out."

"Why?"

"I don't know. He says it's a gesture. He says it's momentous."

"Because he's flirting with you."

"How is hard copy flirting with me?"

"I have no idea," Petra says.

The next day at school I hand the cartridge over to River from both my hands into both of his. The task he's undertaking feels heavy to me, and I know he feels it too. I guess that's why he wanted to print out whatever he finds on actual paper. Plus, we've driven all that way; I don't want him to drop it. I also give him two brand-new packs of paper, five hundred sheets apiece. Probably he won't find a thousand pages' worth of secret memos, damning internal correspondence, buried transcripts, and incriminating emails, but who knows what he'll find? Better to err on the side of too much than too little. Better to make sure no one notices all that missing paper and ink.

"I shall put it to immediate good use, my liege" — he bows his head and pretends he's receiving a sword like I'm knighting him — "and honor you in the doing of it."

It's awkward, the way he talks sometimes, but I get that our relationship *is* kind of awkward. On the one hand, I did save him from getting beat up, which was nice but not very ladylike of me, not super respectful of his manliness. On the other, it's not like I beat the offenders up myself; I just asked them, as old friends. On the one hand, his family did poison mine. On the other, we weren't involved or even there, neither one of us. It makes me think of Romeo and Juliet again, how they had nothing to do with starting the feud, only with ending it, and how they ended it only by also ending their lives, and whether that means River's not just flirting with me and talking like an Elizabethan courtier but actually destined to help put to right our ancient grudge with the Templetons or fall in love with me or die. *And* die, Monday would insist. Though of course Romeo poisoned *himself,* and that's a whole different thing.

So my thoughts are dark, but my feelings are pure joy anyway, bubbling up, curling the corners of my mouth, my feet dancy little cheerleaders waving Pooh's silver tassels like pom-poms. It is the irrepressible giddiness of doing something. It's hope and optimism and expectation. Who knows what he might find and what it might change and what new differences it might kick off? ("Engender," Petra would say.)

I guess it's good to be the liege.

But when he comes into the cafeteria the next day already halfway through lunch period, River looks grim.

He hands me a folder, a thin one, and three ten-dollar bills, damp and crumpled.

"You're paying me?"

"Returning your money for the ink and the paper. I didn't use much. I only got one little email thread."

Shit. "Why?"

"The only time he doesn't have his phone on him is when he's in the shower, so I figured I'd take it then, look through it, forward anything pertinent to myself."

"That's a good idea." I smile encouragingly.

"Yeah, but he takes really short showers here. So we don't run out of bottled water. I only had a couple minutes. I barely had time to scan through his inbox. My grandfather wrote him yesterday. They went back and forth once. Three dumb emails. That's all I could get."

I press the thin folder to my chest.

"I apologize," he says, "that I was not more worthy."

"You are worthy." It seems like the right thing to say, but I'm wondering: Worthy of what?

"I wanted to help but have fallen short."

"You'll get more." Am I trying to convince him? Or me?

"I regret that I've failed you."

I make myself look right into his eyes. "Thank you for helping us." I try to mean it. I was picturing reams of documents, all unambiguous and implicating and accompanied by dates and signatures, and instead I've got one email thread. But he tried. And that's more than we ever had any right to hope. It is a kindness, and maybe kindness from a Templeton is worth more than incriminating documents and smoking guns anyway. Maybe kindness leads to better things than emails would, no matter what they said. It is, in any case, quite a bit more unexpected.

TWO

Mama and Mirabel saw Nathan at the bar (until Mama kicked him out). Tom Kandinsky saw Nathan at Bourne's Best (and Worst) Pizza. Zacharias Finkelburg saw Nathan at the grocery store where he was buying cottage cheese and sliced turkey and diet cola. Mab and Petra saw Nathan driving on Maple, and he waved to them from his shiny black car. They pretended they did not see him, but they did. Pastor Jeff saw Nathan at church and said he did not sing, but he did stay after for the part where there is juice and cookies, but he did not drink the juice or eat the cookies, but he did talk to a lot of people and shake their hands. Kyle R. said he saw Nathan buying clothes at the Fitwit, and Kyle M. said there was no way someone like Nathan would buy clothes at the Fitwit, and Kyle R. said there was nowhere else to buy clothes in Bourne and Nathan was not going to go around naked, especially not now that it is getting cold out, and Kyle M. said he probably had his old clothes sent from Boston, and that is possible because Lulu Isaacs saw Nathan at the post office.

But no one has seen Apple. It can be assumed that she must leave her house to buy food, water, clothes, shoes, and supplies, but no one has seen her do it. And even if she brought or had sent her old clothes from Boston like her husband might have, it can be assumed she did not bring food and water from Boston, and even if she did, it can be assumed she would have run out by now because food is perishable which means it does not stay good forever.

Unless she is dead.

She could be dead because she did not buy any new food and starved.

Or she could not need to buy any new food because she is dead. Dead people do not get hungry.

Both of these scenarios are possible explanations for why no one has seen Apple anywhere which is why it is a relief but also a shock when the doorbell rings and I open the door and Apple Templeton is standing on the front porch. And relief and shock are opposites.

"You are not dead," I say.

She looks surprised, but I do not know why because she must have known all along she was alive.

"That's true," she eventually agrees.

Her family likes Truth or Dare and a Lie as much as ours. Maybe she is here to play. So I start. "Truth or dare?"

"Pardon?"

So I try again louder. "Truth or dare?"

"You're inviting me to play Truth or Dare?"

"Truth!" I answer although that was an easy one.

"I . . ." she begins but then looks like she does not know what to say. "Um. Monday, right?"

"Truth!" She is making this too easy.

"Ah, yes, well." She is winning, but she looks embarrassed anyway. "I wonder, Monday . . . I hear the library is run out of your home now. Isn't that lovely?"

This is cheating because half of this statement is a truth and half is a lie. So I do not say anything.

"I understand you have some materials from my home. House. Uh, from the library. The old library. Not just books. Boxes. Files."

"Truth."

Bourne does not have a town hall or a

courthouse or a department of records. The town council meets at Bourne's Best (and Worst) Pizza. The mayoral mansion is a one-room office above the laundromat. It smells like dryer sheets and has a desk for Omar to sit behind while citizens sit in front and yell at him. It has only three filing cabinets with only five drawers apiece. So some of the town paperwork and files and documents used to be stored in the library, back when we had a library. Now they are stored with me.

"Wonderful," Apple Templeton says, though I do not know why she thinks so. "Can you point me toward them?"

I turn away from her in the doorway and point at some of the places the boxes of files from the old library are: in the closet under the stairs, in the cabinet under the canned goods, in the living room behind my yellow chair. There are lots of places the boxes are, but it is easy to point to them all because our house is small.

"Ah, yes, thank you." Apple Templeton's eyes do not want to look at my eyes, and that is good because my eyes do not want to look at hers. "But I suppose what I meant was can I just look around a bit? You know, browse? Is that possible?"

"That is not possible, for you are living in

the library."

Her eyebrows rise up. "I see."

"I have enough space for the lending of books, but, unlike you, I do not have enough space for the browsing of books."

"Well" — even though I thought her eyebrows were already as high as they could go, they keep going up more — "I guess you better lend me a book then."

So I let her in. She follows me through the kitchen into the living room. Her eyes look all around our house, and her face looks sadder and sadder.

"What a . . . full home," she says.

I do not know what that means, and she looks like she does not know either, so I remember to be professional. "What kind of book are you looking for, Apple Templeton?"

"I don't know," she says. "Surprise me."

"I do not like surprises," I inform her.

"How about . . ." She keeps trailing off for long pauses like she cannot find her way out of her sentence. "I bet you have a good writing section."

"Lie," I pronounce.

"Oh. Or just . . . old composition textbooks maybe, editing tips, what have you."

At last a question I can answer. "What I have is many books piled many places. If you tell me what book you think you need, I will find what book you actually do."

"Ah. Yes. Well. I see." A lot of words are coming out of her mouth, but she is not saying anything. "My son — well, you've met him — needs to start thinking about applying to college. Among other things. He needs tips. Say, for writing good admissions essays. I fear he's losing focus, forgetting the plan for his future, settling in somewhere . . . unsettling."

"Do not move or touch anything," I say.

But when I come back four and a half minutes later, she has both moved and touched something. Many things. I can see some piles of books have been pushed and some have been displaced and some have been rearranged. She has moved to behind my yellow chair. She has touched a picture that sits between the children's books about gnomes and the children's books about owls. She has touched it by holding it. It is a photograph of my mother and father at their wedding.

"Your father was a handsome man." She says "was" which means either she thinks my father is ugly now or she knows he is dead, and it can be assumed it is the latter because why would she think my father is ugly now?

I nod. She nods.

"Your mother was a lucky woman."

"Lie," I say.

Her eyes move quickly to look at mine then quickly move away again. She puts the picture back on the shelf and takes a deep breath. "You have my books?"

I hand over what I have chosen for her: a videotape of the movie *Animal House,* a paperback (old but reissued) of *Love Story,* and the copy of *Charlotte's Web* I took back from Nellie when her reading group was finished with it.

Apple Templeton considers them.

"I don't have a VCR," she says.

"You can borrow one from a friend," I suggest.

"No one has a VCR," she says. Then adds, "And I don't have any friends here."

"Would you like a book on how to make a friend?"

She squints like she is having trouble seeing. "*Love Story?*"

"*Love Story* is a novel about two people who go to college in Boston" — it can be assumed, since he will not stay in Bourne, that River will return to Boston for college — "but then half of them die."

"Uh-huh." She is smiling a little bit now. "And *Charlotte's Web*? What does *Char-*

lotte's Web have to do with writing college applications?"

"I do not have a copy of *The Elements of Style* because *The Elements of Style* got sold when my library closed, but fifty percent of *The Elements of Style* authors wrote *Charlotte's Web*."

"I suppose, but —"

"In addition, *Charlotte's Web* is about using writing to change your life and gain admission."

"To the county fair."

"Exactly."

"The county fair is not an institution of higher learning."

"Both have cotton candy," I point out.

"I don't think that's quite right."

"Then I have been misinformed," I say.

"Truth!" She grins like she made a joke.

On Apple's way hurrying down the driveway, she encounters Mab hurrying up the driveway. Even though it is sunny out, Mab is carrying a green folder I have never seen before. When she spies and identifies Apple Templeton, she tries to stuff the folder in her jacket. It is too big, but Apple does not notice anyway. They both look away when they pass each other as if they do not like it when people look in their eyes. Mrs. Radcliffe likes to pretend that it is only me who does not like looking in people's eyes and the rest of their faces, but it is more accurate to say lots of people do not like it. I have just been not looking too hard to see that I am not the only one.

THREE

Love stories are only love stories if they go somewhere. Really, that's true of all stories. They require a beginning, a middle, and an end. Rising action, climax, denouement. Conflicts sorted, strife overcome, or challenges succumbed to. Plot. Change. Lessons learned. That's what makes a story. Otherwise it's just a description. Otherwise it's just conceit.

Maybe the point is that's true of all stories, but it's *most* true of love stories. Boy meets girl and all that. They meet, one of them resists the inevitable, then finally they fall in love. They meet, encounter barriers, love anyway. They meet, encounter barriers, love then lose, love then die. Die then love, sometimes. Love stories often end badly, but their bad ends are what make them good stories.

Unless nothing ever happens. They meet, but love was never really on the table. They meet but don't imagine it will be requited or even expressed or even noticed. They meet and one of them loves and then nothing happens next. These are not stories.

But they're all the story I've got at the moment. If it's unsatisfying to hear, imagine how unsatisfying it is to tell, to live. But there's precedent. Think of courtly love. Dante met Beatrice when they were nine, so requited wasn't on the table for them either, and after that he loved her from afar. He loved her more because he could only love her from afar. The question is why. What did he love about her if they never spoke, never joked together over sunset-colored spritzes, never shared a gelato on an early summer evening, never got close enough to find out if they had sexual chemistry? Modern readers assume she was hot, but modern readers are shallower than Dante. He says she made him a better person; she made him wholer; she made him worthy. He says she brought him closer to the divine and the eternal. Tell me that's not better than popcorn and a movie and a make-out session in the backseat of a car. Not that I wouldn't like to make out in the backseat of a car.

If you look closer, if you go slowly, there can be story even without progress or plot, life in small change, like Dante and Beatrice, like fish swimming hard against the current just to stay where they are. They're not getting anywhere, neither Dante nor the fish, but that doesn't mean there isn't effort, growth, triumph, and beautiful poetry. Trust me, stasis is challenging. And challenge is story.

So maybe these are my love stories: Girl meets boy, loves him, and makes her sister save him. Girl meets boy, loves him, and makes her sister make him save her family. There's story there, at least a little. It's tragic, yes, but the best love stories are. I think you know that.

And it's not like I'm not in good company. I am surrounded by tragic love stories. In Bourne there are more than most, but it's also probably true that anyone who sat in on as many therapy sessions as I do would conclude there are no happy endings.

Chris Wohl this week is about as good as it gets, and that's what I mean — sometimes anticlimax is less satisfying but better than the alternative. Sometimes quiet is just like joy. If you squint, you could mistake Chris and his cup of urine and disinclination to chat as cause for jubilation.

"Leandra had an okay week so I had an okay week." From the doorway, Chris sounds almost apologetic for not being an emotional wreck, but really he's just sheepish about what he says next. "I don't want to jinx it by talking about it."

"That's not how it works," Nora says.

"I know."

"Then sit down."

"But just in case."

"So talk about something else," Nora suggests.

"Next week, maybe. Probably," Chris says, then winks at me. "Bye, Miracle Mirabel."

I wave and he leaves, and Nora smiles at me. "Speaking of miracles, looks like you and I have a whole unscheduled forty minutes to ourselves. What shall we do with it?" An unanswerable question — there is not a lot to do in Bourne, and anyway I have biochem homework (though it's true I assigned it to myself) — so it is only luck, or maybe fate, that what happens next happens next.

A knock on the doorframe and on the other side a woman neither Nora nor I have ever seen before. Which means she can only be one person.

"Uh, hi. I'm not sure I'm in the right place." She is little. Not just small. Slight. Winnowed. She has on vertiginous heels which somehow make her look shorter and a skirt straight as a drafting tool keeping her upright. Her face is so thin it's concave in spots. She looks hungry and, with her movie-star makeup, like she's overreacting — to this town and its empty afternoon and the weary week that yawns ahead. "I, um, I'd like to make an appointment?" A question at the end, that question being: Is this town so podunk your medical clinic is really just a house and doesn't even have a receptionist? It is.

"Sure." Nora sits behind her computer, pulls up the scheduling tool. "With me or Dr. Lilly?"

She blinks. "I wanted to make a" — her voice drops — "therapy appointment?"

Nora looks at her screen. "I'm pretty booked next week. There's a hole the Friday after next." Her gaze catches on the woman's eyes, filled suddenly with tears. Nora looks at me. I nod. "Or, as it happens, I have some time right now —"

"Perfect," the woman says, but without conviction, like at the grocery store when they ask if paper is okay and should they put your receipt in the bag, as if there being a virtually unheard-of opening the moment she seeks it is to be expected, as if the world is nothing but automatic doors that slide silently apart before her as she glides

366

through.

"I usually take insurance information at the start of the first —" Nora begins, but is waved off before she can finish.

"Oh, it doesn't matter. I'll just pay out of pocket."

"And, of course, if you would feel more comfortable, my daughter can wait outside." Nora gestures in my direction, but the woman, who has been struggling to keep her cool eyes away from mine, flicks them over me and concludes it is as if Nora has asked if she's comfortable being overheard by a lamp in the corner. "Nothing leaves this room," Nora assures her. But needn't.

The woman nods, unconcerned, at least about me. She comes into the room from the doorway and extends her hand. "Nice to meet you. I'm Apple Templeton."

I almost laugh. It's such an ill-fitting name now that I've seen her. There is nothing flushed or full or natural about her. Maybe she's like a Granny Smith — tart, acerbic, hard, and pallid. Or maybe her parents imagined someone different than she turned out to be which, best I can tell, seems to be the trick of parenting.

"Nora Mitchell. Please, sit."

"Thank you. My apologies for my unfamiliarity with the appointment system. I'm new to town."

"I know," Nora says.

"You do?"

"It's a small town."

"It really is." Apple looks glad to have some corroboration on this point. "In fact, I believe I just came from your house."

"You did?"

"I needed to look through some . . ." she begins, then trails off, then begins again. "I needed a library. And it seems, in different ways, we're both living in one. It's just yours has all the books."

"Well," Nora allows, "some of them."

"I was hoping to help my son aspire to what comes next. Your daughter . . . made some interesting choices."

"Which one?" Nora wonders, and it's a good question actually.

But Apple looks taken aback. "The librarian?"

I exchange a smile with my mother. We can imagine exactly how interesting.

"I'm not sure the materials she selected will be much help," Apple says, "but I can see you don't have a wealth of options here."

"That's certainly true." Entirely neutral. "Help with what?" Which was going to be my question as well, if probably not for the same reason.

"Parenting's so exhausting, you know?" Apple sighs. "River did not want to come here. Me neither, I said. But he's been moody, secretive, short with me and his father. I thought perhaps a reminder that we won't be here long might help."

"You're leaving?" Not a flicker on her face of the jumping for joy she'd do now if she could.

"As soon as we possibly, possibly can," Apple says.

"You're not enjoying Bourne?" Nora asks gently.

"It's . . . hard."

"I bet. More so than you expected?"

"I guess, though I couldn't tell you why. None of it's a surprise. It's not like I didn't know you all were . . ." She looks embarrassed. But not as embarrassed as I think she should look.

"I understand," Nora assures her.

"And of course, to grossly understate it, it was not my choice to come."

"Why did you?"

Apple shrugs. "Family. You know."

Nora smiles. She does know.

"I begged him to say no to this move, but he never says no to his father. I refused to go, said we were staying in Boston, me and our son, and he could visit on the weekends if he liked, but he said our coming was the whole point. If he didn't bring us, there was no point in going at all."

"Those feelings of anger and powerlessness can't be helping ease the transition any," Nora imagines.

"No. To say the least. I'm just supposed to be understanding when he puts the company before his own wife? When he puts that family before this family? I'm supposed to just overlook the fact that he's willing to risk our lives to —" She cuts herself off. Takes a breath. "And then there's my own father if I'm being honest, speaking of family." She pauses, waves that half thought away. "Anyway, I'm here. I wish I weren't. And neither my son nor my husband is helping matters."

"If you told your husband how unhappy you are, what do you think he'd say?"

"I have told him. He says I haven't given it a chance. But some things you know right away, you know?"

Nora nods. She knows. Then she says, "What if you just returned home? Took your son, left him a note, and went?"

"He'd go ballistic."

"He might be angry at first," Nora concedes, "but once he sees how much it means to you, don't you think he might give in?"

370

"Nathan never gives in," says his wife.

"If he knew how much his family was hurting," Nora muses, "his wife and his son, I bet he'd nix his plans here and just go home."

Apple opens her mouth to reply, but Nora is on her feet suddenly, palm up and out like she wants Apple to wait on a busy street corner. "Actually, before you answer that question" — Nora puts the hand to her mouth and frowns with her whole face — "Apple, I'm concerned I might not be the right therapist for you."

River's mother pales, which you wouldn't imagine possible.

"Did I say something wrong?"

"No, no, of course not. I'd be happy to work with you, but there's something of a conflict of interest here."

"Why?"

"Your business is Belsum Chemical, no?"

"His family business, yes."

Nora takes a deep breath, then says gently, even apologetically, "There's some awfully bad blood in this town between us and Belsum."

River's mother puffs out her sunken cheeks. "Which I have to tell you, I never understood until I saw you with my own eyes. Man, you all have some legit complaints."

"We do." Nora nods graciously.

"But I'm on *your* side," Apple protests. "You guys got screwed. I'd want out if I were you. Hell, I want out *because* of you. Not you specifically, you understand, but . . ."

Nora nods again. No one looks at me.

"Besides, do I have another option?"

"It's true I'm the only therapist in Bourne," Nora admits, "and fifty percent of the medical professionals at this clinic, which is the only clinic in town, but there are a few folks I can recommend who see patients online. You'll find wifi spotty in Bourne, but it may be better than the alternative."

"Which is you?"

"Me and my conflict of interest, yes."

She considers. "I don't mind. You — all of you — must hate my husband even more than I do." Apple's voice is full of awe. "This might be the best therapy I've ever had."

Meeting Apple Templeton at last, listening to her complain about her husband, worry about her son, wish she could ditch this town and the family business and all of Belsum's plans for here and for us, this would have been enough for one day.

But on the way to the bar, Nora's phone rings.

She glances at the screen and then, because she is driving, puts it on speaker.

"Russell?"

"Nora."

A whole conversation right there. She already sounds panicked. He already sounds full. He has news — he's never the one to call; it's always her — he doesn't want to tell her but must need her to know.

"You okay?" She's a little breathless.

"Yeah. You?" Him too.

"Yeah. Just leaving work and going to work."

"You driving?"

"Yeah. You're on speaker. Say hi to Mirabel."

"Hi, love," he calls. I wave from the back, not that he can see, not that he expects me to answer otherwise. And then, "Hey Nora, do me a favor?"

"Anything." She's aiming for breezy.

"Pull over."

She waits. She waits until everyone gets there. She says nothing as her guys file in. She takes their orders, which she needn't because she knows them by heart, and serves them calm as ever. She waits until they're into their second rounds. She does not let her face show fury or fear or even distraction. She does not weep or rend her robes, which are a stained button-down belonging to her dead husband over a pair of faded black leggings, or roll her eyes or raise her voice to either the heavens or the patrons themselves, her friends and compatriots and fellow survivors. She unearths great reserves of strength or, maybe, hunkers down for a long night coming and waits and eventually finally says, light as she's able, "So. Russell called."

Their heads all rise like the bubbles in their beers. They do not need to ask, "Russell who?" They do not need to ask why he called or what he said.

"Aww, Nora, honey," Tom begins, but she raises a hand that says stop, that says she doesn't want comforting or gentleness or her ass kissed, that she'll cry or scream or probably both if they don't just tell her quickly what they know they must.

"The suit isn't going anywhere," Hobart says quietly. If she notices he's used the present tense, I can't tell.

"These things take time." She bites her lips. She interrupted, and she didn't mean to. She is trying so hard to seem loose, cool.

"Twenty years?"

374

"It hasn't been twenty years."

"Sixteen."

"Yeah. Sometimes," she says. "Sometimes it takes sixteen years. We're making progress."

"We aren't, honey." Tom tries to match her calm, her pretend calm.

"How would you know?" she snaps.

"Forget gaining ground, we're losing it."

"We aren't."

"We are," says Zach. "They're back. They're reopening the plant. That's how not worried about this lawsuit they are."

"It's a ploy, Zach. It's all for show. Tell me you don't see that."

"How do you figure?" Maybe he's genuinely willing to hear what she has to say. Or maybe letting her lay out her case is the first step to poking holes in it.

"That's why they're back. Because they're worried about the suit. So they can show they aren't worried about the suit."

"That doesn't make any sense." Zach sounds like he's talking to a small child or a scared dog.

"Maybe you're right," Tom starts.

Nora snorts. "Then what's your excuse?"

He shrugs, helpless, but raises his eyes again to hold hers while he answers her question. "They offered us jobs, Nora."

"In exchange?" she demands, even though she knows, even though Russell warned her.

"Not in exchange." Hobart winces. "But yeah, as a condition of employment, we had to take our names off the lawsuit."

"It's blood money."

"Maybe," Tom says, "but it's still money."

She opens her mouth, but Zach starts in before she can say anything. They've been waiting to have this conversation with her, dreading it no doubt, but ready now and eager to have it over with finally. "They're good jobs, Nora. Full-time, good salary, benefits." And when she still won't look at him, "Health insurance. Life insurance."

"You don't need benefits." Her eyes are wide, too much white. "Pastor Jeff —"

"Could stand to get paid more for his services," Zach says. "You too. I mean Mirabel's doing a great job with the books over there" — he smiles at me, my tray piled with Frank's receipts, not that I've looked at so much as a single number this evening — "but it can't be enough."

"We're fine," Nora says, a statement so absurd, on so many fronts, Zach laughs.

"You're underpaid. And you're overworked. If more of us had insurance, more doctors would come. More services, specialists. Maybe we'd get a hospital close enough to make a difference. If we had a choice —"

"You have a choice," she interrupts.

"We don't." Zach stands then. So she can take his measure, I guess. Maybe to remind her how many legs he has left to stand on. Maybe to remind her how much he's lost as well. "We don't. They took that —"

"Yes, they did. So why would you —"

"Because what else can I do, Nora? Buy more buckets and more blankets and stretch the roof through yet another winter? Stay home all the time because it hurts like hell even limping with this piece-of-shit prosthesis? No offense, man." He turns to Tom who's keeping Zach's leg functional with will, plumber's tape, and a bike wrench.

"None taken."

"Make my career at the Greenborough 7-Eleven? Cross our fingers the suit finally goes to trial *and* we win *and* the award is big enough for everyone *and* they don't appeal *and* the judge upholds the award *and* we live long enough to see it paid?"

"Yes." She's desperate.

And he steps all the way up to the bar and reaches across and takes both her hands in both of his. "We can't anymore, Nora. We've tried. We've tried for so long. We talked about it." He waves around at everyone staring guiltily into their beers. "The whole town's talking about it. The only reason anyone's come up with to turn down these jobs is to not make you angry." He meets her eyes again, takes in her face. "More angry."

That's a good reason, I think. That, and we might finally be making some progress on the lawsuit. We have River getting us access to information we've never had before. We have proof that Duke and Nathan are up to something, even if we don't know what yet. We have a sister pact and the resolve that comes with it. It's not much, but it's not nothing, and it makes everyone's mass and sudden loss of faith that much more tragic. Nora doesn't know any of that, but it doesn't matter. For her, it's tragic enough already.

"They're. Evil." Nora's own eyes look witchy, black and bottomless.

"Maybe." Zach steps back, away from her. "Maybe not. Maybe they've changed. Maybe Nathan is different from his father. Maybe mistakes were made, and it's time to forgive and move on. What's the worst that can happen?"

She flings her arms wide to enter into evidence all of them, all of us, all of it — Bourne-that-was versus Bourne-that-is and our whole world.

"Right," says Tom. "The worst already happened. It can't happen again."

"Of course it can!" She didn't mean to be so loud. I can see it in her face. "You think they're chastened? You think they're sorry? They're triumphant. They learned they can fuck us over with not a single repercussion. They learned they can fuck us over, and not only won't anyone out there notice" — she waves around at the rest of the world — "no one here will notice either. Or if we notice, we'll move on soon enough. They *should* fuck us over because they make a shitpile of money doing it, and when they're done, we bend over and beg them to go again."

"They're the answer to our prayers," Hobart says, emboldened now because she's yelling.

"You prayed for death, poison, and destitution?" Nora spits.

"We need jobs, Nora. We need money. We need something to do all day besides sit in here and drink. We can't leave. We're stuck here. Our property ain't worth shit. Our houses. Our land. That ridiculous excuse for a school. What are my kids gonna do? Huh? Belsum is our last best shot. We have to give them another chance because they're giving us another chance. If they come in and make good this time, it'll be like they promised before. Growth. Opportunities. Our property values go up. Our town becomes less of a dead end. Our kids have a chance."

"But at what cost?" Nora is shaking. Or maybe it's me. Probably it's both of us. "What about the principle here?"

"Well, now those are different questions." Zach is making his voice sound reasonable. "We don't know at what cost. Last time didn't work out for them either. Must have cost 'em a fortune in lost revenue when they shut down. You figure they'd really rather not poison us if they could." Weak smile. "They've worked out some kinks maybe. They're less willing to take that kind of risk. They can't afford to do it again. So probably no cost."

"You can't know that," she interrupts.

But he keeps talking. "And we can't afford to stand on principle, Nora. We literally can't afford it. Only rich people get to stand on principle."

"And besides," Tom begins, then stops.

"Go ahead." She knows what's coming.

"You're right." He shrugs. "We're already ruined. They can't ruin us again. They've taken our livelihoods, our dreams, our confidence, our prospects. What the hell else is there? There's nothing. We might as well let them come back and try. We've got nothing left to lose."

She pauses, shakes her head, crosses her arms over her chest. "They're not going to hire you."

"They are, Nora."

"They aren't because you're too fucking stupid. How are you going to work at a chemical plant when you're this goddamn dumb? Frank wouldn't hire you to mop the floors in this bar because you don't have the brains for it. He wouldn't hire you to carry rocks because the rocks are smarter than you are."

"Frank," Tom appeals to a higher authority. They're cowed in her presence, and they're sorry, but they'd still like not to be abused by their bartender.

"Don't cry to Frank," Nora says. "Frank's the only one of you who's not an idiot. Frank's got sense and faith and isn't about to let himself get fucked again by these ass-holes. Every goddamn one of you" — she's calling out to the whole bar now — "dropped off the suit except me and Frank."

"Nora." Frank clears his throat. Everyone stops and looks at him, and he clears his throat again and then again. He's been quiet, listening to all this. He owns the place after all, so it doesn't seem so weird he's observing but not saying anything.

She turns toward him, eyebrows raised, face open, completely unprepared.

"Nora, I took my name off too."

"No you didn't." This is so impossible she doesn't believe him.

"I had to."

"What are you talking about? Why?"

His hands rise then fall back against his sides. "I couldn't stand in their way." He waves at his customers, the guys at the bar, the couples whispering at tables and trying to ignore us, takes them in, me too maybe. It's my future more than anyone else's here, after all.

"What about my way?" she hisses.

"You have a job. Two actually. I have a job. I can't stand in the way of someone else having one too. I get it. These folks need the money, the bennies, the whole thing really."

"And you get rich too," she adds darkly.

"Not rich." He laughs, mirthless, forced. "But yeah, Norma's needs Belsum's good-will and patronage to stay afloat."

"It hasn't so far."

" 'Cause these guys never get off their stools." That mirthless laugh again. "When they go back to work, think of the hit. And think of the business from execs just out of their last meeting, managers at the end of a long week, new wives in town, new families. I can't just tell them they're not welcome here."

"They're not," says Nora.

"They're not," Frank agrees, "unless they're coming anyway."

"Russell said there were two names left on the suit. And one of them's me."

"I'm sorry," Frank says.

"I just assumed —"

And then, out of the darkness by the door where the lights don't reach, "It's me. Okay? It's me. I'm the other one. I'm sorry, guys." This to the barflies. "You know — I hope you know — I'll do whatever I can to support you. But I owe her. And I . . . . believe her. It's me."

I didn't see Omar come in. Nora obviously didn't either. She looks not just stunned but like she might actually fall over. In fact, apparently no one noticed Omar's entrance, everyone too busy arguing, stating their cases, standing up to Nora's dressing-down. Now he's standing behind me, behind all of us, and everyone's turned to look at him.

"You can't not have taken your name off the suit," Nora sputters. "You were never on to begin with."

That he understands this, which even I don't follow at first, is saying something. "I signed on a couple weeks back. I told Russell not to tell you. Didn't want to make a big deal. But it was time."

There has been attrition over the years as people died or moved away. There have been abstainers, like Pastor Jeff, who believes in heavenly justice rather than the earthly variety. But it's always been Omar's holding out that's most rankled her. He's the one whose name and title seem like they would lend the whole thing weight and import. He's as wronged as anyone. But he's always refused, claimed he has to remain impartial, be available to appear as a witness instead should it ever come to that.

"Why?" She has actual tears in her eyes. "I mean, why now?"

He walks straight toward her like he honestly can't help himself. Stops a few feet away and looks awkward and embarrassed. Smiles nervously around at everyone. Decides he doesn't care and not only comes up to the bar but ducks under the flap and right over to her, inches away. Holds his hands out toward her then pulls them back in fists then tucks them in the back pockets of his jeans. "You were right. We can't just let them back like nothing happened. Everything happened. They have to know we know it. They have to know we're watching this time, paying attention."

"What happened to 'We have to be nice to them because it's our best shot at being treated well'?"

"We tried that already. It didn't work out that great. So I'm standing with you. We'll try something else this time."

"Tried that too," Hobart grunts. "We've been suing them sixteen years now."

"Omar has a job too, you know," Tom says.

"You want it?" Omar's standard response, but he hasn't taken his eyes off Nora.

And I see why. She glows, like her face is lit up from inside. She stands looking at him for a while, letting him look back, letting him stand close, their eyes holding, but neither of them saying anything more. Then she points at a place on the other side of the bar with her chin, and he ducks back under and doesn't meet anyone's eyes — never mind every single one is on him — and slumps onto the stool she picked for him, battered, like he's swapped the weight of one world for another, but unbeaten as yet.

She brings him a beer and a bowl of pretzels, a meager offering maybe but an offering nonetheless.

"Thank you, Omar."

"Anytime, Nora."

She raises an eyebrow at him.

"Well," he hedges, "at least this time."

ONE

"So!" Petra says, eyes shining, an un-measurably small amount of time after River gives me the folder with the emails and leaves the cafeteria. "Read them!"

"Not yet."

"What do you mean 'Not yet'?!" Shrieking.

"You sound like Monday," I inform her.

"I DO NOT SOUND LIKE MONDAY!" she disagrees.

"I have to wait for her."

"Who?"

"Monday."

"Why?"

"And Mirabel."

"Who drove you all the way to *and from* Greenborough?"

"We studied on the way," I say.

"Compendiously," she says.

"They're my sisters."

"So am I."

"Tomorrow," I promise, because she's right about that part. "Tomorrow I'll tell you everything."

Pooh also opens with "So! Read them!"

"I'm waiting for my sisters."

"What about me?"

"I'll tell you tomorrow."

"What if I'm dead tomorrow?"

"Then you won't care anymore."

"Nothing exciting ever happens in Bourne."

I nod. She's not wrong.

"And when it does, it's because everyone's being poisoned," she allows, "which is almost worse."

I nod some more.

"Why did you even come by if you weren't going to let me see?"

"To give you incentive not to die before tomorrow," I tell her.

On the way up my own driveway, I run into Apple Templeton. She's on her way out of my front door. She looks surprised to see me, but not half as surprised as I am to see her — *I* live here, after all — and I worry that if she looked at me closely she would see at once that her son picked me, picked us, that he betrayed her family to help mine, that I hold in my hands a thing he gave me which might break open the lawsuit, bring Belsum to its knees, and change everything forever. But as soon as her eyes meet mine, she looks away.

Inside, I find Monday reorganizing the periodical section, which lives under the bathroom sink. It's mostly old magazines from the eighties, many missing covers, most missing pages, all water damaged and molding. Usually she arranges them by topic. Sometimes by color. Today, though, she seems to be going for alphabetical by the first name of the issue's first contributor.

"So things didn't go well with Apple?"

"We played Truth or Dare and a Lie."

Well, one of them did probably. "Why was she here?"

"She wants River to leave Bourne."

"Leave?" My chest feels strange.

"She does not want him settling in. She does not want him to forget his plan to go."

"Was she here to see me?" I knew it from her face in the driveway.

"Why would she be here to see you?"

Because she knows he's helping us, knows what he told me at the dam, knows what he delivered in the cafeteria. She knows we've spent time together and everything's changing, and she wants it to stop.

"I don't know," I lie.

"She came to borrow books about how to get your son into college when his grandfather is rich but evil and his parents steal other people's libraries."

Oh. Strange as this sounds, it actually makes more sense than what I was thinking (though even for Monday, this would be a hard title to find).

"He gave us something." I show her my folder.

"What is it?"

"An email thread."

"What does it say?"

"I haven't looked yet."

"Why not?"

"We should do it together. Mirabel went to work?"

"Yes, but you and I can —"

"Not without her," I say. "We'll just have to be patient."

"But I am not patient," Monday points out.

We just manage to wait until Mama and Mirabel get home, but then they have news. Over a dinner Mama makes but cannot eat, she tells us what happened at the bar, what happened with the lawsuit, what happened with Omar.

"Does that mean everything is dead?" It's unlike Monday to speak so figuratively, but she's right. It feels like everything is dead.

"No," Mama says.

"What does it mean?" Monday asks.

"I don't know," Mama says.

When we finally get back to our room, I don't even have time to open the folder before Mirabel's Voice launches into a paragraph she's been saving all afternoon. It doesn't seem like there could be yet more news, but there is. "Apple came to therapy. She wants to leave Bourne as soon as possible. She knows River is hiding something. Nathan forced them to move here. She said it isn't safe. She said risking their lives. He said the whole family had to come. He said there was no point otherwise."

We listen then sit there blinking at one another.

"Why?" Monday finally asks.

"Because it's just for show." My words feel dark and thick as sludge. "They could run the plant remotely like they did before, but if they bring their nice family and their growing boy, it demonstrates to anyone paying attention how safe it is now. It's just like pretending to drink the water." We've known this from the beginning, but it's more appalling, more shocking now that the family has faces, that growing boy a name and a voice. They risked our lives and well-being, but now they're risking their own kid's too, and why would they do that? They're risking River when they're the ones who are supposed to keep him safe. His very own mother knows this is happening, and even if she's not happy about it, she's still letting it go on, and for the first time, including when he was getting beat up every day after school, I feel truly sorry for River. At least our mother values us above all things. If the ship has sailed on our lives and well-being, at least our mother stands on deck with us shouting at the crew to make the voyage as pleasant as possible.

"Why is it not safe?" Monday asks.

Mirabel's hand flips up and out. She doesn't know.

"You don't know yet," I say, "but maybe you can find out." My eyes lock with Mirabel's.

"How can she?" Monday asks.

"Next appointment." I lick my too-dry lips. I'm anxious to get to my folder, but this is important too. "When Apple comes back, we have to make sure you're there."

"Maybe," says Mirabel's Voice, and we wait while she types. "Nora said conflict of interest."

"Why?" Monday asks.

"Why do you think?" I can't believe even Monday doesn't see this immediately. "She's been suing the woman's family for the last two decades."

"That is not what I meant, One. Not why is it a conflict of interest. Why did she say it was a conflict of interest instead of learning what she could from Apple Templeton and then helping the lawsuit by telling Russell?"

A much better question.

"Because Nora is," Mirabel's Voice begins, and we wait while she types the rest, "better than they are."

We sit and contemplate the incontrovertibility of that until Monday can stand it no longer.

"River gave Mab a folder with an email thread between River's father and River's grandfather," she tells Mirabel. "She said we had to wait for you to read it so we do not know what it says so do not ask. There is only one email thread, and River tried to get more but could not so do not ask that either."

Mirabel smiles at me, a complicated smile, and I smile complicatedly back.

"If you are not going to read it" — Monday does not understand non-straightforward facial expressions but would not have any patience for them even if she did — "please allow me to read it."

So I hand her the folder. I can't bear to look anyway.

"There are three pieces of paper in this folder" — she counts them four times to make sure — "which are three emails. I will read the first email first. It is from Duke Templeton to his son Nathan Templeton. 'WHERE ARE YOU???? WHY AREN'T YOU PICKING UP????' "

I clap my hands over my ears. Mirabel has to settle for one hand over one ear. "Oh my God, Monday" — she's so loud I'm wincing like she's broken some kind of sense barrier — "why are you yelling?"

"The email is in all capital letters," she explains.

"We get it," I assure her. "Read it regular."

"I have to be true to the text."

"You do not," says Mirabel's Voice.

Monday turns back to the folder. "The next email is a reply to the first email, and it is in a normal font, and it is from Nathan Templeton to his father Duke Templeton."

"We know who's who," I say. "We don't need the cast of characters or the voice acting. Just read."

"Fine," she says. "It is your loss. 'I'm running between meetings, Dad. I'll call you back in an hour. But please, try to relax. I know you're anxious to get started on this, but I promise there's no rush. I'm taking care of it, making sure everyone sees it's safe now, reestablishing trust, spreading goodwill, offering jobs. We don't need the workarounds. It'll be better in the long run if we do this aboveboard this time. Besides we can't risk a worker saying something and tipping someone off. Remember, all they have to do is look and they'll realize. So please let me do this from the other direction.' " Monday finishes and looks up. "Tipping someone off what?"

"Tipping someone off *to* what," I amend. "But yeah, that's the question."

Mirabel taps at her tablet. "And look where? And realize what?"

"Read the last one," I tell Monday.

"The last one is from Duke Templeton replying to his son Nathan Templeton."

"WE KNOW!"

"Please stop yelling," Monday says, "unless you are quoting someone yelling."

I lower my voice and beg her through my teeth. "Just. Read. It."

"Okay, but prepare yourselves because there is a swear," she warns. " 'Bullshit. We don't need their trust or goodwill or cooperation. What we need is to get started before anyone down there finds the damn paperwork. Deeds, deals, contracts, who the hell knows what kind of paper trail, but whatever it is, we need to be well underway before anyone thinks to look for it. We don't want that headache. Money and power buy a lot of things, but I'm telling you, they won't buy this. They have to start by Thanksgiving, otherwise we have to wait until March. And since you can't seem to get this done, I had to. Soonest available was 11/22, so I took it. In the old days, they did it when you goddamn told them to, but now there's a lawyer for fucking everything. Maybe this whole thing was badly set up in the first place, but we're not going to let it destory us.' Now plug your ears," Monday advises. She props the paper up on her lap so she can plug her own and screams, " 'CALL ME THE MINUTE YOUR MEETING ENDS.' "

Then she flips the paper around and holds it out so we can see. "What is 'destory'?"

That's her most pressing question? I look. "I think it's just a typo," I say. "He must mean 'destroy.' "

Which you'd think would raise more pressing questions. But Monday says, "I do not like typos."

"We know," I assure her.

"How do you know?"

"We've met."

"I do not like typos," she says anyway, "because typos are lies, inaccuracies, and an abbreviation all at once, and they mean that your brain can be thinking one thing, but your fingers can rebel all on their own which should not be possible but is."

"So you've mentioned."

While Monday figures out how to move on, Mirabel and I try to figure out the rest of it. There is so little there. There is so much there. There is so little that's clear. But one thing that is clear is this: there is something somewhere that somehow could destroy them. And this: we could find it if only we knew where to look.

"So Duke Templeton does not want us to find paperwork?" Monday says finally.

"Yes."

" 'Damn paperwork'?"

"Yes."

"Because he is mad at the paperwork?"

"Probably mad we might find it," I offer.

"Why does he want us not to find it?"

"I don't know."

"What does it say?"

"I don't know that either."

"Why not?"

397

"Because I don't know what it is."

"Oh." Monday thinks about that for a bit. "Then how do we know we want to find it?"

"Because he doesn't want us to. And because if we do, they can be destroyed."

"It is October twenty-third."

"So?"

"There are only thirty days until November twenty-second." Monday stops looking confused and starts looking panicked. "Thirty days is not enough to find paperwork we do not know what or where it is."

But Mirabel is shaking her head.

"No what?" I say.

"Muh," she says.

"More what?"

She taps at her screen. Monday fidgets. Mirabel's Voice says, "Christmas?"

"What about it?" Sometimes I can guess Mirabel's point from just a word. Sometimes she has to type the whole thing.

She taps for a while. "Happens between Thanksgiving and March," her Voice explains.

I see what she means.

"To be more accurate, there are many holidays besides Christmas which occur between Thanksgiving and March," Monday informs us. "Hanukkah, New Year's Eve,

New Year's Day, Martin Luther King Junior Day, Groundhog —"

"Stop listing holidays," I snap at Monday. To Mirabel I say, "Shopping? They're trying to manufacture something in time for the holiday rush?"

Mirabel shakes her head.

She's right. It doesn't make any sense to me either. "Even if they were up and running tomorrow, they wouldn't be able to make it, whatever it is, package it, ship it, and get it into stores in time. And definitely not if they didn't open until Thanksgiving."

"Valentine's Day," Monday shrieks. "Presidents' Day. Chinese New Year!"

Mirabel is tapping at her screen. "Winter?" her Voice says.

"They can't reopen the plant once it gets too cold." It dawns late, like winter mornings themselves. "But why? Chemical plants aren't seasonal. They're open in the winter. They're not birds. They don't —"

"Who cares?" Monday interrupts. "It does not matter if they are birds." What she means is that this logic isn't logical enough. What she means is that suddenly the calendar pages are spinning away, the clock's ticking down, and we don't have time to waste anymore speculating, guessing, getting things wrong. And she's right, at least in one way. It doesn't matter what they've scheduled to begin on November 22. It doesn't matter why they can't do it December through February. It will be hard to find what we're looking for because we don't know where or even what it is. But it won't be as hard as not knowing whether it exists at all. It won't be as hard as when it exists but turns out not to matter. Now we know. It could destory them. Whatever it is, it matters. So it's quickly becoming the only thing that does.

Two

A saying when something is hard to find is that it is like looking for a needle in a haystack.

This is a stupid saying.

It would be easy to find a needle in a haystack because it would be the thing that is not a piece of hay. It would be the thing that is short, shiny, and stiff instead of long, tan, and bendy. Even in the dark, a needle would be easy to find in a haystack because the needle would be the thing that stuck you in the finger.

A better saying for something that is hard to find would be that it is like looking for an important piece of paper in many stacks of unimportant pieces of paper. This is because all pieces of paper are pieces of paper, and none of them are needles, and all of them look the same until you read them, but there are too many to read them all, and none of them will announce themselves by sticking you in the finger. And even if I did read them all, it would not help because I do not know what I am looking for so even if I found it I would not know that I had because I do not know what it is.

Mirabel thinks River getting us the emails was heroic. Mab thinks River getting us the emails was kind. But I think River getting us the emails was pointless because the emails do not say anything useful or, to be more accurate, the emails do not say anything useful we can understand.

What they say that we *can* understand is something is scheduled for November 22, which is thirty days from today. They also say River's father and grandfather do not want us to find some paperwork. We do not know if the paperwork is related to November 22, but since River's father and grandfather do not want us to find it, Mab and Mirabel do. Fortunately there is a lot of paperwork in our house. Unfortunately Duke Templeton did not specify what paperwork so finding it is like looking for an important piece of paper in many stacks of unimportant pieces of paper. Exactly like that, in fact.

The auction house that came to sell our books went into the library and made two piles: what they wanted to buy and what no one did. I got what no one did, but it was a big pile, and some of it was stuff no one did *including me* (because boxes of documents and papers and forms are boring) so those boxes could stay in the library attic "till kingdom come" said the man from the auction house which Pastor Jeff said meant until Bourne became heaven on earth which Mama said meant forever. The boxes-no-one-wanted could stay in the library attic forever.

All of which means I might not have the paperwork Duke Templeton does not want us to find because it might be at Omar's or it might be in the library attic or it might be lost, but it also means I might have it because I did choose many boxes from the kingdom-come pile, and I could look for it if I knew what it was or who wrote it or why or when or on what grounds, literal or metaphorical. But when a random email warns that it is very important no one finds the damn paperwork, it could be cursing about anything.

The documents in the boxes are all in folders, and the folders all have labels that were labeled long ago, but those labels do not always tell me what is in the folders. Not labeling folders is very bad, but it is not as bad as labeling folders incorrectly or ambiguously.

One box has folders about fauna:

Brown Bear Sightings 1947–1967
4-H Fair Entry Forms: Livestock
Fishing License Applications
Dog Poo Removal Reminder Signs

One box has folders about flora:

Daffodil Bulb Order Forms
Mulching Sign-ups
Elm/Hickory Grove
Tree Doctor Contact Info (Greenborough)

One box has folders about the opposite of fauna or flora which is high school:

BMHS Field Trip Permission Slips
BMHS Parking Permits, Blank
Sheet Music: BMHS Graduation Ceremony
Reorder Form: *Lord of the Flies* (I consider throwing this entire folder away — even though it is more accurate to say it is already thrown away by being here with me, even though its being here with me has not prevented them reordering and us having to read this book in class — which, I would argue if pressed by a library disciplinary tribunal, demonstrates that I

404

understood the book which is about anarchy, but I would never destroy library property, even ex–library property, because my duties as a librarian are sacred.)

Some of the folders contain nothing but paperwork related to ramps. Ramp designs, ramp repair, ramp refurbishment, ramp specs, site guidelines, handrail requisition forms, ramp signage. There is an entire box on nothing but ramps.

Then I find a box of folders, each of which has a single piece of paper in it. The folders are all labeled "Request for Aid," and there are 117 of them. The first one is dated right after what happened happened. The last one is dated right before the library closed. The others are all in between. Inside each folder is a letter from Omar telling how hard things are in Bourne, how much we need help and also money and also compensation, addressed to "Representative" or "Congressperson" or "Senator" or "Your Honor." Each one is stamped with the word "DENIED."

None of it is anything I can imagine Duke Templeton or Nathan Templeton caring about never mind hiding from us never mind destroyed by. I do not know what we are looking for, but I can make an assumption it is not any of this.

Aside from the paperwork, the email gives two other hints. One is Duke Templeton has to do something you cannot do in winter. One is you used to be able to in the old days.

There are no files I can find specifically about seasonal activities in Bourne so I turn instead to my books and make a pile of all the ones in my library about things you cannot do after a freeze:

Surfing

Building a deck

Swimming laps for fun and exercise

Planting tomato starts

Planting really anything (so I put all the gardening books on the pile)

Spending a day at the beach (Technically, you could spend a day at the beach even if it was freezing, but the two books I have on the subject are both mystery romance novels marketed to teenage girls, and what their protagonists do at the beach is lie topless on towels to achieve a tan, run

406

in the sand in bathing suits with boys, bounce in the waves with a beach-ball, build a bonfire after dark, canoodle in bikinis, and solve crimes. While you could solve crimes or build a bonfire — to be more accurate, you would have to — if it were extremely cold, you could not do those other things without freezing to death or losing all of your extremities to frostbite which these protagonists could not because that would not make them very attractive to the boys which is their principal goal. So I put these books in the maybe pile.)

In his email, Duke Templeton says you could do whatever he wants to do anytime "in the old days," but he does not say how old the days in question are. I consider my pile of books to see if any of the activities you cannot do in winter now you could do in winter years ago, but the only one that seems possible to me is the one about swimming laps. You cannot swim laps for fun and exercise now between Thanksgiving and March, but maybe there used to be an indoor pool and then you could. So that is what I must find out. Did Bourne use to have an indoor pool?

Bourne does not have a newspaper any-

407

more because Bourne is too small a town to need one because nothing ever happens here, and when something does happen here everyone knows about it right away because we are such a small town. But there used to be the *Herald Bourne,* back when even small towns had newspapers, back before we were even alive. In the old days. Back then, there was no internet, so the *Herald Bourne* is not saved online, and it is also not archived on microform or microfiche like a real newspaper in a real library, but Mrs. Atholton, who was the librarian before Mrs. Watson, who was the librarian before me, saved some of the *Herald Bourne*'s articles by pasting them into scrapbooks and saved some of the scrapbooks by shelving them in the library as if they were actual books. Where they are now is in the pantry underneath the cereal.

I have looked in the scrapbooks but not a lot because the paper is old and the paste is old, so they are hard to read and delicate and crumble into powder if you touch them or even just sneeze too hard while you are looking (which you do because they are dusty). So I look carefully. There are a lot of scrapbooks, but I am not worried because I can skim the headlines to see if there is anything about an indoor pool or some other unlikely-to-exist-in-the-future winter activity.

What I learn is there was never anything to do in Bourne, not even in the old days.

In the winter of 1958, there was a snowman-building contest.

In the winter of 1959, there was a sled race on Baker Hill.

In 1961, there were record warm temperatures and therefore no snow and therefore no snowman-building contests or sled races.

For Christmas 1962, Bourners decorated a big tree in the middle of downtown. There was a contest for best handmade ornament. The winner was a tiny model of the space capsule *Friendship 7* with an even tinier John Glenn in a tiny space suit inside.

There is no mention of an indoor pool.

In 1963, three Santas stood shoulder to shoulder to shoulder and dangled fishing poles over the river. The bridge was draped in holly and pine branches. At first I think this is an activity you used to be able to do in winter but cannot do in winter anymore. No one fishes in Bourne in winter now. No one fishes in Bourne at all now, but even before what happened happened, it was too cold to fish in winter, and the kind of fish that live in our river are sleeping or frozen or dead between Thanksgiving and March.

However, the caption says the Santas were only pretending to fish which you could do any time of the year.

Then I look at the picture more closely.

It is black and white. Or, more accurately, brown and white. Or, more accurately, brown and beige because it is both faded and dirty, and not dirty in a way you can clean, though I do try, dirty like time got on it and now you cannot get it off.

But there is something very strange about this picture, and it is this: there is an extra river in it.

This cannot be.

But I check. And it cannot not be either.

And those are opposites.

The picture is fifty-five years old so it makes sense that some things would have changed between then and now, but you can see my library. You can see our very same church with its too-short, left-of-center door. You can see the bridge in between, arcing from one bank to the other. And if you look, you can see a river rushing below it.

Which is very, very wrong because there is no river there. The bridge with the river rushing under it is the bridge near the plant. The bridge between the church and the library, which is the bridge covered in

Santas in this picture, is the bridge over the ravine.

I think about it for a long time, and here is what I think: Maybe there used to be many rivers in Bourne but most of them died or left or dried up, just like there used to be many people in Bourne but most of them died or left or dried up too. Maybe the river we know now is a twin of this old one, or maybe even there used to be more, triplet rivers, but the other ones did not survive. A lot of times when there is more than one baby in one womb only one of them lives long enough to be born, and even though I do not like to think about it, it is true anyway.

But this Santa river did not die in the womb. It lived for at least a while. Because here it is, alive and well, in 1963, but now, fifty-five years later, it is nowhere to be seen.

THREE

Nora has her calendar on her phone, her computer, and long-hand in a daily planner, and she still can't keep it straight. But it lives in my head with just about everything else. This is how I know Apple Templeton is Nora's last patient of the day, and it is why I go so far as to aspirate applesauce over breakfast: so Nora will definitely bring me to work with her.

I realize the odds are long that Apple will confess in therapy the nature and whereabouts of a piece of paper her father-in-law is desperate to keep us from finding because it's incontrovertibly damning evidence Nora can give Russell who can present it to a judge who will stop the reopening of the plant and shut Belsum down forever. Not to mention anything she did disclose would be subject to doctor-patient confidentiality and therefore inadmissible in court. But it's all we've got. So here I am.

Before we get to Apple, though, I have to sit through all her other patients for the day. I considered aspirating applesauce at school, getting sent home at lunch, and thereby skipping Nora's morning patients, but I couldn't risk her canceling her afternoon altogether to take care of me.

First up this morning is Pastor Jeff. He and Nora get together every week to take stock of their flock, to discuss who they're worried about, who's fallen off the wagon, who's fallen into despair, who's strong this week and could maybe help, who's not and should be a recipient. They corner, between them, each Bourner's holy trinity — Nora treats their minds, Jeff their bodies and souls — and they have decided, heart to heart, that neither the sanctity of the church nor that of the clinic is breached by their comparing notes and tag-teaming outreach. Working together is their only shot at handling their always overfull patient loads. It's not as if either, at this late date, expects God to intervene.

This morning Pastor Jeff settles into the orange sofa, leans forward, and says quietly, "You know who I'm worried about this week, Nora?"

She opens her notebook to a clean page. "Who?"

413

"You."

She closes the notebook.

"Jeff, I'm fine."

"I don't think you are." He looks at me. "Mirabel, do you think your mother's fine?" I teeter-totter my hand, an impressively comprehensive answer to a complex question.

Pastor Jeff nods like this is the profound wisdom of the sages. "See? Mirabel thinks so too, and she's more observant than anyone. You seem" — he pauses and settles on understatement — "tired."

She snorts. "Not sure that insight requires either a girl genius or a medical man of the cloth."

"Tireder," he amends, and when she doesn't respond adds, "Than usual," and when that still gets nothing, "Remember those weighted mats Tom gave Mirabel?"

"Yeah?"

"I think we can learn a lot from those mats." My mother and I look at him like he's crazy. "It might be time to lay it down and get over it."

Nora's face closes. "It's not time."

"It's not good for you, the stress and anger you're carrying around, have been carrying around for so long."

"You've never supported the lawsuit, Jeff."

414

"That's true." The whole heavenly justice thing. "But I've always supported you."

"Yes. You have. So why quit now?"

"This is how I'm supporting you. I'm inviting you to lay it down and get over it. Admit you tried as hard as you could, and it didn't work. You didn't win." He shrugs. "Sometimes that happens."

"This lawsuit isn't just some game it's fine to lose. It's not sour grapes. It's not me being a spoilsport."

"No one said it was." And when she opens her mouth to protest, he raises a hand and rephrases his point before she can leap on it. "No one *here* said it was."

"Everyone — *everyone* — dropped off the suit. I've been working on this for sixteen years. This was not meant to be my life's work."

"Your life's not actually over yet," he points out gently. "Sixteen years is what, Nora? Twenty percent of a life?"

"Depends." She meets his wet eyes with her wet eyes. He nods. There is no arguing that. "We're finally close, I think, and if I stop now, it dies. If I don't do this, no one will."

"I'm not disagreeing. I'm saying maybe letting it die is okay. In case what you need is permission to quit, to stop suing and stop

415

fighting and just lose, I'm saying it's okay."

"Fine. Noted." She rearranges her face from riled back to professional. "What about you?"

"What *about* me?"

"How are you holding up?"

For he is her only therapist and she his only minister. "Oh, you know, the usual. Doctoring. Pastoring. Learning to sew."

"You're not getting a lot of rest either, Jeff," my mother says gently.

"We've got a lot of work to do."

"Agreed. So what are you giving me shit for?"

"That's my job," he says.

In the afternoon, Apple does a monologue. Most of Nora's patients like the back-and-forth. She asks a question; they answer; she asks; they answer. But Apple is doing a monologue. More accurately, Monday would insist, Apple is doing a tirade.

"It's all my mother's fault I married Nathan Templeton. Isn't that the point of therapy? Tracing your neuroses backward until you can blame it on your parents? Then good news: I'm cured. My appalling marriage is entirely my mother's fault. She did warn me. This I admit. I'd like to say I had no idea what I was getting into, but it

416

isn't true. This is the problem with old-world wealth. It comes off as stuffy and priggish when you're nineteen. First, she brought in my grandmother to talk to me. Grandma said, 'You're too good for him,' but I thought she just meant she loved me so much no one would be good enough for me. Grandma said, 'He's got more dollars than sense,' but she always did love a pun, obviously. But Grandma was — I don't know — bohemian, I guess. What rich people call a free spirit. She never wore shoes. She was always packing picnics. Clearly she had a thing for trees. She was an artist, back when women — especially rich women from good families — weren't artists, or anything else really. She was the one who designed the window in your library, you know."

What?

"You're kidding," Nora says. "How on earth did that happen?"

A great question — I'm thrilled she's asked it — but Apple moves right on.

"Who knows?" Apple gives a dismissive wave with nails as red and shiny as her namesake. "Anyway, when the whole wisdom-of-the-elders approach didn't work, my mother went the direct route instead. 'He's after our money.' And 'We're better

417

than that.' *We* are. Like she was marrying him too, not that she would. That was her point. That, and I was a silly girl who had her head turned around because he was handsome and exciting and in love with me. It sounds mean, right? It sounds like we should be talking about what a bitch my mother was. And she was. However, she was also right. So I blame her because if she could have told me that nicely, if she could have told me in a way that didn't make her seem like a wealthy, privileged bitch, maybe I would have listened. But she didn't so I didn't, and now look where I am."

She pauses for breath. My mother takes the opportunity to interject, "Where are you, Apple?"

"Right? Exactly!" Apple looks like my mother has just proved her point. "Where am I? Stuck in this shithole. No offense. Raising my kid in a goddamn haunted house."

Haunted?

"Married to the man she warned me against — no longer handsome, no longer exciting, no longer in love with me, though don't feel bad: I assure you the feeling is mutual."

"How did you and Nathan meet?" Nora asks, to remind Apple of a time when her

418

feelings were fresher, fonder.

"Oh, I met Nate before I can remember." Another dismissive wave. Apple must do her nails herself because Bourne doesn't have a manicurist. "I met Nate before I was even born. Our families go way back, as they say. Boston society is a small world. So, you know, similar circles: same parties, same dances at the club, same charity benefits. At one of them — I honestly couldn't tell you which one — we were seated next to each other, got to flirting, got to drinking. But I wasn't very much older than she is." With a shiny wave in my direction. "He was older and gorgeous and made my mother furious. There was no way I wasn't going to fall for him. But now I'm paying for it. Suddenly I have to be worried about leaks and cracks and repairmen who won't work over the winter. I mean it's just such a mess down there. Dangerous probably. Who knows how broken really. This should not be my problem. This is not what I signed on for."

"Why is it?" Nora asks. "Why aren't these Nathan's problems rather than yours?"

"Family." Apple does a little shrug. "Legacy. You know?"

"That's what you said last week. Family. But . . ." Nora trails off to ask without asking *Why do you care so much about your*

419

husband when you care so little about your husband?

"I owe them."

"Them?" Nora looks as lost as I feel. "Who?"

"My family. Or maybe not all of them but him at least."

Nora begins, "Your loyalty to your husband is —" Strange? Inconsistent? Misguided? Who knows how she might have finished that sentence.

But Apple laughs. "Not my husband. God, no. My father."

"Your father?"

"I guess probably it makes sense. Just, you know, grief."

But it doesn't make sense. Apple's father has nothing to do with us. And I am starting to realize we need another plan. Of course Apple isn't going to start giving out hints in therapy, in the first place because she probably doesn't know anything but mostly, worse, because she doesn't care. Whatever she's upset about, it isn't what her husband is doing to us.

"What are you grieving?" Nora asks gently.

Apple's eyebrows go up like she's surprised. "My father died." She says this simply, like it should be obvious, like it is something everyone must know, and when

420

she looks back up from the ground at Nora, it is with a melting of her painted face.

"I'm so sorry," Nora says. "When did he die?"

"Just before we came. That's why I agreed. I could give a shit about Nathan's PR stunt. He can drown alone down here for all I care. But some of Daddy's letters are still here."

Still here?

"Letters?" Nora says.

"Daddy was a letter writer. Handwriting, stationery, nice pens. He did all his business longhand. He thought email was ruining the art of correspondence and the heart of negotiation. He was pretty out of it the last few years so he was spared the smartphone, but if he hadn't been dying already, the text message would have finished the job. I know they say you can never really erase an email, but you have to be some kind of tech geek to recover one once you delete it. But letters? Well, you post them, and then they're out of your hands, in both senses. You send them somewhere, and then you can't just get rid of them with a keystroke. They'll remain forever right where the recipient leaves them. I think that's why they call it hard copy."

"I'm not sure I follow, Apple," Nora says.

421

"I can't let his name get dragged into . . . well, any of this. That's the kind of thing that mattered to him, his name. And now he's not around to protect it anymore, it has to be my job. That's why I'm so desperate to find — I don't know — whatever there is to find. That's why I'm here. Not for my husband, and not for his father certainly — I couldn't care less about Duke — for mine. Nathan's here to reopen. Myself, I'm here to re-close, here to make sure anything well lost stays that way."

"Well lost?"

"Sometimes it's important to remember things the way someone worked really hard for you to remember them," Apple says, "rather than the way they actually were."

At the bar later, Nora's in something of a trance, eyes and mind both unfocused and elsewhere.

On the one hand, the guys are relieved she's not yelling.

On the other, "Did we break her?" Tom asks me the third time he's asked for another and she hasn't heard.

"Weird day," my Voice says.

"At the clinic?" Frank, who's working his ass off since Nora is not, is ready to entirely forgive this fact if she will even incrementally forgive everything else.

"You know she can't say." I have that one saved. Frank and I have had this conversation before.

"Yeah, yeah, doctor-patient blah-blah-blah."

"Nora's not a doctor," Hobart says, a point he makes often because it annoys her.

"You'd think a shrink would be saner," Zach adds, same reason.

"They're the craziest ones," says Tom.

They're baiting her. Usually they tease her because it's all in good fun because they know she knows they adore her. Tonight it's an apology, a peace offering, a plea that they might all return to normal, that she forgive them.

This wouldn't work except that her mind is so far elsewhere it's shed even her fury. She's not angry with them at the moment because she's not really here with them. They're relieved — me too — but also confused, worried, waiting.

Then, out of nowhere and to no one in particular, she says, "Do you guys remember when the stained glass was put in the library window?"

"What, all the people reading books?" says Zach.

"Yeah."

423

"Hasn't that always been there?"

"No, no, remember it used to be a house?" says Tom.

"What kind of house?"

"For rich people."

"Obviously."

"Remember when there used to be money in Bourne?"

"No."

They're a chorus of memory, talking too fast for me to keep track from the corner of who's saying what, overlapping and talking on top of one another, remembering together, misremembering together, correcting, hole plugging, tall-tale-ing. It's not often these guys get to remember Bourne before. It's not often they get to revel in recollection: of their childhoods, growing up, being teenagers then young adults, full of promise and in love and having children of their own, their whole lives in front of them, hope and dreams and all that. It's another cruelty you never think of, almost incidental it's so far down the list, but the bad memories paper over the good until the good ones are gone or so buried they're forgotten. Today's Bourne is less upsetting if you don't remember the idyllic Bourne that used to be. I imagine once you're an adult your childhood seems remote no matter where you live, but when your life and that of everyone you know blows apart, everything before isn't remote. It's gone.

"Remember when the library was just a room in the church basement?" says Tom.

"There was also the one at Bourne High" — Hobart laughs — "if fifty-year-old encyclopedias met your research needs."

"Donating a library is serious philanthropy," Frank says. "I mean, I love you guys, but I'm still not donating my home to you. 'Course mine wouldn't hold a library." Frank lives in a storage room above the bar. I live in a house which is nowhere near big enough, though it is, in fact, a library, but I take his meaning.

"Point is, it was a home," Nora says. "A family residence. So they must have put the stained glass in sometime later."

"How do you figure?" Hobart says.

"Because a family home doesn't have a wall of stained glass on the front. And even if it did, it wouldn't be of people reading."

"Is that what they're doing?"

"What do you think they're doing? They're all holding books."

"Yeah, but I didn't realize they were reading them."

"What else do you do with books?"

"I dunno. Even the mountain lion has one."

"Mountain lion?"

"Man, that's a dog."

"It's not a dog."

"It's a dog."

"Fine, it's a dog. Mountain lion, dog, either way, it can't read."

They're so happy reminiscing. They're so happy debating something that couldn't matter less. They feel forgiven maybe, or their sins at least forgotten. Their chatter makes a soft hum, and I might be falling asleep when the door opens and Omar comes in.

Nora takes him in, takes a deep breath. "Omar. You'll be able to answer this question."

For a beat, a look of pure gratitude sweeps his face — something changed when he told her he signed on to the lawsuit, and it's stayed changed — then he wrestles his expression back to blasé, everyday; he's just a guy in his hometown bar, shooting the shit with the bartender.

She pours him a beer. "Do you remember when they put the stained-glass window in the library?"

He thinks about it. "Was it right when they converted it or later?"

"None of us can remember."

"Me neither." He's trying to think but having trouble concentrating because he's so happy she's talking kindly to him. "Must have been expensive."

"Must have been," Frank agrees.

"So I bet it was part of the original agreement."

"What original agreement?" Nora asks.

"I don't know the details — it was before my time — but I think the machinations were pretty complex. A lot of money changed hands, and I can't imagine it was all on the up-and-up."

"You think someone was bribed with a stained-glass mountain lion?" This is beyond Hobart's imagining.

"It's a dog!"

"I think a stained-glass mural like that cannot have been cheap and is not Bourne's usual . . . aesthetic," Omar says.

"Agreed." Zach signals Nora for another.

"So I wonder if it wasn't part of the terms to begin with, whatever they were."

"That's real weird," says Tom.

Omar shrugs. "So is local government. You know who you should ask, though?"

"Who?"

"Apple Templeton."

Nora takes in a hard breath and holds it.

"Apple Templeton?" Frank has obviously never heard this name in his life. It's not a huge surprise Apple hasn't made her way in here.

"Nathan Templeton's wife," Omar explains.

"Why?" Nora's still holding her breath.

"Before it was a library, it was her family home."

Her family home? My mother and I exchange a confused glance.

"How?" Nora asks. She exhales finally but can't seem to manage the inhale. Then she revises her question backward a step. "Who?"

"Her family is the Groves," Omar says.

The Groves? Whose name is on the bridge over the ravine? And half the fancy graves in the cemetery?

"No." Nora can't make this make sense. Me neither.

"Yup. The library's the old Grove place." Omar makes his voice sound like the house might be haunted. He's joking, but Apple said the same and she wasn't. This must be what she meant, though. Not ghosts, at least not literal ones. Haunted by memories and old relatives and the past, her family's history and legacy. That makes sense now, but nothing else about this does. Apple said she met Nathan in Boston. It must have been years before the Templetons darkened our doors, and the Groves have nothing to do with Belsum.

"They've been gone a long time," says Frank.

"Well, right, she never lived here," Omar says, "but her grandparents did, her parents for a while maybe before she was born, an uncle, some stray aunts and cousins I think. You should wait a couple days before you ask her, though."

"Why?" The crease between Nora's eyes could grasp a spoon.

"She came by my office this morning. She was pretty worked up."

"What did she want?"

"Boxes she thought I might have. Said they weren't in the library attic so I *must* have them like there's a law of physics that says anything not in the library is with me. She wasn't making sense. Wouldn't tell me what was supposed to be in the boxes, so how am I supposed to help her find them? Ranted on and on about somebody's father and somebody's family. I couldn't follow it, but honestly, I wasn't trying that hard." Tom grins and clinks glasses with him. "I finally turned her loose on the filing cabinets and let her see if she could find whatever she was looking for, but I wanted to say, 'Ma'am, do we seem like the kind of town that keeps cataloged archives?' " A warm laugh from everyone. "I haven't had a secretary in ten years. Some stuff got thrown away long ago. Some was in the library but —"

"You're living in it now, lady!" Hobart cackles.

"Again!" Zach adds.

Omar is glowing.

"Did she find what she was looking for?" Nora asks.

"No idea. She left empty-handed." Omar opens his to demonstrate. "Something about the plant, I bet," he ventures carefully.

There's a pause.

"Different day, same shit," Tom says finally, and they all crack up, even Nora eventually, even angry as she still is at these guys, even confused as this afternoon's revelations have left us both, as if this is the truest, funniest, most original sentiment anyone has ever expressed.

I spend the evening trying to puzzle all this together, but I'm missing too many pieces to be able to see the picture. Duke Templeton is hiding papers. Apple Templeton is looking for papers. They can't be the same papers. Can they? Is Duke hiding them from Apple as well? His email said deeds and contracts. Apple said letters, but she also said her father used them to conduct business, so maybe they *are* the same or in the same place or at least connected. Because whatever they are, if they aren't in Omar's filing cabinets, if they aren't in the library somewhere, chances are good that Monday was, of all things, right: she doesn't know what she's looking for. Which — she would point out — is not the same as their not being there.

"Apple is also looking for papers," my Voice blurts as soon as I'm alone with my sisters.

I'm expecting shock, maybe confusion, possibly incredulity. A smidge of veneration that I was able to make this potentially revelatory connection would not be out of line.

But Mab says, "That makes sense."

And Monday says, "I already knew that."

"You did?" My Voice cannot believe it.

"I did not know I knew it but now I know I knew."

"Huh?" I say.

"Me too," says Mab.

I make a hand motion that means "What the hell are you two talking about?" It's not

431

a complicated one.

"That day we were at the library" — Mab waves at Monday as if otherwise I'd forget I wasn't part of the "we" — "Apple was up in the attic. She came down covered in cobwebs and dust. Nathan asked her if she found anything. She said no."

"And when she came to my library to borrow a book," Monday adds, "she did not come to my library to borrow a book."

"Huh?" Mab can pronounce infinitely more words than I can, but that's the one we both go with anyway.

"She did need books," Monday explains. "However, that is not why she came. She came to look through boxes and files that used to be in her library and now are in my library."

"Did she?" Mab demands.

"Obviously no. I told her not to touch anything. She touched some things anyway, but I found the books she needed quickly so she did not have a lot of time."

"Why didn't you tell me?" my Voice demands of both of them.

Mab shrugs. "Didn't know it was important."

"To be more accurate," Monday adds, "we still do not know it is important."

"It is," my Voice insists. "Look again in

your library, Monday."

"I do not know what I am looking for so it is impossible for me to —" she begins, but my Voice interrupts her.

"Look again in your library," it repeats, then turns to the other sister. "You have to get into the plant."

"Why?" Mab says, annoyed.

"Because I can't," my Voice answers, also annoyed, and her face softens.

"I meant why does anyone have to get into the plant."

But I knew what she meant.

"Apple said the plant is dangerous," I type. "Leaking, cracked, broken."

Mab looks as nervous as I feel. "Then why would I want to go in it?"

I take a deep breath. "Good place to hide."

"You just said it is not safe." Monday sounds nervous too, more nervous than usual. "Therefore the plant is not a good place to hide. It is a bad place to hide."

"Something," my Voice appends. "It is a good place to hide something."

ONE

"Do not tip your hat," Monday warns.

Mirabel taps the folder that's supposed to help you tell your doctor where it hurts, then the picture of a severed hand, emphatically and repeatedly, so the Voice sounds deranged in its affectless calm as it reiterates like a skipping record, "Hand. Hand. Hand. Hand," but I knew what Monday meant.

"This isn't something I can just casually work into conversation," I tell her.

"Old books say to use your feminine wiles," Monday advises.

"I don't have any feminine wiles."

Monday points to her chest with both index fingers.

I look to Mirabel for help, but she's in the Body Parts folder already. "Breast," her Voice intones, and then we can't discuss anything anymore because we're all laughing too hard.

Mirabel thinks the papers we're looking for might be in Monday's library, in which case the person to find them is Monday. But she also thinks they might be hidden in the plant, so we need someone who can sneak in and look around without being noticed, in which case the person is definitely not Monday and can't be Mirabel. In which case the person is me.

The miracle comes from the unlikeliest of places: World History. Mrs. Shriver long-jumps us from the Atlantic slave trade to the industrial revolution. At first this cheers me up. At least the industrial revolution isn't enslaving humans. At least it isn't war. It's human ingenuity and forward progress, inventions rising up from society, unpredictably, like hairstyles — at least, that's Mrs. Shriver's spin on it. But as the lecture goes on, I slowly realize the industrial revolution *is* a war. Mrs. Shriver wants it to be revolution like the Renaissance we left a couple months ago — great leaps forward made by humans being clever. But the more she talks, the clearer it becomes: the revolution in "industrial revolution" is like the revolution in "American Revolution," revolution like war. It remapped small towns and big cities and nations, destroyed communities, willfully refused to consider the long term in favor of immediate blood and power, and demanded the sacrifice of scores upon scores of soldiers for the glory of the men getting rich. It was the industrial revolution that conscripted towns like mine and con-signed their citizens — us — to the bottom of every pile yet to come.

So I am thinking of armor. I am thinking of arrows and muskets and cannons. I am thinking of the longbow and the M16, armadas of ten thousand ships, rows of white crosses repeating into infinity, which is why when Mrs. Shriver calls on me to catch me out for daydreaming by the win-dow instead of paying attention in class — "Mab, something on your mind?" — I ac-cidentally blurt out the answer to that ques-tion.

"Why aren't factories like museums?"

She's amused. Bored maybe. Gives me an indulgent smile and decides to play along. "I don't know, Mab. Why *aren't* factories like museums?"

"No. It's not a joke. Remember last month when you showed us all those pictures from the British Museum? Helmets. Guns. Swords. All that stuff?"

"Right. What does that have to do with factories?"

"Other artifacts of war go in museums.

Why don't punch clocks or conveyor belts or fake emergency exits? Why aren't munitions factories and mill floors and chemical plants preserved the same way, like for tourists to wander around and have perspective on history and stuff?"

Mrs. Shriver looks at me for too long before answering. "No one would pay to go in," she says finally. "Plus, what would you sell at the gift shop?"

But after class River steals up next to me and whispers, "You want to see the inside of a chemical plant?"

I am about to tell him that wasn't the point I was making when I realize the point I was making was entirely beside the point. I nod mutely.

He smiles then blushes then smiles a little more widely. "I can totally get us a key."

Two days later I am on my way to tutoring after school — Mrs. Radcliffe and Petra and I have compromised on once a week — when River takes my elbow and steers me to an old, disused classroom.

"Pick a hand." He holds out both in closed fists. I hear Mirabel's Voice intoning, *Hand. Hand. Hand. Hand.*

I pick a hand. He turns it over, peels it open. It's inevitably empty. Obligingly, I tap his other fist. It's empty too. He grins at me. I grin back. Can't help it. He reaches behind my ear, comes out with a fist, opens it. Empty. I'm still grinning, waiting patiently for the reveal. He's patting himself all over, looking confused and increasingly alarmed, but it's not until he starts cursing under his breath that I realize this isn't part of the trick. He takes both my shoulders in both his hands, looks into my eyes, and says very seriously, "Can I please turn you to face the wall?"

"Not a chance."

He waves his arms in the air frantically like he's walked into a swarm of gnats and, when that yields nothing, undoes his top two buttons, pulls both arms inside his shirt, and wriggles around like the weekend Monday and I spent trying to take off our bras without taking off our tops as if this were a necessary life skill. No luck. River looks at me dolefully. I smile.

And because I do, he smiles back. And because I do, or maybe just because he's embarrassed already, he doubles down. He yanks off his belt dramatically, lassoes it in the air a few times, and wiggles his hips back and forth, around and around. But that's as far as he can go.

"Please?" He twirls his finger in a circle

and hopes I will follow suit. "The first rule of magic is misdirection."

"Of the audience."

"At least close your eyes."

"If my eyes are closed, how will I see what happens next?"

River blazes red, unbuttons his khakis, starts excavating around down there, first in his pants, then in his underpants. I try to pretend the reason I'm blushing is because I'm laughing so hard.

Finally his hand reemerges from his underwear. "Ta-da!"

"Neat trick."

"It's all in the sleight of hand."

"I can see that."

"For you." He holds it out to me gallantly, offering me the key to, well, everything.

"Thank you," I say. "You carry it."

So I skip tutoring.

It seems impossible, but it's true: I have never before followed anyone on a bike. Petra has a car and even when we were little never had a bicycle. "You know how my mother feels about outside," she always said when I complained. When I ride with Monday, I go first or at least alongside. When I don't ride with Monday, I ride alone. So it's all new to me: the way a person's shoulders

439

and back flex beneath his shirt as he shifts through gears on his handlebars, the way a person's calf muscles ball like cookie dough and release, ball and release. I have to pedal hard to keep up.

He slows so I can pull alongside him. "Can I ask you a question?" he says.

My heart speeds, and it's not from exertion. *Are you flirting with me just to make me easier to manipulate? Are you being nice to me because you're using me? Are you tricking me into taking you into my family's lair so you and your crazy sisters can destroy us?*

"How come no one in this town celebrates Halloween?" he says.

It's November already today. We're a week closer to the twenty-second and still have no idea what's coming.

"We used to. When I was little." It's hard to shrug when you're leaning over handlebars. "Maybe people figured we had enough demons around here already. Maybe there were too many ghosts to make dressing up like one seem fun anymore."

"Yeah, that makes sense." But it shouldn't, not to him anyway. And probably this is the strangest thing of all: we're not so strange anymore. He's getting used to how things are around here. "Kind of a bummer for little kids though."

440

I try to shrug again. "It's too far between occupied houses to trick-or-treat anyway."

He looks so sad about that — about *that* — that I change the subject. "So are you just super trustworthy or what?"

"Completely," he answers at once. "I'm completely trustworthy, Mab. I would never betray you."

Which is not what I meant.

"Your father," I clarify. "Your father must trust you. He doesn't lock his phone. He leaves the key to the plant just lying around."

"The key's completely hidden. In fact, the key is under lock and key. A second key I mean. Not the same one. That would be stupid." He grins. "He didn't leave it lying around. I sleuthed it out."

"In two days?" I'm impressed.

"One."

"One?"

"One day to find it. One day to copy it and put it back so he wouldn't notice — it's a good thing Mirabel already told me you have to go to church to get a key copied around here. But it only took dinner to trick him into giving up the clue."

"Are you a magician or a detective?" I ask.

"Both. The plant has dozens of keys. It's not like he carries them around in his pocket. But there's one master, and I needed to know where it was. So I lost mine."

"Your what?"

"My keys. So then he has to make a big production at dinner about how I'm growing up, and a man keeps track of his things, and a man has responsibilities, and now I'm sixteen years old, and it's reasonable to expect me to be mature enough to keep track of my own house key, and how can he buy me a car if I keep losing my keys." All this in a mock-deep voice, looking down his nose at me, poking the air with his index finger like he's scolding a dog, and riding impressively one-handed. "Then Dad's all, 'You should do what I do. Devise a system. My house keys and car keys go on a hook by the front door. I hang them back in their spot the minute I get home, and then when I'm ready to leave again, you know where they are? Right where I left them and right where I need them to be. Smart, right? Remember the garden shed in the backyard in Boston? We kept that key at the backyard door. Work keys? Locked in the bottom drawer of my desk in my office. Get it? Backyard, shed. Work, desk. Simple.' So then my mom in her super-sarcastic voice finally goes, 'But where do you keep the key to your desk?' And he's all, 'Behind Uncle

Hickory. Of course.' "

"Who's Uncle Hickory?"

"My great-uncle. Remember that super-big, super-ugly oil painting in my dad's office? Point is, his tone — like *Where does anyone keep a desk key? Behind Uncle Hickory. Duh* — shows you exactly what kind of weirdo my father is. And the reason he drives my mother crazy."

"What if your mom hadn't asked where he keeps the desk key?"

When he turns his head to look at me, the hood of his sweatshirt blows over his eyes, and he sits upright to pull it back off his face, riding in the sun with no hands, eyes closed, open as a dying tulip. He laughs. "What kind of magician would I be if I couldn't bust open the lock on a desk?"

"The kind who loses the key in his underpants?"

He beams. "Exactly."

When we cross the river and pull up at the plant, though, the cockiness fades a little and then a lot. There's a truck parked out front, an old beat-up Ford pickup.

"Shit. Someone's here."

"Would your father be caught dead in a twenty-year-old Ford F-150?"

River laughs nervously. "Not even twenty years ago."

443

"Then I think we're fine." I'm striding toward the front door like we own the place. In fairness, one of us does.

"Mab, stop. He must have security on already." River grabs my sleeve. "I didn't think he would yet, but we'll have to get in some other way."

I keep walking. I don't recognize the pickup, but I'm not worried.

At the door, there is indeed a security guard behind giant mirrored sunglasses, sitting on a desk chair that looks totally out of place outside though I guess a security guard in a lawn chair would be even stranger, and there's no one here but us so there's no need to stand. River is still clutching at my sleeve, still begging me to turn back, even though, clearly, we've already been seen. I look to see if security has been issued a gun. He has.

"Mab," he says. "Mr. Templeton."

"Hey Hobart," I say. "How's things?"

"I'm not —" River starts, but Hobart's answering my question.

"Not bad. Got a job." He spreads his hands to show me, as if I couldn't already see, as if I didn't already know.

"Congratulations."

"Thanks. How are you?"

"Fine," I say. "Same." Even though that's

444

less true by the moment.

"Your sisters?"

"Them too."

"Glad to hear it." A short pause. "You kids headed in?"

"Yup," I say.

He turns to River. "Your dad know you're here?"

"We've even got the key," I assure Hobart and gesture at River to show it to him.

"No need, no need." Hobart reaches around us and unlocks the front doors, glad to be of service. But on our way inside, he puts a hand on my arm.

"Mab, listen." I pause and do. "This job? Your mom knows, but she doesn't know, you know? She doesn't know I started yet. If she's upset, would you tell her? I just really, really needed it."

I was picturing derelict, dusty expanses, nails and washers and stray parts scattered across a stained and cratered floor, cobwebs and mouse shit and broken glass, hulking machinery so out of date even I would recognize it was beyond repair. I was picturing leaking, cracked, and broken because that's what Apple said. But what I see is shocking, and the longer we look around the more shocking it gets.

There is, at first, no hint of a chemical plant, no hint of a plant of any kind. It looks like an office but an office in a magazine, much nicer than anything we have in Bourne. There's a lobby with comfortable-looking chairs and sofas surrounding a thick gray rug with splashes of red like uneven sunburn, a coffee table with fans of never-read magazines, a water dispenser with cold and hot and a variety of tea bags and cocoa packets and sweetener choices, a matched set of mugs, a coffee maker. A fireplace. Behind that, offices and conference rooms, some glass-walled so you can see inside, some with the glass frosted so you cannot.

"Wow" is all I can manage.

"That's what you're supposed to say," River tells me grimly. "Come on. This is just the front office. That's not what you wanted to see."

It's not? I have no idea what I wanted to see.

"Let's find your revolution," he says.

A series of corridors, all pristine. Shining. A series of rooms, and River's key opens them all. One holds nothing but office supplies. Another paper towels and tissues and toilet paper. Another is filled with brand-new desks and chairs wrapped in plastic like sandwiches. Another is empty save for

446

maybe a dozen phones trailing cords from the wall and dotting the carpet like weeds.

Finally, behind another nondescript door, row after row after row of filing cabinets, filing cabinets to the moon. This is the room I've come for. This is the room Mirabel's sent me to find. But even if it's in here, even if I knew exactly what to look for, I'm no closer to Duke's buried paperwork now than I was at our house. It could be right in this room, inches from my fingertips, but given all the time there is between now and the end of the world, I'd still die in there before I found it.

But River is on to the next door anyway. It opens to a garage like an airplane hangar full of forklifts fitted together like vertebrae, tires full and black as ticks. You can tell just by looking that, unlike the equipment on the torn-up grass outside, these have never been driven. You can tell just by looking they have never even been turned on. The door next to that reveals another enormous garage, this one of demolition equipment — bulldozers, backhoes, dump trucks, excavators — some dirt-caked and mud-splattered, some fresh and untouched and yellow as buttercups. If real backhoes shipped like toy ones, most of these would still be in their original packaging. I realize: This is not a factory that's been through a war. This is a factory gearing up for one.

At last we reach the floor of the plant, the heart of the beast. We're up above it on a kind of walkway enclosed in glass, peering down like far-off gods. There's something very strange about looking out windows and seeing inside. You expect trees when you look out a window. Or, if your view is unlovely, then cars, parking lots, the outside of the house across the way. But to look out a window and see in is dizzying. Also, because we're so high, the floor so far below, I can't quite make out what I'm looking at. But slowly it resolves. Vats upon vats upon vats, pipes snaking into their tops, out from their bottoms, crisscrossing in layers of chrome and steel, bending hard at right angles and veering away, plunging into the floor only to reemerge somewhere farther along, like loons. They are punctuated at intervals even as railroad ties by bolts that rise like nipples from their rounded hulls.

I don't know if Apple was wrong or lying or being lied to herself, but this place is not a leaky mess in need of repair. This place is perfect, pristine, and ready to go.

I'm having trouble catching my breath.

"You okay?" River looks at me, worried.

I nod. He takes my hand. This does not

make it any easier to breathe.

"You're kind of pale."

"I'm fine. Really." He looks unconvinced. "It's not what I was expecting."

"What were you expecting?"

A fair question. Smaller. Dirtier. Brokener. Less whole.

Less ready.

"It's so . . ." I trail off because I cannot tell him any of that, can I? But he seems to get it anyway.

"They hauled so much out of here. You can't believe the cursing my father does into his phone every day. All new this, all new that, tear out those, get rid of that other thing. They had to fly in some kind of special cleaning crew."

"Why?"

He shrugs. "I don't know. I guess the stuff that was already here was too old?"

"For what?"

"For whatever they're going to make next."

And when I don't say anything to that, he says, very gently, "What did you think reopening the plant meant?"

I shake my head. I do not know.

He smiles. "Don't worry. We'll find what you're looking for." He holds out his fists, and I choose one. He opens it, empty, waves it over the other, also empty, and shows me the first again with its prize gleaming in the center of his palm. "After all, we have the key."

So I lean over and kiss him.

I don't know why.

It's terrible. Atrocious. My sisters would scream if they saw. My mother would be dismayed beyond the power of speech. But I can't think what else to do. Being in here is so overwhelming and strange that what's steady and safe is actually River. Though he's new and the plant's older than I am, comparatively speaking he's what feels familiar and comforting. Possible.

And even though my mother would label me treasonous right now, I'm here on her quest. She started it. She's the one who told us to find out what we could from River. Plus, he's betraying his parents more than I'm betraying mine, and he's done it for us, for me. Stealing those emails, stealing that key, these are the nicest things anyone's ever done for me. When I started kissing him, it was just spontaneous, a thing to do, an opportunity — and maybe the only one I'll ever get — but now it might be something more than that because after I start I don't stop. It was kind of him to bring me here. It was kind of him to worry about me. It was kind of him to promise me his key. I doubt he did it so I'd kiss him. But I don't know why he did do it. Or, really, why I am either.

It's terrible, it is, but also it's amazing.

First he tastes surprised.

Then he tastes euphoric.

Or maybe it's not taste but some new sense that's feeding that information straight into my brain. When he puts his arms around me, I can feel him pressing that key against my lower back. When I put mine around his shoulders, I can feel those muscles that flexed when he changed gears. I can feel his mouth, outside and in, and his breath, bated as mine.

We kiss for a little while which is surprising because when you think about your first kiss, you think of it like a finite thing, measurable, contained, begun in a blink and over just as fast, but this is not contained. This sprawls and wanes, except the waning is actually waiting, the begging of more to come, and then more does come, and that's all part of it, a small thing that proves to be part of a much larger, growing one. Expanding. Like the universe. But eventually, we part.

When we do, he takes my hand again. "It's not really a museum, I guess."

"No," I agree. Museums preserve the old.

This is all new, gravely new. "More like a monument."

He smiles like I'm making a joke. I'm not. "To what?"

"To what's to come."

TWO

The days we have left before November 22 are precious now and shrinking in number, but for nine of them, I did not tell anyone about my Santa picture because it was not a clue to the mystery of how to not reopen the plant. We are looking for paperwork, and the Santas are not paperwork. We are looking for activities you used to be able to do in winter, but the Santas were only pretending to fish which you could do anytime. We were looking in the plant for something leaking, cracked, and broken, but that was Mab's job not mine, and those issues do not apply to Santas.

But it turned out it was more accurate to say the Santa picture was a clue, it was just not a clue to the answer. It was a clue to the question. The Santa picture was a clue to what the mystery actually was.

On the day I showed my sisters the Santa picture, which was yesterday, Mab got home from school even later than when tutoring got out, and I knew she did not go to tutoring. When Mab finally got home the reason she was late was because she got River to take her in the plant, and since she went in the plant she wanted to talk and talk and talk about all the things she saw and one she kissed. Mirabel was listening hard for clues, but it sounded to me like a boring description of the difference between what Mab was expecting (a plant that had been sitting vacant for seventeen years) and what Mab actually saw (a plant that is about to reopen). Since we already knew the plant is about to reopen, the only clue I could find was that Mab is not as smart as she appears.

Mirabel was also interested in hearing about the kissing. I was not.

I sighed, but they ignored me, so I sighed louder and then I sighed louder and then I sighed louder, and then Mab talked again about the kissing which she had already talked about a lot, so I started running around them in circles so they would know that I wanted them to talk about something else. We were in our room where there are three beds. Mirabel was lying on hers. Mab was lying on hers with her legs up the wall in a funny position because her part of the wall is covered in postcards I sent her. So the circles I ran in were small, but I have had a lot of practice running in small circles.

"Jesus, Monday, this is kind of important." Mab said this as if kissing River Templeton were the key to not reopening the plant.

"This will not work," I told her.

"What won't?" Her face made a face that meant whatever I was going to say next was going to be stupid, but she did not know that because I had not said it yet.

"I do not think River will go to his father and say, 'Father, I have kissed Mab Mitchell, and it was nice, so I do not think you should reopen the plant,' so his father will say, 'Okay, River, you have convinced me.' "

"No one's saying that," Mab sneered but she did not say what anyone *was* saying. "At least I'm trying to help. What are you doing?"

"I am looking at scrapbooks to see if there used to be an indoor pool," I said.

"What does an indoor pool have to do with anything?"

"I do not know," I said because I did not.

"Did there?" Mab asked.

"Not that I could see," I said.

"Not much of a clue," she said.

I was going to say I could not find clues if I did not know what clues I was looking for. I was going to say scrapbooks were more likely places to hold hints about the past than the inside of River's mouth. I was going to say she should just shut up because I could not think of a better comeback. But instead I said I did find one clue.

They both stopped looking at each other and looked at me instead.

"About the river," I said, and I thought they would say who cares because nothing in the emails said anything about a river.

But Mab sat up and looked at me. "What about it?"

"There used to be two," I said. "Twins at least. There might have been triplets. We cannot assume," and I felt stupid because rivers are not twins or triplets, but I said it anyway because I could not think of another reason why the river was where it was not and also because they are my sisters and I know they love me even when I am stupid.

"Two?" Mab said, and she did not mean me. She meant two rivers.

"It is probably not important," I admitted.

Mirabel typed. "River is important," her Voice said, and I thought she meant because Mab kissed him, but then I realized she meant *the* river is important.

"Why?" I asked because the river has nothing to do with paperwork or winter activities.

Mirabel looked at Mab. Mab said, "Because it runs next to the plant? Because that's what got poisoned in the first place? Because it smelled and ran contaminated water to our taps and turned green? Because that's what killed us last time Belsum was up and running?" Her voice made questions at the end, but I did not know what the questions were. "What do you mean there used to be two?"

So I showed them the Santa picture that could not be but could not not be either that revealed how at Christmas 1963 there was a river running right through the middle of downtown.

Mab looked and looked, and Mirabel looked and looked, and Mirabel made a squeak, and Mirabel started to type, and then her Voice said, "What did the fish say when it swam into a wall?"

And I said, "Fish cannot talk."

And I said, "There are no walls in the ocean."

And I said, "You might think fish are stupid because their brains are small but fish are not stupid and —"

But Mab interrupted, "Oh." And then Mab said, "Damn."

457

Or, to be more accurate, Mab said, "Dam."

Mirabel explained that the rivers were not triplets or even twins. Mirabel explained that the river in the Santa photograph was our very same river but in a different place. It took all night for Mirabel to explain because her predictive software did not predict you could move a river just like I did not and because she did not have anything saved already on the subject of river diversion so she had to type every single word. It also took a long time because I did not understand. When she told me you can move a river I was thinking you would have to fill a bucket with water and carry it somewhere else and dump it out and then go back and fill it again and carry it again and dump it again and then do that over and over and over. I said no matter how many times you did that it would not work because more water would keep coming. But Mirabel helped me understand you can turn the river itself which is the difference between big dams and little dams. The big dams you think of when you think of dams generate power which is called hydroelectric, but smaller dams like ours are used to make lakes and divert rivers which means move them, and then the place where the

458

river used to run would be a ravine and fill with vines and plants and brambles so you would not think that a river used to run there but it did.

Which means sometime between when the Santas pretended to fish in 1963 and every single memory we have, someone put in the dam.

Mab got very excited and started asking questions we did not know the answers to. I do not know why she did this since we did not know the answers, but Mirabel kept nodding her head and tapping her screen and her Voice kept saying, "Yes. Yes. Yes."

Mab said, "When was the dam put in?"

Mab said, "No, wait, why was the dam put in?"

Mab said, "No, no, no! Who put the dam in?"

Mirabel's Voice did not answer any of these questions. Mirabel's Voice said, "Yes yes yes yes yes."

This morning we are very tired because we were up too late last night understanding dams, but it is Saturday so Pastor Jeff is here so we get out of bed anyway. We have many questions we cannot remember the answers to because we were not born yet, but he and

Mama probably remember because they were.

By the time we finish getting up and dressed, Pastor Jeff is already eating. Mama has made blueberry danish and chocolate brioche plus lemon muffins for me, but Pastor Jeff is eating one of my muffins, even though he is a man of God. (He does not care what color his food is, and also what if he touched all the muffins when he took one?) But then Mama puts out a separate plate of untouched lemon muffins for just me. This is nice of her.

"When did they build the dam?" I shout which I did not mean to, but I am very excited. Mama stops pouring coffee. Pastor Jeff stops chewing my muffin.

"Good morning to you too, Monday," says Pastor Jeff.

"When did they build the dam?" I say again.

Pastor Jeff and Mama share a look which means confused but also laughing at me.

"Why are you asking about the dam, love?" Mama says.

"We cannot remember before it was built," I explain, "because every time we can remember it was already there."

Mama looks at Mab who sometimes explains me when I am too confused or excited or upset to explain me myself, but Mab is just sitting there looking like she is wondering the answer too, so Mama figures that the question I am asking is the question I am asking. Her face does a funny thing. "It was right before . . ." But she does not finish.

"Right before what?" I ask even though I should not have to because people should complete their sentences.

"It was right before Belsum came to town," Pastor Jeff says quietly. "Before they broke ground on the plant even."

"We thought . . ." Mama begins, then has to clear her throat. "We thought everything was about to get so great. And instead everything got so terrible."

"But the park was nice," Pastor Jeff says.

"Briefly." Mama snorts.

"Why did they?" I ask.

"Why did they what?" says Mama, as if I have changed the subject which I have not.

"Why did they build the dam?"

"To make Bluebell Lake," Mama says like this is obvious.

Pastor Jeff does a better job of saying more. "In the summer, kids used to wade in the river to cool off." I try to picture this. I cannot picture this. "Splashing contests, prying up rocks, catching tadpoles in jars, that kind of thing. But the water moved too fast out in the middle. Parents started to worry about some kid getting swept away. I think there was a petition or something. People lobbied the mayor — this was the mayor before Omar — until finally they dammed the river to build the lake and the park so we'd have somewhere to hang out and swim safely."

"Did you?" I cannot picture anyone swimming in Bluebell Lake or anywhere in Bourne. It is like Pastor Jeff has admitted he spent his summers swimming in something gross and also dangerous like a vat of drooling wolves.

"Sure we did. It was really nice."

"Briefly," Mama says again.

"It was nice to have somewhere to swim instead of just wade," Pastor Jeff continues. "And the park was pretty all year long."

"Your dad proposed to me there," Mama says. Suddenly my sisters and I are alert as birds because we have never heard this story. "It had snowed, and it was late, and we were walking around the lake holding hands, just, you know, to be out in it, throwing snowballs at each other, hugging to keep warm. And it was so pretty, all white and moonlit and quiet. Clean. It was one of those nights you could stay in, perfectly

462

content, forever. You know?"

I do not know. I have never heard her talk like this. She is not looking at me or Mab or Mirabel or Pastor Jeff. She is looking above our heads.

"And then he tripped over a branch or something. It was buried in the snow, and he couldn't see it. He fell right over, and we laughed so hard, and when I tried to help him up, I slipped too, and then we were just lying in a pile together in the snow, laughing, tears streaming down our faces. I made it upright finally, and I reached out to pull him up, and he took my hand but resisted when I tugged his, and then he said, 'As long as I'm down here . . .' and he was on his knees and I was standing there, and he said, 'I think you better marry me.' And I said, 'Yes, I think I better.' And then he got up, and he walked me home. And then at my door he said, 'I am pretty sure I love you more than anyone has ever loved anything ever.' "

She is quiet then. Even I can see there is more to say, but she does not want to say it. She has sucked her lips inside her mouth like she is afraid of what will come out of them next and wants to keep the words in. Her eyes are wet and pink and still not looking at us but no tears fall out. Then she closes them and scrunches them up and then she opens them and makes them wide and then she blinks and shakes her head and shakes her head some more. And then, after a long time, she starts talking again like she is right in the middle of her sentence and did not interrupt it with a very long silence. "And he said, 'But wait until tomorrow. Tomorrow I'll love you even more.' " Then she swallows a lot and does a little cough and then she says, "And you know, they never shut the park. All these years, the park's still there. Hardly anyone goes anymore because you wouldn't go in the lake for anything, and going to the park with that lake just calling to you and you not being able to go in, that's just cruel. Plus, you know, all those memories. It's hard. But it used to be a really nice place."

Pastor Jeff reaches over and squeezes Mama's hand which squeezes his back.

No one has anything they can think of to say next.

I look at my sisters. Their faces show confused which is just how I feel too because Mama and Pastor Jeff answered the question. But it did not answer the question.

THREE

I'm doing English homework in the clinic waiting room. *King Lear.* Now *there's* a character with three daughters who has a rough time of it. Aside from that, though, he and Nora don't have much in common. Lear bought his own troubles, and that's a luxury Nora's never had. Maybe he's right that he's more sinned against than sinning, but Nora is not sinning at all. Nora is sinned against *instead* of sinning. Maybe if she'd had the chance, she might have liked to sin a little in her life, but her whole world has been taken up with being sinned against, so there hasn't been time. It's not that the well-connected, well-endowed, and powerful don't have troubles. It's that they're so much more likely to have earned them than the ones who are isolated, poor, and defenseless. And not the king of anything.

My own sins include telling my mother I wasn't well enough for school this morning when really I just wanted to come to work with her so that I could be here for Apple Templeton's appointment this afternoon. I don't know why it's important that our library is her lineal home, but it must be. Bourne is too small for it to be a co-incidence that her forebears lived in this town and then she married into the family that destroyed it. I don't know whether what she's looking for has anything to do with what we're looking for, but I do think if it were in their attic, in their plant, or in the files Omar let her look through, she'd have found it already. After all, unlike me, she knows what it is. All of which means, whatever it is, there's a chance it's in our house and has been there all along. And if only I knew what it was, we could find it.

Chris Wohl emerges from his appointment, pulls his jacket off the coatrack in the waiting room, and winks at me. "Miracle Mirabel, how's it hangin'?"

"I am good, thank you," my Voice says mechanically. "How are you?"

He stops like I've unplugged him. "I'm not so great right now, actually."

"No," says my Voice, and I hope he knows I don't mean "No, don't talk to me" or "No, I don't believe you" but "No" like "Oh no."

"The usual." He gestures over his shoulder. "I was just telling your mom. Leandra's cancer is back. Soon there won't be anywhere left for it to spread. I know it's my job to cheer her up, but who's going to cheer me up? There are drugs that help, but only she's allowed to use them. It blows."

"No," my Voice says again.

"But at least I can say so whereas you . . ." He waves at me, my chair, my Voice. Chris has no filter. Nora says it's part of his recovery. You stop doing drugs, you also stop lying, even the little ones that make conversation less awkward. Not that non-awkward conversation is an option available to me either. Or maybe when all your energy goes into staying sober and taking care of your wife, you have no reserves for masking your social anxieties.

"It is okay," my Voice whirs.

"It is?" I am surprised to see he has tears in his eyes. "Life is kicking my ass up and down Main Street. How are you okay? How do you do it, Mirabel?"

He waits patiently while I type. Then my Voice says, "I am Miracle."

"Miracle Mirabel." He grins through tears. "Yes, you are."

He squeezes my hand and leaves. This happens all the time, as if I'm an extension of my mother: patients leaving her sessions

467

only to confess to me in the waiting room, even the ones who aren't recovering addicts.

Nora comes and stands in her doorway.

"You are, you know."

I duck my head at her.

"You are a miracle. Some people's bodies make it easy for them to get through life." I am thinking of Apple and wondering if Nora is too. "And some people's bodies make it hard, but your body, your body makes it miraculous." She pauses so I can agree or reject this. I do neither. "I'm so proud of you."

Yes, I nod. *Yes I know,* not *Yes I agree.*

"You know what else? You're great at this."

At what? I flip my hand up.

"This. You'd be a great therapist."

A pause again. Again, I neither yes nor no.

"For one, you've had a lot of practice." She laughs. "You listen well. You're thoughtful, which is the most important part. You raise good questions."

Raise, she says, as if I cannot ask them.

"I don't mean the sight of you or the fact of you." Nora, of course, can read my mind. "I don't mean you inspire people with how brave you are or any bullshit like that. I mean you are mindful, and mindful is contagious. You have perspective, so the people around you seek some too. Your effort is apparent, which reminds people of its virtue and necessity. You could help people if you want to, Mirabel. And you should. Because you're good at it. And because people need help. And because it will help you too."

Part of the perspective she means is *If Mirabel can smile in the face of such soul-crushing constriction, my dead end doesn't look so bad.* But it is true I look for bright sides, not because I am an optimist by disposition, not because I don't know any better — I do — but because I am so slow. It takes me so long to do everything I do. And if you go slowly enough, every moment of the day becomes its own journey, either its own triumph, which you get to celebrate, or its own failure, which you get to move on from, by definition, in the very next moment. If you operate at speed, each word is not a victory, each swallowed piece of food or sip of water is not a conquest. If you operate at speed, you need bigger things to vanquish than a sentence or a muffin or a single line of *King Lear*. It's not that slow is not also frustrating — for me, for Nora, for my sisters — but frustrated is what people are supposed to make their sisters feel, what teenagers everywhere are always provoking in their mothers. It's not that slow isn't painful, maddening, restrictive. It is all of those things. Plus it's not like I have a choice. But slow is also one of the blessings of being me. *Mixed* blessings. Slow is one of the mixed blessings of being me.

As I've said — though not, of course, to Nora — there's no way I'm going to be a therapist, but as for what I'll be instead, I'm still narrowing it down. There's a lot you can do when you can use one arm, one hand, when you control your Voice and your thoughts, when you can study and read and type. When you are smart and curious. When you have learned forbearance and acceptance and generosity of spirit the hardest of ways. My skies may not be the limit, but they are less clouded than they seem.

Whereas Apple's are flat-out stormy. She's nothing but weepy today. I feel bad that she feels bad. I feel worse that because she feels bad, she's talking in circles and not about anything useful.

"Daddy worried these last years. Or, I don't know, maybe he was worried all along. But especially at the end. I want to do what he wanted me to do. I just don't know how."

"You're not a mind reader." Nor, at the moment, is Nora, who's not sure what Apple's talking about but says all the right things anyway. "It's just as hard for children to know how to make their parents happy as it is for parents to know how to make their children happy."

I exchange a secret smile with my mother. We do read each other's minds most of the time. We do share happiness and unhappiness like we're splitting a sandwich.

"He had a good heart, my dad." Apple nods, sniffles, nods. "Lots of people couldn't see it — wouldn't see it — but it's true. Maybe he didn't always do the right thing all the way, but he did the right thing some of the way, when he could, and the truth is that's more than most people do."

"It's hard." Nora might mean doing the right thing all the way. Or she might mean having a father who split these particular hairs. Or she might mean honoring that father now that he's gone.

But Apple isn't really listening anyway. "Dad was a man who saw the value of compromise. Doing things halfway gets a bad rap, but a lot of the time it's better than not doing them at all. When it's the most you can expect, you'll be happiest if you learn to settle for it."

I imagine Apple's version of settling looks different from ours. Still, this strikes me as an unusually Bourne-like sensibility.

We are closing up. Nora's filed her patient notes and progress reports, powered off her computer. Pastor Jeff left ten minutes ago, so she turns the lights off and the heat down. We are on the front stoop at the top of the ramp, and she's got her key in the lock when there's a sound.

It's a throat clearing. Then a voice. "Nora?"

She turns, surprised. Takes him in, more surprised still.

"Dr. Mitchell," the voice amends.

She turns back to the door and thunks the dead bolt into place. "I'm not a doctor."

"I know I'm not on the schedule, but I wonder . . . is there any chance you have time for one more today?"

She does not say she's been here nine hours already. She does not say she is due at the bar in twenty minutes. She does not say anything. So he keeps talking.

"I do realize it's a lot to ask, but I . . . well, I could really use someone to talk to for a few minutes."

Nathan Templeton looks at her, fully, right into her eyes. She looks right back. Their gazes are hard — not hard like cold, hard like challenging, thorough. I feel like Monday. I cannot read either of their expressions (too complicated) or emotions (too many), but neither of them is shying away from whatever this is.

"I'm just . . . well, to be honest, I'm having a rough time," he says. And when she still doesn't reply, "I can make an appointment for next week or next month or whenever you have an opening, of course. I just thought I'd take a shot that maybe you had time right now. It's a pretty small town after all." Big, conspiratorial grin. "This is one of the good things about small-town living, right? I figured how many people in a town this size could possibly need a therapy appointment on any given day?"

Her jaw clenches, and the back of her neck flushes. It's the certainty of his presumption that he'll still be here "next month or whenever." It's his blindness to just how much therapy the people of our little town need — and why. It's that she has a second job to get to, which he knows but which does not occur to him anyway. When she opens the office back up, turns the lights back on, it's to tell him no, not on the street where it might seem flippant or even punch-pulling but in a clinical setting where it will be clear who's in charge. She motions him onto the orange sofa, where he sits while she leans against the front of her desk and regards him.

"First of all, your wife is a patient of mine."

He shakes his head, unconcerned. "I understand that, but —"

"Second of all" — she puts up a hand to interrupt and make him listen — "there would be a significant conflict of interest in my working with you."

"I appreciate that" — Nathan nods this time — "but I have confidence in your professionalism." That flashed we-two-have-an-understanding smile again. "I like people who are good at what they do."

"And as you can see, my daughter is here." She's wavering. She indicates me with her chin but does not offer to make me sit in the waiting room. Probably she feels beggars of on-demand after-hours therapy appointments can't be choosers. Only afterward does it occur to me: maybe she wanted a witness.

Nathan Templeton does me the favor his wife did not of doubting whether he can discuss whatever he needs to with me sitting in the room. His eyes dart my way, and the wattage of his smile falters like when there's a storm and the lights flicker but you don't lose power altogether. He must feel just that bad though because the spark of his smile catches finally and flares. "Oh, Mirabel and I go way back. My secrets are safe with her." He winks at me then beams at my mother. "You've got a gaggle of whip-smart girls, Nora. You must be so proud. Raising kids is hard work — believe me, I know — and you haven't had the easiest time of it. Apple and I, we're two against one. You, you're one against three. I don't know how you do it."

And that's what does it. That's when she decides to lay rough timber over the morass of ruin between them and help — because he comes to her at last, parent to parent, because she is wooed by his praise of her daughters, because he's stopped short of admitting why she's had such a hard time of it, but he's come close, and that's something. And because he needs help and she's the only one here and that, after all, is her job.

She moves from standing against her desk with her arms folded to her chair, where she tucks her feet up and says, soft but clear, "So, Nathan Templeton. How can I help you?"

"Well, Nora, I'll tell you." But then he doesn't. He's wearing a silky cream shirt with tiny just-pink stripes — even the buttons look fancy and perfect — but it's untucked from dark jeans, jeans nicer and more expensive-looking than anyone else's entire wardrobe around here, but jeans nonetheless. He's leaning forward on the sofa, toward Nora, his hands loosely clasped between his knees, his eyes on the floor. "It's all a bit of a strain at the moment," he finally manages, with a laugh that says this is pretty silly and not a big deal, but with eyes that admit he's here, isn't he? "I guess I'm not telling you anything you don't already know since you saw my lovely wife just a few hours ago."

She opens her mouth to explain that she can't reveal anything Apple has discussed in therapy, but he's got his hands up already. "I know, I know, I would never ask you to comment on anything you two chitchatted about together." Like they're teenagers at a sleepover or old friends who insist on ditching their husbands for a girls' night out once a month. "I know she blames me. I know you do too, for that matter." He smiles at her, half sadly. "It's hard to see, I realize, but I really am trying to help here. I have only the best interests of Bourne at heart."

Not hard to see, I think. Impossible.

Not help but hide.

476

Not best but self.

She would not say any of that, but he keeps right on without giving her a chance to respond anyway.

"I meant what I said in the bar, you know."

"About what?" As if she's at a bit of a loss, can't quite remember what he's referring to, hasn't given it another thought since.

"About the jobs. They'll pay well. They'll have good benefits. They'll be good jobs. Stimulating, safe, regular hours. That's what Bourne needs now. Hell, that's what everyone in the whole world needs now."

"Sounds wonderful," she says.

"It is, it is," he agrees.

"Why are you here, Nathan?" Gentle and not a question really. More like permission. It's okay to tell me. It's okay to say.

"And we're also supporting other families' businesses." He's spinning his wedding ring around and around on his finger. "We're the go-between, Nora. Facilitators. Helpers, if you will. We enable other families to run their businesses, innovators to be able to afford to follow their dreams, companies to produce right here in America instead of having to ship the manufacturing part of their production overseas. Honestly, we're just a small cog in the great wheel of local entrepreneurship, and I can't think of any part I'd be prouder to play."

He peeks up at her — involuntarily I'd imagine — to see if she's buying this.

"Plus, if we weren't here, it would be someone else, someone who doesn't care about you the way we do. Bourne feels like home to us, and we want what's best for everyone. You get someone else in here? They won't be so invested. They won't be so careful and caring. There's a lot of corruption out there, Nora, a lot of people with their hands in one another's cookie jars, a lot of CEOs who would ruin this town and everyone in it out of greed and sheer myopic disregard. We would — I would — never let that happen here."

Again, she does not add.

Instead she repeats, quietly, "Why are you here, Nathan?"

He doesn't say anything. He screws his eyes shut. He holds his head in his hands. Finally he looks up at her. "I have, you know, misgivings, Nora. I have misgivings."

He looks done, like that was the confession. I am barely breathing.

"What kind of misgivings?"

"Just." He waves around vaguely. "You know."

She waits.

But suddenly he stands, smooths his

expensive shirt and jeans. Runs a hand over his flushed face. "Thank you, Nora. That helped. It was kind of you to fit me in. I appreciate it. I know you've got places to be. I'll see you both" — he's fumbling in his back pocket but pauses to wink at me — "all around the town." He finds his wallet and extracts a pile of machine-new fifties, pulls two of them free, pauses again, pulls out two more, folds them in half and in half, clears his throat, and holds them out toward Nora awkwardly, his face ablaze now, flustered or maybe just sorry.

She does not move. Her office is so small, all he has to do to lay his fold of money on her unkempt desk is lean forward. He gives it a little pat.

Her eyes do not leave him. "Nothing you say here leaves this room, Nathan. Not under any circumstances."

He looks at the floor and nods, chastened as a toddler, then holds his hands out, helpless. Without the wallet to occupy them, they're shaking. The blood has drained from his face like a downspout, and I see what I've missed before. Fear. This man is terrified.

He tries to pace, finds there's nowhere to do so, and sits back down, resigned to it now, ready to get it over with. "I have a PhD

in chemistry. Bet you didn't know that."
He's going for breezy, but his voice is shaking as much as his hands. "Over my father's vehement protestations. He thought school was a waste of time. He said what did I need an advanced degree for since I was inheriting a job. If I insisted on going, he wanted me to get an MBA. But I didn't want advice, a company, or anything else from him. I didn't want anything to do with Belsum. I wanted to teach chemistry at a nice liberal arts college somewhere far away from my parents. That was the plan." He looks up at her. "I had a plan."

"You were a kid," Nora says, pointedly but not unkindly. "Kids have plans. Almost no one does what they thought they would when they were twenty."

"*I* would have." He *sounds* like a kid, a petulant one, sulky he didn't get his way but smart enough to be embarrassed about it.

"Except for what?"

"Well, for one thing, I started dating Apple. She didn't want to be married to an academic. She didn't want to be married to an academic's salary. Her family and mine go way back. When we got together, she assumed I'd be inheriting the business. I didn't know it at the time, but I'm sure that

480

was the appeal."

"Marriage often requires compromise and sacrifice," Nora allows, "and changes of plans."

"I agree." But he doesn't sound like he does.

"And for another thing?" she prompts.

"Pardon?"

"You said for one thing you met Apple. What's another thing?"

He says nothing but nods at the floor. She's asked the right question.

"For another thing . . ." he begins, and then stops. And then says, "It was me."

"What was you?"

He looks at her. Looks back to the floor. "I invented GL606."

He looks up at her again, expecting fury to subsume her professionalism, but she already knew this. Or maybe it's not that she knew it but that she doesn't care. It's Belsum. It's always been Belsum. It doesn't matter to Nora who did the actual legwork. But I'm starting to see what's coming.

"I didn't mean to. People always say that — I didn't mean to embezzle those funds, murder that snitch, cheat on that wife. But no one does those things accidentally. You know what people do do accidentally? Chemistry. So much of what you discover, you discover looking for something else. My research was environmental. Swear to God, I got into this to save the world. My dissertation work was on developing cheap, portable materials, like plastic, except they would biodegrade. Can you imagine? And GL606 is two of those things." He glances up to see if she can guess which two. She can. "I named it Gala 606. After Apple. Gala? Get it? And June sixth, the first night we kissed. God, I was young."

He stops like there's no more to the story, like the emotional trauma of inventing a life-thieving, limb-curdling, town-destroying chemical is the embarrassment of naming it like a middle schooler. If I could, I would leap across the room and shake him.

"But my father, well, his goals were different from mine. He got really excited. Belsum wasn't a chemical company at the time. We were Belsum Industrial. We made containers and container parts — bottle tops, rubber seals, things like that. But my father got how big GL606 could be before I even finished explaining it to him. He was . . . proud of me. Proud of. Impressed by. Thrilled with. Do you know what it feels like to please a man you've been disappointing your whole life? Do you know what it feels like to succeed like that in front of your father? Especially when your father is a man like mine?"

I catch Nora's eye. She has never *not* been proud of, impressed by, and thrilled with me, even when I am nothing special, even when I am nothing but. It occurs to me for the first time: there are some ways, some crucial, breathtaking, shattering ways, in which Nathan Templeton's lot is far unluckier than mine. I mean, there's money and mobility and living in the house on the hill, but which would you choose: parental love and support and pride, or a chemical company mired in public relations nightmares and a tenuous all-eggs-in reopening plan, the thwarting of which is currently being concocted by three tenacious teenagers?

"I can imagine that would be a very seductive feeling," Nora allows.

"So I started testing the 606."

"And?" Nora nods, giving him permission to continue, never mind what's coming. I catch her eye again and remind her to breathe. I remind myself to breathe. "What did the tests show?"

"Increased liver size in rabbits. Birth defects in rats. Tumors and cancers in dogs. DNA damage. The same thing that made it appealing was also the problem with it. It was resistant to degradation, meaning it held up to the manufacturing process, but it was also bio-resistant. It stays in the body, builds up over time, does not biodegrade or break down really ever. I told my father all this, but he didn't . . . It's not that he didn't care. It's just that it wasn't a deal breaker as far as he was concerned."

"But, I mean, it wasn't your or even his decision, right? There are procedures, regulations. Right?" She's trying to allay his feelings of guilt and culpability, which is what she should be doing, but there's an edge in her voice that's desperate, panicky almost. "You had to show the government or the EPA or the — I don't know — oversight bodies of some kind? You had to prove it's safe."

"You'd like to believe that, right? That's what we count on. You believing that. You think if a chemical might be unsafe, it's tested, and if the results are unfavorable, it's banned or at least regulated. But it's not true. Until last year, the EPA only had to test chemicals that had been proven to cause harm. *Already.* And the burden of that proof . . . Well, let's just say, most chemicals never get tested at all. There are tens of thousands of synthetic chemicals in use by companies a lot less scrupulous than we are, and nearly none of them have been tested for safety, never mind environmental impact. They're almost all entirely unregulated."

"But." Nora's mind skitters away from Nathan's crisis of conscience. "But, like, the FDA? I have a patient who was part of a clinical trial a few years ago that required more paperwork and monitoring than anything I've ever seen. And she was sick already."

"GL606 isn't a food, and it isn't a drug. You don't ingest it."

"You do if it gets in your water." Her voice is shedding the downy cloak it wears for therapy sessions.

"We didn't know it would. We thought it might, yes, but we didn't know it would, and we didn't know it would be harmful if it did. Mine were barely preliminary results. Conclusive ones would take years and a team of scientists and a budget well beyond what they give postdocs. Therefore I was being unnecessarily rigorous with the testing, overly stringent, obnoxiously dogged as usual, in my father's opinion. Meanwhile, his experts were pointing out that humans are bigger than lab animals with different biology and can handle significantly higher dosages."

"And that's all it takes?" Nora sounds not

angry but awed. "To make everyone ignore what you don't want them to see? To slip right through?"

"That, and Dad knew a guy. Bunch of guys. He always does. Strings were pulled. Officials looked the other way. Forms got signed. I fought him. I did. But not that much. Not enough. And then I thought, well, if it's happening anyway, better to be on the inside. Maybe from there, I could do some good. Maybe inside, I could help. So I came aboard."

"And how'd that go?" Her tone is less psycho-rhetorical than deep-fried sarcasm.

"That's the sick part." *That* is? "I'm better at running this company than he is. He's always on about how I don't have that cut-throat instinct. I'm not willing to do what it takes to get things done, make the hard calls, put it all on the line, first to the finish at all costs. That's true. But people don't like him. They don't trust him. Everyone likes me." He sounds ashamed, sorry about it. "People like me and believe me. They go above and beyond for me. They want to help me out. They trust me. I don't know who was more surprised, me or Dad, but it turns out, I'm good at this." He looks up, and his eyes meet hers again and hold, steady, unfaltering. "And then I couldn't leave because now, well, now I'm all that's standing between you and him."

"I'm not sure —" she begins, but he reads her mind.

"It could be so much worse."

"It's pretty bad already."

"I'm invested in you," Nathan says. "All of you. I feel responsible for you. What happened wasn't my fault exactly, but there would have been no 606 without me. I owe you. I have to make it up to you."

She blinks. "You can't."

But he shakes his head, won't hear her. "It'll be different this time, Nora. We fixed it. The 606. We had this incredible team of researchers and scientists. We had the budget and the manpower this time. And the years. The test results are astonishing. It's better now. It'll be different this time. I swear."

"So you're here for a do-over."

"Not a do-over. A do-better. All the good things we promised before. None of the bad ones. My dad thinks I'm stalling. Dragging my feet. 'Pussyfooting around like the pussy I am.' " He nods an apology in my direction and makes quotation marks with his fingers to show me such language is beneath him and it's only his father who would use it. But it's not his language that offends me.

"I keep telling him it's easier said than done to get work started in this town. But honestly? It's true. I want to slow down and do this right this time."

"Are you sure?"

"Sure I want to do it right?"

"Sure it's fixed."

The faintest of doubts flickers over his face like a hair got caught in his eyelashes for a moment. "Sure as you ever get in this business. Or any business. Sure enough."

"Sure enough for whom?" Nora asks.

But he answers a different question. In fairness, it's the pertinent one. "He's my father, Nora."

"So you care about us, just not as much as you care about your father."

Nathan shrugs but holds her gaze. "He's family."

"There are more important things than family." She turns her head away from me when she says it, as if I won't hear if I can't see. "And there are other families besides yours."

He smiles sadly and opens his hands, like what can he do. "It's my legacy."

I don't know if he means GL606 and what it wrought are his legacy, or the need they engendered for him to risk everything by trying to fix it. But it doesn't matter.

Because I'm starting to realize: so far, we've been doing everything wrong.

ONE

I am learning magic.

I am learning everything.

I have stopped going to tutoring altogether. Mrs. Radcliffe gave me shit about it. Petra gave me shit about it. Even the Kyles gave me shit about it. I could tell them it wasn't helping anyone anyway. I could tell them they should hire someone with training and a degree in teaching kids with poisoned blood instead of foisting it off on Track A as if the only skills required are average intelligence and showing up. I could tell them I don't owe them anything since drawing the long straw was just as likely as drawing a shorter one, and I didn't get to pick my straw any more than anyone else did. But among the things I don't owe them is an explanation. So I don't tell them anything.

Instead, I am learning magic. Making small objects disappear and reappear, picking your card, reading your mind. River isn't supposed to show me how. I know the whole magician's code thing sounds cheesy, but I get it too — it's not really magic, so if everyone knew how to do it, it wouldn't be cool anymore. Sometimes in order to preserve the enchantment, you have to know less.

In history, from across the room, he palms a quarter then motions for me to look in my shoe, and there it is. In calculus, he passes me a note folded like a rose. I unfold it, and instead of lying flat, it makes a heart. In the cafeteria, he guesses what Monday has in her lunch. (She is unimpressed, and in fairness, how many sandwiches besides egg salad and how many fruits besides bananas are yellow and easy to pack in a paper sack?)

After school, we hold hands and walk with lovely lazy slowness (if she weren't annoyed at me, Petra would say "perambulate") in the woods behind my house or around Bluebell Park. We hang out downtown and wander in and out of the few stores, feed each other bites of whatever's hot at the Do Not Shop. We sit on the steps of the church and just talk. You wouldn't think we would have anything in common, since he has been so many places and I have been so few, since his dad is rich and mine is dead, since what his family does for a living took living away from mine. But I might never run out of things to say to River. We sit and talk for three hours after school and then go home and call each other. We stay up late whispering into the phone, and I still have so much to tell him by first period that I have to write him a letter instead of taking notes in World History. It's not because he's new anymore since I'm getting used to him. It's because everything about him makes me feel bright — luminous — and there is nothing to do with that feeling but put it into words.

It's freezing in the mornings, chilly all afternoon, the sky clouding up right after lunch or staying gray all day, fall racing toward its end. It's not like there's much of anywhere for us to be together inside, though. We can't hang out at his house where his angry, brooding mother is, or at mine with Monday and all her books and anxieties and yellow things. We can't go to the coffee shop or the drive-in or the mall because we live in Bourne instead of on TV. So we bundle up and stick to our outdoor haunts. It's a good excuse to hold hands, to stay close.

The steps of the church are cold through my jeans the day he is teaching me the disappearing-key trick. We are sitting there, freezing, giggling, wriggling the key free from our sleeves, when Pastor Jeff trudges up the wheelchair ramp pushing Pooh. I haven't seen her in ages. Guilt grabs me by the ears and shakes my face. I stand to go over and give her a hug.

"Don't you dare," she says, and my heart drops.

"Oh Pooh —" I start but she interrupts.

"Don't you apologize to me, Mab Mitchell." Then her voice dips to a too-loud whisper. "This is what we trained for!"

"It is?"

"A secret boyfriend. An affair that just might kill your poor mother. Heavy petting and who knows what-all else." I blush so hard it hurts. "So don't you feel bad about not coming to read to a blind old lady. I can read to myself, thank you very much."

While I am thinking about whether I can play this off to River later as the ramblings of what Petra would call senescence, it gets worse. "Still, I need to hear all the details. Obviously. I think you'll agree I've earned them. Come for bulgogi and hamburgers soon as you can, and plan to tell me absolutely everything. I miss you. But don't hurry. I'll wait. I'm very patient."

I nod mutely, but she's not done.

"And Mab, honey? Try not to sin actually

493

at the church. It's bad for your karma."

Pastor Jeff laughs. "I should do more with karma. That's a good angle." And they continue inside. We hear her say to him, "Romeo and Juliet, those two. I'm so happy for her!"

To cover my embarrassment, I take the key back from River and try the trick again, but my palms are sweaty and I have the same problem he did the first time he tried to do it for me. The key slips from my palm, up my sleeve, and when I try to wiggle it out, it goes the wrong way, down my shirt and into my jeans. Since I'm not going to take them off in front of him, I excuse myself, slip inside, use Pastor Jeff's facilities — I think of Pooh's advice not to sin at the church, but what can I do? — and bring the key back out to River.

"Speaking of taking your pants off," he says, "I have a great idea."

Which is how I find out there is something to do with that bright feeling besides put it into words. The place we can be alone, the place that isn't my house and isn't his house and isn't the church steps or the park or the school, the only place really, is the plant. And after all, we have the key. I just retrieved it from my underwear.

Same as last time, Hobart is there and no

one else. He's thrilled we've come and wants to chat — about the weather, about the holidays coming up, about the enormous dog Donna Anvers bought last week to help guard the nursery. "Is she crazy? No one wants anything she's got in there anyway," says Hobart, which is a fair point though I wonder whether he's just miffed that a dog got the job over him, a professional security guard. But we're anxious to be inside, so we say goodbye and hustle in and pull the door shut against the chill behind us. Inside is just like last time: sleeping. I smell nothing — no chemicals, no people — and all around us is quiet, deep, no machines running, no one there to talk, but everything building, waiting, nearly ready to go.

We stop on the threshold of the only room that looks lived in, which must be his father's office. There are papers on the desk, a computer, phone, and printer, and against one wall, a long, soft-looking blue sofa.

"What if your dad comes in?" I say.

"He won't. He's hardly ever here. He says his work is at the grocery store, the bar, the Little League games."

"There are no Little League games," I tell him.

"No, but you know what I mean," he says, and when I don't look like I do, he makes his voice deep like his father's. " 'You can't spread goodwill behind a desk, son. The most important work is always fieldwork.' " His voice returns to normal. "So you don't have to be nervous."

I am anyway. But that's not why. He unlocks the office door, then stops and turns toward me.

"I was just kidding about taking off your pants, you know."

"You were?"

"Not kidding exactly," he hedges. "Trust me, I meant it when I said you taking your pants off gave me an idea. This idea."

This is very honest.

"But I did not mean to suggest that what happened next would necessarily have to involve you taking them off again. Though you could. You know. If you wanted."

I consider this. "Not by myself," I say finally.

"No, no," he agrees. "It would be a real shame to be the only one without pants."

"Not first," I add in a whisper because if we're going to keep talking about what we're talking about, I don't want to do it out loud.

"Maybe together?" he suggests.

And that seems okay, and he reaches over and opens the door and takes me by the hand and leads me in and closes it behind us. And then, while we're still fully dressed, he kisses me, standing there, first a little, then a lot. And then he leads me over to the blue sofa, and first we're sitting on it and then I'm lying down on it and he's lying over me, still with our pants on, stopping every once in a while to make sure it's all still okay. It is. More than okay. Dizzying. When I said before falling was nothing like flying? I was so wrong.

And then he says, "Ready?"

And I wonder, for what? For taking my pants off? For what comes after that? Or for what comes after that? And since there's no way to know what that is, how can I possibly know if I'm ready for it? But that's Monday-logic, so I swallow it and breathe. "Yes, I'm ready. Yes I am. Are you?"

And we've been kind of laughing about everything, but now he stops and looks in my eyes and holds my hand against his chest and just nods. So I guess we're both ready. Except I feel like he should know something so I say, "I've never done this before."

"That's okay," he says.

"Have you?" I ask, and my heart beats hard while I wait for the answer, though that may or may not be why or what I'm waiting for.

497

"Are you kidding?" he says. "Loads of times. I take my pants off every night."

Later, when Monday and Mirabel ask what this is like, which they will, which they should, I will have to lie. They have a right to know, I know, but I can't tell them. There are words for it, but they don't describe what it feels like. It feels like full. It feels like singing but not out loud. It feels like opening, like everything is opening, like everything in the whole wide world is suddenly open to me. It feels like magic.

After, we are lying together on the blue sofa, and I say, "What will he do with this place?"

"Who?" He is tracing a line on my shoulder with his finger.

"Your father."

"When?"

"When we shut it back down. He's got all this new equipment. All these new supplies. Do you think he'll be mad?"

"My grandfather will be furious. My dad will just be taking it."

"Will your grandfather be mad at you?"

"Me, you, my father, my mother, your mother, everyone."

"I'm sorry," I say but that's not it, not exactly. I'm not sorry to be doing it. I'm

498

desperate to be doing it. I'm not sorry his grandfather will be mad. It's his turn. But I'm sorry River will have to bear it.

"It's okay." He pulls the back of me against the front of him. "I'm used to my family."

"You think they'll raze the whole place or convert it into something else or just leave it here to rot?"

"I don't know."

"I mean not right away, of course. I know it'll take a while. But when it's a done deal and they have to give up. When they realize it's dead."

And what River replies is "If."

But I'm not really listening.

I get home distracted, floating, a little bit sore in the best, most secret way.

I would like the house to myself.

I would settle for the bedroom to myself. For an hour to myself. For a little bit of time alone to consider what just happened and replay it without anyone watching me or demanding to know what I'm daydreaming about or making fun of the stupid smile on my face or pestering me with questions or wanting me to think about what they want to think about instead of what I want to think about.

But, as usual, what I would like has nothing to do with what I find when I get home.

"Mirabel found the gun," Monday reports before I even have my coat off.

Gun?

"Smoking gun," Mirabel's Voice corrects.

"At therapy," Monday continues. "Nathan Templeton invented GL606 in college for his environmental chemistry dissertation, and he tested it, and the tests showed it caused bad things, and he wrote them all down, and he told his father, but Belsum Industrial changed its name to Belsum Chemical and made GL606 anyway, and now we know they knew."

"Apple said all that in therapy?" This doesn't sound right.

"Lie," says Monday. "Nathan himself came to therapy because he feels worried about what the GL606 did and worried about what it will do next when they reopen the plant but not that worried because they fixed it."

I hear and I follow and I understand, but I don't believe it. Not quite. It's too big a thing.

"Was it a trick?" I ask.

Mirabel shakes her head no. "He was scared," her Voice says.

I nod. The room is spinning. "Mama must

500

be . . . Is she celebrating? Buying party supplies? Buying fireworks?" I'm happy for her, for all of us, but "happy" isn't really the right word. Even Petra wouldn't have a word for this I don't think. Or maybe the point is more like I have just had a big beginning, the first of firsts, which makes it feel unsettling rather than joyous to come home to such an unexpected, unnameable end.

"She will not use it," Monday says.

"Won't use what?" I don't get it. Maybe it's the spinning room. Maybe Monday is just maddening.

"The gun."

I look at Mirabel, wordlessly, and she looks back the same way. It's slower for Mirabel to explain, but it's often the more direct path to get where you're going.

"Doctor-patient confidentiality," her Voice intones like it's nothing, like the world hasn't just been offered and then snatched away.

Ahh.

And what I do is laugh. It's the wonder of the day and the magnitude of something like this coming on the heels of something like that. It's the cumulative hours and weeks and years we've spent thinking about this and this and nothing but this. It's running errands and just happening by the one restaurant in all the world you've been longing to try for sixteen years, and they have a table and your favorite food on special, and your dish comes out, and it smells like a dream, but they haven't brought you any silverware so you just have to sit there, smelling it, knowing how great it would taste if only you had a fork while eventually it gets cold and eventually the place closes and eventually your perfect meal molds and then rots and then dries and turns to dust and blows away. Except that doesn't make sense because you'd just use your hands, right? Even in that fancy, perfect restaurant, if you had to, if you didn't have another choice, you'd plop your face into your plate and eat up like a farm animal. Want of utensils wouldn't stop you. Nothing would stop you.

"Did Russell say it was completely inadmissible?" I wipe my eyes. "Maybe there's a loophole."

"She says," Mirabel's Voice begins, and I wait until I realize that's all there is. Emphasis is hard for the Voice. What Mirabel means is *She* says. It isn't Russell who won't use it. It's Mama.

"No. No way." Not appalled. Incredulous. Less than incredulous. There's not a part of me that believes it.

"Doctor-patient confidentiality," Mirabel's Voice repeats.

"Is that why he came?" I ask. "Somehow he knew we were close, and he thinks that since he told Mama in therapy she won't use it?"

"I don't think so," Mirabel's Voice says.

Monday is rubbing her bottom lip with her left thumb. Me too. It's a weird thing to turn out to be genetic, or maybe we've just been mirrors for so long. You'd think she wouldn't because it can't be sanitary. You'd think I wouldn't because she does. But maybe this is how it gets toward the end — everything stops making sense.

"Fine," I finally sputter. "*You'll* tell them."

"No," Mirabel's Voice says.

"What do you mean?"

"No," she explains.

"Why the hell not?"

"Doctor-patient confidentiality," she says a third time.

"You're not a doctor."

"Neither is Mama," Monday points out, predictably.

"You're not a medical professional," I amend, though I needn't, not for Mirabel's sake. "You aren't a therapist. He wasn't getting treatment from you. You were just there."

She types. "Nora told him nothing he said would leave the room."

"She was wrong!" I shout.

"No," her Voice says.

"Why the hell not?" I demand again, louder.

"Wrong," her Voice says.

"It's not wrong. What they did was wrong. What they're doing is wrong. The whole thing is wrong. They're corrupt and morally bankrupt and ethically void, and they play dirty, and they've shown very clearly for two decades that they don't give one shit about us. And you're going to die on the hill of a tiny stupid technicality because you'd be breaking a pinky swear?"

"Yes," says her Voice.

"Are you nine?"

"No."

"Are you joking?"

"No."

"Then why do you even go to therapy?" My arms are wide, my head flung back so I can rail at the heavens but really at my sister and not the usual one.

"Didn't know he was coming."

"But you knew Apple was. You've been eavesdropping on Apple's sessions for

504

weeks. It's not like it was ever much of a plan — that she would just happen to mention something to her therapist about some documents her husband and father-in-law were hiding — but if you weren't going to use it anyway, why bother?"

"Point," she says.

"How is that the point?"

But she shakes her head, annoyed, frustrated I'm not getting it. ". . . us," she adds, and now I have even less idea what she means.

She rolls her eyes and types, ". . . to what we need."

"So you've actually overheard the evidence we've been desperately searching for, which would end a battle your mother's been fighting since you were born and avert a crisis for an entire town, but you won't tell our lawyer about it because you overheard it in therapy. But if something Apple said, also in therapy, pointed us to evidence you could find yourself, that would be fine."

"Yes."

"You're not Nancy Fucking Drew."

"In addition to the Nancy Drews in our clothing drawers, there is a copy of *The Clue in the Old Album* on the fifth stair from the bottom on the right side as you are going up" — Monday sounds even more nervous than usual. She does not like yelling — "and a copy of *Nancy's Mysterious Letter* under the rubber bands in the junk drawer."

"Tell me that's not why," I say to Mirabel. Implore. Plead. Beg. Whatever. "You're having such a good time putting together clues and solving mysteries and being at the center of the action for once in your life you hate to see it end."

"No."

"If he just tells you, it's too easy."

"No."

"Nathan's all, 'We did it. We're guilty.' And you're like, 'No, I want to be the hero. I want to prove it with my own cunning.'"

"Feel bad for him," she types.

"Oh, so you're stupid!" I shout. Monday clamps her hands over her ears and is pressing herself into the wall. "Naive, manipulable, and stupid. He needs therapy because he feels so sad he poisoned us, especially since he's trying really hard to do it again, and *you* feel bad for *him*?"

"Yes."

"You got played." I can't even look at her. She shrugs the one shoulder she can shrug. Then she types, "Moral high ground."

"Bullshit," I say.

"Difference between us and them."

"They're smart, and we're dumb? They're solvent, and we're destitute? They're living in the real world, and we're dying here? In the unreal world? Abandoned, forsaken, and dumb as rocks?"

She's ignoring me, typing while I yell at her. Her Voice says, "If we behave like them, we are no better."

"Sure we are."

"No."

"Fine, then. I can live with that."

"No."

I grab fistfuls of my hair at both temples and pull hard. Mirabel and I usually understand each other without the Voice, and it is part of the genius of her that she says what she means in fewer words than you can. But right now her nos are more than succinct, more than stubborn even. They're petulant, dismissive, a refusal to defend herself, not because she knows she's right but because she doesn't care whether she is or not, doesn't care what I think, has already made up her mind and will not be moved. Which is not how it works between us.

"Just because you can't talk doesn't mean you get to make decisions unilaterally."

"Big word," her Voice mocks. She's had that one saved since Petra and I started SAT prep, but it's been a while since she used it.

"Just because you can't talk doesn't mean I don't get a say."

"Yes." Mirabel has the luxury of her Voice speaking one thing and her face doing something else. Can you stick out your tongue and talk at the same time?

"I won't just acquiesce. I won't just bow to your pronouncement. I'm not other people."

"Truth," Monday says from the corner. "You are you."

"No," says Mirabel.

"Just because you can't walk or move or speak or eat or do really anything for yourself doesn't mean you always get your way."

"Lie," Monday whispers from beneath her hands. Getting her way tends to be exactly what Mirabel's limits mean.

"I don't care what you think anyway," I say.

"Lie," Monday says again, but I keep right on going.

"*I'll* tell Russell."

"Hearsay. Inadmissible," Mirabel's Voice says immediately. She must have known I'd get here eventually and saved that in advance.

"Fine." I am talking through my teeth, but it's so they won't chatter. "Then I'll tell

River. He'll tell his father you told, and then it won't matter whether you respected his privacy and confidence — which you didn't, by the way. You told Monday. You told me. He won't believe you didn't tell everyone else in the world too. Mama will lose her job. He'll warn his lawyers. And this whole thing will be in vain."

"Stop!" Monday's hands do not move from her ears. "One, Three, stop, stop!" She sounds like a stuck video game.

"You would," Mirabel's Voice says.

"Truth," I say. "I would unless you —" but she interrupts because she wasn't done.

"You want the plant to reopen so your boyfriend will stay."

This takes my breath away. When it comes back I get all debate-clubby. "If I wanted the plant to reopen, why would I be begging you to tell Russell what Nathan said in therapy? If I didn't want you to tell, why would I be standing here screaming that you have to tell?"

"Deep down," her Voice says while her face does smug and angry and hurt and scared and superior all at once.

"You're the one who won't use what you know," I throw back at her. "Maybe you're the one who wants the plant to reopen deep down."

"Why?" her Voice asks. Then there's a pause while she adds, "He's not my boyfriend."

My mouth opens again, but nothing comes out. Monday looks terrified. And frankly, I'm with her because either Mirabel truly believes this appalling thing about me, or she's stooped to lies and slander. Either is low and mean and unlike her.

And untrue.

But not entirely untrue.

It's not true that I would sacrifice my mother, my sisters, my father's memory, our town, and our future just so River won't move back to Boston. I would not. I would never abandon our sister pact to make sure the plant does not reopen, even if it means losing River. If that's what it takes, I will let him go. I will have to.

Also, it's her — not me — holding the smoking gun in her hand but refusing to pull the trigger. Or pull it again, I guess, since it's already smoking. Or whatever the stupid metaphor is. Point is, she's the one who has the information that could stop Nathan, and she's the one refusing to use it to do so.

But it is true that for the first time since Belsum came back, for the first time in my life really, I'm starting to see other things that could happen and how they might not be so bad. It would be bad if the plant reopened, but it would not be so bad if the plant not reopening dragged out a few months or years until we graduated, during which River and his family had to stay to fill out paperwork or something. It would be bad if Belsum got rich off our suffering, but it would not be so bad if the possibility of Belsum getting rich reduced our suffering, either because of an influx into Bourne of promise and hope and a little cash or because I finally met a guy I like.

We still have to take them down, but they are becoming less evil by the moment — River, of course, but also his homesick mom and, apparently, his heartsick dad. We are wavering in our commitment — Mirabel because of technicalities or, as she would call them, principles, Monday because she can't take raised voices or muddled morality. And me? I guess because I'm young and in love. Which, of course, makes me think back to Romeo and Juliet. They were young and in love, and it got them killed, and not only them — a bunch of other people too. They were young and in love, and it made them abandon beliefs and loyalties and — yes — grudges that had been serving them their whole lives, their parents too, their entire families for generations.

But the other thing about Romeo and Juliet? Both only children. Not a sister between them. And you can tell because even when you're happy and don't want to hear it, sisters won't let you settle a blood feud or fake your own death. Sisters don't care how he's magic or how it feels when his hands touch your face and his eyes meet your eyes or how much he changes your life and opens your world and everything in it, especially you. They won't green-light your ill-founded, life-ruining plan just because you're in love. With sisters, at the very least, you're going to need a much better reason than that.

TWO

If their house is small enough, even two sisters who are not talking to each other still have to talk to each other even if one of them cannot talk. After Mab and Mirabel fight, Mirabel goes straight to our room, but she cannot slam the door behind her so I pretend she just went in there to do homework or read a library book. Mab *can* slam the door behind her, and the door she slams behind her is the front door because she is so mad she leaves the house, but four minutes later she comes back because it is cold outside and too dark to walk in the woods. She comes into the bedroom and slams that door too, but we are already in there so I do not think it works.

I am on my bed and Mirabel is on hers so the only places for Mab to sit are in Mirabel's wheelchair, which she would not do, or her own bed, but she lies on it and faces the wall and the postcards instead of sitting and facing us.

And she does not say sorry.

That is all the mad you can be in our house.

But Mab is also impatient so she only waits two minutes before she rolls over and says, "Fine. We'll compromise."

Mirabel is very patient so she does not say anything so neither do I. So Mab says, "Also I had sex."

Mirabel wants to be mad, but I think she also wants to hear about the sex. I do not want Mirabel to be mad, but I also do not want to hear about the sex. Or, to be more accurate, I want to not hear about the sex.

"Let us start with the compromise," I say.

Mab does a big sigh. "I get that Mama won't tell Russell what Nathan said in therapy," she says to Mirabel, "and I get you won't either. But he's no different from Apple, so what if we did your plan for her sessions where something she told would just point us in the right direction? What if we used what he said to find evidence ourselves?"

Mirabel makes a motion with her hand that means *Like what?*

"Like what if we found his dissertation?"

A dissertation is less than a book but more than homework, so it is not something you can buy online and have shipped to your house, and it is not something that will be on the shelf in any library you visit, not even any library you visit except one that is just leftovers in someone's home. But Mirabel says it is something that might be on the shelf in one library, and that is the library of the college where it was written, like how not everyone's picture frames hold a photograph of you but your mother's picture frames probably do.

"We cannot visit Nathan's college library because it is too far away," I object.

Mirabel types. "Interlibrary loan."

"We don't have a library on this end," Mab says.

"Lie!" I shout.

And that is how I find myself on the telephone dialing the library at Nathan's college.

"Library," says the person who answers, which I like because it is simple and direct. No one ever calls me, but if they did, that is how I would like to answer.

"Good evening," I say politely. "I am calling to ask one librarian to another if you will send me a copy of Nathan Templeton's dissertation via interlibrary loan."

"I'm sorry," says the other librarian, but she does not sound sorry. She sounds

515

confused. "Who is this?"

"This is Monday Mitchell," I say. "A librarian."

"You sound very young, Monday."

"I am sixteen."

"I see," the other librarian says. "And what's the name of your library?"

"My library does not have a name."

"Why doesn't your library have a name?"

"It is in my house."

"Ah," says the librarian. "I think I see your problem. A library is not a house."

"That is not my problem," I correct.

"Who is Nathan Templeton?" she asks.

"He was a student of yours, and he did homework we know about but cannot discuss without reading."

"I see." The other librarian laughs, but I do not know why because I have not made a joke, but I do hear typing. "Well Monday Mitchell, Librarian, I'm not finding any record of a dissertation or any other publication by a Nathan Templeton, and I'm afraid we don't keep student homework, nor are we able to send materials via interlibrary loan to someone's house."

"Even if their house is a library?" I ask.

"Even if. However, I like your style."

I look down. I am wearing a yellow cardigan over a yellow T-shirt over mustard-colored pants and socks. "You cannot see my style."

"I like your spirit, I mean," she says. "Being a sixteen-year-old librarian is impressive."

"Thank you," I say, both because it is polite and because her words make me feel grateful.

"Keep reading, Monday, and keep librarying."

" 'Librarying' is not a word," I say.

"Doesn't mean you can't do it, though, does it?" the other librarian asks, and it is surprising but that is an accurate thing to say.

After we hang up, Mab says, "Google?"

And I say, "It is an exaggeration to say we have googled Duke Templeton and Nathan Templeton and GL606 and Belsum Chemical a million times, but it is only a slight exaggeration."

Mirabel types. "Gala 606," her Voice says because we have never known the full name of GL606 before or even that GL606 was an abbreviation. I do not like abbreviations.

But when we google Gala 606, the only thing we find is pictures of people at fancy parties and pictures of apples.

"Is it not strange" — I am scrolling through all the pictures on the screen —

"that Apple's name is Apple, and when we search for Gala 606, we find pictures of apples? That is a good coincidence."

"No," says Mirabel's Voice.

Mab rolls her eyes, which is usually at me but which right now is at Mirabel who is answering in one word only instead of explaining what she actually means.

So Mirabel adds, "It's a pun."

"What is a pun, Three?"

Longer typing. "He named the chemical after her and the night he kissed her."

"Why?" I ask.

"Love," her Voice says, which does not answer the question.

Mab agrees because she says, "What kind of loser thinks the way to a girl's heart is puns?"

"Her name," says Mirabel's Voice.

"Huh?" Mab's face shows irritated again.

"Her maiden name," Mirabel types. "Apple Grove," Mirabel types. "Apple said in therapy" — many of Mirabel's sentences to us start that way recently so she has that part saved, but then we have to wait while she types the rest — "her grandmother liked puns."

"Weird," Mab says. But then she sits up. "Oh. Like Uncle Hickory."

"Who is Uncle Hickory?" I ask.

518

"River's great-uncle. Remember? That giant painting at their house? It's in his father's office so I thought he was his dad's uncle. But he must be Apple's uncle. Uncle Hickory. Hickory Grove. I get it."

"Ha ha," I say rather than actually laughing because I get it too but it is not funny. "Probably the painting is in Nathan's office, even though he is Apple's uncle, because that is where it fit best based on its size or color scheme, but on the —"

That is when I stop talking right in the middle of a sentence.

Because that is when I remember a folder in the box called Flora.

Mirabel was right. It was in the house all along. I found it and did not know I found it, not because I did not know what I was looking for, which is what I have been thinking, but because I did not know what it was. I had it right in my hands the day I found the Santa photograph, a folder labeled Elm/Hickory Grove, filed in the Flora box because whoever put it there thought what I thought, which is that a folder titled Elm/Hickory Grove must hold papers pertaining to trees. But Elm/Hickory Grove are not trees. Or, to be more accurate, they are not only trees. They are also brothers. They are

Apple's uncle, Hickory Grove, and Apple's father, Elmer Grove.

At first I think the most important lesson I learn is do not name your children puns because it confuses everyone in the world for all of time to come who is not your direct descendant. But when I refind the file, I realize that there are other more important lessons than that.

In the file are four letters. They are handwritten, so harder to read than typing, but with neat handwriting, so we can still read what they say, and on paper that is yellow (good) because it is old (less good). So I am very careful when I hold the pages and read them out loud.

Dear Hickory,

Ran into Duke Templeton at a party at the Gladstones' last night. He's an insufferable ass, worse with a few drinks in him, but now that the kids are together, he seems to consider us family and has zero compunction about cornering me at a social occasion to make unreasonable business propositions and demands. Nathan seems like a nice enough kid, but I fear Apple will outgrow him. In fact, I'm certain she'll outgrow him. It's just that I imagine she'll marry him first.

Every time the phone rings, I'm expecting it to be Nathan Templeton requesting my daughter's hand in marriage. I long for the days when asking the father's permission was something other than an old-fashioned gesture you cannot possibly say no to.

Therefore, Duke presumes not only that we'll sell him the land he wants but that we'll give him a great deal on it. He's eager to buy about twenty acres in Bourne for some kind of chemical plant they are hoping to have up and running by late next year. I said you were there at the moment with Mother and Dad, and I'd check with you and get back to him. I reiterated your offer of the land below the orchard and told him I considered the rate you quoted him quite generous. He explained though that their operations require a river — apparently for some pretty questionable effluvia so the less we know the better — so he's interested only in the land by the river. I said that though we do indeed own all the land by the river as well, there's less of it, and it is quite a bit more expensive, even for almost-family. Between you and me, I would much prefer to talk him into that vacant land instead because then we'll be able to sell both. We get the money for the orchard land, and then, when his plant opens and brings in lots of new workers, we'll be able to jack up the price of the river properties. It's win-win. If you disagree with any of the rates I quoted, let me know soonest. Otherwise, I will proceed by holding firm and awaiting his reply.

Yours,
Elmer

"What is effluvia?" I say.

Mirabel taps at her tablet. "Run off." Her Voice seems to be giving me a command.

"Run off where?" I ask.

"Not run off," says Mab. "Runoff. Effluent. Shit that's leaked by a chemical plant into a river that then runs downstream and poisons the water and the soil and everyone who lives there."

"So Nathan's parents knew and Apple's parents knew and everyone's parents always knew?"

"Not everyone's," says Mab, and she means our parents. Our parents did not know.

That is all anyone says for a while because it is hard to think about how some people so far away so long ago said okay to a thing that would totally change or, to be more accurate, harm my life before my life had even started because some wanted to sell land and some wanted to sell chemicals. And maybe the reason it is hard to think about is it is mean and a sad statement about human nature, or maybe the reason it is hard to think about is because maybe those people poisoned us.

Here is what the rest of the letters say:

Dear Hickory,

Your solution to all this is a stroke of genius. I know it's tiresome being there, but I wonder if you would have come up with it from Boston. If it took actually walking the land to think of this, it was worth it. That's easy for me to say from here, but I'm grateful, and you'll be home soon enough, sooner now that we're sure to make progress.

Harvey is on the Cape for a month, but another of the partners and two of his associates all assure me that your idea falls under the category of infrastructure and therefore, in this case, is the purview of the local government, not the landowners. So you have to get the mayor and town council on board, but once you do, they, not we, will incur the expense of both construction and maintenance going forward. Harvey's partner had an engineer who sometimes does work for him take a look. That guy told us that the diversion of the river to the orchard will create a greenbelt where the river is currently and a small lake just upstream. So Harvey's partner thinks the way to sell the mayor and town council on this is by pointing out there will be a greenbelt, a lake, and a pretty new park. You'd know better than I, but last I was there, Mother was telling me that the mayor's finally retiring later this year. Perhaps he'll be eager to leave a legacy in the form of a beautified town and be unconcerned about the price tag as it will soon no longer be his problem.

Will keep you posted.

Elm

Dear Hick,

Thrilled to hear the mayor and town council have agreed to finance construction. Smart of you not to even mention the Templetons or their plans for a chemical plant. Why muddy the waters, so to speak? That battle will belong to whoever wins the race for the next mayor anyway. It's not this guy's problem, and it's not ours either.

I invited Duke Templeton for lunch at the club yesterday. Because the orchard land will now have a river running through it, I significantly raised the asking price. When he balked, I cited increased expenses owing to having to build such substantial infrastructure. Who exactly is paying for what is not a detail he will have or could even reasonably expect to have access to. And regardless, the land is now quite a bit more valuable, so of course the price has gone up. It took some doing, but we settled, at last, on quite favorable terms.

I have to admit to being secretly pleased that the outgoing mayor put a caveat on all this. I like a worthy adversary, negotiators who do something other than roll over and die, and I happen to agree with him that an in-kind donation is appropriate in this case. They should get something out of it. His argument that a growing town ought to be able to grow their minds as well is quaint, so I say we agree to the stipulation that we build the town a real library as a bit of tit for tat. I understand your concern over the cost, but they're right that lending moldy old books and dated reading material out of their church basement is pitiable. I have a solution which, while maybe not as heaven-sent as yours, will, I think, make you quite happy. What if we converted Mother and Dad's house? I know Mother likes it there, but how much more small-town living can Dad possibly take? And now that there's a wedding to plan, Mother will want to be here to help Apple pick china patterns or bridesmaids' dresses or whatever else needs butting into. The house is enormous so we can bequeath it for use as a library, and the only real expenses will be shelving and some new books. And then you can all leave poor little Bourne for more civilized climes. As I keep saying: win-win.

Yours etc.

Elm

Dear Hickory,

It's done. The moment Bourne Town Council signed the paperwork and broke ground, our land deal went through with the Templetons for more than we dared hope. What happens next is Duke Templeton's business to negotiate with Bourne and whoever they elect as mayor, not ours. I will be thrilled to wash my hands of this and have all of you out of there.

I don't know if she mentioned it to you, but as a parting gift, Mother's designing a stained-glass mural to re-place their living room picture window in the hopes this will make the old place seem less like a cast-off house and more like a library. I see why she likes it there — it's a pretty little town — but I've never had a good feeling about their prospects. We did well to buy up so much land so inexpensively and sell on the upswing. But I fear it will not last. There is something about that place that makes me think there is more standing between them and good fortune than a lake and a park and a library. Perhaps the plant will bring an influx of new jobs, but between you and me, I don't trust the Templetons and will be glad to have you all living somewhere where your well-being is not dependent on their integrity.

No one on the Templetons' side has thought to ask for the deed or anything else, and why would they? The sale is contingent only on the river running through the land they've bought, and we have assured them it will do so. They don't care how, and even if they did, they wouldn't ask in case it's not been on the level. They certainly don't want to take responsibility for any more than they have to, so I doubt they'll think to ask for a very long time. What Bourne does next regarding the Templetons is their own decision to make, and we are lucky that we will all be somewhere else when they do so.

Your loving brother,

Elmer

I finish reading.

No one says anything.

Then Mab says, "Oh."

Then she gets up and rummages around on her desk until she locates the emails River gave her.

First her face gets very white and then it gets very red. First her face gets very serious and then it smiles, but it is not a smile that means happy. It is a smile that means crazy. "I don't believe it." She laughs. It would be more accurate to say she cackles. "It's a typo."

"What typo?" People should proofread. It is a critical step because it ensures you have conveyed your intended meaning, and meaning is important. Otherwise, why would you bother to write it down?

"They're not worried we'll find the *damn* paperwork." Mab's face shows happy, surprised, and angry all at once which should not be possible but is. "They're worried we'll find the *dam* paperwork."

I think she has forgotten all about the sex. So that is one good thing.

THREE

Usually Nora goes into another room to call
Russell. Leaves us in the kitchen and goes
into the living room. Leaves us in the living
room and goes up to hers. It's a small
house, so it's more the illusion of privacy
than the fact of it, but even the illusion of
something precious can also be precious.

Today, though, she puts the laptop right
on the coffee table with us gathered around,
prays to the wifi gods for a strong enough
connection, and lets Monday read Russell
the letters she found. We are expecting tight,
tentative optimism, but it's been a long time
since we've seen Russell or he's seen all of
us.

"Amazing!" he enthuses when Monday
finishes reading.

"Really?" Nora breathes.

"Look at you girls!" He is grinning and
shaking his head. "You're all grown up!"

We forget that Russell knew us before we

530

knew ourselves, back when we were brand-new. We forget that Russell began fighting this battle long before we did. We forget that Russell has loved not just our mother, however complicatedly, but the three of us as well for a very long time.

Last night, we looked — now that we finally knew what we were looking for — through Monday's boxes in case the town deed to the dam was also hiding, misfiled, in the house all along.

"It could be like in a horror movie where the girl locks herself inside so she will be safe," Monday said, "but the zombie or madman or monster or alien or deranged ex-boyfriend is already in there."

"He's only already in there if the girl is stupid," Mab said, dismissing her, "or slutty."

"You had sex," Monday said, "so let us look through all the boxes again."

Monday read over a great many pieces of paper herself, and I read over the great many pieces of paper she piled on my tray, and Mab lay on her bed with her legs up the wall and said things like "It's so amazing. It's beyond words. I really can't tell you what sex is like."

And Monday responded things like "Lie.

That is all you have been doing since you had it."

And Mab said, "Would you just concentrate on what you're doing?"

And Monday said, "Why cannot you help us?"

And Mab said, "You're the one in charge of pointless pieces of paper."

And Monday said, "On television, sex makes people happy, but you are still annoyed and annoying."

And I tried to remind myself that if I killed them both I would never be able to use the toilet again when my mother was not home.

Looking through all those papers was fruitless maybe, but not pointless. It was distracting. And I needed a distraction. It's not like River and Mab having sex was a surprise, but that doesn't make it any less of a betrayal — not by her and not of me, but a betrayal nonetheless. It's not that I'm jealous — at least not exactly — more like I don't want River to have sex with anyone. Not in an if-I-can't-have-him-nobody-can way. In that I want him to be beyond — above maybe — his body's baser limitations. I transcend mine every hour of every day. Is it too much to ask him to do the same for one afternoon with my sister?

Because I was trying to ignore Mab talking about River, because I was trying to ignore Monday talking about Mab, I was concentrating hard on the documents before us and can say this with confidence: Monday's boxes do not contain the deed to the dam or anything relating to it or the land sale.

In their stead, Nora reads Russell the emails River got off his father's phone in which, it is finally clear, on November 22, Duke Templeton plans to start repair work on the dam. Our dam. It was brand-new when he built the plant, but two decades later it's as worse for wear as the rest of us. This is what Apple meant when she said Nathan could drown down here, the leaks and cracks she was worrying over in therapy. You can actually see them on the wall of the dam. Mab remembers brown curls of water wending their uneven way down the side from when she and River sat along its top and discussed leaping off the one in Switzerland. And those are only the cracks you can see. There must be at least as many on the lake side, but no reputable contractor would begin underwater work around here December through February. That's why Duke was in such a hurry. Without a sufficiently functional dam there is no river there, and without the river there is no chemical plant.

The papers Duke was hoping stayed hidden and the papers Apple was desperate to find may have pointed the same place, but they are not the same papers. Neither wanted anyone to know about the dam but for different reasons. She wanted to destroy the letters that showed her father knew Belsum's plan hinged on dumping chemical waste, knew the diverted river would be polluted and ruined, but sold them the land anyway, addressing the problem only by donating a house and taking his riches and moving away.

Apple knew her father's actions were good profit-strategy but bad human-being, bad citizen-being, a bad legacy. What she didn't know was that they were the missing link in the lawsuit, the elusive, irrefutable, incontestable proof Nora's been after for our entire lifetimes.

What Russell says when Nora's done laying all this out is "You're gorgeous." He is shaking his head in awe. "All four of you. Just gorgeous."

"Russell. Focus. Are you listening? This is what we've been waiting for all these years. Proof Belsum knew before beginning operations that there was harmful effluent they needed to hide. In our river!" She discloses not a single word of Apple's therapy sessions. She does not so much as hint at Nathan's PhD or the reason for Belsum's shift from container parts to chemicals or the question of GL606's provenance. She does, though, report Omar's story about Apple's frantic search through the town filing cabinets, which, after all, is not a doctor-patient confidentiality breach, only hearsay.

"Just gorgeous," Russell says again.

Nora blushes with exasperated pleasure, and also, of course, she is used to his cautious pessimism in the face of her surely-this-time enthusiasms. She hugs Mab with one arm, squeezes my foot with her other hand, bends her head toward Monday who gives Nora a small smile of thanks for not touching her.

"My girls," she says.

Maybe she senses his sense that it's too late. Maybe it's all these revelations, finding everything she's been searching for for so long and finding also that it doesn't mean what she thought it would. Maybe it's that the question Mab and I wrestled was never a question for her. I can see Mab grinding her teeth and know she's wondering what I'm wondering. If we told him about Nathan's tests would that be enough? Or would it not matter because we could never prove he shared them with his father, or that his father, without a PhD in chemistry himself, knew what they meant? But Nora was never going to use anything Nathan disclosed in therapy anyway. Maybe her sad smile is because of any of that, or maybe she's just tired, or maybe she finally sees what Russell's been trying to tell her for years now.

"It's not enough?" She's smiling with wet eyes.

"Probably not." He smiles back. "Especially not now that nearly everyone's dropped off the suit. Especially because this brings in other parties, the Groves, mostly deceased and with whom your beef is not. Especially not after so much time."

"I can get more emails," Mab says weakly. "I can look more places. There's more evidence out there." She looks at me. "I know it."

What we three feel is desperate. What Nora and Russell feel is more like goodbye. This is its own victory — maybe the most important one — but we're not ready.

"The problem is you have all the proof you need of their disregard and their scheming and their willingness to do you great harm. It's just not enough to take them down or make them stop. However — Hey!

Look who's here! It's Matthew Pumpkin! Come on over, Mr. Pumpkin."

Matthew in a pumpkin costume wanders on screen and also lights up to see us, his huge grin mooning larger. He throws his arms wide. "My friends!"

"Do you remember the Mitchells?" Russell prompts his son. "This is Mab, Monday, Mirabel, and Nora."

"Hello!" he calls cheerfully. "I'm a pumpkin for Halloween."

"It is November," says Monday.

"I'm a pumpkin for Thanksgiving." He waves vine-laced arms at us, shimmies his pillowed orange middle like he's hula-hooping.

"You're such a big boy, Matthew." Nora is smiling the same smile Russell gave us. "I'm so proud of you."

"Why?" He's delighted but puzzled.

"Because look what a good job you've done growing up."

She's teary still but grinning now, Russell too, surrounded by four impatient, awkward, embarrassed kids, looking across too many miles and too many years into each other's eyes like they are in the same room, which they will never be again.

"However what?" says Monday.

No one has any idea what she's talking about.

"You said we do not have enough to take them down or make them stop however."

"However what?" says Russell.

"That is what I am asking you!" Monday shouts.

"No idea. Here's a thought, though." Russell's face changes. "You won't get any money, and I can't guarantee Duke Templeton won't come back, but if all you want to do is stop the plant from reopening, you don't need to win a lawsuit. Just take away his dam."

"How?" Nora looks perplexed. My sisters look perplexed. Even Russell looks like he's still puzzling this out. But all at once, I see it. I see everything.

"He doesn't own it," Russell says. "Bourne does. Who knows how he's planning to get this done — forged paperwork, shady contractors — doesn't matter. There wasn't any way for us to keep them from coming back because they own the land the plant's built on and those extended land-use rights, but we can stop any work he's doing on the dam simply on account of its not being his."

Because I was wrong. Duke wasn't in a rush to get dam repairs underway before winter. Duke was in a rush to get dam repairs underway before anyone thought to look for the paperwork and realized the most astonishing thing of all: that it's been in our power all along to say no. The land is theirs but the dam is ours, meaning all we have to do is nothing.

"How?" Nora asks again, though in a different tone this time, less incredulity, more wonder.

"We file an injunction to halt work on the dam. You believe that's scheduled for November twenty-second?"

"Yes," my Voice and my sisters all answer at once.

"I'll prepare it now so it's ready to file the minute construction starts."

"What do we do in the meantime?" Nora asks.

"Nothing. Keep quiet. Call Omar. Get the deed and whatever other pursuant paperwork."

"Just like that?" says Nora.

"Just like that," says Russell.

"It can't possibly be that easy," she breathes, "can it?"

"Of course not," Russell says cheerfully. "They'll appeal the injunction. They'll countersue. They'll go to some judge who owes them a favor and suspend the suspension. But all of that takes time, and we'll have a head start."

"And then what?" Nora says.

"And then we'll see," Russell promises.

"Trick or treat!" Matthew screams.

"It is November twelfth!" Monday shrieks.

"Bye, Matthew." Nora gives a little wave.

"Bye, girls." Russell holds his hands to his heart.

"Bye, Mab, Monday, Mirabel, and Nora," Matthew sings.

"Bye, Russell," Nora whispers.

"Bye, Nora," he says and reaches forward to disconnect.

In all the years, it is the first time I have ever heard them say goodbye.

She calls Omar.

"Apple Templeton was both right and wrong," she says without preamble. "It's true you don't have what she was looking for. But the answer is in your files."

A pause while she listens then announces triumphantly, "The dam is leaking."

Another pause.

"I'm sure a few small leaks *are* nothing to be concerned about if your goal is just to maintain a nice park and a pretty lake no one would be caught dead swimming in anyway. But if your intention were, say, to reopen a disgraced chemical plant and dump poison into the nearby river, it's apparently in desperate need of repair."

This time her face opens into its widest smile as she listens.

"Good question. The person who gives the go-ahead for repairs to a dam is the person who owns the dam."

Pause.

"Also a good question. The person who owns the dam is you. Us. Bourne."

Forty-five minutes later, he's at our front door.

He is wearing a tuxedo jacket and shirt and bow tie over jeans and sneakers.

He is holding flowers.

And a tiny velvet box. A ring box.

We are sitting around the kitchen table when he knocks, and she is laughing before she's even got the door open.

"Omar Radison. Why on earth do you own half a tuxedo?"

"Work-study job at college. Catering and Events."

"I'm impressed it still fits."

"Nothing ever changes around here" — he pats his belly — "except my waistline, of course. The pants went long ago."

She laughs, touches the top of her own pants absently. "And where'd you get

541

these?" She takes the flowers — yellow mums in a pot — with reverence. They are blooming things, after all.

"Donna Anvers grew these herself. A good sign, no?"

"The best." Her other hand cups her flushed cheek like he's told her they've struck oil underneath the Do Not Shop.

"And you were right, Nora."

"About what?"

"Everything, probably. You've always been right. I've known it . . . Honestly, I guess I've known it all along."

A pause then as she looks at him and he looks at her and neither looks away.

He clears his throat. "But among other things, you were right about the dam. The dam belongs to Bourne. The decision as to what to do with it is ours. If it's leaking, if Belsum needs it repaired to get up and running, we've got the chance to answer a question I only ever got one shot at answering. And that time I chose wrong."

"What question?" Nora's trembling.

He gets down on one knee, holds the tiny box up to her. "Say no."

She's half-laughing, half-crying again. "Omar Radison, you've made me the happiest woman in the world."

"Open the box," he says.

She does. Inside is a piece of paper, ori-
gamied to fit. She unfolds and unfolds and
unfolds until it lies flat. The deed to the
dam. Witnessed by Hickory Grove. Built
perhaps at his behest. But inarguably,
unambiguously, notarized right there in
black and white as belonging in its entirety
to Bourne Town Council and Municipality.

"You mashed it all up!" Monday shrieks.

"It's a copy." Omar's eyes do not leave my
mother's. "This one's only for dramatic effect."

She hugs it to her chest. "And sentimental
value."

"Sentiment is for the past." He says it very
softly because by now he is standing quite
near her.

"This is from the past," she points out.

"No" — his eyes are shining — "this is for
our future."

Her eyes are shining too, and when I
search them I see that she can't quite
believe it, this promise of a future. But I see
that she can't quite not believe it anymore
either, that her permanently reined-in
expectations are slipping their leads, taking
first tentative steps, then running wild.

ONE

The plan is simple. All we have to do is wait, which should be easy since we've been waiting all our lives, but you'd think I would have learned by now: nothing is easy.

It would be nice to march over to the library and wave the deed to the dam in Nathan Templeton's face, and he would know we knew and had him beat. Now that we know permission is ours to withhold, we'll never let him repair the dam. Maybe it'll leak, then crumble, and Bourne will flood and drown, but at least then we'll be cleansed and reborn and returned to our rightful state via the removal of the barrier that started it all. Realizing that's a sacrifice we're willing to make, a sacrifice Belsum has forced us to make, a sacrifice Belsum has made less of a sacrifice — there is not much Bourne left to save — Nathan Templeton will give up in defeat and slink off in shame, never to darken our doors again.

We can't do that, though. Because he can't know we know.

The reality is disappointingly less dramatic. First, we have to wait ten days. Then, on the twenty-second, when they try to start repairs, Russell will file the injunction to make them stop working on Bourne infrastructure without Bourne approval. Then we'll wait some more while Belsum scrambles to do whatever they're going to. Maybe a judge will finally be persuaded they're evil when we show how they were trying to keep our own dam a secret. Maybe a judge will finally be persuaded by the proof we have at last that the effluent was not an accident but something Belsum knew and took measures to hide going in. Or maybe March will prove too long a delay, and fighting our injunction will prove too tiresome, and Belsum Chemical will decide Bourne is more trouble than we're cheap and move on.

The waits — ten days till the twenty-second, then waiting to see what they'll do in response to the injunction, then waiting to see what happens after that — feel torturous, but actually, they're the best thing because the reality is once he knows the plant's not reopening, Nathan Templeton will take his family and go back to Boston.

So, hard as it is, all this waiting is really a blessing. The plant will not reopen, but no one will know it, so all the bad things that are going to happen when everyone does — there will be no new jobs after all, no influx of customers for new shops and restaurants, and, worse than any of that, River will leave and I'll never see him again — won't happen yet. As Elmer Grove would say: win-win.

The worst part of this plan though — the part it hinges on — is keeping it a secret. We cannot squander our head start. Russell's injunction has to be a surprise to Belsum, a shock even. We want them scrambling and wrong-footed and delayed and behind and outsmarted. No one knows we know about the dam, neither who owns it nor Belsum's secret plans to repair it before we realize we can say no, and we have to keep it that way for as long as possible. We can't tell anyone, not even River. Mirabel says especially. Especially not River.

"We don't keep secrets from each other," I say, and she laughs, I think unkindly. "Besides, he's on our side."

"He is sixteen," her Voice says. We are lying in the dark in bed waiting for sleep to come.

"So?"

"Young," her Voice says.

"We're sixteen," I remind her.

"Yes."

"He spied on his father, gave us those emails, got me into the plant. He's been helping us."

"So —"

"So he deserves to know what's going on." But she wasn't finished yet.

"— far."

"You think he'd betray us?"

"Don't know."

"You don't understand. He wouldn't do that to me. He l-likes me." I trip over the *l* because I was about to say "love." "We tell each other everything."

"*We* tell each other everything." Monday, from out of the darkness on the other side. I didn't even know she was awake. "And sometimes I do not like you."

"We're sisters. That's how it's supposed to be. It's different with boyfriends." Oh, what that word feels like coming out of my mouth. Even in the dark, I can see it rising to the ceiling, like a balloon, that buoyant but mostly that joyous, that celebratory.

"Don't tell him," Mirabel's Voice warns, back where we started.

So I hold my tongue, guard our secrets. I wait seven days.

And then I tell River anyway.

I tell him because of what I told Mirabel. He's on our side. He's been helping us, helping me. This is his victory too. I tell him because I do not want to keep it — or anything — from him. I trust him. I know he will be thrilled for us, like Russell, like Omar. I tell him because the weather is turning for good, and the cold is coming for real now. There will be snow. I want to drink hot cocoa with my boyfriend and hold his hand while we watch it fall.

So I tell him. I tell him not to tell anyone. I swear him to secrecy. He promises. He crosses his heart and hopes to die. He thanks me for trusting him. He pulls me to him and whispers into my hair that he would never betray me. And that might be the best feeling of all — trusting, having faith — better than the kissing, better than the sex, better than the magic.

Briefly.

TWO

It is November 21, so there is only one night left to wait, and we are eating dinner, and the doorbell rings, and Mama's face looks happy, and I can guess that is because Omar has come to visit twice since he brought over the deed to the dam, and that makes me feel squiggly because Mama hated Omar until very recently. And happy and hate are opposites. But when Mab opens the door, the person on the other side is not Omar. It is Nathan Templeton.

"You're eating," he says, which is accurate but not the point anymore. "I can come back later."

But I am alarmed he is here, and I cannot eat while I am worried about why, and I can make an assumption that that is true for Mama and Mab and Mirabel too so he might as well come in now. Mama opens a new bottle of water and pours him a glass of it. He thanks her, and he sits down, but he does not drink the water or say anything. Mama looks tired and afraid but patient. She will just wait to hear what he will say. I am afraid too, but I am not patient.

"Why are you here?" I ask.

"Monday," Mama warns with her warning voice.

But Nathan looks relieved I asked, probably because he wants to say why he is here but did not know how.

"Listen," he says, and then he does not say anything else, and then he says, "I know you know about the dam."

It feels in my stomach like I swallowed something very hot without waiting for it to cool first. I look at my sisters, and they look like they feel the same way. Mab's face is the color of a marshmallow. Mirabel's eyes look like they might try to exit her head.

"How do you know?" I ask because no one else does even though it can be assumed that everyone wants to.

"Doesn't matter." Nathan looks down at his water glass. Mab stands up and leaves the table, and even though I cannot see where she goes, I know it is into our bedroom because I hear our bedroom door slam. I look at Mirabel, but her stretched-out eyes are stretching toward Nathan. "I wanted to come here as a . . ." He trails off.

"Friend?" my mother asks. Her question is not, *Is that the word you were going to say before you stopped talking.* Her question is, *Do you think you are my friend.*

"Yeah, I guess." He laughs a little bit of a laugh. "I felt I owed you I suppose. You helped me, my family. You've put up with . . . Well, over the years, you've put up with a lot from us." He breathes in a big breath. "It's true my father didn't want anyone to realize the dam was yours rather than ours. And it's true he's not been taking the, uh, highest of roads. But first of all, the idea that this is going to stop him? There's no way." He holds his hands up and out like he will balance a pizza on each one. "So there'll be a slight delay. So he'll be angry and annoyed, and there'll be a lot more to finagle than he anticipated. Fine. But then he'll build his own dam. Or he'll get someone at the state level to override your rights. Or he'll pay someone enough money to ignore your injunction. He hasn't worked it out yet, but trust me, he will."

"And second?" Mama's voice sounds like she does not care about the answer, but her face shows that her voice is lying.

"Secondly, more importantly, as I think you know, I haven't always agreed with my father's approach. Personally, I was never in favor of hiding your rights to the dam or trying to sneak anything by the citizens of this town. Myself, I've had a different plan all along. A better plan."

He stops talking and looks at Mama, and I can guess he wants her to ask about his plan, but she does not, so he starts talking some more. "As you know, the fate of that dam is up to this town."

"As we *now* know." Mama's voice means correcting. "As we discovered ourselves, despite your best efforts."

"As you discovered" — Nathan bows his head and hinges the palms of his hands open from a prayer shape to a book shape — "what happens with that dam is up to this town. Without a dam, Belsum would have to shutter the plant and leave." I think he will look sad about this but he looks happy. "And the people of this town want Belsum to stay. We've done so much hiring, Nora. Everyone's on board. Everyone's excited."

"Not everyone." Mama means she is not excited.

But Nathan does not mind that she is not excited. "I got the final write-up of the R&D. That's why I came tonight. I thought you'd want to see." I think back to that day we met him in my library and how he looked so smooth. He still looks smooth but not as smooth because his hair looks like he has touched it with his hands a lot, and his pants look like regular pants instead of expensive smooth pants, and his shirt looks like a fancy shirt but a fancy shirt he slept in. He has his same smooth smile, but he does not look like he believes it anymore. "The QA numbers are high as they go. We commissioned the most rigorous testing we could find. I insisted on it. Harburon Analytical is the most exacting, state-of-the-art independent testing and chemical analysis company in the world. They're famous for shutting down all sorts of would-be products that passed every other set of testing they were subjected to with flying colors. And they gave us their highest rating. They were absolutely reservation-free."

He holds out to Mama a binder, and she takes it, but she does not look inside.

Nathan breathes another deep breath. "I know last time was terrible, Nora. I'm sorrier than you can know. But chemists far more experienced and talented and well funded than I was have been working on GL606 for two decades now. I was a student. These are world-class scientists. A team of them. They've overhauled the whole thing. It's safe. I've been over and over those

553

results myself." He points to the binder on her lap. "I give you my word."

"I will take that for what it's worth," Mama says.

Nathan nods like she asked him a yes-or-no question, which she did not. Then he says, "You don't have to. I'm going to Omar."

"For what?" Mama looks surprised but happy but mad. It is confusing.

"For the mayoral go-ahead. For official permission to repair the dam."

"He'll never give it," our surprised happy mad mother says.

"He will" — Nathan also looks like more than one feeling — "because that's what the people of his town want."

"Omar's on our side." Our mother crosses her arms over her chest.

"Omar's on Bourne's side," Nathan Templeton says.

"Me too," says Mama.

"Me too," says Nathan.

But this cannot be accurate. Nathan's side and Mama's side are opposites.

THREE

I go to the bar with Nora, mostly so I don't have to look at Mab, don't have to think about what happened to bring Nathan Templeton to our door, don't have to consider the hard-won, blown-glass-delicate, slight-as-corn-silk victory which has been squandered here and how and why. If she hadn't gotten up and left the table when she did, I would have had to, and it was good she couldn't raise her gaze from the floor because I could not have met my sister's eyes.

But the other reason I go is to take care of our mother, who is pretending unconvincingly not to be rattled by Nathan's visit, by Nathan's confidence, by Nathan's conviction that he's a better man than his father, when what he wants and what he'll do to get it have come straight down the bloodline.

It's a perfectly ordinary night at the bar.

Even though the cat's so far out of the bag as to render the very notion of bags immaterial, she doesn't tell the guys about the dam. She's sorry, of course she is, about their jobs and their plans. She wants to let them be hopeful a little while longer. She's not worried — she's certain as sunrise Omar will pick her over Nathan Templeton a thousand times in a thousand — but she's maybe a little bit worried. For their part, the guys are just happy to be back in her good graces. It's a quiet evening.

Toward closing, the door opens, and Nora's head bobs up and her eyes light, but it's not Omar. It's a face no one's ever seen in here before.

River.

At first only his head and shoulders come in. His legs and torso remain outside. But the cold air is earning him dirty looks — that's not the only reason maybe, but it's the one he can address — so he comes all the way in and lets the door close behind him.

But before it even meets the jamb, Nora's pointing back out. "You can't be in here."

He raises his hands. "I know. I'm sorry. I know. I just wanted to talk to her."

Me. He's pointing at me.

"No." Nora shakes her head. "No way.

You're not twenty-one. Get out of here."

If River were a hundred and eight, she still wouldn't let him in this bar. But the rest of it's not her decision. He turns, cowed and embarrassed, and walks back out the door. And I start after him.

"Mirabel!" Nora gasps. The *Get back here young lady!* she'd roar if she could is all over her face, but she can't say that to me. That's not how it works between us, but more importantly, she and I have fought so long and so hard to make it possible for me to flout my mother's wishes and storm away from her in a fit of pique to follow a boy she disapproves of. However much it looks like heartbreak, this is a moment of triumph. *Also* a moment of triumph. "No," she says, but it sounds more like *Please.*

I don't ignore her. I meet her eyes. And I tell them the truth of it with mine: *I have to. I have to go.*

A small sound escapes from deep inside her, but she can't utter the words she longs to any more than I can.

I press the wall switch to open the door and follow River out into the night.

Outside it's cold, dry and windless and star-scattered, but I am warm, deep in the bones warm, deep in my muscles even. He's come to find me. He's come to *me.*

The first thing he says is "Thank you, Mirabel."

I shiver and nod.

"Thank you for meeting me. Thank you for talking to me."

I start down the sidewalk, away from the bar. He follows.

"I know my dad came to your house. I'm sorry."

"For what?" my Voice asks, and he nods. Yes. That's the right question.

"I'm sorry I told him. I didn't mean to."

We don't really know each other very well, but even still, River can read the skepticism on my face. How does something like that happen accidentally?

"Yeah, okay. I guess I mean I didn't plan to. I know I promised not to tell, but deep down my father's a good guy. I knew he'd find out eventually, so I just thought I could, I don't know, spare everyone the suspense."

I close my eyes then open them to type, "We wanted the suspense."

"I know." He looks away from me to explain, "My parents were fighting all the time. My grandfather kept screaming at my dad about how no one can know this big, stupid secret I know they already know. I just . . ."

He trails off, so I don't get to hear exactly

558

how he was planning to finish that sentence, but I know the sentiment: *I just picked my father over your sister. I just put my feelings over your needs. I just chose what's easy right now instead of what's right and two decades in the making. I'm just sixteen, far from home, with sense enough to see I'm in over my head but not very much else. I'm just sixteen and have no idea what it means to love someone, and anyone who thinks I do is deluding herself.*

"I didn't know what to do." He looks up and meets my eyes again. "I'm sorry for everything, Mirabel."

He should not be sorry for everything. It's not all his fault. It's not all Mab's fault certainly. It's not all his father's fault or even all *his* father's fault. It's not all Omar's fault for believing them all those years ago or all the Groves' fault for selling them the land. It's not the barflies' fault for dropping the suit or Russell's for keeping his distance. It's not the river's fault for being so easily diverted or the dam's for holding so much back.

There are so many people who have sinned a little and a lot. There are so many people who deserve some of the blame. But that means there is never anyone whose responsibility it is to take responsibility.

There is no one who must make it right, no one who must make amends. There is so much, therefore, that stays wrong and unmended.

River should not be sorry for everything. But he should be sorry for some things.

"I don't know what's going to happen next," he says.

"Me neither," my Voice admits.

"I don't know what *can* happen next."

I nod and wait. Shiver and wait.

"I didn't betray her," he says. "Not really. You know it's not that simple."

I do not know that. But I know what he means.

There's a pause, and then he says, very quietly, "You're all I have here." He does not mean me. He means us. He means Mab. "I'm worried I ruined everything."

For whom? I wonder, but my Voice replies, "Wouldn't be the first time."

At Norma's door I find Omar taking deep breaths, psyching himself up to go in.

"Mirabel!" He looks surprised to see me — must wonder what I'm doing on this side of the door as much as I'm wondering what he is — but asks like it's the most everyday of pleasantries, "Headed in?"

I nod, and he taps the push plate to open

560

the door and follows me in.

Nora's head snaps up. Her face washes white with relief to see me, edged with confused gratitude to find me with Omar instead of with River.

She turns to him first. "Thanks for bringing her home." She gives him the smile they've been exchanging this week — tentative, possible — and tables for the moment the clamoring teeming swarms of questions.

"Anytime," he says.

And then me. She exercises restraint. "You okay?" She looks me all over.

My eyes assure her I'm fine.

"We closed three and a half minutes ago." Her exactness makes her sound like her middle daughter, and she pretends she's admonishing Omar, the lone customer in the bar, but I know this is directed at me: *You were gone a long time.*

"Is it too late to get a soda?" Omar asks.

She pours it for him, and he stirs it with a swizzle stick. She starts cleaning up, glancing at him, glancing at me, holding her tongue, doing her job.

"Listen, Nora." She stops drying the glass in her hand and turns to him. Me too, I'm alarmed at once. It's his tone. His eyes too: sorry, bated. How can this night be about to get more strange? "Nathan Templeton

561

came to see me."

She exhales. *Already?* "Me too."

He nods. He knew this. "He showed me the test results. Did he show you?"

"Well he *gave* them to me." A laugh small and dry as an almond. "He told me what they said," she adds. "Not that I . . . you know."

Omar nods again. He does know. He takes a breath. "He's not his father, Nora."

She looks away from him. "I know."

"What he says those tests prove may or may not be true," he admits, and her eyes spark with gratitude, but he keeps talking and they dim again, "but everything else he says is. We do need the jobs. We do need the opportunities. We do need the growth." He pauses, then adds, "Reopening the plant is what lots of folks in this town need and want."

"Think they need," Nora amends. "Think they want."

"Nora, I read through his binder." There's an edge in his voice, a warning not that what's coming is bad, but that it's good, which is worse. "The test results are impressive. Reassuring. It seems like he's done his homework. And if the GL606 is fixed —"

"A big if," she interrupts.

"Yes. Exactly. A big if. But *if* it is, then the

reason to keep them out isn't safety any-more. It's spite."

"That's a plenty good reason." Nora's face is red. Blazing.

"For some people."

"Yes! Us!" she says, and then, when he doesn't say anything, "I can't believe it," her voice changed completely, her face too, like she's become a different person in these few sad seconds.

"What?"

"When he told me he was taking this to you, I was thrilled. Overjoyed. Because I knew — I *knew* — you'd never pick him over us. Over me. But it turns out —"

"I would never pick him over you," Omar interrupts. He won't let her say it, won't hear it.

"That's not what's happening here? That's not what you're telling me?"

"Nora. It's not."

He stops and she stops, and they look at each other while long moments pass. What-ever's going on between them these last weeks has broken her rage like a fever, but it's left her fragile, vulnerable. Without the anger toward him, all she has is fear, fear and unguarded hope and the likelihood of being hurt some more. She drops her head.

"I am not choosing him over you or over

Bourne," he says slowly. "Of course I'm not." A pause, then, "Among many other reasons, it's not my choice."

Her head snaps up. She was expecting him to take her side. Then, when it seemed like it would go the other way, she was expecting to be devastated for failing to expect that of course he was taking Belsum's side. Again. But she was not expecting this.

"I'm calling a vote," he says, sorry but sure.

It takes a moment for her brain to catch up. "You're kidding."

"No."

"Omar —"

"I have to."

"You do not."

"This isn't your decision, Nora."

"No, it's yours."

"It's not."

"Omar." She makes herself take a deep breath, lower her voice. "This is our chance. Our one chance. You said you chose wrong last time. This is how you — we — make it right."

"It wouldn't make it right, Nora. It can never be made right. But that is the choice I'd make if this were my decision." He pauses and holds her eyes, making sure she's heard him before he continues. "But

564

it's not. We need to decide —"

"Yes! Exactly!"

"Not we, you and me." He puts his hands over his heart. "We, all of us. Bourne's citizenry. We need to decide — we all need to decide — if this is a risk we're willing to take as a town in exchange for what Belsum is offering. If we believe them this time. If we think they've earned another chance. If we think they haven't earned another chance but we're going to grant them one anyway. I told Nathan I'd give him a couple weeks to make his case around here, put that R&D in layman's terms for people, and then we'll hold a vote. If the majority wants to give Belsum another go, we'll repair the dam. But if the vote goes the other way, we'll proceed with legal action immediately to force Belsum to desist on the grounds that the infrastructure is unsound."

"You don't owe him a vote or anything else." Her voice breaks and she lets it, allows herself to sound — to be — vulnerable before him, allows herself to ask him for this one thing.

"You're right, Nora." But he's shaking his head no. "We don't owe Belsum anything. But I owe the people in this town." He looks like his heart is breaking. "At least it will be fair this time. At least you'll get your say."

She nods and meets his eyes as hers fill. "It'll be a landslide," she says. "Right? Of course it will. It has to be."

"I agree." Does he? Or is he just saying that to comfort her? "I bet it's ten to one, a hundred to one, kicking them to the curb. We'll get the best of both worlds: everyone has their say *and* we get rid of Belsum."

She squeezes her eyes shut and wills his words to God's ears.

He puts his hands on the bar, palms up, and whispers, "I'm sorry."

Everyone is sorry tonight.

Slowly, she goes over and presses her hands on top of his, not holding but palm to palm, and whispers back, "I know," dazed by this latest twist of shared misfortune, which is, however, an improvement over the usual kind which she has to burden alone.

ONE

He doesn't answer his phone or return my texts, but maybe he's not getting them because his reception's so bad. I can't call his landline because anyone might pick up. So the only place to have this conversation is at school. And wc cannot have this conversation at school.

Or maybe it's that I don't really want to have this conversation.

There might be a perfectly reasonable, totally logical explanation, a really good and fair and legit reason why River betrayed me, betrayed all of us, double agented, pretended to be on our side, and then consorted with the enemy. Maybe he got tricked into telling, or his grandfather came into town and kicked him till he confessed, or they threatened to make him drink tap water or bribed him with something great even I couldn't expect him to refuse, like that box you put people in to saw them in

567

half. Maybe he was hypnotized.

But I don't ask him, not because these scenarios aren't possible, but because they aren't possible enough. Much more likely explanations include: *I kissed you, but I was faking. I said I cared about you, but I didn't really. I only pretended to be interested in you so you'd spill your family's secrets so mine could get richer. I can't believe you fell for it. I'd never be interested in someone as pathetic as you.*

So I make sure not to be alone anywhere he is. When the bell rings, I'm already packed, the first one up and out of the room, like he used to be when he was getting beat up. When he tries to catch my eye, I flick mine away from him at the last second. When I see him coming in the hallway, I pretend I forgot something and turn back the other way. When a note makes its way to me hand over hand in history, I refuse to take it.

"I shall extirpate this missive for you." Petra deposits it in the trash can with a flourish, so we know he sees. He looks miserable. But not as miserable as I must.

And plus there's the vote, which is all my fault. Or, to be more accurate, as Monday would insist, it's River's fault he told his father, and it's his father's fault Omar had to call a vote, but it's my fault for telling River in the first place, and if I hadn't, there wouldn't have to be a vote.

Which could go either way. On the one hand, no one in this town but Omar and Nathan ever had an opportunity to say yes or no to Belsum. Omar was lied to, and apparently Nathan can't say no to his father. Lots of us would very happily say no to Duke Templeton, but Duke Templeton never asked us. So maybe now that the question's finally being posed, enough of us will answer it the right way. Not all of us — not Mama's guys at the bar, not all the ex-employees who dropped off the lawsuit when they got the opportunity to be ex-ex-employees instead — but enough. Sure, some of us will choose jobs and another roll of the dice. But most of us — enough of us — will choose anger and comeuppance and what's fair and what's right and having learned our lesson the really, really hard way.

I say *us,* but actually it's them. We can't vote. We're not old enough. So even though we're the ones whose future's being voted on, we don't get a say, and that's too bad because we'd vote the right way for sure. I remember the Kyles explaining they had to kick River's ass because someone had to take up the cause when their fathers dropped it to take jobs. I remember Mirabel saying it's our turn now.

It is, but no one's asking.

Still, it's my fault, and I have to fix it. Pay penance. Make amends. Propitiation, Petra says, for what I've done. I make her come with me, and we start campaigning.

When Pooh answers the door, we plunge right in with "You have to vote against Belsum."

"Obviously." She rolls her eyes. "But your pitch needs work."

"They're flagitious." Petra's counting off on her fingers. "They're pernicious. Their specious claim that they're innoxious now is a spurious one."

"I know what you mean," Pooh says, "and I have no idea what you mean."

"How would you put it?" I ask. "Tell us from the heart. Why are you voting no?"

"My dotage, decline, and eventual demise will be much less depressing if I'm leaving a world without Belsum in it."

I wrinkle my nose. "It's a little wordy."

She rainbows her hand across the air in front of her, imagining a billboard or maybe bumper stickers. " 'Belsum. Don't die before they do.' "

"Pithier," I grant her, "but you're not dying."

"Well not yet," she says. "How's your love life?"

"Miasmatic," I admit.

Pooh makes a sympathetic face and promises to vote against Belsum. Petra makes a sympathetic face undercut with relief that even in the depths of my despair I'm still studying for the SATs.

We find Pastor Jeff at the clinic instead of the church, so we take a medical approach.

"You have to vote against," Petra says, "because of your obligations as a doctor. First do no harm?"

"Bourne's not a sick patient," he says. "And many of its citizens who are wouldn't be — or wouldn't be as often — if they had health insurance and more providers."

So we switch tactics.

"What about your pastoralism?" I ask.

"That's not what that means," Petra warns.

Pastor Jeff smiles. "My divine duties overwhelm my civic obligations."

Petra looks confused.

"He's too sacerdotal to vote," I explain.

"Heavenly justice works every time," he says.

I raise my eyebrows at him without comment.

"You look exactly like your mother," he says. "It works *much* of the time."

"What about *your* mother?"

"What about her?"

"And your dad. They were activists. They were freedom fighters. They'd want you to vote against. What would your mother say?"

" 'Eat something,' " says Pastor Jeff. " 'Get more sleep. Put on a sweater.' "

"Same thing," says Petra.

"Probably true," agrees Pastor Jeff.

We stay after school one day to talk to Mrs. Shriver.

"We're here to ask you to vote against Belsum," I say.

"Of course." She nods, distracted though, not looking up from the essays she's grading. "Just don't get your hopes up, girls."

"We're campaigning inimitably," Petra assures her.

"I'm certain." She smiles at us, one of those smiles that somehow means sad. "But people move on." I consider her husband who cannot work and her children who cannot be born and her life which cannot ever be what she had every right and reason to believe it would. I consider how "move on" is exactly what she cannot do. "Some things are terrible enough it's better to forget if you can."

We're staring at her with our mouths open. "What?"

"You teach history."

That sad smile again. "History and memory are unreliable narrators." I think back to that first assignment, how galled I was to have to write it over still-summer, how much everything has changed since then. "It's hard to remember when it's so painful. It's hard to remember when you're dead."

"I guess, but if —"

"It's hard to remember the past," she interrupts, "when it won't pass."

"So what do we do?" I ask.

She takes off her glasses, holds my gaze. "Anything you can."

We find Mrs. Radcliffe at home. She regards us on her front stoop over crossed arms, already mid-sigh when she opens the door, and does not invite us in.

When we finish our spiel, she says, "If you both come back to tutoring, I'll vote against."

We agree to these terms. It's the least we can do.

Petra's mother resolves to leave the house

for the first time in five years to vote no. Le-andra is going to have a hard time getting to the polls, but Chris says he will carry her if necessary so they can both vote emphatically against. Donna Anvers says she will vote for flowers so against Belsum. Omar will vote for Nora maybe or for Bourne or for second chances, but in any case, we know, he will vote against.

Nathan is campaigning too. All over town, he's put up posters with his face looking trustworthy. Every time Mama sees one, she draws a mustache on it. She mustaches so hard she breaks her marker and stains my father's favorite shirt with ink. But excepting this sartorial tragedy, I know how she feels: better to be distracted, better to be doing something. Petra and I feel it too. Maybe we can't vote, but we can convince lots of other people to vote the way we want them to, so that's even better. It feels good to say our piece, to tell our side, to be heard for once. It feels good to think that this time, maybe, it'll be different. It's not hard to go to everyone's door because they're our neighbors after all, our friends. They're us, and there aren't so many of us.

For a little while, memory being unreliable and also, apparently, easily distracted, I almost forget all about River. But not really.

TWO

Mab will not come with me because she does not want to see River. Or, to be more accurate, she wants to not see River.

Mama will not come with me because when I ask her if she wants to she says, "Over my dead body." Which means no.

Mirabel will not come with me, but she turns away and will not say why, but it does not matter because it means I am out of people and have to go alone.

Nathan Templeton's first campaign action was he brought me two binders containing Harburon Analytical's extremely exacting, extremely thorough, extremely reassuring test results to lend from the library in case anyone wanted to borrow them. I said this was nice and responsible of him, but Mama and Mab and Mirabel all said that, to be more accurate, it was manipulative and disingenuous, so I shelved the binders behind the toilet, but no one came needing

575

or even asking to borrow them anyway.

Next Nathan Templeton made his very own frisbees that read "Harburon Analytical Gives Belsum A+," and he left these for anyone to take for free at cash registers and checkout lines and Frank's Norma's Bar and even, Pastor Jeff reports, at church. Mama said a stupid plastic toy in exchange for their lives not to mention justice not to mention self-respect is not a trade Bourners will make, but they are fun (the frisbees, not the Bourners) and come in many colors including yellow as well as green (so you could play in the rain since they are also waterproof) so Mama might be wrong.

Then Nathan Templeton printed posters and flyers with highlights from the test results and pictures of himself and put them up all over town. Mama defaced them, which should mean she removed his face but does not. But it was still funny.

Now, the night before the election, Nathan Templeton is having an open house, which means a party you can go to late and still not be rude. There are cookies and coffee and champagne and a slide show, and the slide show runs on a loop — in case you come politely late — and is all about the extremely exacting, extremely thorough, extremely reassuring test results.

I do not go just because I am invited. Everyone is invited.

I do not go for the cookies, even though he flew them in specially, because everyone knows cookies made by your mother are better than cookies bought from a store, even if that store is in Boston.

I do not go for the slide show because I read one of the binders he dropped off at the library (I did not have to read them both because they were exactly the same) so I know what the slide show shows.

I go to see Apple Templeton.

I ride my bicycle to my library all alone, even though I never ride anywhere all alone, even though it is very cold out, even though it is not my library anymore, and this time when I go in my eyes remember the last time they were here instead of all the times they were here before that. It looks less like a library now and more like a home because the Templetons have unpacked since the last time I was here but also because, now that my eyes know the history, they can see the home it was in the first place. And also the third place. The second place, when it was my library, turned out to be the short one. So my eyes feel very sad. The fancy kitchen in the Children's section is full of the fancy cookies and other fancy treats, like tiny quiches that smell nice and are yellow, but I do not eat them anyway. There are a lot of people hanging around eating the snacks and watching the slide show and shaking hands with Nathan Templeton whose pants have become his expensive ones again and whose shirt and hair have both been ironed smooth. And in the corner, looking like how I sometimes want to be in the corner where it is quiet and safe and no one will touch you, is Apple Templeton.

No one is talking to her which is good because it means I can talk to her.

"Hello Apple Templeton," I say politely.

"Monday Mitchell." She makes a little smile which might mean happy to see me or might mean almost anything else. I cannot tell. "Glad you could make it."

"You are?" I ask.

She looks surprised and like she does not know what to say but decides on "Sure."

"Is it because of what I have brought you?" I ask.

"I don't know." She smiles more now. She might be happy someone brought her something. Or she might be laughing at me. "What have you brought me?"

I take the Elm/Hickory Grove folder out of my backpack and hand it to her. She looks at it, and her face gets yellow, but not

578

in a good way, and I can tell that she can tell from the label what I could not, which is what is in the folder.

"I was looking for this," she says, but she is not looking at me when she says it and might not even be talking to me.

"I know," I say because I do.

"You do?" She looks up at me so my eyes look away. "How?"

"Omar told us you were looking through his files but did not find what you were looking for." This is not a lie. Omar did tell a whole bar full of people including my mother and my sister that Apple Templeton was looking through his files and did not find what she was looking for. But it is sort of a lie in that it is not the whole truth or even the part of the truth that led us to this folder. *That* truth is hard to understand though, even for me, and might get my mother or sister in trouble, which I know would not be fair, so I do not tell her that part.

Her eyes looking for my eyes have tears in them. "Why are you giving these to me?"

"Because it is not accurate to say they are yours, but they are closer to yours than anyone else's."

She nods, and she hugs the folder, and she says, "That is very, very kind of you,

Monday."

So I say, "You are welcome," which is polite, and then I turn around to leave, but then she asks me another question.

"Did you read them?"

"Yes," I answer. "Many, many times."

She nods and seems like she will not say anything else and then she says, "Are they bad?"

And I am surprised so I look at her to see what she means so she looks away because her eyes do not want to look at my eyes any more than my eyes want to look at hers. I do not know what to say so I do not say anything.

"My father didn't know what was going to happen." Her voice is very quiet.

"Lie," I say.

Tears fall out of her eyes so she rolls them up to the painted-over ceiling of the Children's section like it is still covered in rainbows and clouds. "He didn't know it was going to be that bad," she says. Then she adds, "This bad." Then she adds, "What happened after my father sold the land wasn't his fault. Our family wasn't even here anymore."

"Then why do you want the letters?" I wonder.

She nods like I have asked her a yes-or-no

question to which the answer is yes. "People might not understand if they read them. They might not believe that what happened had nothing to do with my family."

"Truth," I say for they might not. As an example, I do not.

"Dad was just doing his job. Buying and selling land. That's what he did. He didn't know the chemical was poisonous or that it would get in the water or what would happen if it did."

"He said effluvia," I tell her. "He said he did not trust Duke Templeton. He said he was glad his family would be far away from Bourne when the plant opened."

"It wasn't his job to protect you," Apple says.

"Truth," I say for it was not his job.

"Maybe he wasn't perfect," Apple says, "but he did the best he could."

"For himself," I say, "and for you, his family, it is accurate to say he did the best he could. But not for us. For us he could have done much, much better."

"Truth," she whispers. Then she says, "Thank you, Monday. I hope you win tomorrow."

"Because you want to go home?" I ask, for I have learned that home is not just where you live. Home is also where you want and need and are meant to live. Home is also the people who are there with you, who are the people who will help you live, who are the people who will do the best they can, not just for themselves, but for you, their neighbors and friends, as well.

"Because I want what's fair," says Apple Templeton.

THREE

Monday wore green to school today, but the rain keeps switching over to snow flurries then sleet then back to rain again, none of it lasting long enough to accumulate but relentless, sopping, and deep-in-the-bones cold. They say voter turnout is lower when the weather's bad and the issues local, especially for whoever's ahead in the polls, but in our case, there are no polls, and however near, the stakes could not range wider. The voting booth is a wooden box with a slit in the lid into which you insert a red poker chip if you want to rebuild the dam and reopen the plant and a green poker chip if you want Belsum to leave and never return. The jars of chips are helpfully labeled in case you're color-blind or confused. It is extraordinarily appropriate that in Bourne voting literally feels like gambling.

Pastor Jeff, who as a man of God is what passes around here for trustworthy and unbiased, serves as election chair, but it's a weekday so he must also serve as Dr. Lilly. The voting box, therefore, sits in the clinic waiting room. As do I. People with appointments today come in and vote and then sit and wait their turn to be seen. People without appointments come in and vote and then sit and chitchat with the waiting patients. Some people come in and vote and then wait for nothing in particular except for the rain to abate. It is not a festive atmosphere exactly, but it is communal, all in, everyone here, at least for a little while. I would bet that counting uncomfortable glances at me and/or my mother's shut door would be an effective exit poll. If so, at lunchtime, we are neck and neck. My mood, however, mirrors the weather.

Because win or lose, I am at every turn betrayed.

Not just by River, who told what he shouldn't have, who chose his family over ours — which might maybe be understandable except he also chose wrong over right, cowardice over integrity, fear over fair, and, worst of all, reversion to form instead of change, growth, and becoming the person I had faith he was, or at least could be. His apology was heartfelt I'm sure, but also empty — too easy — and also too late.

584

I am betrayed by my eldest sister who also told what she shouldn't have, who also chose someone else over our family, though at least in her case it was because of love, at least some of it was. But mostly it is this: We have shared a room, a life, a heart all these weeks and months and all the years before these weeks and months, and she has fallen in love without ever once noticing that I have fallen in love as well. Worse than not ever once noticing. Not ever once imagining. We communicate, Mab and I, without language, without motion, without space, passage, sense, or sometimes even purpose. We are so much the same — for two people who navigate the world so differently — it is appalling that she could love another and not realize that I would — of course I would — do the same.

I am betrayed by the adults whose job it is to look out for me because if you asked us, we who are coming slowly of age, we would vote Belsum out — without pause or pang or division — no matter what wonders they dangled before our innocent eyes. I am betrayed by my town, my neighbors and friends, these people with whom I have strived and struggled and suffered, the only people I have ever known, my entire world, roughly half of whom have come before me today to vote that it's okay with them, or okay enough, what was done to all of us. And what was done to me.

Then the door to Nora's office opens, her last patient of the day shuffles out, and my mother stands in her doorway regarding me through red, weary eyes.

"You okay?" She is tired but smiling, hopeful, willfully optimistic.

I nod and point to her.

"Oh yeah, me too, better than okay actually. It'll be close, but I think it's going to go our way finally."

She glances at my face to see if I know something she doesn't yet. I don't. An hour ago, Pastor Jeff came out of his office, told me to cross my fingers, and left with the box of poker chips tucked inside his raincoat.

"Cheer up, Mir-Mir." Nora's bouncing a little. "Everything's great. This time, I know it, I feel it, everything's going to be just great."

And it is the stress of the day maybe, of the damp quicksilver chill of the weather, of watching every single member of this entangled town trickle in to vote, or perhaps it is just one betrayal too many, but it is too much for me.

"It is not great." I turn the volume on my

Voice all the way up to shout at my mother. "And it is not going to be great."

She is alert at once in case I've been withholding information about the vote. "What happened?"

"Nothing," my Voice says. "Ever."

"Mirabel, you scared me."

"You should be scared."

She is. I can see it in her face. And I feel bad, but not bad enough to stop. She waits while I type.

"No matter how the vote goes, I already lost."

Mab thinks it's not fair this town is so boring. Monday thinks it's not fair that sometimes it's raining in the morning but sunny in the afternoon and she didn't bring a change of clothes to school. But what's not fair is what's not fair, the ways they feel they've been wronged by fate versus the ways I have.

"You have to look on the bright side, love," my mother tells me. "It's the only way."

"No," my Voice says, and she waits while I type. "You have to let me be on the dark side."

"Never," she says.

"Aaaaaaaahh!" I scream, I cry, I roar, and then I close my eyes to gather the energy necessary to type. "Even if everyone votes the right way, I will still be this way."

"I love you this way," Nora says.

"That is not enough," my Voice says, and we are both stopped by it, for it is heartbreaking and it is worse than heartbreaking. And it is true. It is not enough to be loved by your mother. It is a good start, and you wouldn't want to do without, and it helps, but it is not enough. You need also the love of your community, the love of friends and admirers, the love of strangers who don't know you but still wish you well, the love that comes from passion and from commitment and from someone who will never, never betray you and not just because they're related to you. You need more love. We all need more love. And here — in this town, in this body — love is abundant but it is not sufficient. It is not enough.

She crosses the room and takes my head in both her hands, makes me look into her eyes when she says, "You are wonderful exactly as you are, and I wouldn't have you any other way."

Tears snail down my cheeks which make tears snail down hers, and we sit there looking at each other through our mollusky eyes. I know that she means what she says. And I know there are ways she does not mean what she says.

Because why wouldn't she want me different than I am? Why wouldn't she wish it for me? Anyone would want a child whole and limitless. Anyone would wish it for themselves as a parent, and anyone would wish it for their child, for any child.

"I mean it." She can see me doubting her. "You are so strong. You do a whole body's worth of work with one hand and one amazing brain. You are so gentle. You are so smart. I know there are things you can't do, but it's a package deal. And it's such a lovely package I think it's worth the trade-off."

She is still holding my face so I can't see my tablet to raise my Voice. If I could, I would say I don't want a trade-off. I want both.

"I know it sucks," she says. "I know it's not fair. I would trade places with you if I could. You know I would."

I acknowledge the truth of this statement with my eyebrows.

She smiles, but a sad smile. "But if your body didn't limit you, if it didn't make you sit still and watch and listen and process, if you didn't have so much time to think, you wouldn't be you. And I love you." I roll my eyes, but there's more. "You wouldn't be so wise or so observant or the smartest person

589

I know."

For she is my mother. Of course she thinks the part of me that works best is beautiful.

And this is Nora's permanent, impossible bind.

If her children are perfect just as they are, then why is she so angry at Belsum?

If they've caused such damage, where is her proof?

And if the proof is us, doesn't that mean we are broken indeed?

She sees my skepticism, or maybe it's my scorn. "It's possible to want two things at once, you know."

I do, of course.

"Even opposite things. Even things that contradict and contraindicate. We don't talk about that enough."

I don't talk about anything enough.

"Not we," she clarifies. "They. In the world. Out there." She waves at it, a world beyond Bourne. Sometimes it seems so close I think I'd be able to see it if only I could get up a little higher, like from the roof of the school maybe or the crest of the cemetery. Sometimes it seems so far I don't even believe it exists. Opposites. This is her point. She means she is angry at what was done to her — what was done to *hers* —

590

but she still loves us as we are. She means she can live in the past and still drag it along with her into the future. She means — or maybe she doesn't but it's still true — that this lawsuit is killing her and this vote is killing her and this battle is killing her. But she would not survive without it. So it's hard to argue Nora can't fight while she's moving on just because those things are opposites.

"It *is* because of you I do this," she allows, "but not the way you think. I want you to know you can fight. I want you to know you *should* fight. You will be treated carelessly and cruelly, unfairly and maliciously, shortsightedly and selfishly in this world, and when you are, I want you to know you do not have to take it like you deserve nothing better and you're powerless to protest. I want you to know you can win."

Another impossible paradox: how to show your children they can keep getting up when all they ever see is the part where you fall.

She lets me go. I turn back to my Voice. "I am angry and sad I cannot have what I should have."

"Me too," she says. Maybe she means she is also angry and sad I cannot have what I should have. Or maybe she means she is angry and sad she cannot have what she should have. Both probably.

"It is okay we are angry and sad," I type. "You have to be okay."

Nora wants to comfort me, wants to praise me, cheer me, bolster me, applaud me. But not as much as she wants to hear me.

"Okay," she says.

What else can I ask of her?

The bar is closed on account of the vote as if it's a polling place. Truth be told, voting at the bar makes a lot more sense than voting at the medical clinic, but that's not how it is and it's not why Frank closed. He wants to go back to being neutral territory. He wants the bar to be a place of succor and comfort not hostility and rancor. He doesn't want to spend all night looking at everyone looking at each other like they've all been betrayed. So Nora and I bundle up and head for home. She makes dinner. Mab cleans up — by herself and without complaint. Monday sits and squirms like she sat on a crab.

At last, the phone rings.

It's Omar.

And it's official.

The truth is, it wasn't a vote. Not really. You can't ask people to vote if they can't make a choice. The question was not was

Belsum culpable all those years ago. It was not are they repentant and reformed now. It was not do we believe improvements were made and operations are safe going forward. It was one thing. Are we more angry or more desperate? Which is a measure of our souls. It may be a question, but it isn't a choice.

Still, we were asked. *They* were asked. And the voters of Bourne — not all of them but enough of them — voted to repair the dam and take their chances and their jobs and the rest of us down with them. It is not okay. Not remotely. But Belsum wins anyway.

ONE

The next night there's a knock on the door after a dinner no one ate anyway.

River.

I exchange looks with my sisters. Petra would call them inscrutable.

We didn't go to school today. None of us went to school today. Maybe school was canceled, for all I know. Maybe we all — my whole sick and sorry generation — boycotted en masse without discussion. But apparently even burning the place down wouldn't have been enough to keep avoiding this conversation.

We go for a walk.

It's cold, even though I've bundled up, even though we're moving, even though he holds my hand and I let him, even though it's not that cold. The leaves are gone now, all of them, so you can see straight into the woods, moonlit, which should be romantic but instead makes me feel naked too, ex-

posed. It is very quiet out. There is no noi⸱
— no wind, no cars, no one talking, n⸱
streetlight buzz even — nothing but us. I
can see our breath, which feels somehow
like a step backward, relationship-wise, like
his breath used to be only mine to share
but now it's out there for any raccoon or
owl or other nocturnal creature with good
eyes to see.

As far as steps backward relationship-wise
go, that's probably the least of them.

"What you told me and made me promise
not to tell . . ." He starts and trails off. Mad-
deningly.

I hold my breath. But what he says next
knocks the wind out of me anyway.

"I already knew," he says.

He can read minds. He can tell the future.
He really is magic. "How?"

"Mirabel told me."

I drop his hand. I stop walking. I understand suddenly what it means to be struck
dumb. You think it means "struck" like it
happens all at once, but no, it means
"struck" like you've been slapped. You think
it means "dumb" like you can't talk, but no,
it means "dumb" like stupid, like all sense
has all at once been removed from my brain.

My fingers and toes get very cold. My face
gets very hot. Like a bad line of dialogue, I

ant to say "Mirabel who?" because there s no way Mirabel told him.

"After school one day. After the last bell. You were at tutoring," he explains. Like that explains anything.

"Why?" I say.

"Why what?"

"Why did she tell you?"

"I don't know." He shrugs. "Why did you?"

A pause, our breath all around us like evidence.

Instead of answering, I ask my own question. "Why did you tell your father?"

Mirabel has already told us how he apologized for this when he met her at the bar. I thought he went to her because I was avoiding him. But that turns out not to be why. And who knows how much Mirabel's told me that wasn't actually true?

"I don't know," he says again. He doesn't know anything. "He's my father? If Belsum fails, what will we do? I was scared?" It's like he's asking me. "I got impatient?" We couldn't wait anymore, any of us. "I'm sorry," he says.

But that doesn't make it better. I start walking again.

"I told him I'd been helping you," he offers.

I'm getting colder. Shouldn't I be afla...
by now?

"And I told him I thought he was being ...
jerk. But he's not a jerk, you know? He's an
okay guy really. So I thought it was worth a
shot. Talking to him."

"Did it work?"

"I asked him how Belsum could do this to
you again after what happened last time. I
told him I thought he had a responsibility
to make it right and then leave you the hell
alone."

I keep walking, one foot in front of another, careful, matching my steps to my
breathing, knowing both will falter if I take
my mind off them even for a moment.
"What did he say?"

"He said, 'Do you want to become
poor?' "

"And?"

"I don't."

"No one does," I agree, and when he
doesn't say anything, I add, though it seems
obvious, "We don't."

"I know. I said that. But he said —" River
stops, which is how I know, though it
doesn't seem possible, that what he says
next is going to be even worse than what
he's said already.

"What?"

597

He said you can't become poor because
ou already are poor."

"So?"

"You always were."

"What do you mean 'always'?"

"He said you were poor before we —
before Belsum — even got here. You would
have gotten rich if the plant had been suc-
cessful. That was the plan before, and that's
the new plan too now that we won the election, and that would have been — will be
— great."

He stops again and seems to be waiting
for me to — what? — express excitement?
Gratitude?

"That's not what happened," I say. Again,
this seems both obvious and somehow
necessary to say anyway.

"No," he agrees, sadly, "last time it didn't
work out, but my dad's point is now you're
right where you always were. You didn't
make any money, but you really didn't lose
any either. Why should we?"

"Why should you what?"

"Lose money," he explains. "He says
Belsum took the risk. Why should we be
punished?"

"Why should *we*?" I ask.

"You're not being punished," he says.
"You just didn't . . . get better."

I take enough deep breaths to be a[ble to]
say without my voice shaking, "You [de]
stroyed us."

"My father says that wasn't us."

"Who was it?"

"Someone before us. My mom says
Bourne wasn't that great to begin with."
His shoulders rise, fall. A shrug or a sigh.
Resignation or regret or defeat. I don't
know. "Plus my dad says sometimes bad
things happen. It's no one's fault. It's nothing anyone can control. Anywhere you go,
some kids are born okay and some kids are
born with problems, some people are rich
and some people are poor. That's just how
it is."

"What do *you* say?" My teeth are chattering.

"Me?"

"Yeah. You said what your dad said, and
you said what your mom said. What do you
say?"

"It never matters what I say."

"It matters to me." *Mattered,* I think.

"I guess I'm just trying to keep everyone
happy."

"Not everyone."

He winces but has nothing to say to that,
and though I would like to walk away with
some dignity, I would rather walk away with

answers.

can't believe you did this."

"I just had a conversation with my father."

"I can't believe you did this to me," I clarify. "You promised. And we —" I stop. "And you promised."

"Not you."

"What?"

"I didn't do this to you. Please, Mab. I didn't break my promise to you because I already knew. It was Mirabel. Mirabel told me."

"We are the same, Mirabel and I." I am shaking so hard he looks wavy before me. Or maybe he's trembling too. "We are the same person. We are exactly the same."

We have turned and headed back toward my house. I am almost home. There is so much left to say. There is nothing left to say.

But it turns out I'm wrong about that.

"We're leaving." His eyes dart to mine, then away again as soon as they meet. "I came to say goodbye."

I stop walking. I stop breathing. "But you won."

"Exactly, so my mom says we don't have to be here anymore. She says my dad can run the plant remotely now. Our actually being here was mostly a publicity thing, a

gesture of goodwill." He shrugs aga.
guess it doesn't matter anymore."

"I guess not." The list of things that .
parently don't matter anymore is long ai.
winding as a river, long and winding as his
tory. Literally.

At the front door, I don't know what to
do. Something violent? Something tender?
Do I kiss him goodbye? Promise never to
forget him? Tell him I'll write? I stand and
look at River, really look at him, and force
myself to know: I will never see him again.
He can't look back at me, can't say goodbye,
can't walk away, can't bring himself to
touch me. Or maybe it's that I won't let him.

"I really liked you, Mab." The past tense.
The past tense might fell me.

But I say anyway, "Me too," because it's
true, and it's important that it's true. I don't
want him to think — I don't want to think
— I did all I did on a whim or for fun or
just to see what would happen. I was in love,
I'd plead before the court, if we ever got to
go to court. I'd plead before my sisters. It
wasn't my fault. I was in love.

"I wish I didn't have to go."

"Really?" I am genuinely asking.

He blushes. So he *is* lying. "I wish I didn't
have to . . . leave you," he amends. "I get

reception in Boston. We can keep in
n."

Why? I think, but I just nod at my shoes.

"I have something for you," he says. I look
up. He reaches into his not-a-backpack and
hands it to me carefully, ceremonially even,
without taking his eyes off mine. And I
receive it. But when I tear my eyes from his
to look, it's just a college catalog, one of
those glossy brochures that fill the mailbox
as soon as you sign up for the SATs. I don't
know what I was expecting. Or would have
wished for. Something sentimental maybe,
anything really, but this is nothing.

"For your escape," he says, "and all your
future endeavors."

My stomach clenches like I've eaten
something off, rotten, like I've stuffed his
stupid catalog into my mouth page by page
and swallowed it.

"This is where my father went to school,"
he offers.

I know this from when we called the
library in search of his dissertation research,
but I can't tell River that.

"And where his father went to school. So
it's where I might go too. Maybe we could
go together. Take a look."

When I still don't say anything, he pulls
his wand out of his back pocket. Waves it

around half-heartedly. Offers it to
"Want to say the magic words?"

I cannot even shake my head no. I cann
say a word. Magic or otherwise, there a.
none left to say. So I do the only thing lef
to do: Turn away. Turn away and back to
my worn front door and my worn life. My
body is Mirabel's. It can listen, but it can't
not listen, and it can't reply. It is sapped of
strength, control, and agency. I have my one
hand. I can turn the doorknob and let
myself inside and close the door behind me.
That is all.

In bed, I can hear Mirabel typing, but her
Voice is silent. I can hear her and Monday
listening to me cry, waiting for me to be
done. Mirabel must know I know what she
did now. What we both did. Monday can't
have any idea why I'm so upset, but in some
ways it doesn't matter to her. She's upset
I'm upset. And that's enough.

Still, I can feel her itching to ask — she
doesn't like to not understand — and itching to comfort me too. They both have so
much they want to say. But instead of tears
it feels like words are leaking out of my eyes,
and soon I won't be able to tell them
anything at all. And I have a question I need
answered before I surrender forever the

er of speech with no magic Voice to
ace it. I wipe my face off and roll over.

You told him," I say into the darkness. A
uestion. An accusation. But more than
anything, a plea. *Please let there be some
kind of explanation to make me stop feeling
like this.*

"Who told who what?" Monday sounds
relieved to hear my voice, any voice.

"Yes," says Mirabel's.

"Why?" I beg because if she has an answer
it will halve the number of people who've
betrayed me.

She types. "You said," she says.

"And you said he was too young. You said
he wasn't trustworthy. You said we had to
keep the secret from everyone, even him.
You said especially him."

She types. "You convinced me."

"But," I say, and then I don't say anything
else. I turn on the light. We squint at each
other as our eyes adjust. I look at my sister,
and she looks at me. What I want to say is:
*If someone was going to tell him, it was my
place not yours.* What I want to say is: *Did I
convince you it was okay to tell, or did you
convince me it wasn't so you could?* What I
want to say is: *At least I can speak. Or I could
before this.* What I want to say is: *Why and*

604

how could you?

But I know how she could: Slowly. D̶̶
erately. And — dawning, incredulous –
also know why. The fact that I haven̶
known before, that it hasn't even crosse̶
my mind until now, is maybe the biggest
betrayal of all.

Monday is just getting her head around
what happened. She stands up on her bed.
"Three! You told?"

"So did I." I am so angry at Mirabel and
so hurt by Mirabel I don't know which of
those I am more. But that instinct to protect
her — and share her burden whenever possible — runs deeper still.

Monday's head whips to me. "I am not
stupid. I figured that out. But I do not
understand why."

"We don't know," I answer for both of us.
And then, "I can't believe you would do that
to me." I sound pathetic, but they've both
heard me sound worse.

"You mean you cannot believe *River*
would do that to you," says Monday. "Betray
you. Tell his father."

"I don't mean River," I say. "I mean Mirabel. Why?" I want to hear her say it.

"I do not know why," says Monday.

But there's only one reason, isn't there?

...bel must have told for the same reason
...d.

You love him?" I ask.

"I love who?" Monday says.

"Yes," says Mirabel's Voice.

"But that's" — my brain rolodexes through every vocabulary word it's memorized in the past five years and lands on — "impossible."

"No," says Mirabel's Voice. There's more there, sentences and paragraphs and tomes waiting to spill, but we don't have time right now for her to tell them.

"How can that be?" This is crudely — cruelly — put because of course it's not impossible. It's exactly as possible for Mirabel to fall in love as for me or River or anyone. Mirabel-champion is my most important job, not just telling her she can do it, whatever it is, not just helping her do it, but believing she can. She's brilliant and funny and strong and, yes, lovable, and I'd fight anyone who said otherwise, but there are some things she just can't do. So why does she have to do them with River, who, in addition to being the scion of her enemy, is mine? I feel terrible for asking these questions, even in my head, but mostly I just feel terrible.

"I don't know," her Voice answers.

"For how long?"

She types. "All along."

"I do not know what that means," Monday says.

Me neither.

"That's no excuse," I say.

"No," she agrees.

"Just because I told too —" I stop. "I was wrong but only once and understandably. You were wrong twice —"

"Because you told when you said not to tell and because you betrayed your very own sister!" Monday cannot help but put in. Enthusiastically.

"And not understandably," I finish.

"Yes," Mirabel's Voice insists. I hope she means yes, she was wrong, twice. But she could as well mean, yes, it was understandable. And the fact that I don't know might be the greatest loss of all. I wait, but she doesn't clarify.

Finally I admit, "He gave me this," because I have to sometime, and it might as well be now. It's mortifying really, but they are my sisters, so I hand over the brochure.

"He wants to help you go to college." Monday is puzzled but trying. "That is nice."

"It's condescending," I spit. "It's pity. It's tossing me his scraps. It's rubbing in my

e that he's leaving and I never will. And
en if it weren't all that, it's just mean
ecause he knows damn well I can't afford
t."

No one says anything for a moment.

Then Monday reaches over. "I will take it.
For the library."

On top I am furious, raging at River, raging at Mirabel. And underneath that I am
destroyed, betrayed by both of them, in pain
from everywhere at once. And underneath
that I am bereft. He is leaving, and how will
it be here now without him? It will be the
same as it was before, and I think I would
rather go anywhere — *anywhere* — than
back.

I feel what it feels like to know I will never
be happy again.

I feel what it feels like to know not only
do I have to feel this, I have to feel it alone
because I've lost my sister, both of them
probably (for we do not come in ones), and
the only people who could help me find my
way through are as lost in the woods as I
am.

I turn off the light and turn back toward
the wall.

I can hear Mirabel snuffling too.

I can hear Monday turning the pages of
that stupid catalog. I should never have

given it to her because I would like t
it in the woods or I would like to set
fire or I would like to feed it to a
animal, but of course she has to read it w
a flashlight under her covers.

And of course she has to do it out loud.

Probably because there was never any chance she wasn't going to, however, it is closer to soothing than grating. I can't stop thinking about a million things I wish I could stop thinking about, so listening to Monday intone the first-year experience at the Templeton alma mater is as good a sheep-counting sort of exercise as any. Students take five courses each semester and can join any of hundreds of clubs. There are three dining halls for them to choose from plus two coffee shops. They live in coed dorms with roommates specially matched for compatibility.

"There is a sidebar with photographs of famous alumni who used to be roommates," Monday says. "Remember that blond guy from that movie we watched about dogs? He used to be roommates with that other blond guy from that other movie we watched about dogs. That is a good co-incidence because ‒"

Monday stops reading, but I wasn't really paying attention anyway, so it takes me a

while to notice. Then she starts keen-
om under the covers.

Monday?"

The keening gets louder. I turn on the
ght.

"Shush! You'll wake Mama." No one slept
much after Omar told us the election results
last night. If Mama can get some rest, she
should.

But Monday can't stop.

"Tell us what's wrong, Two." Mirabel has
that one long saved.

I pull the covers off her. Her hands are
clamped over her ears, so the college catalog
River gave me as the sorriest of parting gifts
has fallen to the floor. I pick it up and look.

And there, grinning back at me, is River
himself. *"My only love sprung from my only
hate!"* (*"Too early seen unknown, and known
too late!"* I'm realizing belatedly the important part of that quote is the second bit.)
He has his arm around a guy I've never seen
before, standing on a cobblestone path in
front of a brick building covered in ivy. The
pileup of love and hurt and anger and
confusion — or maybe it's just his sweet
smile — makes the room spin. So it takes
me longer than it should to realize this
makes no sense. This cannot be a photo of
River.

The caption clarifies. And then se
world on fire.

"A match made in heaven! Roomm.
Duke Templeton ('68) and Scott Blak
('68) on move-in day freshman year. Ten.
pleton went on to become owner and CEO
of Belsum Basics. Blakely is owner and
CEO of Harburon Analytical."

The most exacting, state-of-the-art independent testing and chemical analysis
company in the world.

I would like to join in Monday's keening,
but not as much as I would like my mother
to sleep through this. I would like to hold
Monday and rock her and tell her it will be
all right, but Monday would never let me
hold her and rock her, and I do not see how
it will be all right ever again. Instead, I pull
Mirabel into Monday's bed and climb in
myself, and we huddle there together,
insofar as it is possible to huddle without
touching, our warmth eventually melting
Monday's shrieks to cries to sniffles to silence.

Finally she says, "Independent testing
does not prove anything if the independent
tester is your roommate from college specially matched for compatibility."

"Truth," I say.

"We will tell everyone what we have

d and hold another vote."

nat's not how it works," I tell her.

nen you don't like the outcome of a vote,

u don't just get to ask again."

"But they voted wrong."

"So they have to live with it."

"Me too," she points out. "And that is not fair."

"Truth."

"But they did not just vote wrong," she says. "They voted with incomplete informa-tion because they were lied to and tricked, so they deserve to know the true and com-plete information and then have another chance to vote the right way."

"It's too late," I say.

"For what?"

"For everything."

And then Mirabel's Voice out of the black darkness pricked only by faded, stapled-on stars. "The lawsuit was never the way. The vote was never the way. Nora's way was never the way."

"What way?" Monday says.

"Forward," says Mirabel's Voice.

"What is the way?" Monday says.

We wait while Mirabel types. "The dam needs repair because it is cracked and leak-ing already."

"Truth," Monday agrees.

612

More typing. "What if we help it?"

"Help fix it?" Monday asks.

"Help crack it," Mirabel's Voice correc "Tear it down. Open it up."

"Who?" Monday asks.

"Three." She does not mean herself. She means we three. She means us.

"How?" Monday asks.

Mirabel types. "Dynamite?"

"We do not have dynamite," Monday says.

"Demolition equipment, backhoe, bulldozer, jackhammer." This must be a folder buried deep in her Voice app for the toddler set, and she's just going through and tapping each picture.

"We do not have a backhoe or a bulldozer or a jackhammer," Monday says.

But I sit up, blow my nose, and turn the light back on again. Because it's true we don't have any demolition equipment. But I know where we can get some.

TWO

When I first found the newspaper photograph of the pretending-to-fish Santas, I thought it was just Bourne.

Then I realized it was Bourne of the past.

Now I realize it is Bourne of the future, Bourne to come, the river — and everything — back where it belongs.

Very, very carefully, I cut around the edges with a utility knife, cutting the photograph from the article and caption and cutting through the glue and cutting through the extra-thick scrapbook paper the glue has glued the photograph onto. I feel bad about defacing library materials, but a scrapbook is not officially a book, and the back of a newspaper clipping is more newspaper whereas the back of this scrapbook page is blank for writing on.

I leave the Santa-postcard in the middle of the kitchen table for Mama to find when she wakes up in the morning and comes downstairs to start baking yellow thing

It would be nice to give her a nice sur
But we do not know what will happen.
in case it is a not-nice surprise or one t
takes a long time to come, I do not war
her to worry. She has already worried
enough.

Dear Mama,
It is okay. We are taking care of it.
One, Two, Three

THREE

Remember I told you this at the beginning.

That I can tell stories but slowly, more dripping faucet than rushing flow, more drizzle than hard, cleansing rain, but letter by letter I can get us there. And I was not in a rush, I said. I had plenty of time, I said.

That is no longer the case.

The metaphor is always David and Goliath.

Goliath is big and strong and well funded. He's made so much money, either off your suffering or off not giving a shit about your suffering, that he can buy whatever and whoever he needs to ensure that his profiting off your suffering remains allowed or at least overlooked, which Monday would point out are not the same thing, but Monday would be wrong.

And then there is David. He is poor and small. He is weak, overmatched, under-funded, outclassed. But he is right and he is

616

righteous, quick of wit, fast of finger, of heart, helping those whom Goliath destroyed. The good guy.

And so it's done in an instant. One well placed rock, quick as a tick, and it's over.

I hate this metaphor. It's offered all the time, but it's apt as balloons at a funeral, suggesting, as it does, that if only you were more nimble or more right or more good, you would prevail. Suggesting, as it does, that you are destroyed not by other people's shortsightedness, other people's greed, or other people's deciding you're disposable, but by being yourself too slow, morally compromised, wicked, and weak. Goliath is not at fault in this story. Goliath is just a giant, following his giant nature, laid low by nothing more than a lucky shot. And David, David's just a boy with a sling and a stone, kind of whiny and moralistic, a little bit of a pissant.

In fact, I think it is a metaphor perpetuated by the Goliaths themselves.

Because really Goliath is not the size of a giant. Goliath is the size of the sky. Goliath is the size of a mountain from the base of it, so it takes up everything, everywhere you look, all the room, all the air, all the past and the future as well, until there is nothing anywhere but him, and you have no choice, remember ever having had a choice, this is just the way it is, unfortunate inevitable, inarguable, like how someday e'll all die, Goliath taking, and taking up, verything, including you, including yours, including even the whisper of a suggestion that he might not be right or fair (for a mountain is not right or fair, it just is), including even the whisper of a suggestion that this might not be good for us, for any of us (for a mountain does not care what's good for us), including even the whisper of a suggestion that there might be a different future than this (for a mountain in the future is still a mountain, long after you're gone, long after your descendants have forgotten why they tell this story, long after whatever comes after humans has forgotten our name).

Mountains change, it is true. Grain of sand by speck of dust by infinitesimal layer by drop of rain by whisper of current by time by time by time, a mountain is worn away over eons and ages and the unremitting change of seasons.

But we can't wait that long.

Why did I tell River, when I knew it could cost us our head start and our upper hand and our stealth injunction and ruin everything, when I knew, unlike Mab, that his loyalties probably didn't lie with h[...] definitely didn't lie with me, when I [...] unlike Mab, that he is nothing but a sixt[...] year-old, a boy, sheltered and privileged a[...] nearly as naive about the ways of the wor[...] as we are? Why did I tell him, when I knew he would probably tell his father and we'd lose our desperately honed, two-decades-in-the-making edge of getting there first, and not just getting there first but crossing the finish line before they even arrived at the track or really realized they were participating in a race to begin with? Why did I tell, when I knew it would break my sister's heart?

Because I am also sixteen, with all the vain hopes a teenager is due and all the good sense from which she is absolved.

Because it was my turn.

Because I have a heart as well.

And because I was tired of waiting. Because it is time.

This is what they say about justice too, by the way, that it is slow. So that's the other reason I told. It has taken Nora sixteen years, but she has finally exacted justice — by raising daughters who will see it served. She doesn't see that yet. I'm only just starting to see it myself, a revelation seeded by, of all people, Nathan Templeton. This was started slowly to realize the afternoon nfessed everything to Nora in therapy. was just trying to do right by a fallible ent. Apple too, for that matter. And, I'm nally realizing, us as well. We've been gathering wood for Nora's fire, fanning the embers of her desperate, righteous cause. It feels different because she's so good and she's so right. But even Apple couldn't quite believe her father's "good enough" was good enough. Even Nathan knew he was wrong to bow to his dad's corruptions. And us, we've been pure of heart, yes, on the side of the angels, on the side of our mother who is even holier than angels, but we have also hewn too close to her side.

Now we're on our way. Our own way. Monday is trying to be brave about it. Our new plan is incautious and impulsive and unstable as dynamite. Not that we have dynamite. We will have to blow everything up without it.

"How will we get in?" Monday demands as quietly as she's able, which is not very quiet.

From under puffy eyes, Mab smiles, which an hour ago we all imagined she might never do again. "I have the key."

"He gave you the key to the plant?"

Monday can't believe it. Me neith…
ally.

We have bundled up because it is lat…
and the temperature's dropped. We …
worn our darkest clothes, even Mon…
who did have to borrow some from us b…
did not require much cajoling to see that i…
was necessary to blend in with the night as
much as possible. We are all breathing great
puffs of white in the darkness. And Mab is
forgiving me. She has not forgiven me yet,
but she is working on it. And I am working
on forgiving her back.

"He didn't give it to me," Mab says. "I
copied it. I pretended to lose it down my
underwear when he was teaching me magic,
and when I went in the church to get it out,
I used Pastor Jeff's key-cutting machine."

"Why?" Monday asks.

" 'I have an ill-divining soul,' " Mab says.

"I do not know what that means," Monday
says.

"It's *Romeo and Juliet,*" Mab explains.

"I do not know what that means anyway,"
Monday says.

Mab looks at me, and I look at her. "Just
in case," she says.

There are Christmas lights winking cheer-
ily from a few houses, our neighbors, our
fellow citizens, survivors. I am praying no

ı hear us, step out onto a creaking step, turn on a porch light, and ask the hell we think we're doing in the dle of this night. But I am confident that they do, and if we tell them, they will join rms and come along to help. We are all in this together now.

But Bourne sleeps on.

We cross Maple and the cemetery, and I find our father with my eyes. I wonder if he would applaud what we're doing or chastise us for the foolishness we are about to undertake. If he were angry, I would remind him that the worst that can happen is we could all die, and then I'd ask him how it is, and if it isn't after all worth it maybe for such a righteous cause. If we could sit and chat and compare stories, my father and I, reflect and philosophize, I am certain he would conclude what we have concluded, that there is nowhere his daughters could be right now but where we are.

If you type much with only one hand — or too fast or thinking of other things — you may have noticed, as I have, as Duke Templeton should have, that there is only one tiny transposition, the merest trip of the fingertips, between "destroy" and "destory." I have long thought of ours as a town destroyed, but it occurs to me now it's not that bad. Bourne is not destroyed, destoried — stripped of our past, memories, our lessons, our sense of shar history and how we came to be. Our desto is not our story, which is what would have been had Belsum never entered our pages, but it does not mean that we have no future. We do. We just don't know what it is yet.

But I do know this: part of our destory is who's telling it. My mother, she's telling Bourne's old story, its should-be story. It's our turn now, and we must tell the destory, what happened instead, what happens next. Revenge, recrimination, restitution — where you prove it and you sue and you win and that's why they leave and that's how you move on — all of that is the old story, and we left that one somewhere along the path, forking off to where we are now, on our secret way in the night. It's not our mother — our mothers, the last generation — who can fix this. They can't. It is up to us now, the daughters, to move our town forward, to save us all, to tell a different story. Her way was lawyers and injunctions and lawsuits and the bounds of the system. Ours will be something else because here is a thing we know which Nora does not: sometimes you have to destroy — or destory — something in order to save it.

pealing as the symbolism would be, ebell Lake is not large enough to flood of Bourne. A catastrophic swell of water ill not drown our town and everyone in it, sleeping in their beds unawares, many of them utterly unable to run away in the event of an emergency or really anything else. The dam itself is so small that even if we somehow destroyed the whole thing, it wouldn't mean an exploding wall of stone and steel and cement flattening Bourne back to earth. All it will do is move a river. Less than that, even. All it will do is return the river whence it came. But without the river right where it is now, the plant can't operate. The dam is such an insignificant thing, not as tall as our house and not much wider, that it's hard to believe it's caused so much trouble. It's even harder to believe its removal will end, and then begin, so much else. But that's what we're counting on anyway.

We traverse the quiet streets of our sleeping town, a parade, a cavalcade, the triumphant march of battle-worn just-barely survivors, midnight riders, three against the world. To me it feels like floating, but that's easy for me to say since all I have to do is sit here and hard for me to say since all I get to do is sit here. As we near the plant and push up and over the bridge, I am

thinking about what we'll say to h
when we show up in the dead of
without River to vouch for us. My first
is to get Mab to show him the key. If sh
been given a key to the place, surely she
allowed inside, and we're her sisters, after
all. My second plan, though, if he balks at
the first, is to admit what we intend. Job or
no job, whose side is he going to be on,
Belsum's or ours?

But it turns out not to matter. The plant
has security during the day; if you come at
midnight, apparently all you need is the key.
Mab fits it into the lock and opens the door
like we're coming home.

Then we are racing down corridors. The
fluorescent lighting after the cold darkness
of the walk, the sudden warmth of being
indoors again, our nearness, finally, after
being so far away for so long, the hurtling
speed of us — it makes every part of me
tingle. I think *Slow down.* I think *Be careful.*
I think we have only one shot at this, less
than one, the smallest fraction of a shot,
and it is now, and it's been coming, and it
is now. I think she will have forgotten what's
where. I think we will get caught before we
find what we're looking for. I think *You are
Mab, queen of the fairies, deliverer of dreams.*
I think *Remember, remember everything.*

she does. She remembers which
ay, which door, which garage even, and
opens it with her magic master key. And
re they all are, machines to demolish,
hich we will use to build instead, some
dirt-spattered and mud-stained and ill-used,
some spotless, unridden, and begging to go.

But Mab says, "Shit."

"What?" Monday is dancing a little on her toes.

Mab is red-faced, openmouthed, panting. She is shaking her head. Under her breath, almost too soft to hear, she says, "We don't know how to drive a backhoe."

I have thought of that, of course, but imagined there might be a manual attached in one of those plastic sheaths, or maybe that it might be self-explanatory. But now, faced with it, I realize that is not, in fact, what I imagined. What I imagined was that operating a backhoe would be hard if you wanted to do a good job, if you cared what the finished project looked like, if you needed to keep any surrounding structures intact. I thought it would be hard if you wanted to make something work, but we want to do the opposite, render something useless. I thought driving a backhoe would be hard if the paramount stipulation were operator survival. If you were willing to

sacrifice that for other goals, I had ima
it would be easy, at least somethin,
could figure out as we went along. No
have that sinking horrible feeling of hav
come so far and not nearly far enough.

Then Monday says, simply, "I know how
to drive a backhoe."

"You do not." Mab doesn't even look at
her. Mab can't take her eyes off these machines.

"Do so."

"How could you possibly know how to
drive a backhoe?"

"I have read *Operating Techniques for
Construction and Demolition Equipment,
Eighth Edition*," Monday says. "I have also
read *The Model TF14 5VC 1985 and Later
Owners' Manual: Tractor, Loader, Backhoe,
and Attachments.* I have also read *Site Safety
and User Techniques: The Complete Guide to
Backhoes, Bulldozers, and Excavators.*"

Mab knows there is no way Monday could
be joking, but she cannot imagine that
Monday is not joking. "Whyyy?"

"They are in my library," Monday says.
"And they are yellow."

Never before has it occurred to me how
odd it is that most heavy machinery is yellow, and never before has that fact seemed
miraculous grace, but the covers of these

picture yellow equipment, and there-
— despite the fact that as far as things
plot and character go, these stories must
pretty boring — Monday has read them
al.

It turns out the ones Nathan has ready
and waiting are yellow as well.

It turns out there are keys in the ignitions
and fuel in the tanks, which makes sense
since half these machines are brand-new
from the factory, since there's a gas pump
in the corner, and since no one expects us
to be anywhere near here.

It turns out sometimes, once every few
decades or so, you get lucky.

Mab presses the button on the wall, and
the door of the garage glides open at once
with a quiet murmur. We choose the backhoe closest to outside, the one with the few-
est barriers to navigate around, the one with
what Monday helpfully identifies as a hydraulic hammer attachment on the back.
She clambers aboard.

And Mab stops suddenly and looks at me,
and I stop and look at her.

The sensible thing, the sane thing, would
be to leave me here. The backhoe's cab is
tiny — however yellow it is, Monday's going to have a hard enough time driving it
without being squished against both sisters.

Even if it were large enough, its seat built to hold my head still or my ar open or my body upright. And beside. we get caught, if we've triggered a sil alarm or security's night shift is about t report, if someone shows up here screaming and raging and demanding to know what the hell is going on, I am an excellent diversionary tactic, the slowest of stalls.

Plus, you know how one of the cabinet secretaries always sits out the State of the Union, and the guys who know the recipe for Coke are never all in the same room together, and some parents fly home from vacation on separate airplanes just in case? If two of us are plunging heedless into this night, one of us should stay behind. Someone has to take care of Nora.

I don't have to lay out these arguments. Mab knows them as well as I do. But I don't have to refute them either. I will not let my eyes leave hers to find my Voice, but if I did I would refuse, come what may, to wait here all alone. I don't need to, though. She knows that too. And mad though it is, she does not protest — not with words, not with her eyes, not even in her heart of hearts (for I can see there too). She holds my gaze and nods. They will not leave me behind.

It is an insane risk and an unnecessary

...d a shattering act of faith and loyalty ...stupidity and love. ...ut my chair has to stay. My Voice too. ...d without them, I am stood down, immobilized, silenced, at once firmly anchored and frantically unmoored. It is, simply and terribly, leaving a part of myself behind.

But we have no other option. I drive right up to the beast. I grasp upward with my hand and pull. Monday pulls. Mab pushes. There's a good bit of grunting, wrestling, and elbows in places elbows should not go. It is good that we are sisters. But finally, I am in the driver's seat, the only seat. Mab straps me in. And it is time.

In front of me, I'm relieved to find a steering wheel. A steering wheel, pedals on the floor, buttons with icons of lights and windshield wiper fluid, a radio, cup holders. Just like a car. Not that any of us have ever driven one of those either, but I think we could. Well, I think they could. That most of the controls and indeed the tools are behind me rather than out front is a problem we'll have to address soon. But not immediately.

By raising the armrests, by being a teenage girl rather than the person for whom this cab was designed, by pressing her leg and side against mine, however unwillingly, Monday wedges in alongside me so she can

drive, her butt half in the seat, half i
air. Mab opens the side window and s
dles it, one foot inside, one on the w.
cover, hands reaching in and gripping i
shoulders to keep us both upright. Sh
blinks at me, and I can feel her shaking. I
can feel Monday shaking. I can feel them
both feeling me shaking. I know if we flip
this thing, if we drive off the riverbank, if
we crash into a tree, we'll be dead before
Mab even has a chance to scream at Monday.

But in fact, this is a brand-new, state-of-
the-art vehicle. Monday turns the ignition
switch, and the backhoe purrs to life like a
Maserati. She turns the headlights on and
illuminates the night before us, black
streaked through with her yellow, the river
aglow in our light, bright white and alive,
the only thing moving in the dark silence.
She releases the parking brake, puts the
backhoe in gear, presses the gas pedal, and
slips out of the garage and into the night.
The cab shudders a bit, jagged as our
breath, as she gives it too much gas then
panics and pulls her foot away, too much,
then not enough, too much, then not
enough, but she's going so slowly she hasn't
needed to use the brake at all. And as I am
always saying, slow is good. At the moment,

...or very many more, we have time.

...crawl away from the plant, our pristine ...biting into the earth, steady, not slip-...ng, down to the bridge over the diverted ...ver, and then up over its sleeping crest. Below, the water is rushing beneath us, the clearest note in a quiet night, rushing on, rushing away, loud from over top and fast and cold, the spray spitting in fits to reach us, calling to us, shouting, a threat and a welcome. It has been flowing as long as we've been alive, which is not forever, but which feels like forever. It prattles away, and it is somehow surprising to hear its babble so late as if they should have turned it off after dark, as if it wouldn't speak were there no one to listen. Day or night, light or dark, witnessed or alone, polluted or clean, this river runs on. And we, we three, we're go-ing to stop its song. If it knew, would this river be angry or grateful to return to its path, its rightful way forward, free from diversion, unencumbered by the violent service into which it has been pressed all these lonely years? It got its share of the vitriol, but the river was never to blame. Now it gets to return to the place where it is natural and appreciated and belongs. Now it gets to go back home.

But homecomings are often fraught, some-

times violent even. Things get broken
the way. Nothing's ever quite as you l
They say you can't go home again, but
not true. You can. But only if you're t
river.

On the other side of the bridge, we leave
the river behind and make our bumpy way
toward the lake, over the frozen field, over
the brambles and weeds, over the old orchard land, over the nothing between the
river and the park, knowing what's behind
was the easy part, knowing that bridge was
built to bear us but the dam was not. As the
lights in Bluebell Park come into view,
Monday brakes hard and cuts the engine,
and the backhoe comes to a shuddering
stop. We sit there, breathing hard, like we've
run here. If only. The water in Bluebell Lake
is so black and still it seems made of different stuff entirely than the river, but it is just
as breathtaking. Both have been here all our
lives, seem as part of our town as Bourne
High or the Do Not Shop, seem as part of
the land as the trees and the fields, seem as
movable as mountains, but we know — well,
hope — that very soon they will be gone.

"Now what?" Mab asks Monday.

"We drive out onto the dam," she says.
"The hammer must be positioned at a
ninety-degree angle to the material you

to break through."

an we do that?" says Mab. "Drive out

the dam?"

Small to medium backhoes such as this ne are the ideal machines for maneuvering in tight spaces," Monday says.

"What if the dam's already too weak to support us?"

No one speaks the answer to this out loud, but we all hear it just the same. If the dam collapses under our weight, we'll go into the lake and we will not come out.

Monday starts the machine again, and we drive forward at a pace that makes our ride so far feel fast in comparison. At the lip of the lake, the edge of the dam, we pause to try for calm, for deep breaths, for a small prayer, to say goodbye to the solid world, just in case, ready to all go down together if it comes to that, though, truthfully, it also feels like life might be about to get better, and we'd just as soon stick around for it if we could. We move forward, an inch an hour it seems like, a slow creep over grass and onto the cement top of the dam which feels like solid ground — not as much give beneath us — but of course is less so, the concrete holding but the timbers beneath shrieking as they bow, but holding too, making our slow way as we leave the part built

over ground and cross onto the pa[...]
ing back water. The spine of the [...]
wider than we are. But it is not a lot [...]
than we are.

To our right, upstream, the lake is st[...]
quiet but deep. Mab and Monday can swin[...]
but I cannot, and unstrapping me from a
sinking backhoe and pulling me to shore
through frigid waters is probably more than
any of us would survive. To our left, below
us, is the ravine, what we've always thought
of as the ravine, which is actually a ghost
river, a once and future river, a dry gully
ready to be filled again. It is not so far
down. It is not so full of thorns. But it is far
and full enough if we should fall.

Out over the middle of the dam, as much
behind us as ahead, water above and brambles below, Monday shifts into neutral and
puts on the parking brake. She lowers the
stabilizer legs down on either side, though I
don't know how much stability they'll
provide since they're only just wider than
we are. And only just fit. We all try very hard
not to breathe.

"We have to turn around," Monday whispers.

I am about to shout incoherent protest,
but Mab gets there first. "We've come this
far. We can't go back now."

. not saying go back, One. The ham-
behind us." They both turn and look.
hydraulic attachments go on the stick
ch is on the boom which is on the back.
e have to turn around."

Monday reaches down and releases something under our seat, turns us in a slow
circle, and suddenly we're facing the other
way. Out our new front windshield, the
hammer looks like a giant metal finger at
the end of a giant metal arm, elbow pointed
at the sky, finger pointing to the ground,
more twisted than I am, also waiting. We
can still make out the plant on the shore we
came from, in front of us once again.

"How do we work that thing?" Mab
breathes.

"Joysticks." Monday points to them. There
is one apiece on little pillars on either side
of us.

"Do you know how?" Mab's voice climbs,
and I will her to lower it. I do not know
how delicate our balance is. I do know
shouting will not help Monday.

"The books say all it takes is training,
practice, and a careful touch," Monday says
confidently.

"You have no training! You have no practice!" Mab's voice goes the wrong direction.
"Your touch is not careful!"

"They are yellow!" Monday yells bac.

"It takes more than being yellow!" Ma
shaking, rattling the entire cab, rattling
where she grasps my chest and shoulders.

"I am an expert in all yellow things!"
Monday is indignant. She needs to get out
and run laps around the backhoe, but it is
as possible for her to do so at the moment
as it is for me.

I am tapping One One One on Mab's arm
as hard as I can, but she is numbed by cold
and terror and cannot feel it. So I muster
all my energy and concentration and shout
into the frozen night, "Maaa!"

Not Mab. Not Monday. Me. I have had
sixteen years of practice. My touch is fine
as cobwebs. I am Miracle Mirabel, a maestro
on the joystick. Even in the dark, I can see
their faces light with comprehension, then
giddy, dizzy relief.

"Hah," I say. Tell me how.

"The left joystick swings us side to side,"
says Monday. "You have to position the
hammer between the front wheels."

The left joystick is on the left side, which
makes sense, but it might as well be on the
moon for as much as I can reach it with my
left hand. Monday swivels the seat around
so I can reach it with my right, but then I
am looking out the side of the cab. Mab

ezes into the space behind me and
es me upright and still and breathing. I
re out over black Bluebell Lake, take the
ystick in hand, and gently move the stick
o the right while Mab calls, "More, more,
little more, back a little. Stop. Okay. Good.
Now what, Monday?"

"The left joystick also pushes the stick in
and out and makes it shorter and longer."

"That doesn't help her, Two. What should
she do?"

"Push the joystick away from you to push
the stick out in front," she says and I do.
"Press up on the button on top to lower it
down," and I do that too. It is better that I
can't see what I'm doing I think. It is better
to be gazing out over a dark, still lake. I can
hear motors purring, though, gears engag-
ing, the knock of metal against stone, the
machine responding to my touch, but so
far, it's all prelude.

Then Monday says, "Okay, now the boom.
You need the other joystick." And that
joystick I can play as it was meant to be
played. Right hand, facing front, watching
what I wreak. She turns our chair. We all
three gaze at the upcrooked elbow and its
pointing finger, the dam before us, the plant
out beyond, the lake bated above.

"Side to side on the right joystick controls

the curl," Monday quotes at us. "Away⸻
ers the boom down. Back toward you li
back up."

"What should she do?" Mab has her tee
clamped so hard together — to keep ther
from chattering or to keep herself from yelling, I do not know — it is hard to understand her. But Monday does.

"Lower the boom, right into the wall,
perpendicular — that means a ninety-
degree angle," she breaks off to tell me. I
nod. "And press down."

I do. Suddenly, our front wheels are lifting
off the dam. We are levitating. We are falling. Mab is screaming. I am screaming.
"No, no, do not scream!" Monday screams.
"That is what is supposed to happen. That
is how we know we have the angle right and
the attachment seated."

I try to breathe deeply. I try to calm down.
I try to calm Mab down too.

"Lower us," says Monday, and I do, only
too gladly. And then she says, "Move the
hammer to the edge. And go. Fifteen seconds. Go."

Fifteen seconds does not sound like very
many, but count it off in your head, one
number at a time, a breath in between each
one, and imagine while you do the very
earth shaking into pieces all around you. It

—ong, slow time. It is an eternity. It is
end of the world.

ne. Two. Three.

There is a crack and a crash we hear over
ne hammering and feel in our bones and
feel in our souls.

Four. Five.

Mab is counting off, slow and even, defi-
ant, behind me, against me.

Six. Seven. Eight.

She gets to fifteen, and I stop. We are panting. We are waiting.

"Now move it over to a new spot nearby
and do it again," Monday says.

"Why a new spot?" Mab shouts.

"I do not know!" Monday shouts back.

I don't either, but I do as Monday directs.
She has got us this far. We will all go down
together. I turn on the hammer. Mab counts
to fifteen. I stop. I move the boom again.
She counts and I move. She counts and I
move. Again and again and again, and soon
the whole world is shaking shattering shuddering convulsing-like-to-break-apart, and I
am certain, as certain as I have ever been of
anything in my life, that we are about to fall
to our death, my sisters, our backhoe, and
I, and I think of our mother and how
heartbroken she will be and how proud, and
suddenly, finally, there is a crack that must

640

be what they mean when they say the
of doom, and Bluebell Lake is water f.
ing faster and faster over the dam now, ←
there is so much debris, and I start to u.
the finger to poke it out of the way, to drag
the rocks and stones and mud and cement
and broken concrete and wood away from
the hole we've made, and Monday screams,
"Stop!"

"What?" Mab pants. "What's wrong?"

"Using the hammer to hoist, pry, sweep,
or move large objects may result in premature wear on the tool or poor long-term
performance."

"No one gives a shit about long-term
performance, Monday! We need this thing
to last for another thirty seconds. Can it do
that?"

"Naaa," I say. No. Look. And we all three
do. And we all three see that there is no way
back the way we've come for we have made
a hole too large to cross, filling and spilling
over now with water, and the only way we
can go is forward, away from the plant and
the river, home again.

"Pull it up! Pull it back in!" Monday
directs, and I do, and she turns our seat
around so we face front again, our backs to
Belsum, to the hole we have made, to the
hole we have left behind.

at I feel is free, no longer shattering, onger rattling, the pulsing hard but only own. I clench and unclench my hand, ench and unclench, working blood back n, relishing its sting. For no doubt the first time in my life, my body is exultant. My body worked and obeyed, complied and triumphed, saved us all. Monday pulls forward one breath at a time over the rest of the dam we have destroyed the middle of, over the barrier we have all but removed, over a past which has not been kind but which is ours and which made us, back to mud, back to grass, back to Bourne, back home.

The thing about holes is their size is deceptive. You can't tell by looking if they're wide but shallow or have gentle slopes to hidden depths. Or maybe it's just that with holes, their size is not what matters. Black holes are infinitely small but infinitely dense, drawing into themselves everything there is. I don't know what that means really, but if I were describing a hole, I'd be more interested in how much can fall into it or leak out of it than the size of the thing itself. You'd think those qualities would be related, but world-class physicists insist I'm wrong, and they seem like pretty smart people.

We have made a hole too big to cross [
over, but not really because of its size. C
ing back was never an option. We can final.
only go forward. We have made a hole too
big to hold water, but that is true of any
hole, no matter how small. We have only
slightly widened a little crack in a low wall
to let a shallow lake trickle back into the
barely-more-than-a-swollen-creek it was
always meant to be, but that small crack is
the size of the moon, that wall the width of
the world. That river flows like all the blood
in all the veins of every person left in this
town. It is not really about size.

Our destory is this: We are no longer waiting, imagining justice deferred but heralded,
on its way. We are no longer left behind,
forgotten but unable to forget. We have been
wronged, but we are no longer wrong, no
longer broken, no longer immovable and
wishing ourselves other than we are. Our
water is no longer green and no longer toxic
because that water has flowed on, and so
have that town, those people, that history,
not gone but diluted, far away, and flowing
farther every moment. We get to rest now,
some of us. And others of us? We're just getting started.

Because the flip side of our destory is the

not yet written, the one that happens next.

Duke Templeton doesn't want word to get out about all he did to make us finally take matters into our own hands, or maybe he's just embarrassed to be laid so low by three girls and his very own backhoe, but he declines to press charges against us for breaking and entering the plant and stealing his equipment. In contrast, property damage to town infrastructure is a municipal matter, which makes what to do about it Omar's decision. Omar concludes that we have already performed more than commensurate community service. And our criminal records are expunged.

Therefore it's a little year — a short little year — until Mab receives a postcard, her first from an address other than her own, congratulating her on her early acceptance to a college far away but also not so far, and six mere months after that until she and Petra pile into Petra's horrible car and make it just into the parking lot of their dorm before breaking down, before meeting the rest of their incoming class, small and close, a poky town's worth of students all new in their new world, young and excited and afraid and away from home for the first time, and though those homes are not like

Bourne — of course they aren't — they're also too small, too strange, too missed.

Meanwhile, the library is vacant aga. Omar redesignates it to Monday — or, be more accurate, as she would insist, redesignates it back to the town *care of* Monday. Tom and the Kyles spend a few days putting up shelves, rough-cut one-by-twelves on brackets screwed directly into the wall, inelegant but easily painted a cheery buttercup yellow. Monday stacks them carefully with the battered titles she's loved and watched over all these years like children.

The relocation of Monday's library — re-relocation, she says — makes our house feel palatial, but the Templetons' state-of-the-art kitchen is still too tempting for Nora to resist. She starts doing her more marathon baking sessions there and then selling pastries from the reference desk, muffins and cupcakes and croissants for fifty cents apiece, day-olds for a quarter.

As the weeks until Mab leaves ebb away, she gets more and more anxious that when she and Petra go to school, we'll miss them too much, or they'll miss us too much, or, simply, they'll miss too much, all that's happening in Bourne. "Nothing will be happening in Bourne," Monday assures them,

Mab is still worried. Change happened it could again, could some more. So maybe because it will ease my sister's mind r maybe because it was the start of the string that unspooled, heroically and unexpectedly, all the way to the dam or maybe just because it's time, I relaunch the *Herald Bourne.* There is no staff. There is no money to print it. But there is the internet, however slow. And there is me, however slow as well, to write and research and listen and understand, me to give voice, to be there. To be here.

For a while, I have a subscriber base of one — or rather One — but Mab shares with Petra, reading her the articles aloud as they navigate their tiny dorm room. (Petra calls it incommodious, old habits being operose to break.) Soon Frank, Hobart, Zach, and Tom all subscribe too, never mind bar gossip is how most of my scoops originate, and Mrs. Shriver, though as a history teacher she hasn't much use for current events, and Pastor Jeff, though his primary news source remains our Saturday morning breakfast table. Pooh is a subscriber until her death: in her home, in her sleep, and — this is the miraculous and wondrous part — of old age, natural causes, nothing more painful or insidious than time.

Wondrous though it may be, Mab is heartbroken. Five minutes after Mona calls to tell them the news, Mab and Pete borrow a friend's more reliable car and drive through the night straight home where Mab finds, of all things, a box of vintage shoes plus a note which reads:

Dearest Mab,

If I had jewels or gold or bonds or property, they would be yours. But I don't. Standing in (get it?!) — and since those silver-tasseled mules look so cute on you — I'm leaving you these. It's amazing how long shoes last if you get around town via wheelchair. But for you, my dear, these shoes are made for walking.

I leave out the part about the shoes, but I write about the funeral, even though every one of the *Herald Bourne*'s subscribers is there, including Pooh herself in some ways, maybe the most important ways. It's a good story, the whole town turned out to file past her casket, struggling to corral their smiles because it is a sad occasion, somber, not a cause for celebration, but they keep forgetting, so long has it been since anyone died in Bourne just from being in their nineties, long was she here and well and loved, as they file past my sister (in a black dress and knee-high pink polka-dotted go-go boots), also a wonder, wandering but home again. The piece reads like a fairy tale, a hint of myth, Odyssean, but every word is true.

Other news is more mixed and easier to believe, though also filigreed with hope and change. Leandra dies — not of old age or natural causes — but a few months later, to keep himself clean, Chris Wohl opens an ice rink. Frozen water — that does not flow or smell or color or relocate — is the kind of water Bourne can handle. I write about the new jobs renting skates, grilling hot dogs, smoothing the ice, plus the sled hockey team and the simple joy of having something different to do on weekends. Greenborough doesn't have an ice rink, so we get visitors even, a few, strangers who come to glide over the ice holding hands under the mirror-ball lights, a small road trip to a sweet little town not so far away.

I write about Bourne Memorial High's about-time restructuring of its classes to amend ableist assumptions that, for instance, someone with my body or Monday's brain could not possibly be as smart as Mab. We are not *as* smart. We are different smart. We are also smart. We are other good things as well.

I write about what we learned from the college catalog River Templeton quietly put into my sister's hands, how the test results that proved GL606 was finally safe were faked, a favor from an old family friend, how Bourne's citizens had cast votes based on lies and therefore had their say denied. Again. I write about Nathan's response to the email I send him where he says he was lied to too, where he claims he didn't realize Duke had his old roommate tamper with the results. "I never imagined Harburon would risk their own stellar reputation to bury proof of unfavorable outcomes as a favor to my father," Nathan tells me. "I assumed they just gave us, like, a discount on the testing." He admits, though, that he is not surprised to learn everything wasn't on the up-and-up and regrets his part in convincing the citizens of Bourne to take their chances with his family again, and he makes good on that apology by supplying documentation, his original test results that we could never lay our hands on, that prove finally — finally, finally — that Belsum knew and knew and knew and knew. And did it anyway.

I do not write about the emails I exchange with his son where he says sorry and thank ou and goodbye and I also say sorry and thank you and goodbye.

But this is the story that gets picked up anyway. At first it's the story of the story — the paper of an only slightly larger town upstate runs something in the spirit of a condescending "Small-Town Girl in Wheelchair Thinks She's a Real Reporter" piece — but slowly a larger paper and a larger one still and other states and countries and wire services begin to understand the real story here. With their greater resources, they start to dig. And Belsum, and all they've done to us, is — at last and fully — exposed.

Nora says she's disappointed because she was hoping for more — an embarrassing public arrest at the country club, copious jail sentences served consecutively, maybe a light hanging — but she's faking. She's ecstatic. Vindicated. The settlement offer is not generous — because what would be overly much, given the circumstances? — but it is a lot: enough to change Bourne forever, to buy us a future, to buy us the world.

Nora refuses on principle.

But Russell explains: It's not settling like compromise, concession, surrender. It's settling like building a nest, a community, a place to live and to be. Home.

And to this, Nora will at last agree.

The money is maybe not enough to dri
Belsum out of business, but something is –
the bad press, the failure to relaunch, the
abdication of the son. And of his son as well.
The river no longer where they need it to
be. Demolition equipment far larger and
more powerful and, one imagines, harder to
operate than our backhoe arrives and, in
the course of only an afternoon, a few
enormous small hours, levels the plant that
has shadowed our town and our lives all our
lives.

That summer Pastor Jeff borrows Hobart's
truck for his thrift-shop tour and returns
with boxes and boxes of used but new-to-
Bourne books. Monday needs more shelves
to home them all and is, momentously, out
of wall space, but when Tom offers to rip
out the kitchen and restore the Children's
section, Nora balks. With the spare change
she's raising fifty cents at a time from her
reference-desk bake sales, soon the town
will have enough money to replace Monday's shoebox card catalog. Besides, Omar
says, if they leave the kitchen in, the library
could double as an event space and catering
could use it, like if someone wanted to hold
a wedding there, say, and though Monday
does not like change or think libraries need

ens, she is well used to lending books
om a kitchen. And though Omar does not
ay who might get married, his eyes, and
Nora's too, shine as if he did.

And I keep writing. For I can write as well
as anyone, writing requiring but one well-
honed brain, a ranging imagination, a
determined mind, and a resilient and wide-
open heart. For I have voice to give we
voiceless few. Or maybe "voiceless" is too
strong. Under-voiced, let's say. I have
perspective. Opinions. Ideas. And more than
all that, it is by writing this down that I will
honor my mother's legacy, take up the
mantle of her life's work — never mind, as
Pastor Jeff points out, that both are ongo-
ing. She gets to lay it down now, as he also
said, for it is our turn. We won't forget. We
won't let you forget, either.

I have stories to tell and, even better,
stories to live.

It's only six months after Mab leaves for
college that Monday bundles me onto a bus
to another bus to another, and we go visit
our sister. Monday spends two hours on
Mab's tiny dorm-room bed with her hands
clamped over her ears shrieking about the
state of Mab's bathroom, shared by twenty-
two teenage girls and professionally cleaned
but once a week. To be honest, it's not

necessarily an overreaction, and besides, she managed the buses and going somewhere unknown and all the unpredictability of me, not to mention those many months of being one of only two instead of three. After she calms down, we go into town, and Mab shows us around, takes us to her favorite coffee place and her favorite restaurant and her favorite shops. In one of them, there's a spinning rack of postcards. Monday turns it round and round and finally buys them all. Watching out the window on the bus ride home, she starts to think maybe she could leave Bourne after all, go to college herself (somewhere they let students live off-campus in en suite apartments with walls you can paint any shade of yellow you like), and then get a job out there, somewhere, anywhere, anywhere she wants.

And me? Our road trip makes me see that needing help doesn't mean there aren't other places to get it besides home, other people who can provide it besides family, that having limits doesn't mean I cannot — must not, maybe — bewitch and bewilder, range far and wander wide and wild. For home is like black holes — no matter how small, no matter how humble, they capture everything in range and trap it inside. The only way to escape their draw is to be far enough away.

Nora will stay as her house empties of daughters, slowly but steadily, like, well, like water flowing out of a busted dam. She'll stay because, after all, it is home. She believes in this town. There are other providers of jobs besides chemical companies. There are more ways to grow than you imagine. She has friends here, more than friends, more than family even, people she's survived a tragedy — and its aftermath — alongside, people who she knows will be there for her, for one another, for richer and poorer, in sickness and health, not forsaking but forsaken certainly. For worse but also for better, for when it gets better. Tough as tigers. Able to forgive. Unbowed. Her girls are leaving, and she's heartbroken, and she's euphoric. Her great loves are leaving, but she has great love yet to come.

Maybe our story won't be exactly that.

But it will be something like that.

For now, Monday turns off the backhoe's ignition. She and Mab pull me out of my seat. We are all three sliding down the side of the machine, scrambling onto the earth, all in a pile, a single, weeping, trembling organism. Since my chair is back at the plant, they prop me up with their bodies, and we watch together, we three, under the frozen stars, under the dark, until the night lightens and the sun comes up, as the lake becomes a stream and then a river again, as the dam becomes a weir and then a hole and then a bridge between one grassy shore and another, water flowing below again, between what we have rendered at last a fallen, slain, and desiccated chemical plant and our very own small town, our home, Bourne again, coming slowly back to life.

ACKNOWLEDGMENTS

You read acknowledgments at the end of a book. I write them in the midst of a journey, a long, winding, sometimes fraught one, but one along which I've had the best company.

Molly Friedrich, you have charted this course, as ever, and I am so grateful, as ever. My well-deep gratitude also to Lucy Carson, on so many fronts, and to Heather Carr. I would not, could not do this — or really so many things — without you all.

Amy Einhorn, you hacked our way through the vines, and they were dense and thorny. I am profoundly grateful and also profoundly joyful that "dozens" seems to both of us the right number of times to edit a book. Conor Mintzer, you can do and do do everything with such proficiency and grace, and you send me the best emails about all of it. My bottomless thanks to you both.

I was surprised and delighted to find

nyself at Henry Holt midway through this journey. There, I have been so grateful for the good, hard work of Pat Eisemann, Marian Brown, Catryn Silbersack, Caitlin O'Shaughnessy, Maggie Richards, Chris O'Connell, Eva Diaz, Steven Seighman, Katy Robitzski, Jason Liebman, Allison Carney, Catherine Casalino, Jolanta Benal, Jennie Cohen, Sarah Bowen, Chris Sergio, and Nicolette Seeback.

I have relied along the way on the generosity and expertise and kindness of strangers as well as friends and family. My many thanks to Paul Mariz, Sue Frankel, Dave Frankel, Erin Trendler, Lisa Corr, Jonathan Corr, Nicola Griffith, Kelley Eskridge, Forbes Darby (who also gets credit for the joke about the fish), Eliza Peoples, Alicia Goodwin, Jennie Shortridge, Dana Spector, Benjamin Dreyer, and Hamilton Cain. And extra, deep, profound gratitude to Julie M. Jones. Thank you, thank you.

I wrote the last words of the first draft of this book at Hedgebrook. I wrote the last words of the last draft of this book at Ragdale. I am deeply grateful to these writing retreat centers, to the wonderful people I met and loved and worked alongside there, to the wonderful people who support these nonprofit organizations. Extra thank-yous to Hannah Judy Gretz, who seeded the next book — an extraordinary gift — but also homed the very finishing touches on this one.

And mostly and always, thank you to my daughter for being you, for growing so well, and for allowing me the space and time to do this. I know this is a sacrifice for you too. And to Paul, everything I want to say is way too mushy for public consumption, and "thank you" doesn't even begin to express it. Words fail me. And when they do, you are there. More than anything in the world, I am grateful that we get to do this — all of this — together.

ABOUT THE AUTHOR

Laurie Frankel is the beloved *New York Times* bestselling, award-winning author of three previous novels: *The Atlas of Love, Goodbye for Now,* and the Reese's Book Club x Hello Sunshine Book Pick *This Is How It Always Is.* Her writing has also appeared in the *New York Times,* the *Guardian, Publishers Weekly, People* magazine, *Literary Hub,* the *Sydney Morning Herald,* and other publications. A former college professor, Frankel now teaches for a variety of nonprofit organizations and writes full-time in Seattle, where she lives with her husband, daughter, and border collie and makes good soup.

The employees of Thorndike Press hope you have enjoyed this Large Print book. All our Thorndike, Wheeler, and Kennebec Large Print titles are designed for easy reading, and all our books are made to last. Other Thorndike Press Large Print books are available at your library, through selected bookstores, or directly from us.

For information about titles, please call:
  (800) 223-1244

or visit our website at:
  gale.com/thorndike

To share your comments, please write:
  Publisher
  Thorndike Press
  10 Water St., Suite 310
  Waterville, ME 04901